THE FALL OF THE
HOUSE OF
WEST

Written by JT Petty and Paul Pope
Art by David Rubin

:01

First Second
New York

First Second

Copyright © 2015 by Paul Pope
Published by First Second
First Second is an imprint of Roaring Brook Press,
a division of Holtzbrinck Publishing Holdings Limited Partnership
175 Fifth Avenue, New York, New York 10010
All rights reserved

Cataloging-in-Publication Data is on file at the Library of Congress

ISBN: 978-1-62672-010-7

First Second books may be purchased for business or promotional use. For
information on bulk purchases please contact Macmillan Corporate and
Premium Sales Department at (800) 221-7945 x5442 or by email at
specialmarkets@macmillan.com.

First edition 2015

Art by David Rubin
Story by JT Petty and Paul Pope

Type set in "PPope," designed by John Martz
Book design by John Green
Printed in the United States of America

1 3 5 7 9 10 8 6 4 2

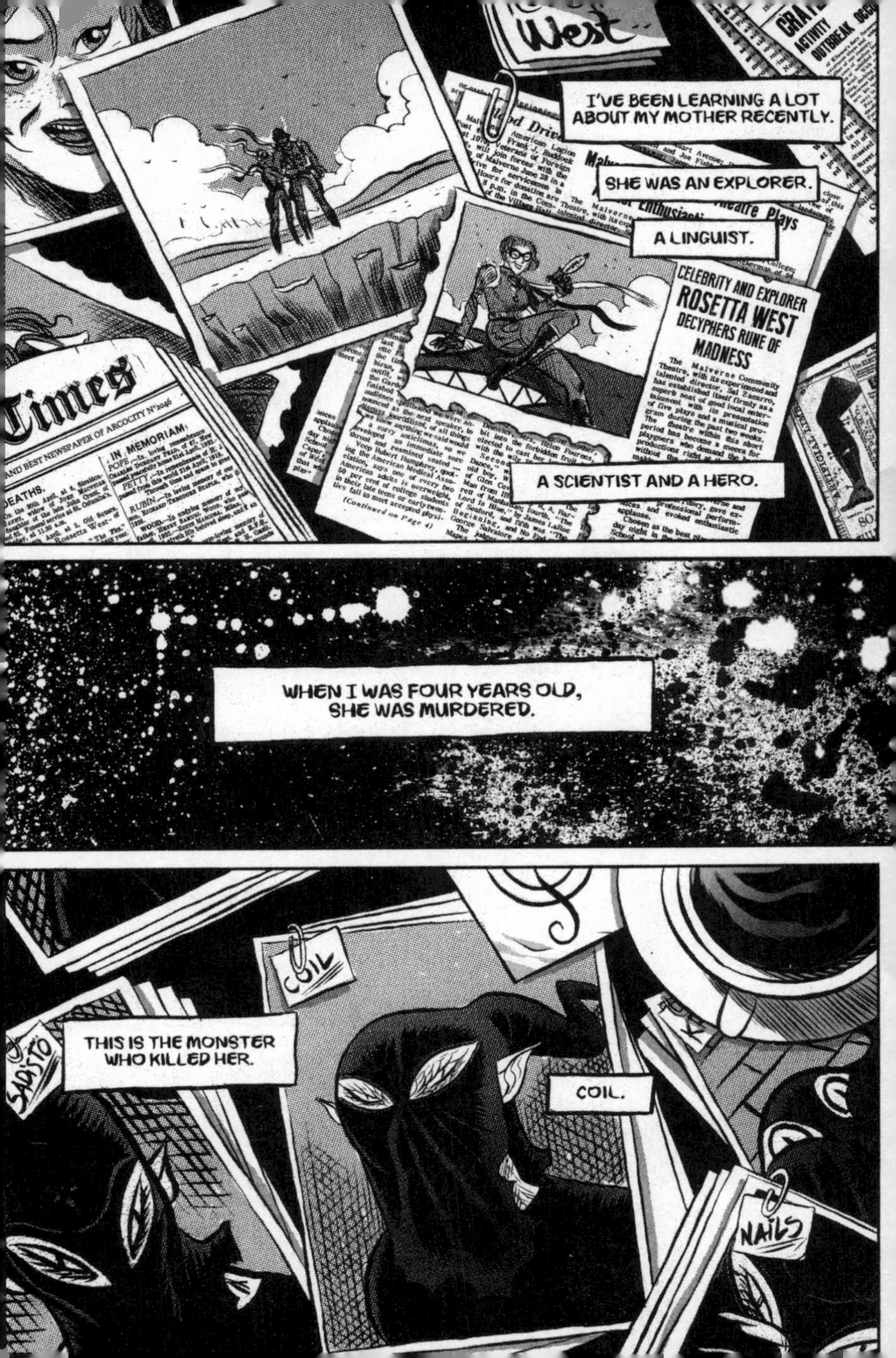

I'VE BEEN LEARNING A LOT ABOUT MY MOTHER RECENTLY.
SHE WAS AN EXPLORER.
A LINGUIST.
CELEBRITY AND EXPLORER ROSETTA WEST DECYPHERS RUNE OF MADNESS
Times
IN MEMORIAM
DEATHS.
A SCIENTIST AND A HERO.
WHEN I WAS FOUR YEARS OLD, SHE WAS MURDERED.
COIL
SADISTO
THIS IS THE MONSTER WHO KILLED HER.
COIL.
NAILS

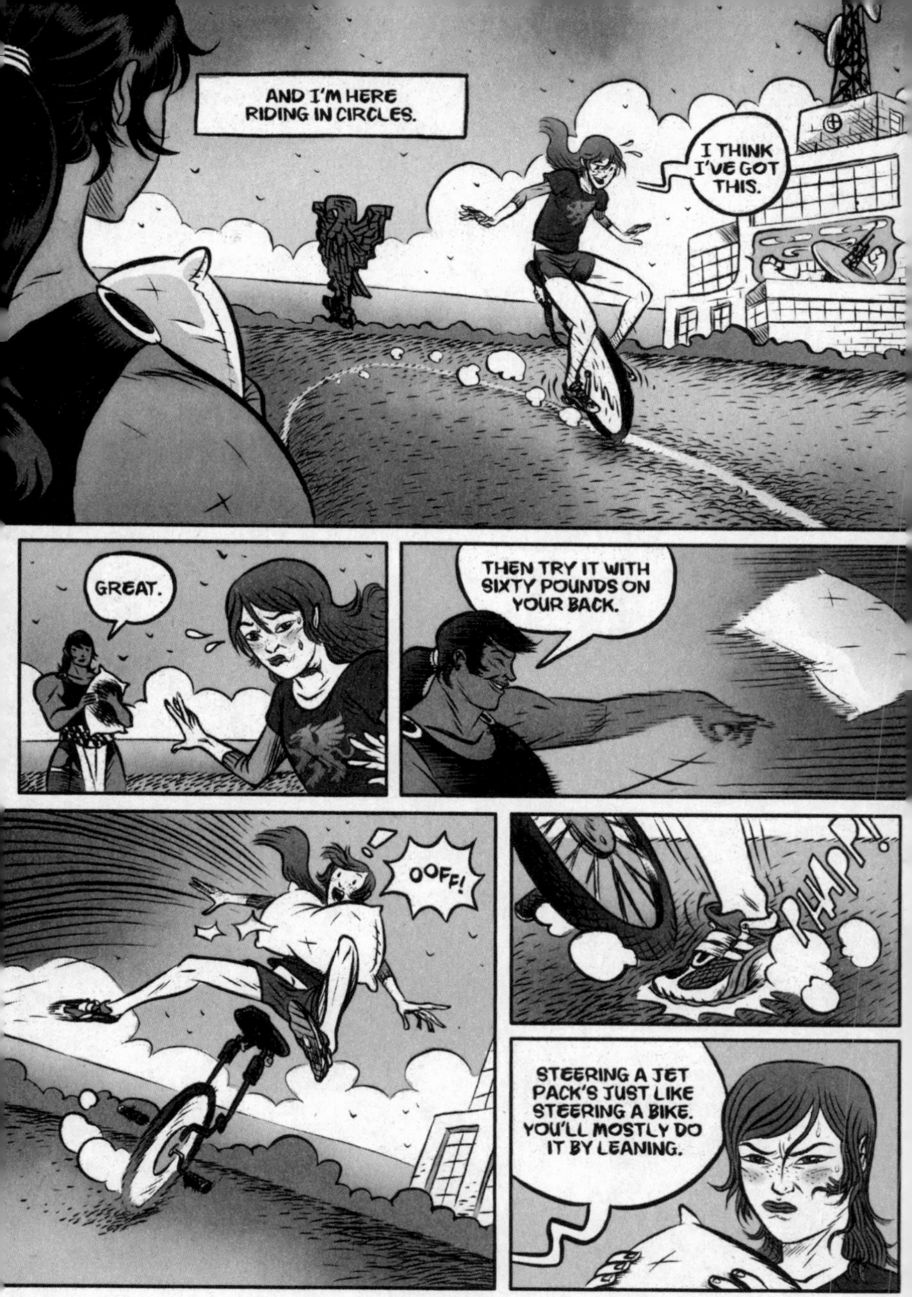
AND I'M HERE RIDING IN CIRCLES.
I THINK I'VE GOT THIS.
GREAT.
THEN TRY IT WITH SIXTY POUNDS ON YOUR BACK.
OOFF!
PHAPP!
STEERING A JET PACK'S JUST LIKE STEERING A BIKE. YOU'LL MOSTLY DO IT BY LEANING.

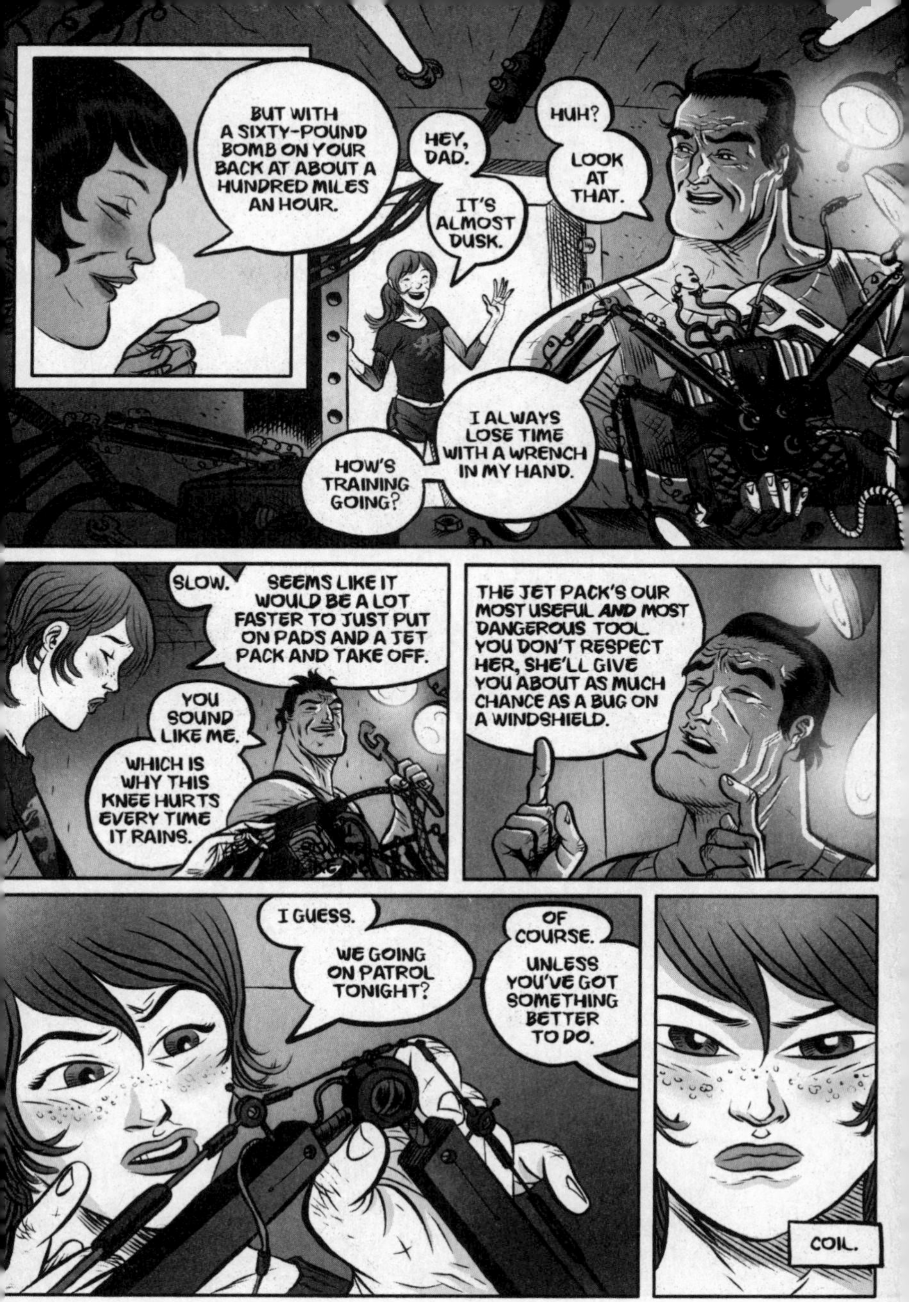
BUT WITH A SIXTY-POUND BOMB ON YOUR BACK AT ABOUT A HUNDRED MILES AN HOUR.
HEY, DAD.
IT'S ALMOST DUSK.
HUH?
LOOK AT THAT.
I ALWAYS LOSE TIME WITH A WRENCH IN MY HAND.
HOW'S TRAINING GOING?
SLOW.
SEEMS LIKE IT WOULD BE A LOT FASTER TO JUST PUT ON PADS AND A JET PACK AND TAKE OFF.
YOU SOUND LIKE ME.
WHICH IS WHY THIS KNEE HURTS EVERY TIME IT RAINS.
THE JET PACK'S OUR MOST USEFUL *AND* MOST DANGEROUS TOOL. YOU DON'T RESPECT HER, SHE'LL GIVE YOU ABOUT AS MUCH CHANCE AS A BUG ON A WINDSHIELD.
I GUESS.
WE GOING ON PATROL TONIGHT?
OF COURSE.
UNLESS YOU'VE GOT SOMETHING BETTER TO DO.
COIL.

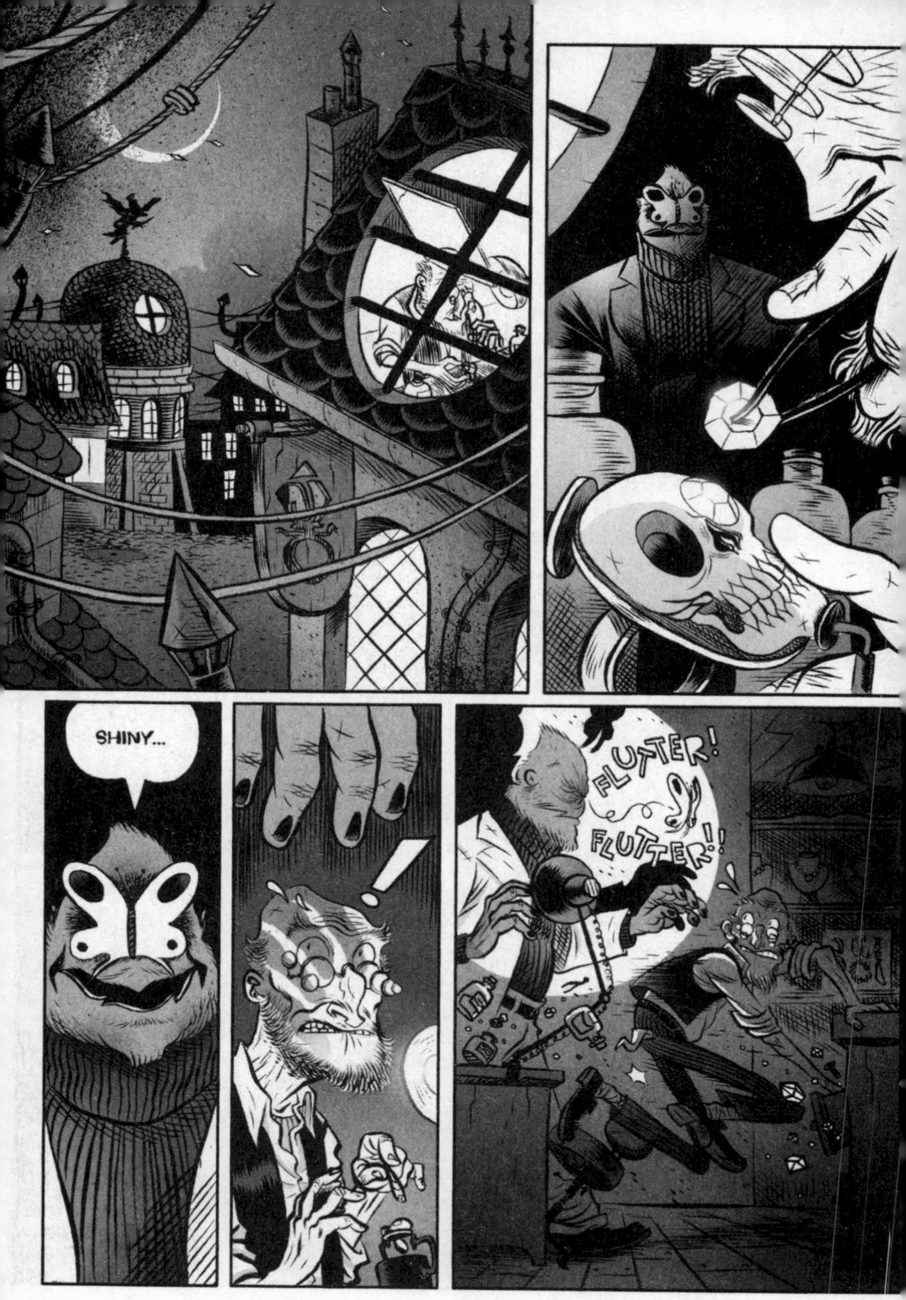
SHINY...
!
FLUTTER!
FLUTTER!!

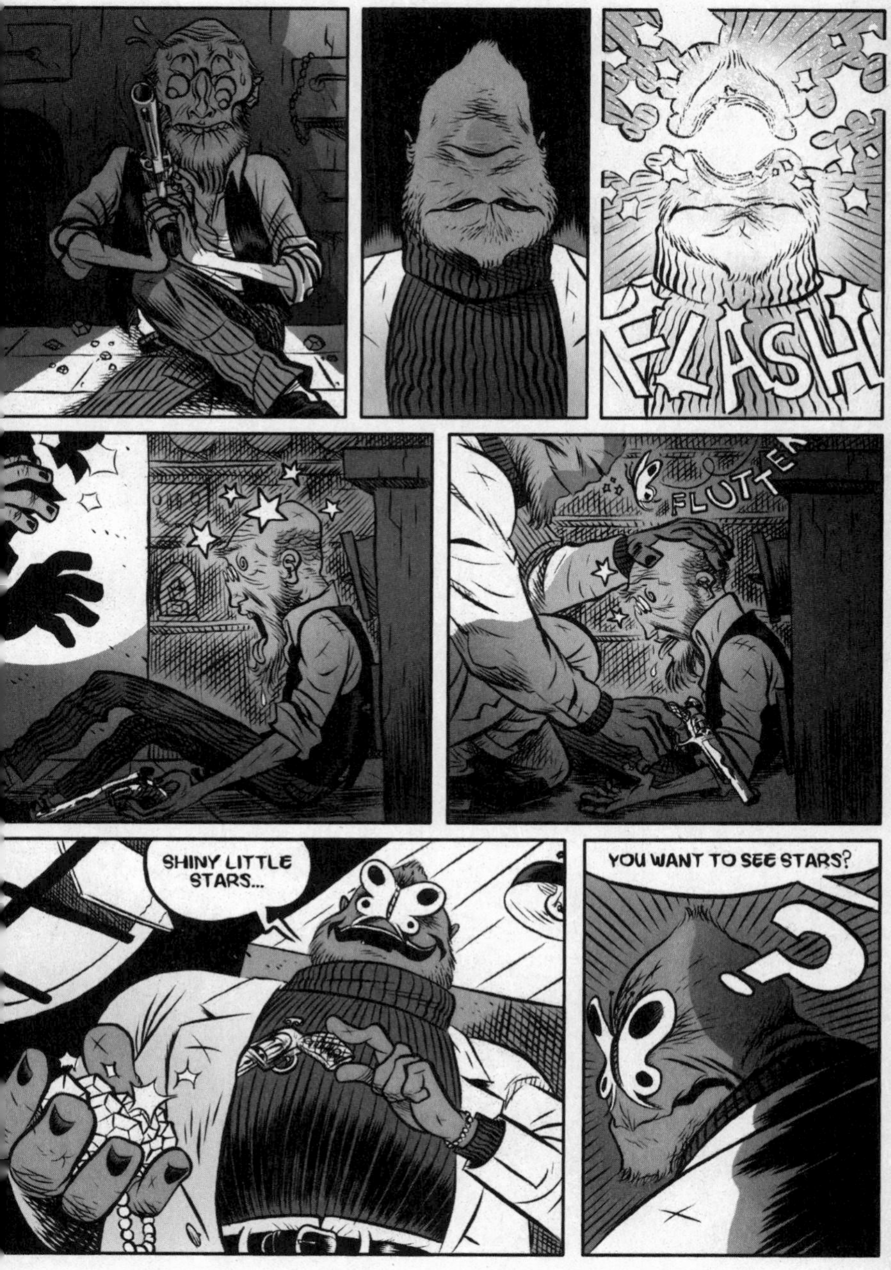
FLASH
FLUTTER
SHINY LITTLE STARS...
YOU WANT TO SEE STARS?

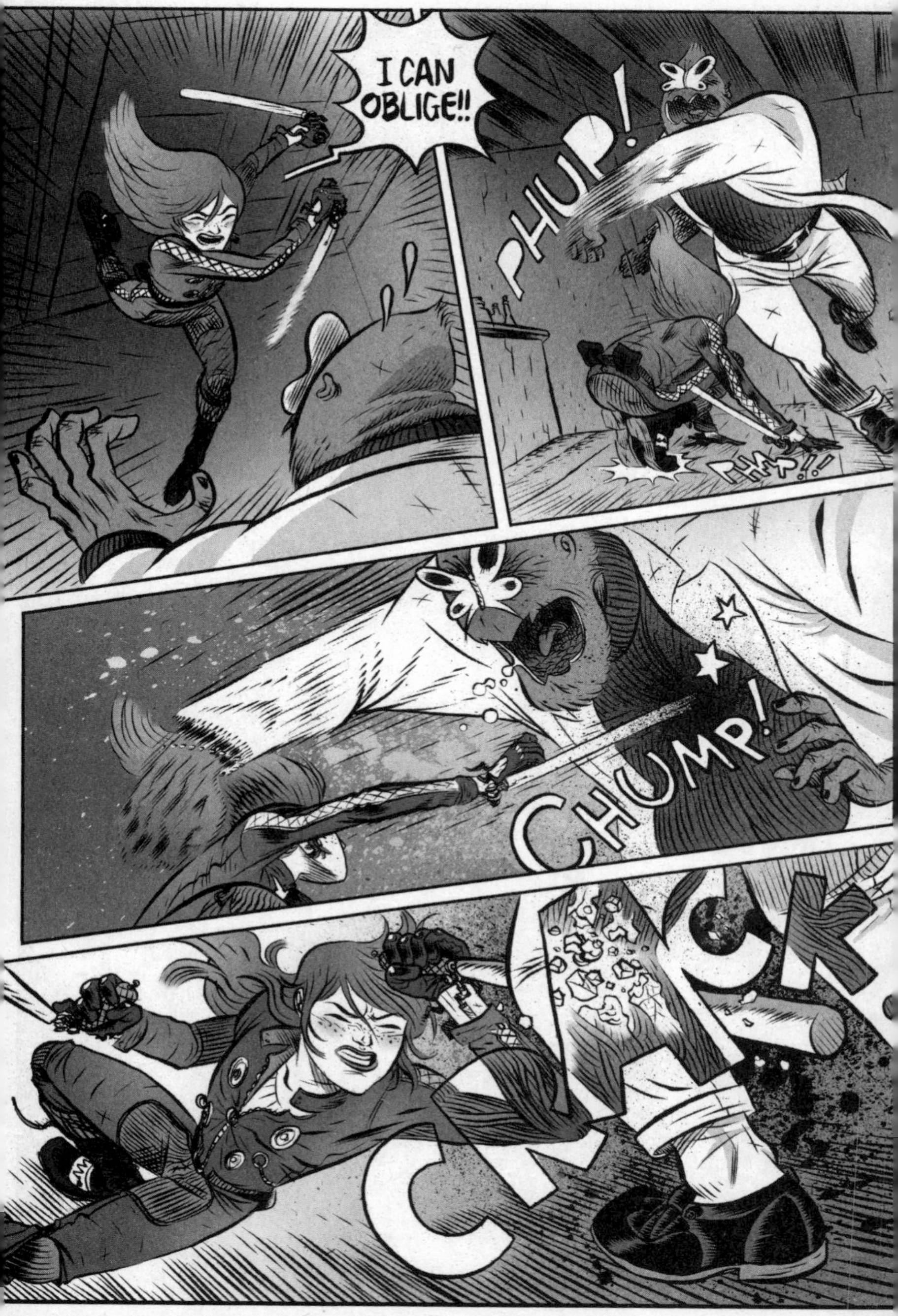
I CAN OBLIGE!!
PHUP!
PHMP!!
CHUMP!
CRACK!

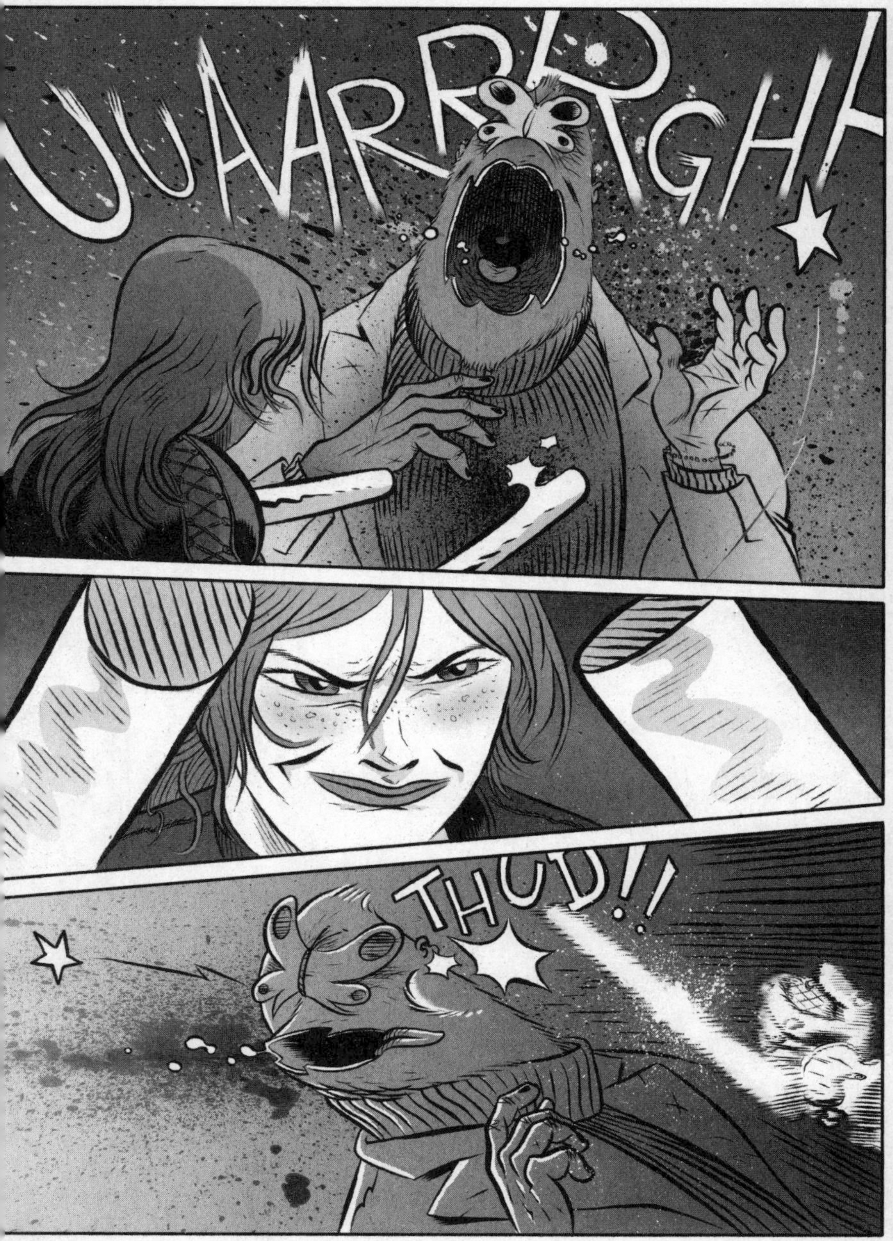
UUAARRRRGH!
THUD!!

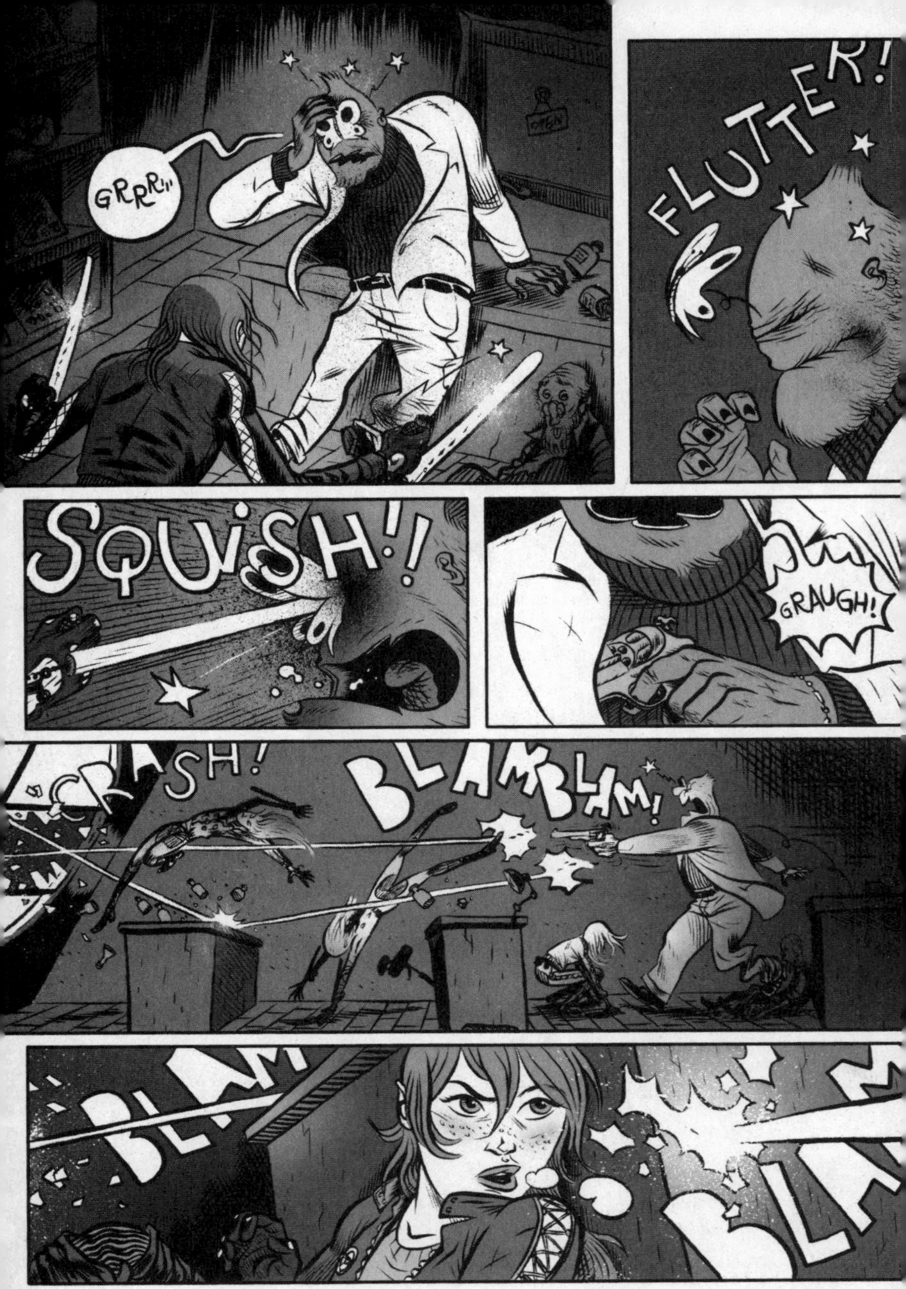

GRRR...
FLUTTER!
SQUISH!!
GRAUGH!
CRASH!
BLAMBLAM!
BLAM

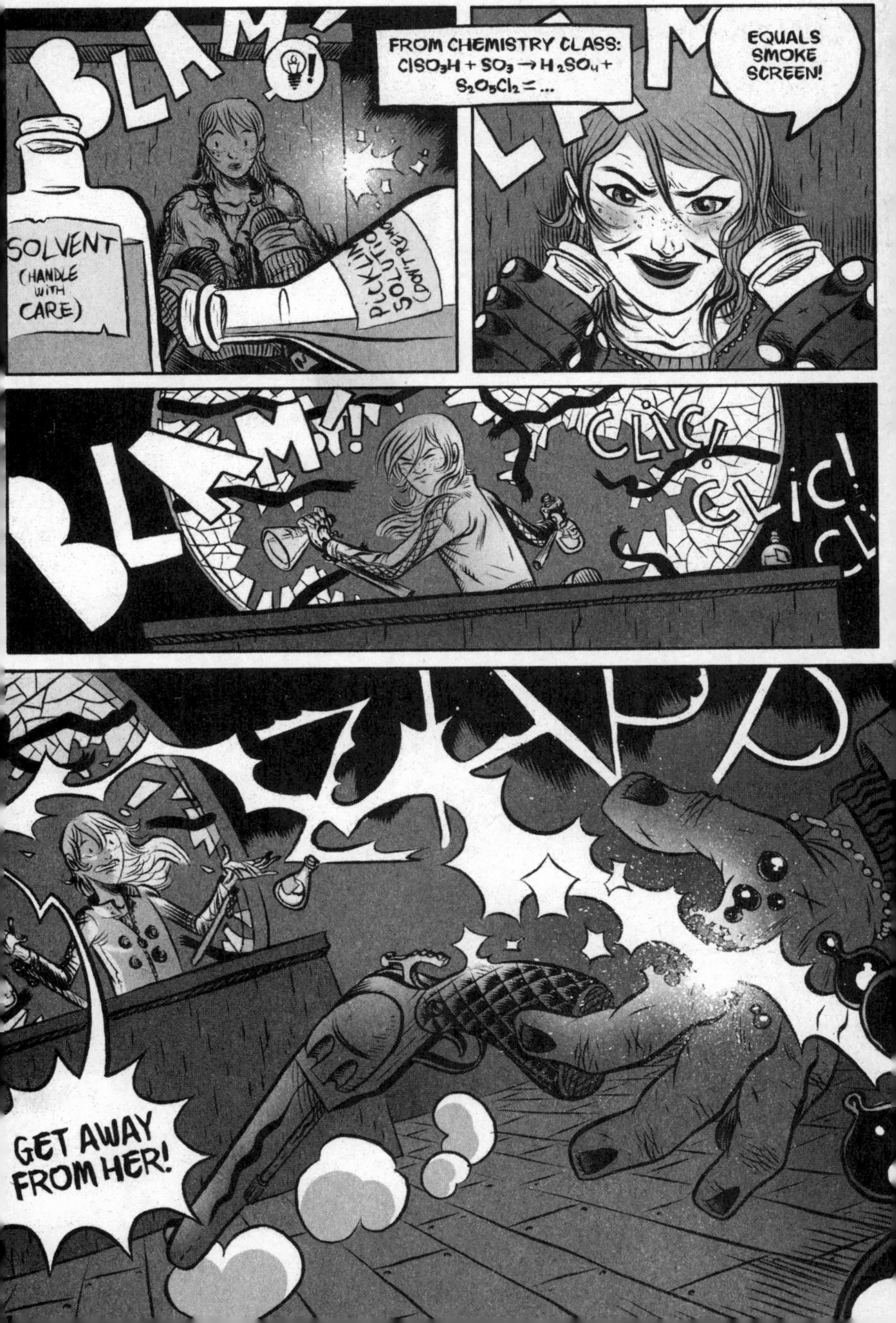
BLAM!
SOLVENT (HANDLE WITH CARE)
FROM CHEMISTRY CLASS: $ClSO_3H + SO_3 \rightarrow H_2SO_4 + S_2O_5Cl_2 = ...$
EQUALS SMOKE SCREEN!
BLAM!
CLIC!
CLIC!
GET AWAY FROM HER!

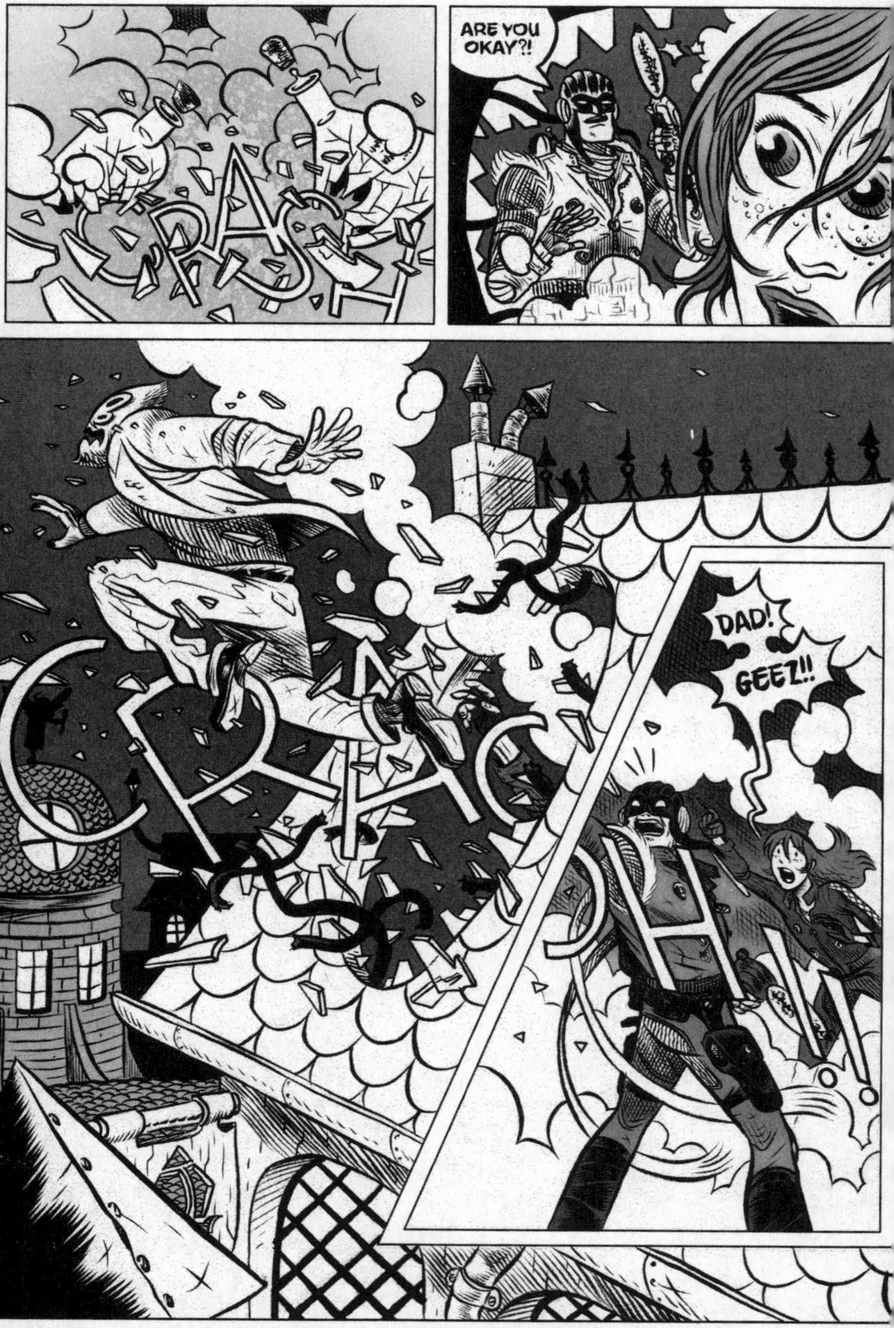
CRASH
ARE YOU OKAY?!
CRASH
DAD!
GEEZ!!

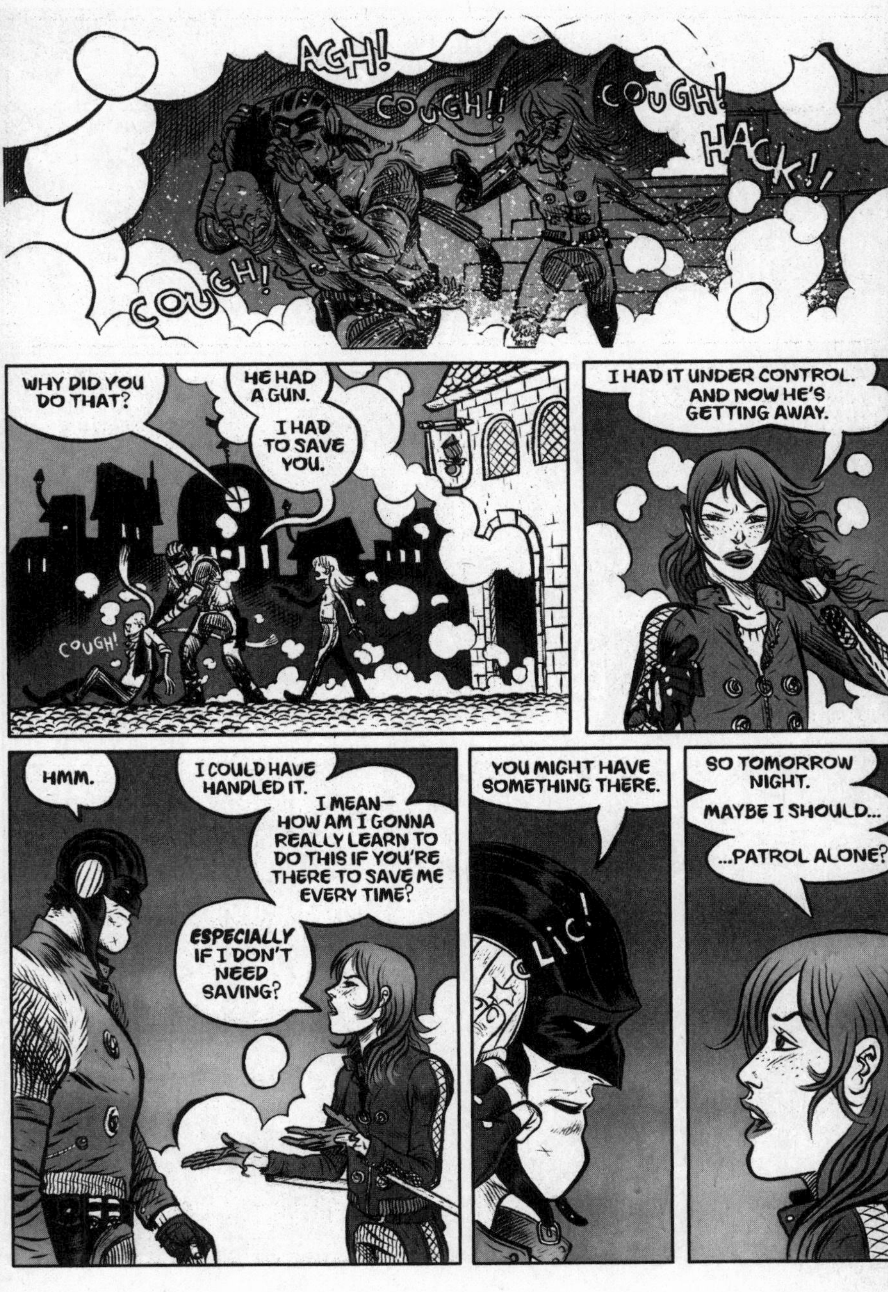
AGH!
COUGH!!
COUGH!
HACK!!
COUGH!
WHY DID YOU DO THAT?
HE HAD A GUN.
I HAD TO SAVE YOU.
COUGH!
I HAD IT UNDER CONTROL. AND NOW HE'S GETTING AWAY.
HMM.
I COULD HAVE HANDLED IT.
I MEAN— HOW AM I GONNA REALLY LEARN TO DO THIS IF YOU'RE THERE TO SAVE ME EVERY TIME?
ESPECIALLY IF I DON'T NEED SAVING?
YOU MIGHT HAVE SOMETHING THERE.
CLIC!
SO TOMORROW NIGHT.
MAYBE I SHOULD...
...PATROL ALONE?

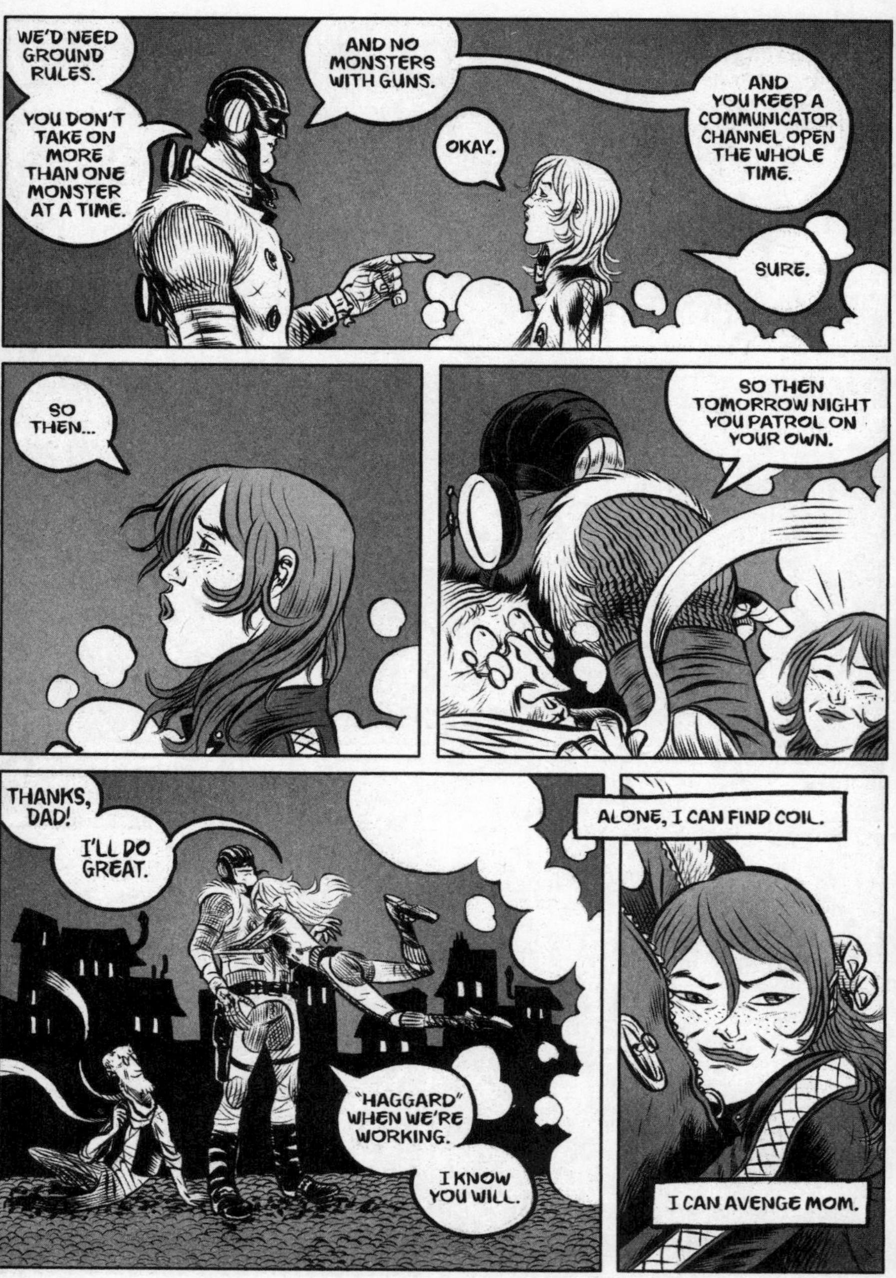
WE'D NEED GROUND RULES.
YOU DON'T TAKE ON MORE THAN ONE MONSTER AT A TIME.
AND NO MONSTERS WITH GUNS.
OKAY.
AND YOU KEEP A COMMUNICATOR CHANNEL OPEN THE WHOLE TIME.
SURE.
SO THEN...
SO THEN TOMORROW NIGHT YOU PATROL ON YOUR OWN.
THANKS, DAD!
I'LL DO GREAT.
"HAGGARD" WHEN WE'RE WORKING.
I KNOW YOU WILL.
ALONE, I CAN FIND COIL.
I CAN AVENGE MOM.

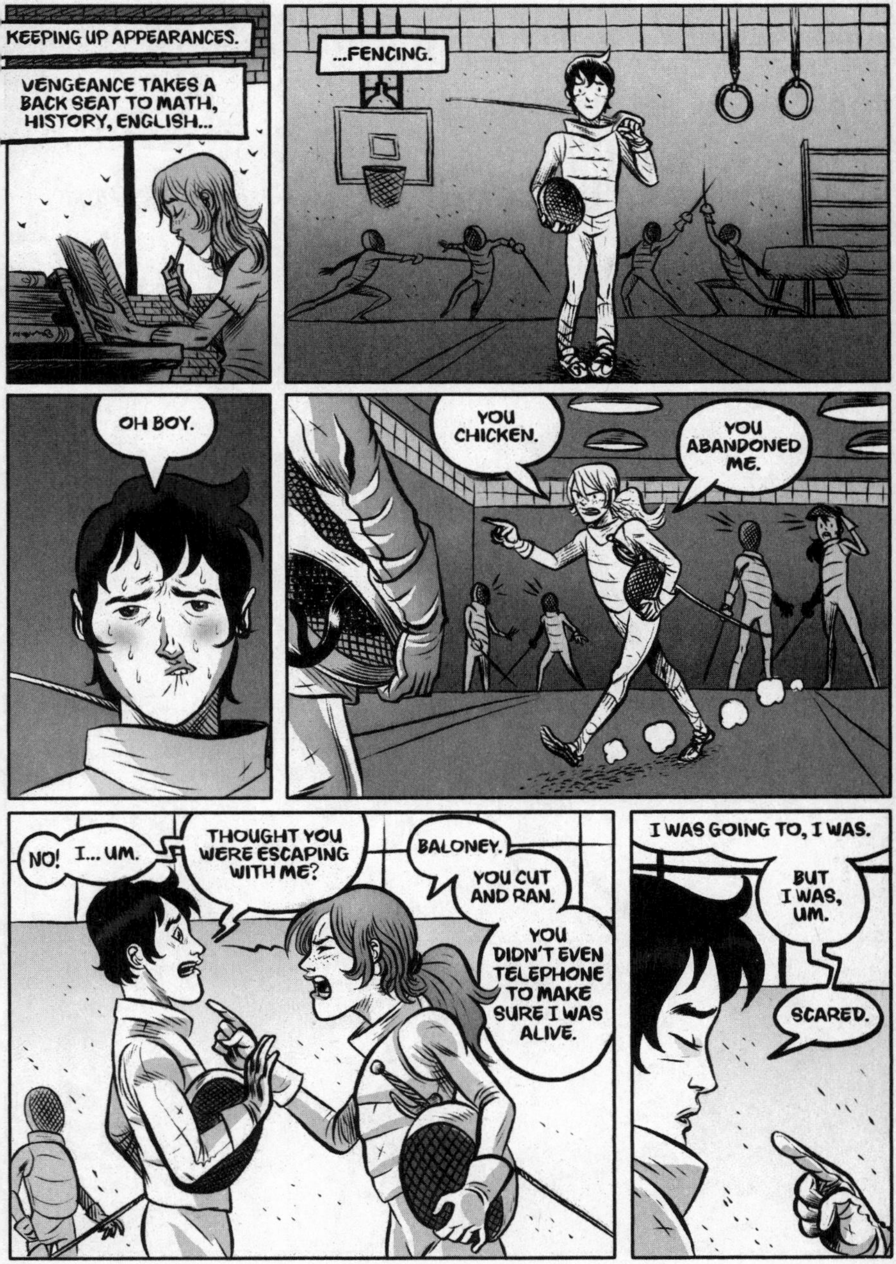
KEEPING UP APPEARANCES.
VENGEANCE TAKES A BACK SEAT TO MATH, HISTORY, ENGLISH...
...FENCING.
OH BOY.
YOU CHICKEN.
YOU ABANDONED ME.
NO! I... UM.
THOUGHT YOU WERE ESCAPING WITH ME?
BALONEY.
YOU CUT AND RAN.
YOU DIDN'T EVEN TELEPHONE TO MAKE SURE I WAS ALIVE.
I WAS GOING TO, I WAS.
BUT I WAS, UM.
SCARED.

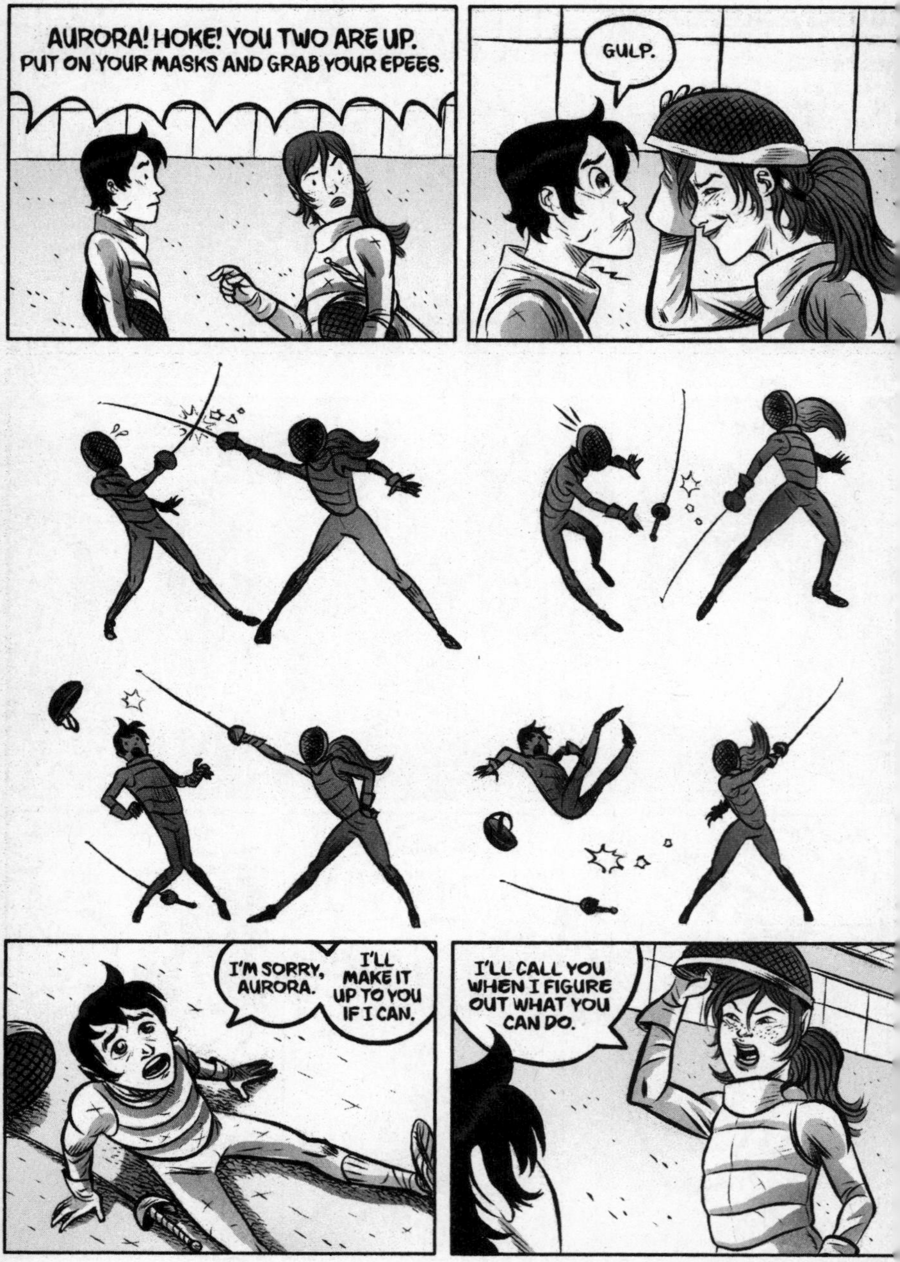
AURORA! HOKE! YOU TWO ARE UP.
PUT ON YOUR MASKS AND GRAB YOUR EPEES.
GULP.
I'M SORRY, AURORA.
I'LL MAKE IT UP TO YOU IF I CAN.
I'LL CALL YOU WHEN I FIGURE OUT WHAT YOU CAN DO.

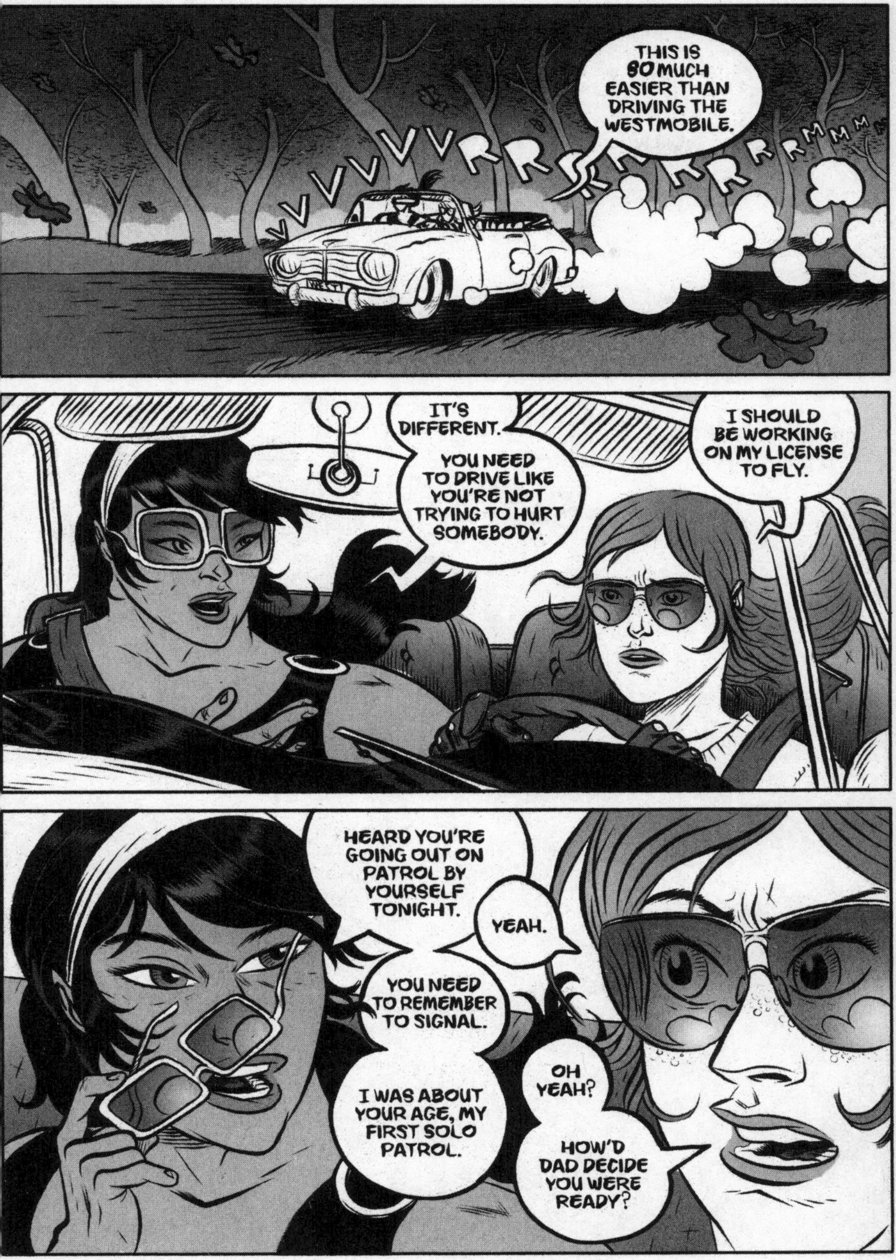
THIS IS SO MUCH EASIER THAN DRIVING THE WESTMOBILE.
VVVVVVVRRRRRRRRRRRRMMMM
IT'S DIFFERENT.
YOU NEED TO DRIVE LIKE YOU'RE NOT TRYING TO HURT SOMEBODY.
I SHOULD BE WORKING ON MY LICENSE TO FLY.
HEARD YOU'RE GOING OUT ON PATROL BY YOURSELF TONIGHT.
YEAH.
YOU NEED TO REMEMBER TO SIGNAL.
I WAS ABOUT YOUR AGE, MY FIRST SOLO PATROL.
OH YEAH?
HOW'D DAD DECIDE YOU WERE READY?

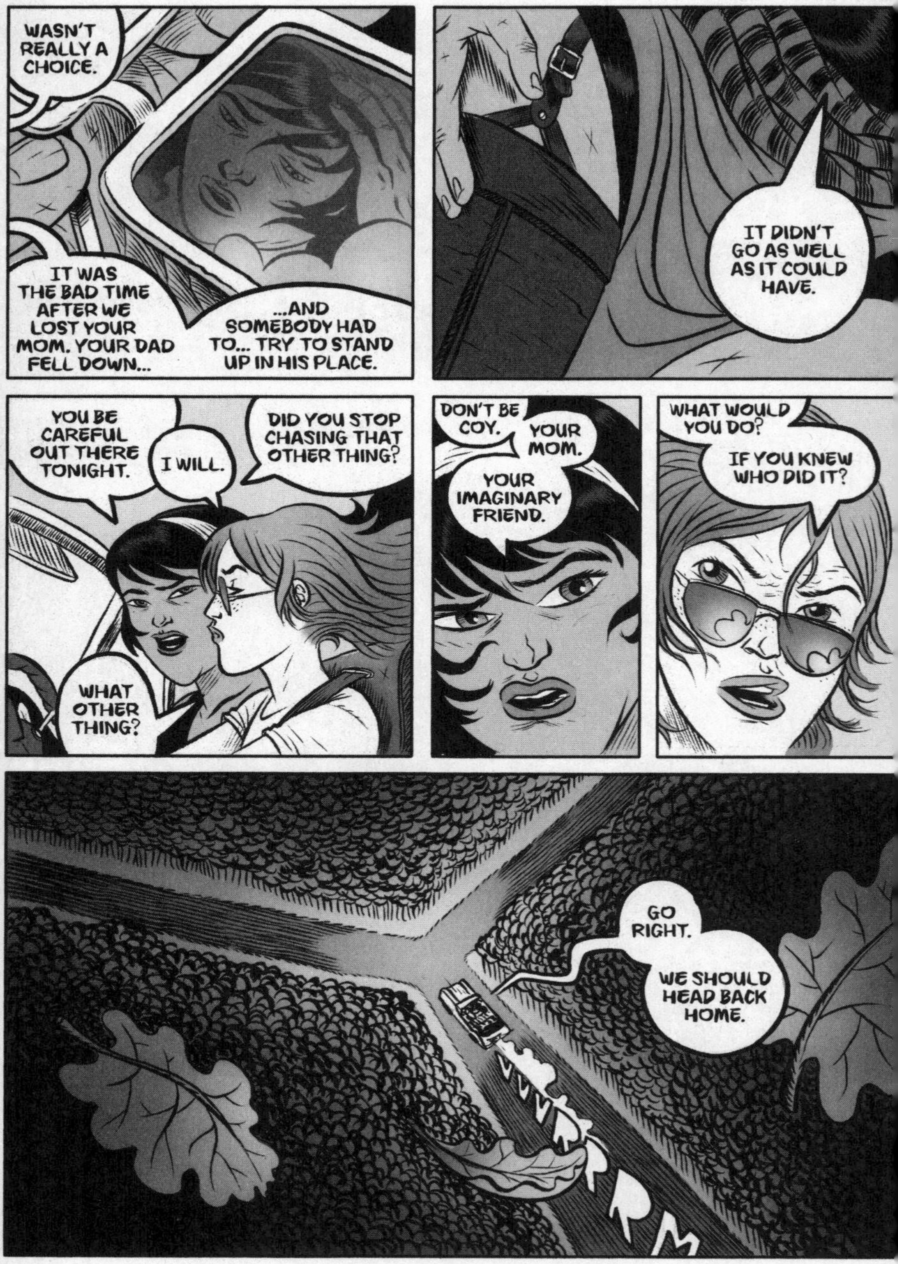
WASN'T REALLY A CHOICE.
IT WAS THE BAD TIME AFTER WE LOST YOUR MOM. YOUR DAD FELL DOWN...
...AND SOMEBODY HAD TO... TRY TO STAND UP IN HIS PLACE.
IT DIDN'T GO AS WELL AS IT COULD HAVE.
YOU BE CAREFUL OUT THERE TONIGHT.
I WILL.
DID YOU STOP CHASING THAT OTHER THING?
WHAT OTHER THING?
DON'T BE COY.
YOUR MOM.
YOUR IMAGINARY FRIEND.
WHAT WOULD YOU DO?
IF YOU KNEW WHO DID IT?
GO RIGHT.
WE SHOULD HEAD BACK HOME.

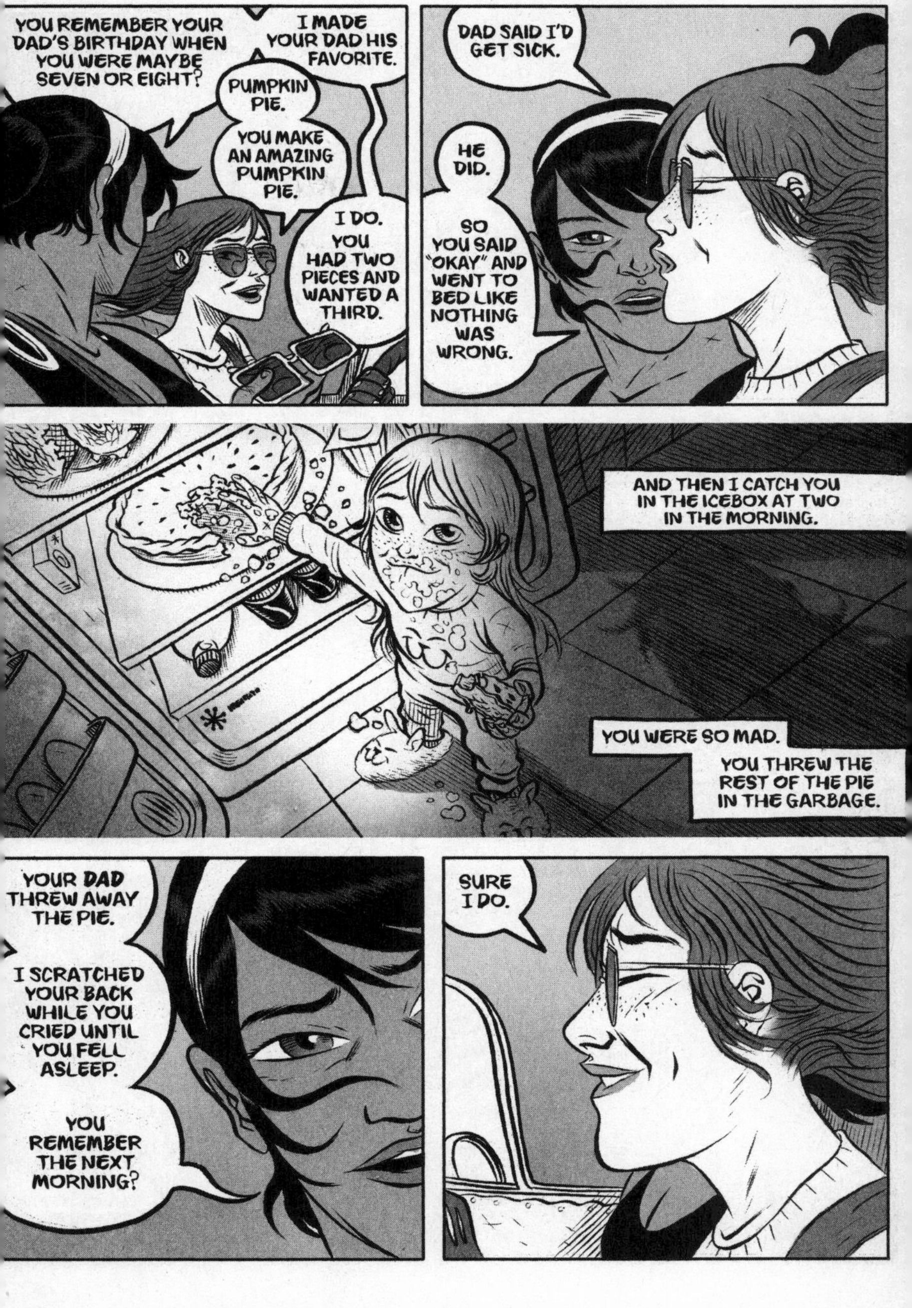
YOU REMEMBER YOUR DAD'S BIRTHDAY WHEN YOU WERE MAYBE SEVEN OR EIGHT?
I MADE YOUR DAD HIS FAVORITE.
PUMPKIN PIE.
YOU MAKE AN AMAZING PUMPKIN PIE.
I DO.
YOU HAD TWO PIECES AND WANTED A THIRD.
DAD SAID I'D GET SICK.
HE DID.
SO YOU SAID "OKAY" AND WENT TO BED LIKE NOTHING WAS WRONG.
AND THEN I CATCH YOU IN THE ICEBOX AT TWO IN THE MORNING.
YOU WERE SO MAD.
YOU THREW THE REST OF THE PIE IN THE GARBAGE.
YOUR DAD THREW AWAY THE PIE.
I SCRATCHED YOUR BACK WHILE YOU CRIED UNTIL YOU FELL ASLEEP.
YOU REMEMBER THE NEXT MORNING?
SURE I DO.

SIX A.M. YOU ATE THE WHOLE REST OF THE PIE.

YUM!

THAT PIE WAS INCREDIBLE.

OF COURSE IT WAS.

ONLY THING THAT TASTES BETTER THAN PUMPKIN PIE IS STOLEN PUMPKIN PIE.

WM2

I WAS SICK ALL MORNING.

YOU WERE SICK FOR *TWO DAYS.*

THAT'S WHY I'M TELLIN' THE STORY, 'ROAR...

...THAT'S WHAT I'M WORRIED ABOUT—

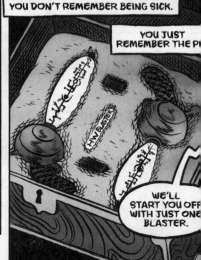

YOU DON'T REMEMBER BEING SICK.

YOU JUST REMEMBER THE P

WE'LL START YOU OFF WITH JUST ONE BLASTER.

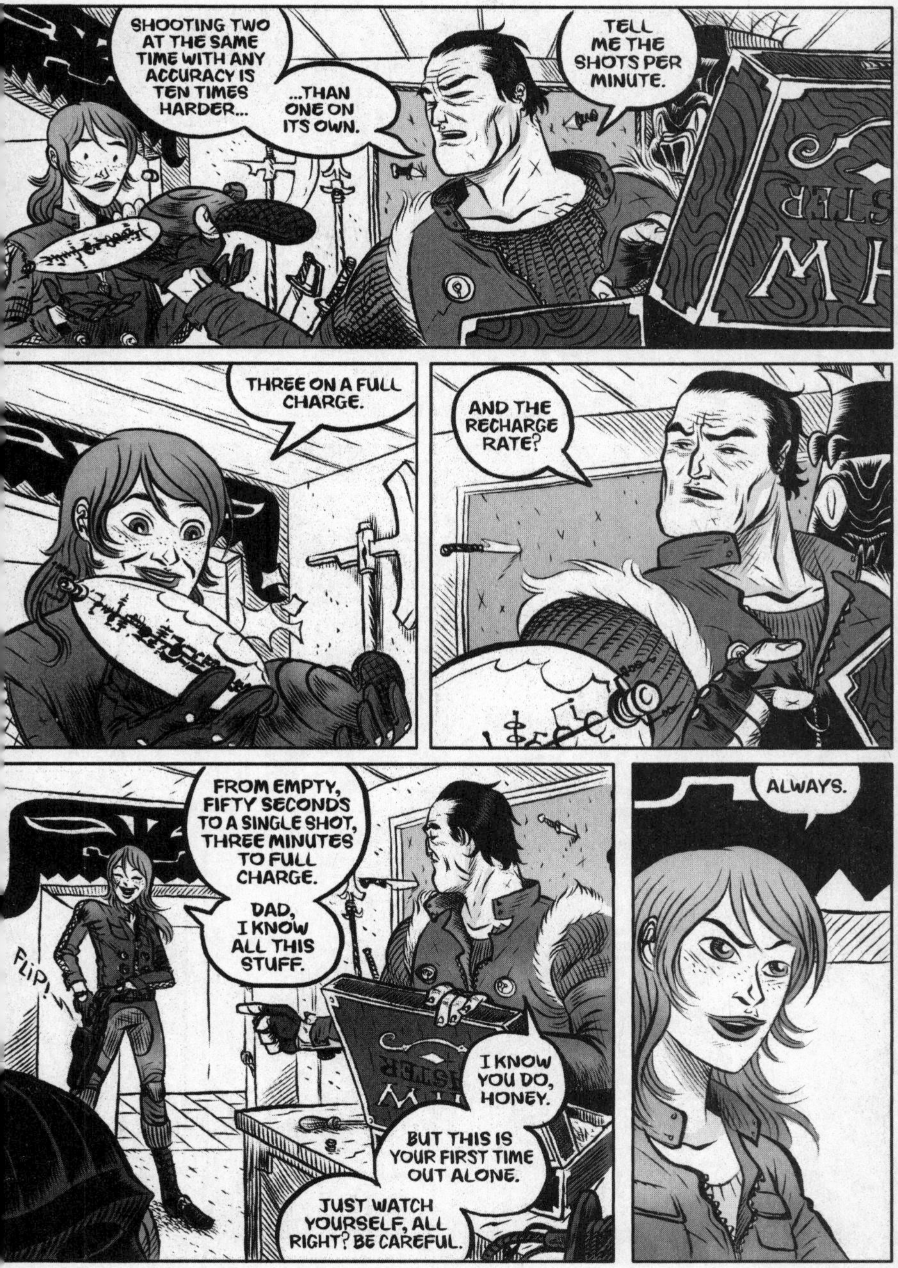
SHOOTING TWO AT THE SAME TIME WITH ANY ACCURACY IS TEN TIMES HARDER...
...THAN ONE ON ITS OWN.
TELL ME THE SHOTS PER MINUTE.
THREE ON A FULL CHARGE.
AND THE RECHARGE RATE?
FROM EMPTY, FIFTY SECONDS TO A SINGLE SHOT, THREE MINUTES TO FULL CHARGE.
DAD, I KNOW ALL THIS STUFF.
FLIP!
I KNOW YOU DO, HONEY.
BUT THIS IS YOUR FIRST TIME OUT ALONE.
JUST WATCH YOURSELF, ALL RIGHT? BE CAREFUL.
ALWAYS.

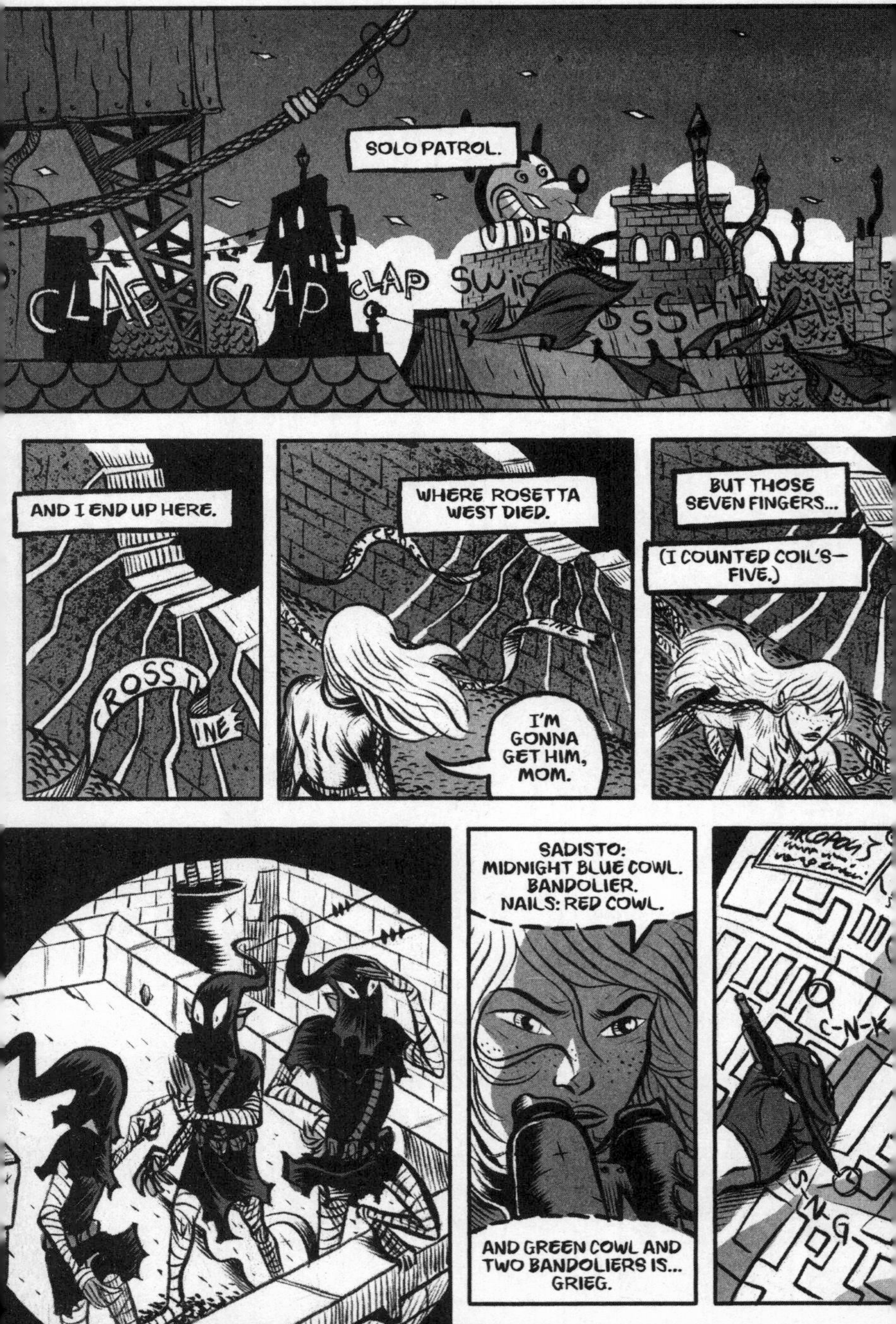
SOLO PATROL.
CLAP
CLAP
CLAP
AND I END UP HERE.
WHERE ROSETTA WEST DIED.
I'M GONNA GET HIM, MOM.
BUT THOSE SEVEN FINGERS...
(I COUNTED COIL'S— FIVE.)
SADISTO: MIDNIGHT BLUE COWL. BANDOLIER. NAILS: RED COWL.
AND GREEN COWL AND TWO BANDOLIERS IS... GRIEG.
C-N-K

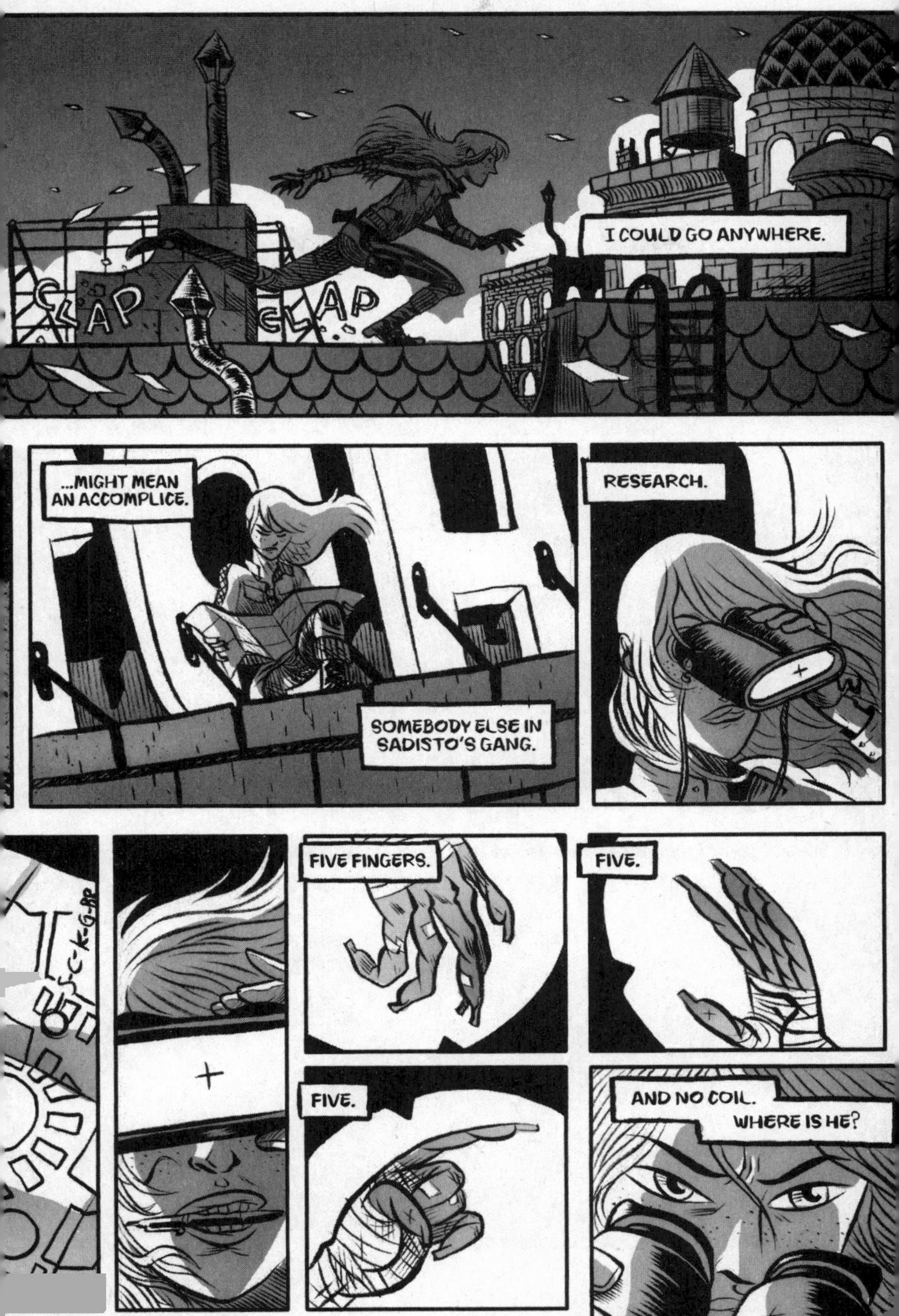
CLAP
CLAP
I COULD GO ANYWHERE.
...MIGHT MEAN AN ACCOMPLICE.
SOMEBODY ELSE IN SADISTO'S GANG.
RESEARCH.
FIVE FINGERS.
FIVE.
FIVE.
AND NO COIL.
WHERE IS HE?

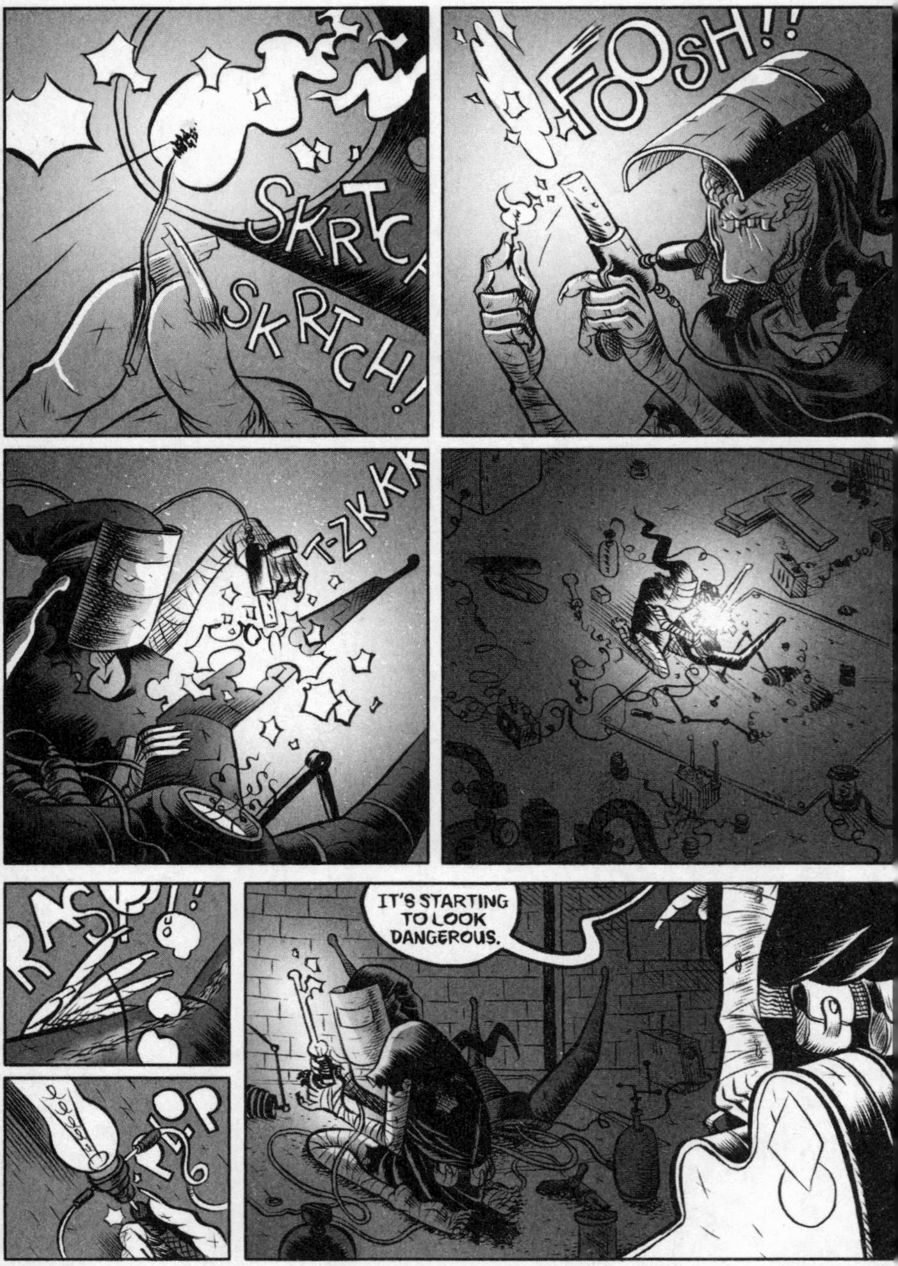
SKRTCH
SKRTCH!
FOOSH!!
T-ZKKK
RASP!!
PLOP
IT'S STARTING TO LOOK DANGEROUS.

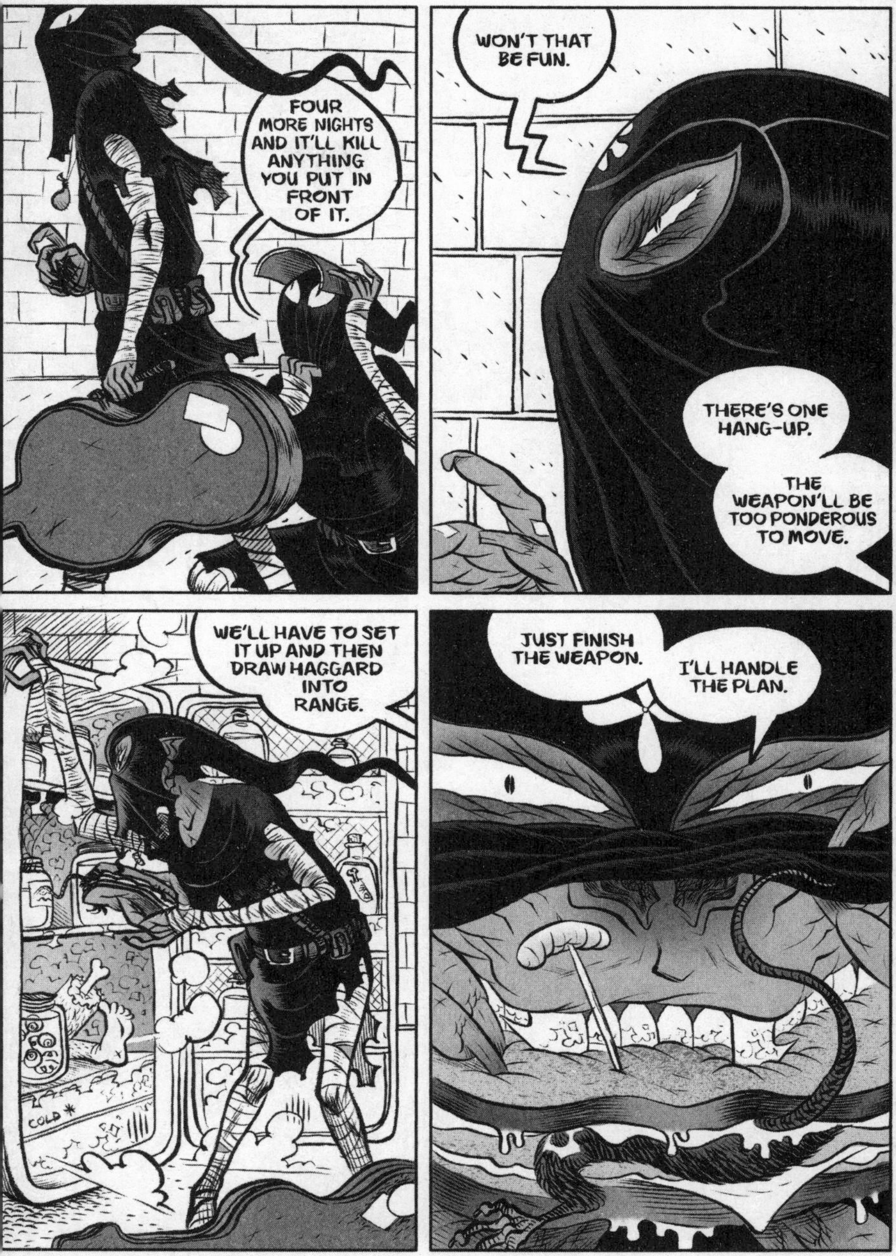

FOUR MORE NIGHTS AND IT'LL KILL ANYTHING YOU PUT IN FRONT OF IT.
WON'T THAT BE FUN.
THERE'S ONE HANG-UP.
THE WEAPON'LL BE TOO PONDEROUS TO MOVE.
WE'LL HAVE TO SET IT UP AND THEN DRAW HAGGARD INTO RANGE.
COLD
JUST FINISH THE WEAPON.
I'LL HANDLE THE PLAN.

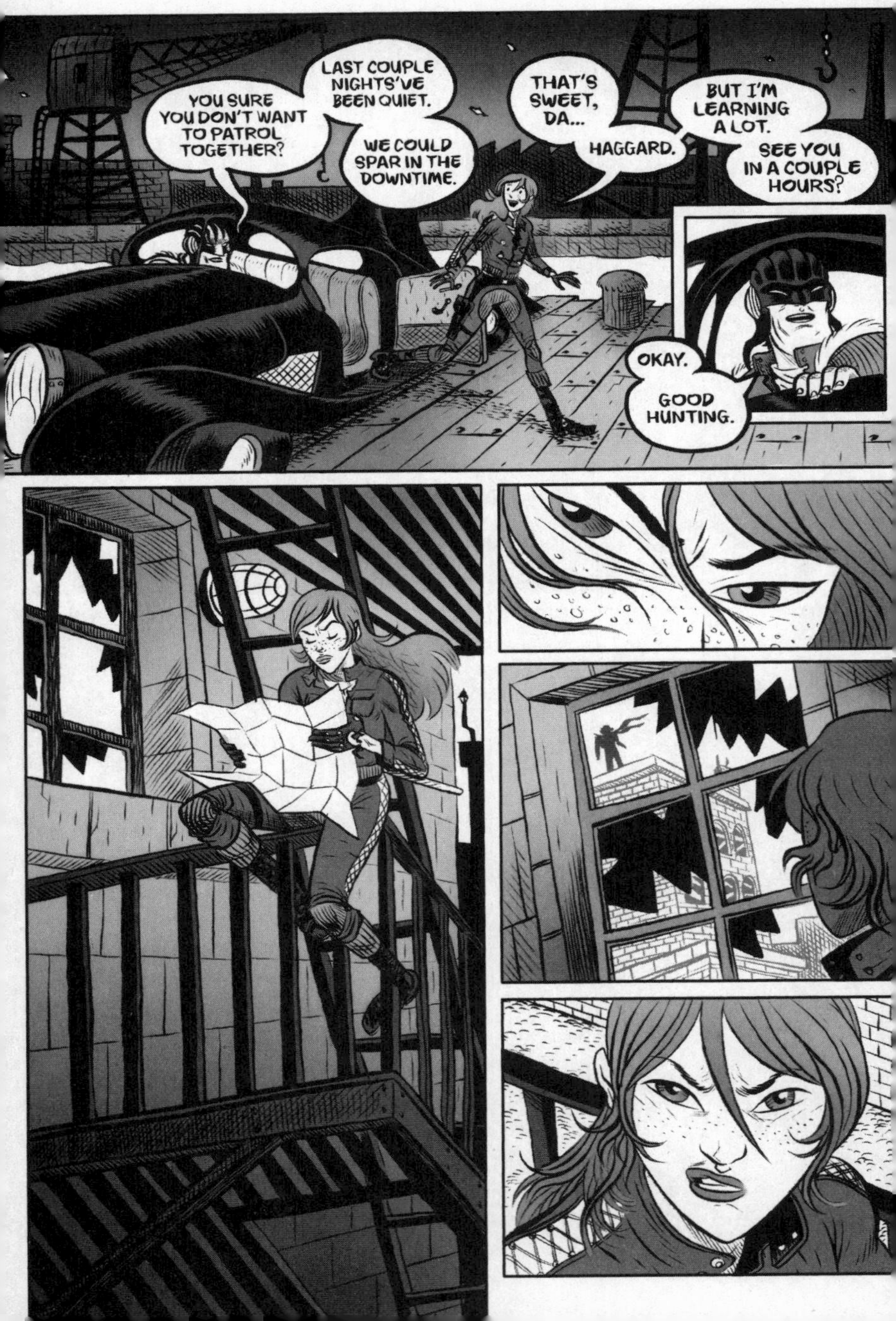
YOU SURE YOU DON'T WANT TO PATROL TOGETHER?
LAST COUPLE NIGHTS'VE BEEN QUIET.
WE COULD SPAR IN THE DOWNTIME.
THAT'S SWEET, DA...
HAGGARD.
BUT I'M LEARNING A LOT.
SEE YOU IN A COUPLE HOURS?
OKAY.
GOOD HUNTING.

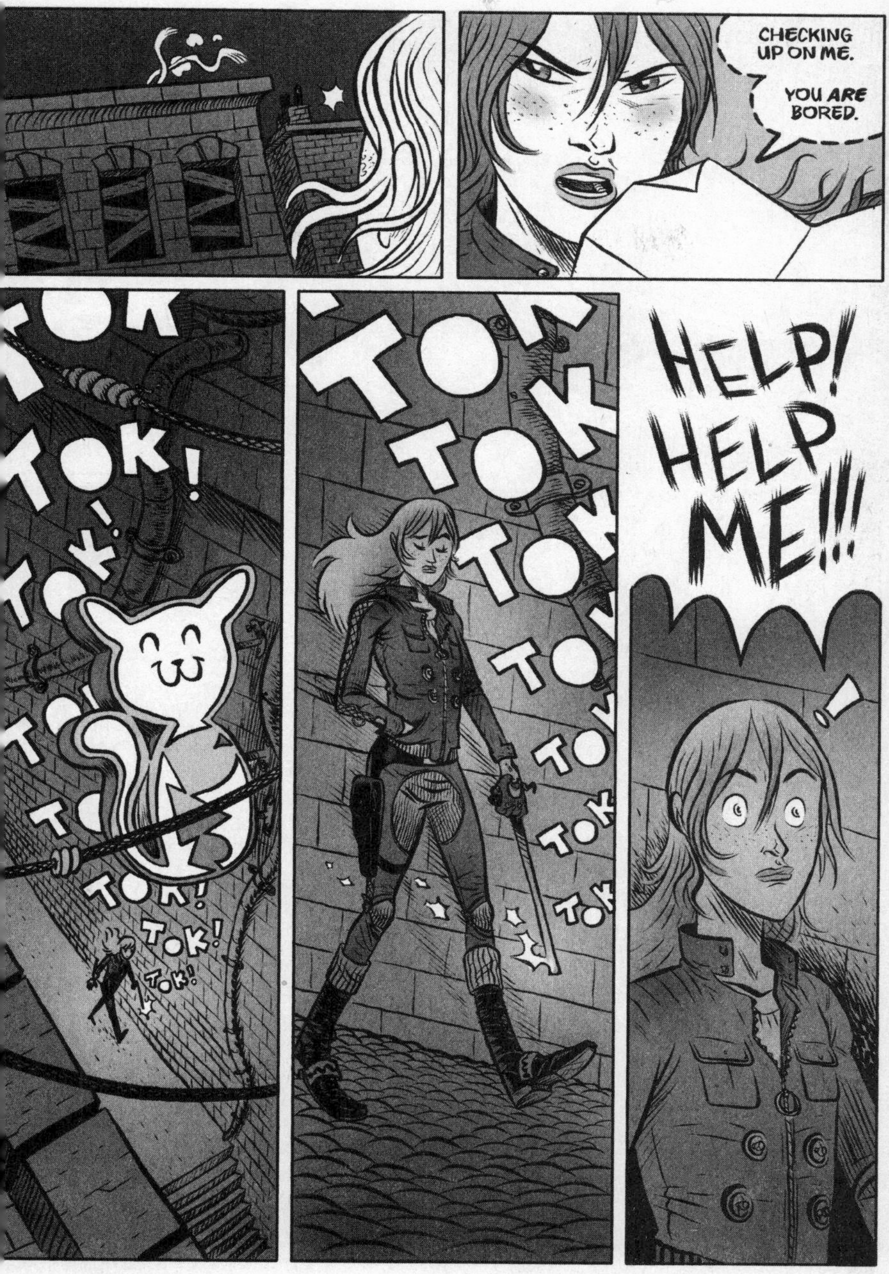
CHECKING UP ON ME.
YOU ARE BORED.
TOK TOK!
TOK!
TOK
TOK
TOK!
TOK!
TOK!
TOK
TOK
TOK
TOK
TOK
TOK
TOK
TOK
HELP! HELP ME!!!
!

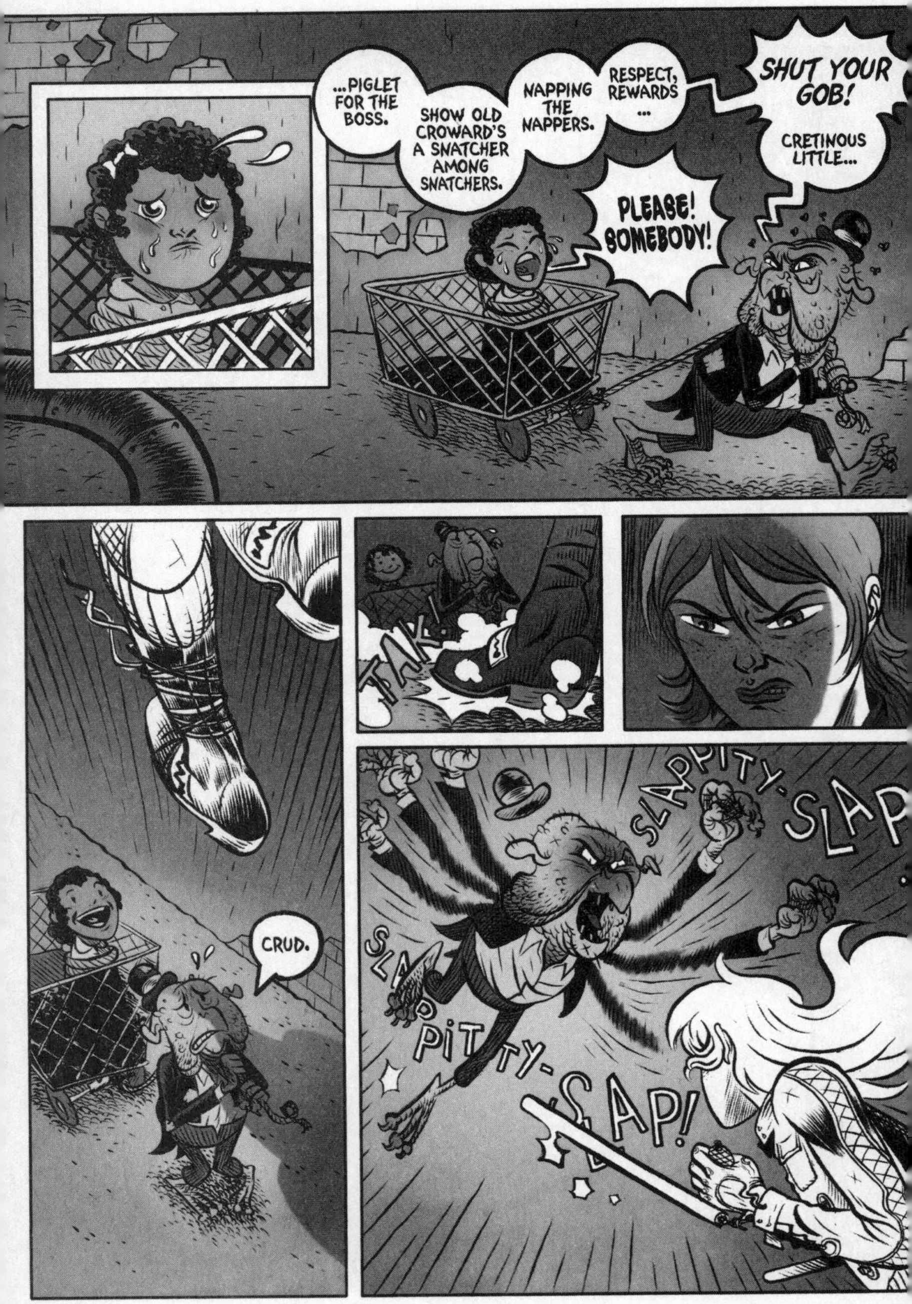
...PIGLET FOR THE BOSS.
SHOW OLD CROWARD'S A SNATCHER AMONG SNATCHERS.
NAPPING THE NAPPERS.
RESPECT, REWARDS ...
SHUT YOUR GOB!
CRETINOUS LITTLE...
PLEASE! SOMEBODY!
TAK!
CRUD.
SLAPPITY-SLAP
SLAPPITTY-SLAP!

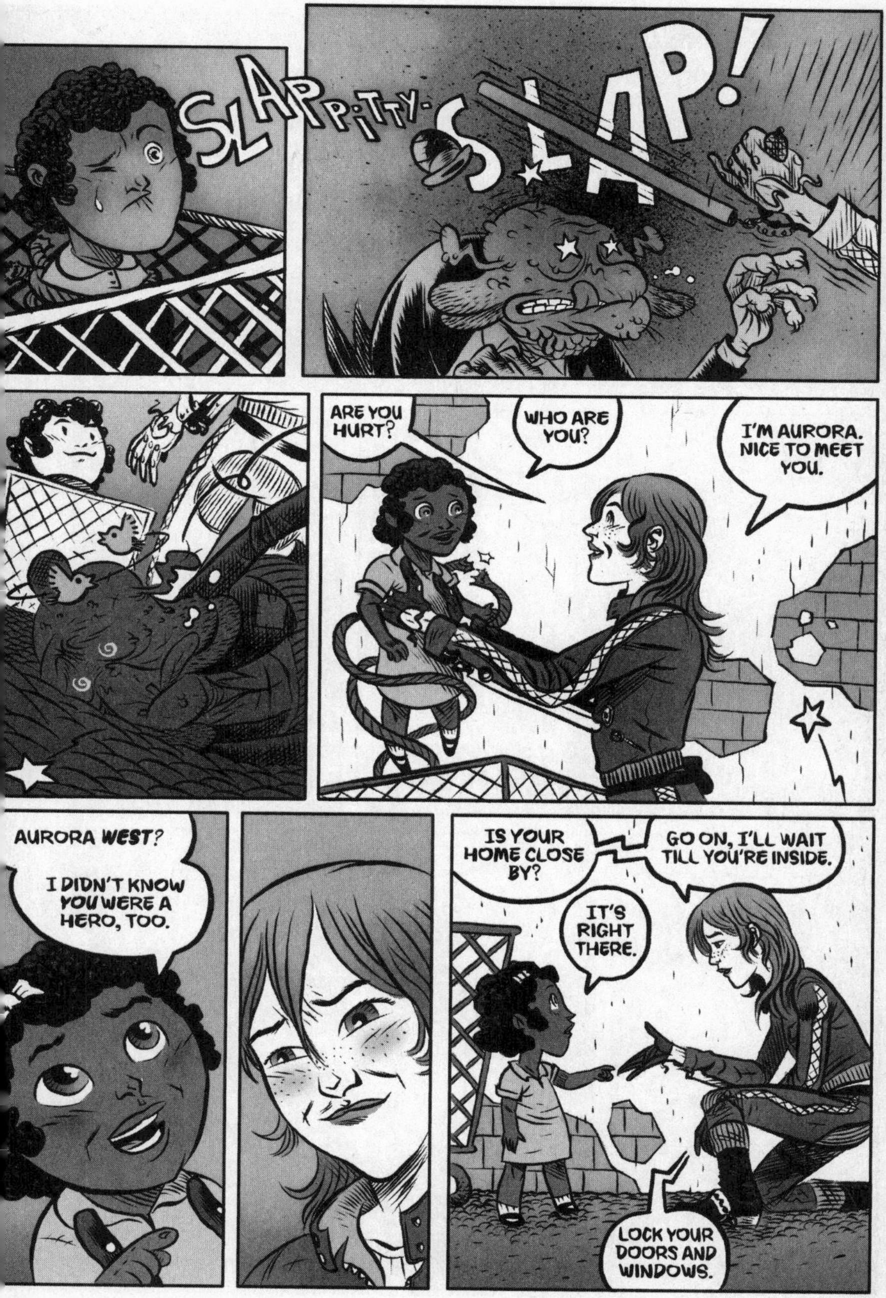
SLAPPITTY-SLAP!
ARE YOU HURT?
WHO ARE YOU?
I'M AURORA. NICE TO MEET YOU.
AURORA WEST?
I DIDN'T KNOW YOU WERE A HERO, TOO.
IS YOUR HOME CLOSE BY?
GO ON, I'LL WAIT TILL YOU'RE INSIDE.
IT'S RIGHT THERE.
LOCK YOUR DOORS AND WINDOWS.

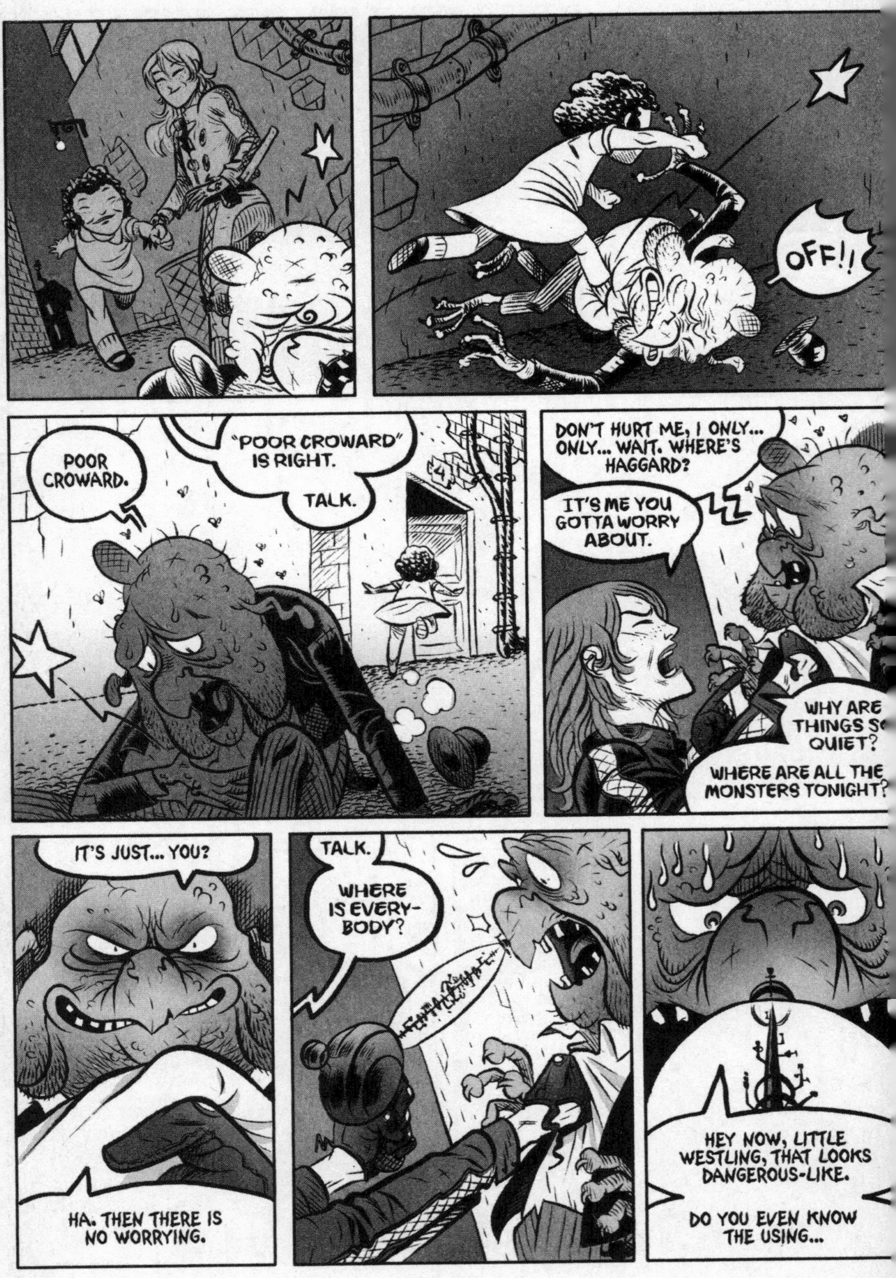
OFF!!
POOR CROWARD.
"POOR CROWARD" IS RIGHT.
TALK.
DON'T HURT ME, I ONLY... ONLY... WAIT. WHERE'S HAGGARD?
IT'S ME YOU GOTTA WORRY ABOUT.
WHY ARE THINGS SO QUIET?
WHERE ARE ALL THE MONSTERS TONIGHT?
IT'S JUST... YOU?
HA. THEN THERE IS NO WORRYING.
TALK.
WHERE IS EVERY-BODY?
HEY NOW, LITTLE WESTLING, THAT LOOKS DANGEROUS-LIKE.
DO YOU EVEN KNOW THE USING...

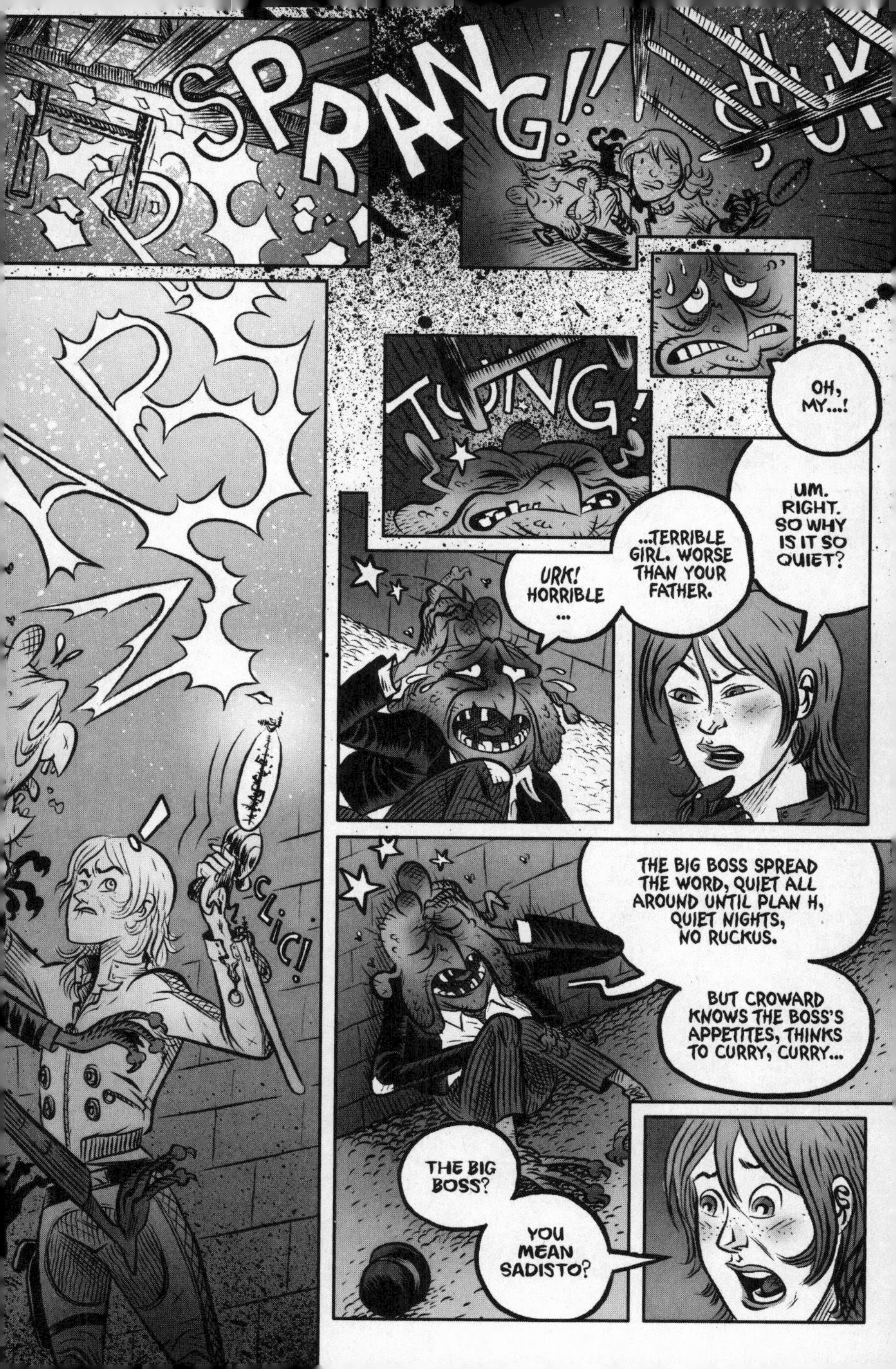
SPRANG!!
CHUK
TUNG!
OH, MY...!
CLIC!
URK! HORRIBLE ...
...TERRIBLE GIRL. WORSE THAN YOUR FATHER.
UM. RIGHT. SO WHY IS IT SO QUIET?
THE BIG BOSS SPREAD THE WORD, QUIET ALL AROUND UNTIL PLAN H, QUIET NIGHTS, NO RUCKUS.
BUT CROWARD KNOWS THE BOSS'S APPETITES, THINKS TO CURRY, CURRY...
THE BIG BOSS?
YOU MEAN SADISTO?

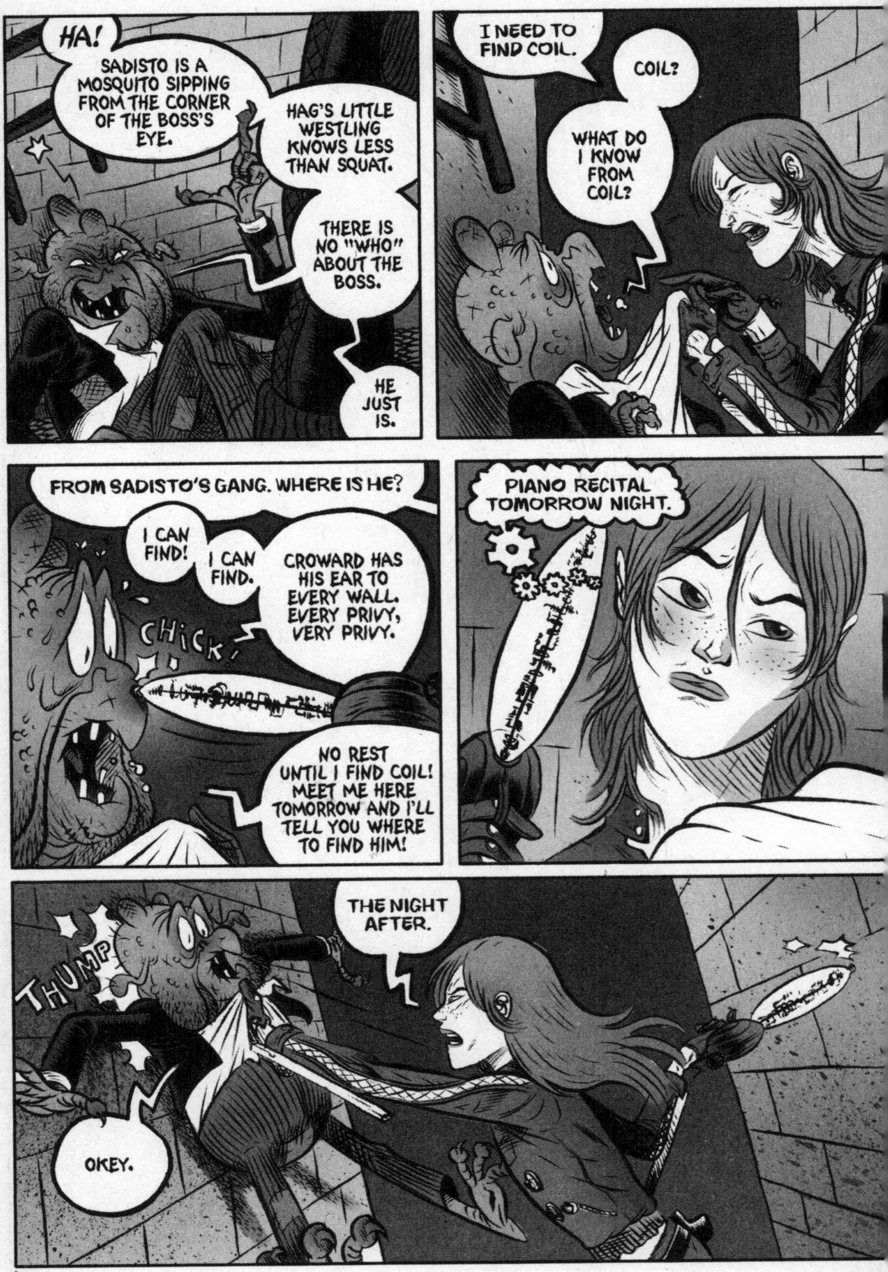
HA!
SADISTO IS A MOSQUITO SIPPING FROM THE CORNER OF THE BOSS'S EYE.
HAG'S LITTLE WESTLING KNOWS LESS THAN SQUAT.
THERE IS NO "WHO" ABOUT THE BOSS.
HE JUST IS.
I NEED TO FIND COIL.
COIL?
WHAT DO I KNOW FROM COIL?
FROM SADISTO'S GANG. WHERE IS HE?
I CAN FIND!
I CAN FIND.
CROWARD HAS HIS EAR TO EVERY WALL. EVERY PRIVY, VERY PRIVY.
CHICK!
NO REST UNTIL I FIND COIL! MEET ME HERE TOMORROW AND I'LL TELL YOU WHERE TO FIND HIM!
PIANO RECITAL TOMORROW NIGHT.
THE NIGHT AFTER.
THUMP
OKEY.

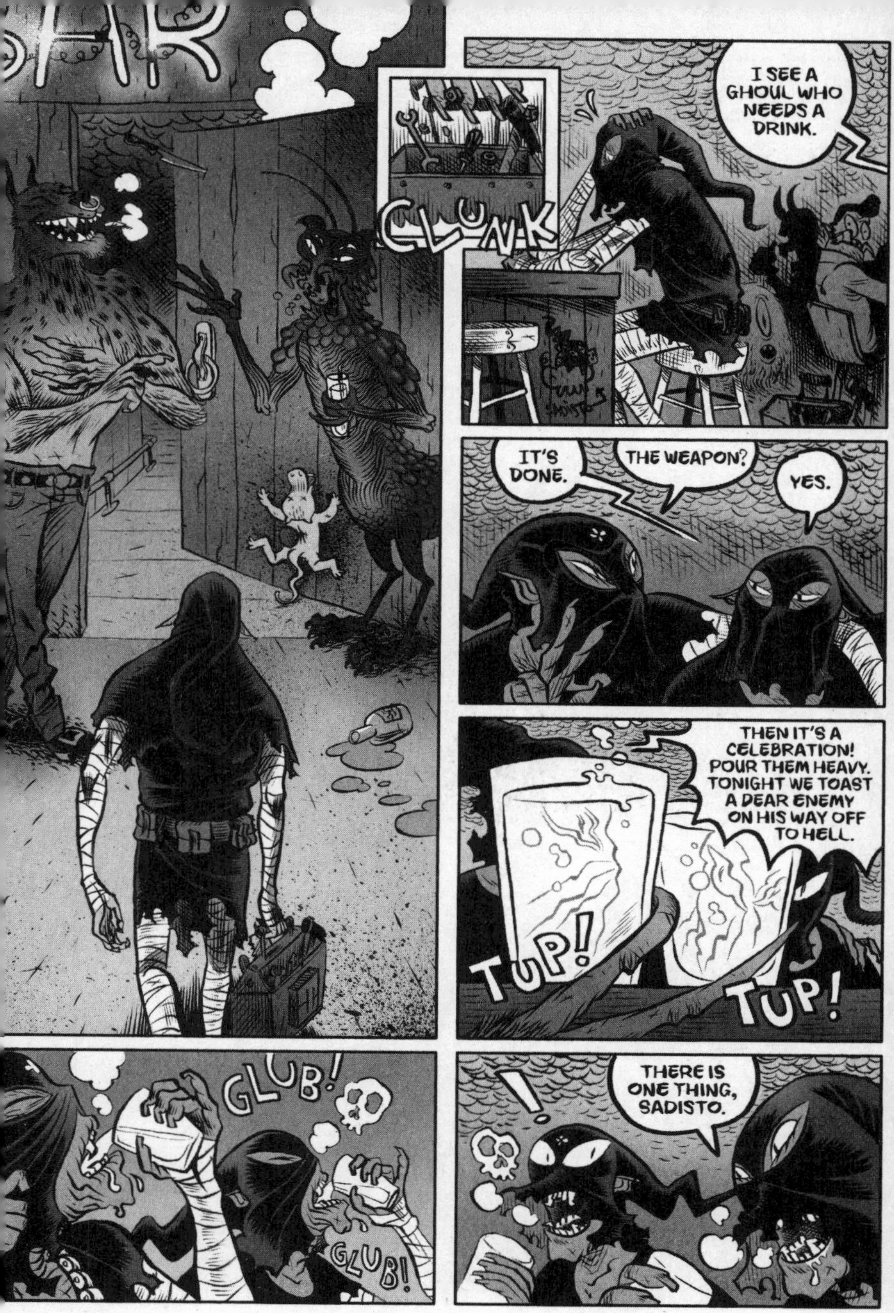
CLUNK
I SEE A GHOUL WHO NEEDS A DRINK.
IT'S DONE.
THE WEAPON?
YES.
THEN IT'S A CELEBRATION! POUR THEM HEAVY. TONIGHT WE TOAST A DEAR ENEMY ON HIS WAY OFF TO HELL.
TUP!
TUP!
GLUB!
GLUB!
!
THERE IS ONE THING, SADISTO.

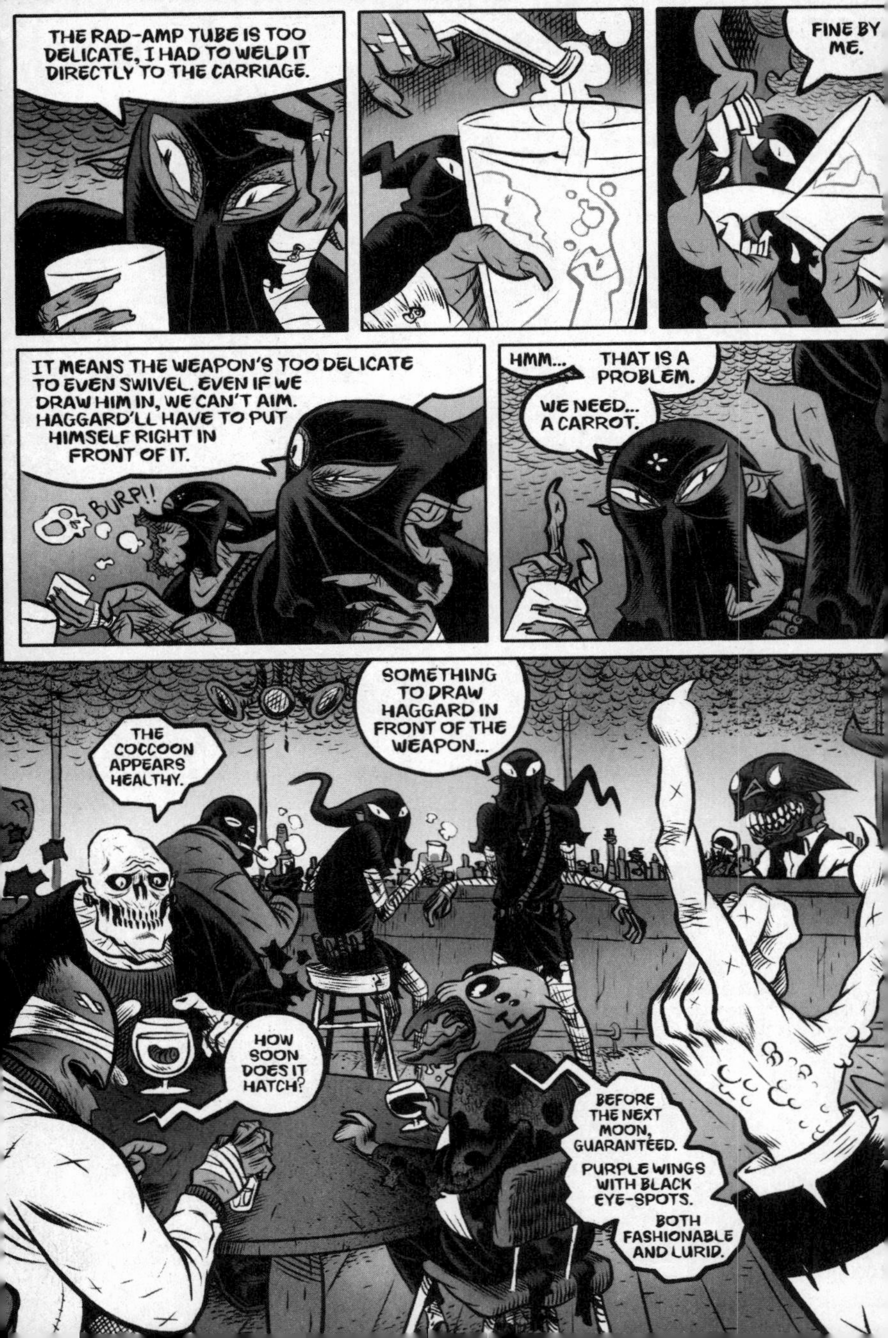

THE RAD-AMP TUBE IS TOO DELICATE, I HAD TO WELD IT DIRECTLY TO THE CARRIAGE.
FINE BY ME.
IT MEANS THE WEAPON'S TOO DELICATE TO EVEN SWIVEL. EVEN IF WE DRAW HIM IN, WE CAN'T AIM. HAGGARD'LL HAVE TO PUT HIMSELF RIGHT IN FRONT OF IT.
BURP!!
HMM...
THAT IS A PROBLEM.
WE NEED... A CARROT.
SOMETHING TO DRAW HAGGARD IN FRONT OF THE WEAPON...
THE COCCOON APPEARS HEALTHY.
HOW SOON DOES IT HATCH?
BEFORE THE NEXT MOON, GUARANTEED.
PURPLE WINGS WITH BLACK EYE-SPOTS.
BOTH FASHIONABLE AND LURID.

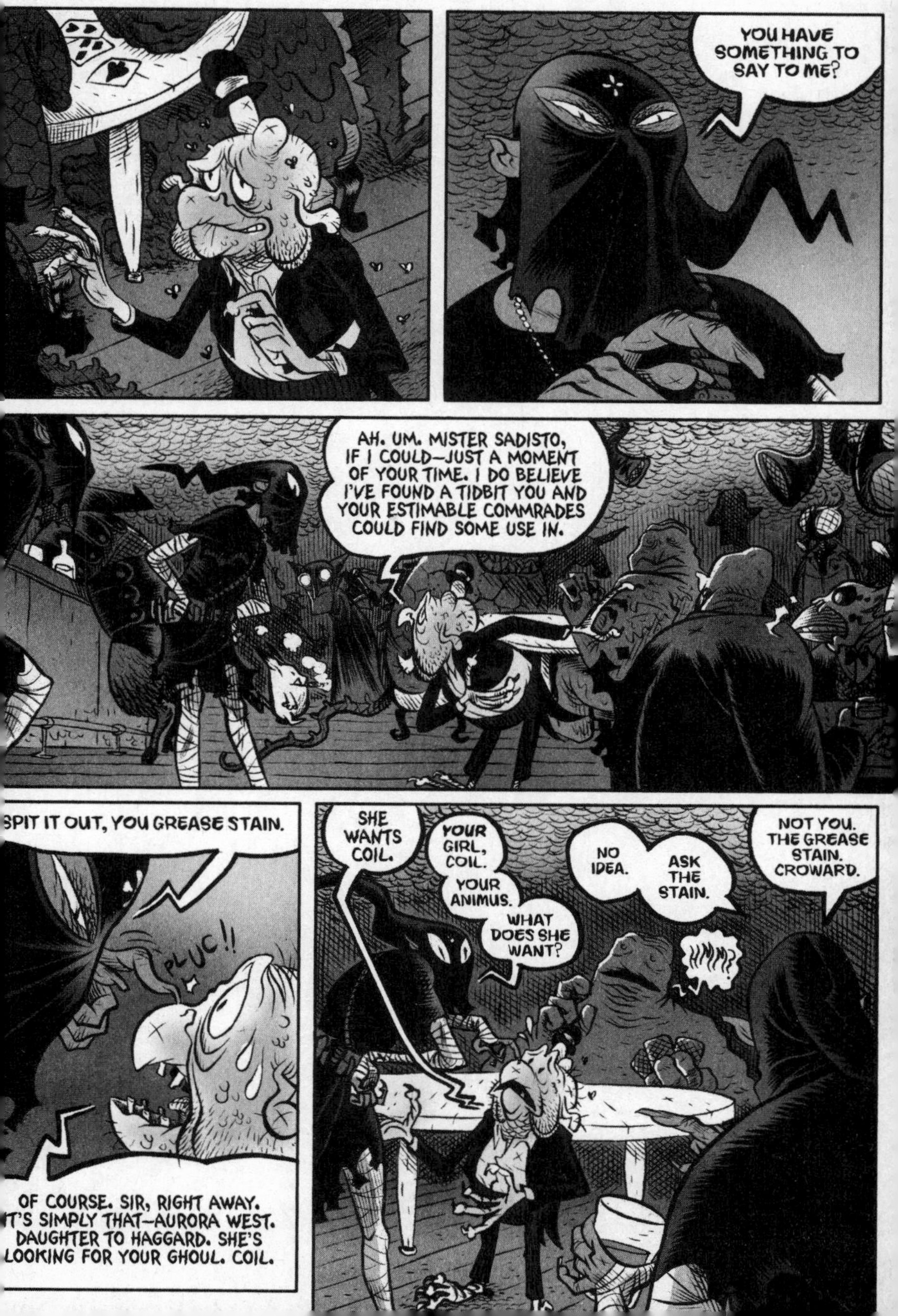
YOU HAVE SOMETHING TO SAY TO ME?
AH. UM. MISTER SADISTO, IF I COULD—JUST A MOMENT OF YOUR TIME. I DO BELIEVE I'VE FOUND A TIDBIT YOU AND YOUR ESTIMABLE COMMRADES COULD FIND SOME USE IN.
SPIT IT OUT, YOU GREASE STAIN.
PLUC!!
OF COURSE. SIR, RIGHT AWAY. IT'S SIMPLY THAT—AURORA WEST. DAUGHTER TO HAGGARD. SHE'S LOOKING FOR YOUR GHOUL. COIL.
SHE WANTS COIL.
YOUR GIRL, COIL.
YOUR ANIMUS.
WHAT DOES SHE WANT?
NO IDEA.
ASK THE STAIN.
NOT YOU. THE GREASE STAIN. CROWARD.
HMM?

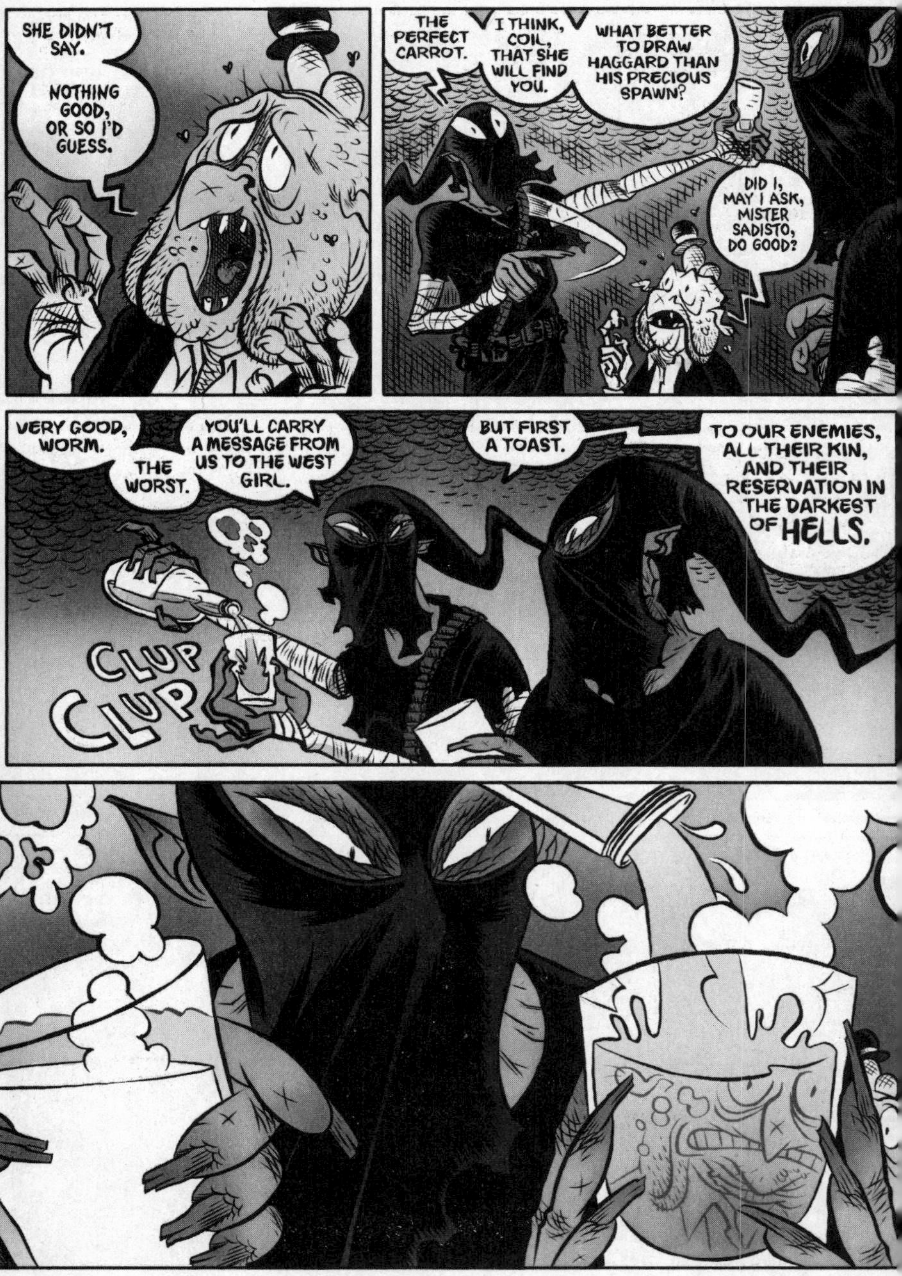
SHE DIDN'T SAY.
NOTHING GOOD, OR SO I'D GUESS.
THE PERFECT CARROT.
I THINK, COIL, THAT SHE WILL FIND YOU.
WHAT BETTER TO DRAW HAGGARD THAN HIS PRECIOUS SPAWN?
DID I, MAY I ASK, MISTER SADISTO, DO GOOD?
VERY GOOD, WORM.
THE WORST.
YOU'LL CARRY A MESSAGE FROM US TO THE WEST GIRL.
BUT FIRST A TOAST.
TO OUR ENEMIES, ALL THEIR KIN, AND THEIR RESERVATION IN THE DARKEST OF HELLS.
CLUP
CLUP

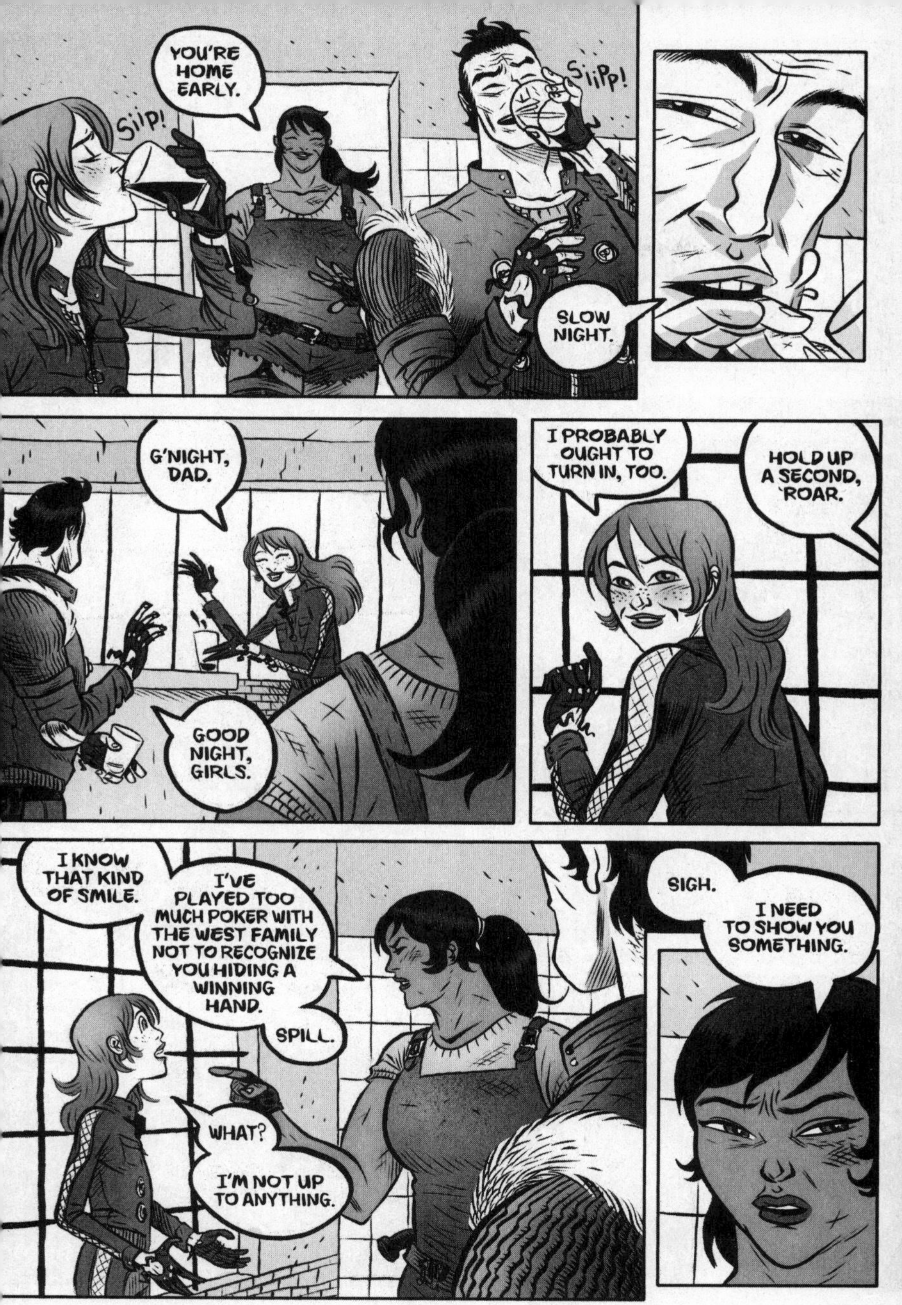
YOU'RE HOME EARLY.
SIIP!
SIIPP!
SLOW NIGHT.
G'NIGHT, DAD.
GOOD NIGHT, GIRLS.
I PROBABLY OUGHT TO TURN IN, TOO.
HOLD UP A SECOND, 'ROAR.
I KNOW THAT KIND OF SMILE.
I'VE PLAYED TOO MUCH POKER WITH THE WEST FAMILY NOT TO RECOGNIZE YOU HIDING A WINNING HAND.
SPILL.
WHAT?
I'M NOT UP TO ANYTHING.
SIGH.
I NEED TO SHOW YOU SOMETHING.

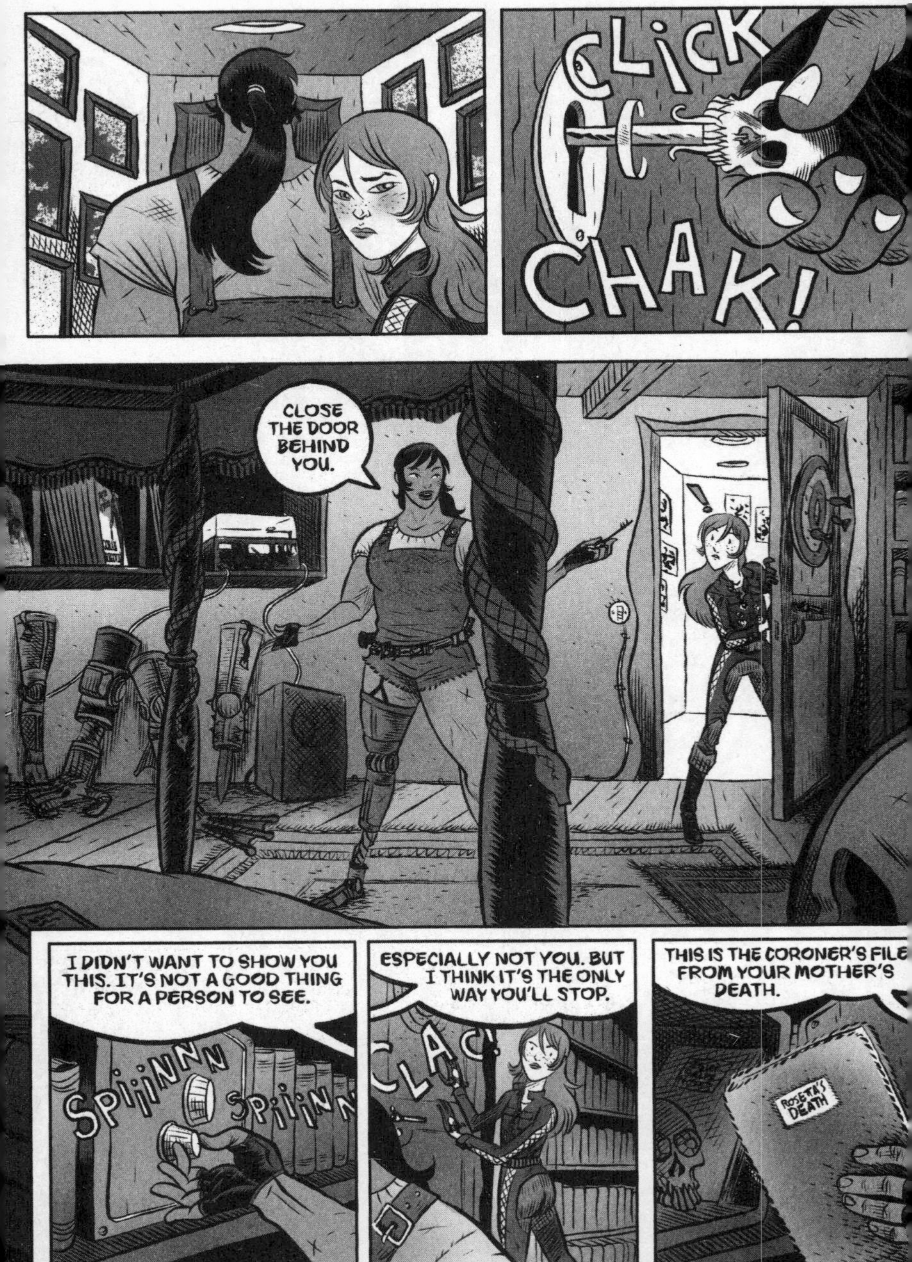
CLICK
CHAK!
CLOSE THE DOOR BEHIND YOU.
I DIDN'T WANT TO SHOW YOU THIS. IT'S NOT A GOOD THING FOR A PERSON TO SEE.
SPIIINNN SPIIINN
ESPECIALLY NOT YOU. BUT I THINK IT'S THE ONLY WAY YOU'LL STOP.
CLAC
THIS IS THE CORONER'S FILE FROM YOUR MOTHER'S DEATH.
ROSETA'S DEATH

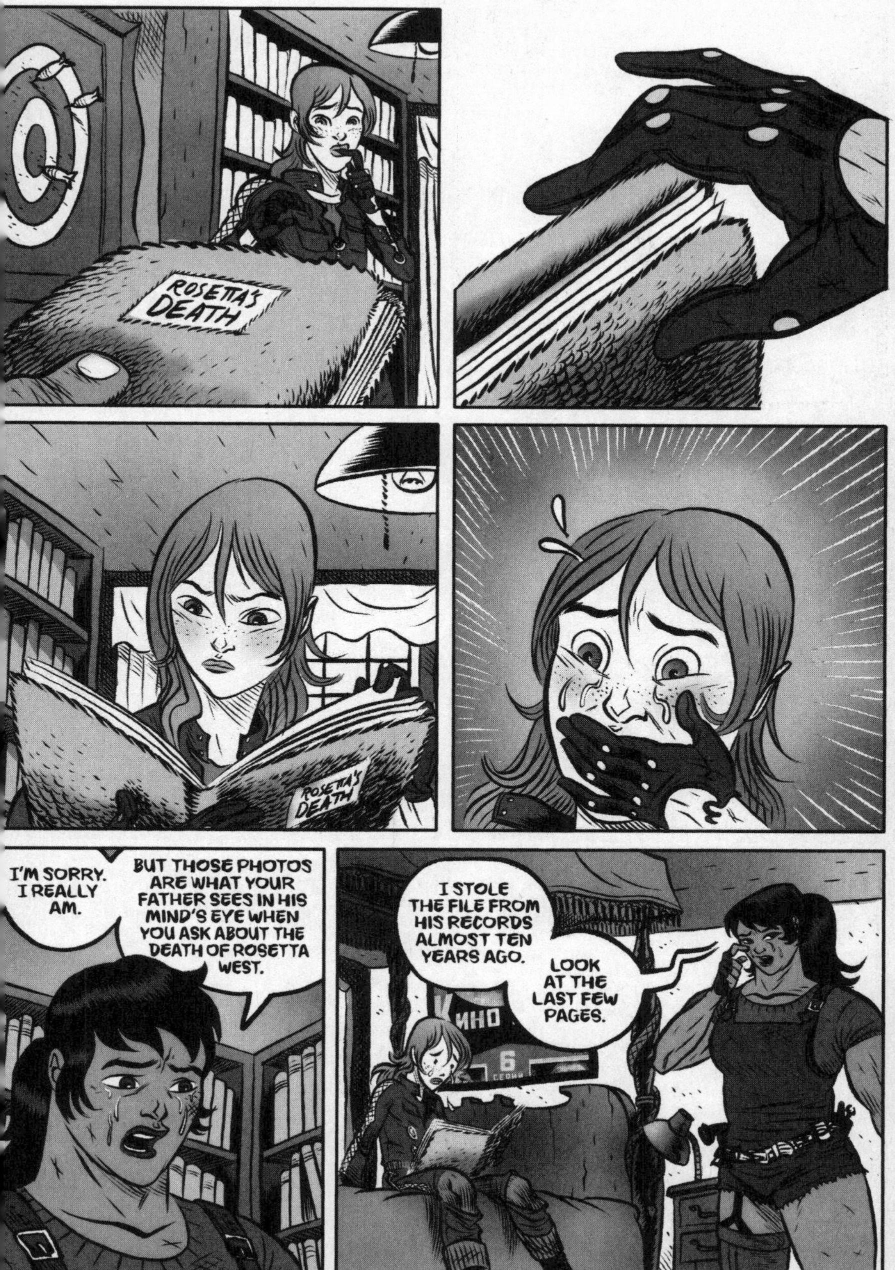
ROSETTA'S DEATH
ROSETTA'S DEATH
I'M SORRY. I REALLY AM.
BUT THOSE PHOTOS ARE WHAT YOUR FATHER SEES IN HIS MIND'S EYE WHEN YOU ASK ABOUT THE DEATH OF ROSETTA WEST.
I STOLE THE FILE FROM HIS RECORDS ALMOST TEN YEARS AGO.
LOOK AT THE LAST FEW PAGES.
КИНО
6

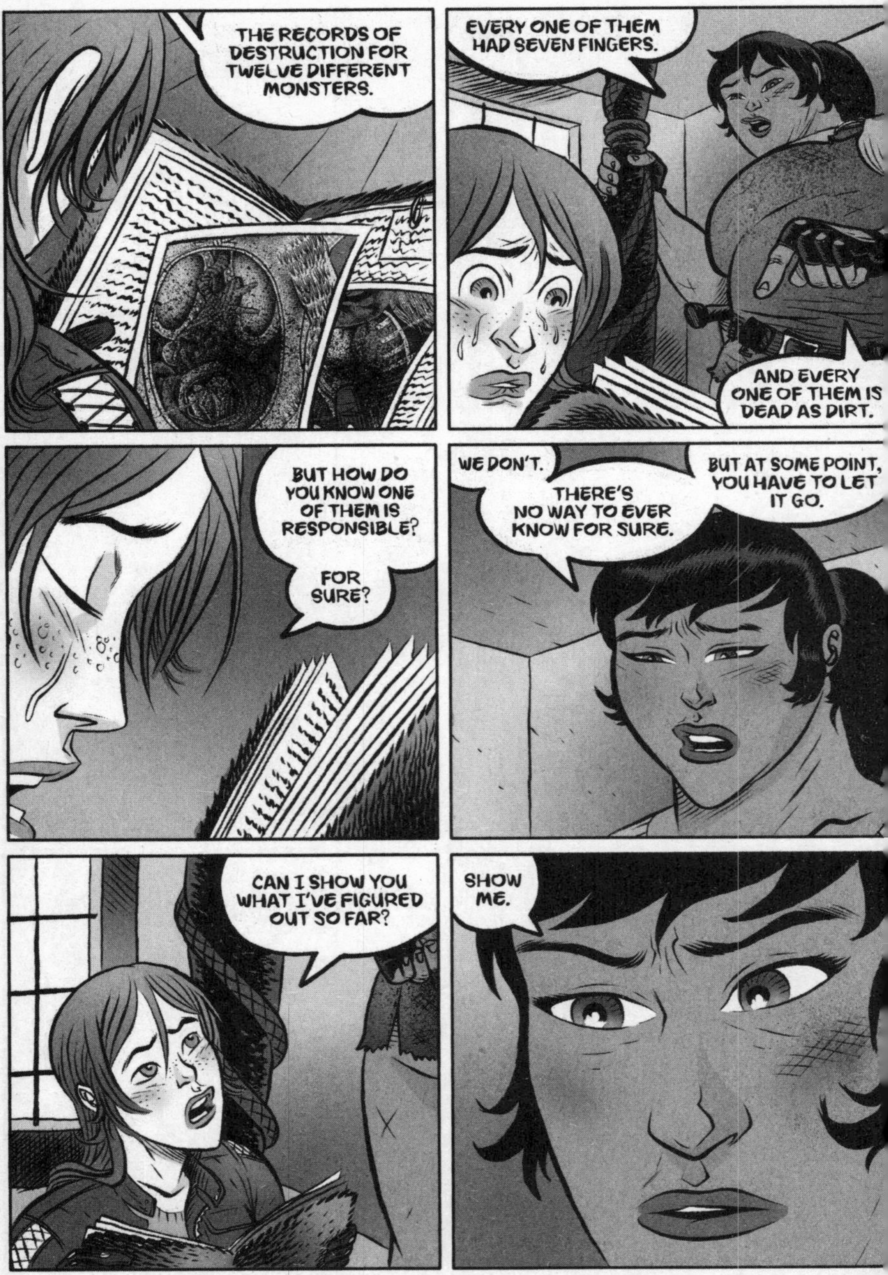
THE RECORDS OF DESTRUCTION FOR TWELVE DIFFERENT MONSTERS.
EVERY ONE OF THEM HAD SEVEN FINGERS.
AND EVERY ONE OF THEM IS DEAD AS DIRT.
BUT HOW DO YOU KNOW ONE OF THEM IS RESPONSIBLE?
FOR SURE?
WE DON'T.
THERE'S NO WAY TO EVER KNOW FOR SURE.
BUT AT SOME POINT, YOU HAVE TO LET IT GO.
CAN I SHOW YOU WHAT I'VE FIGURED OUT SO FAR?
SHOW ME.

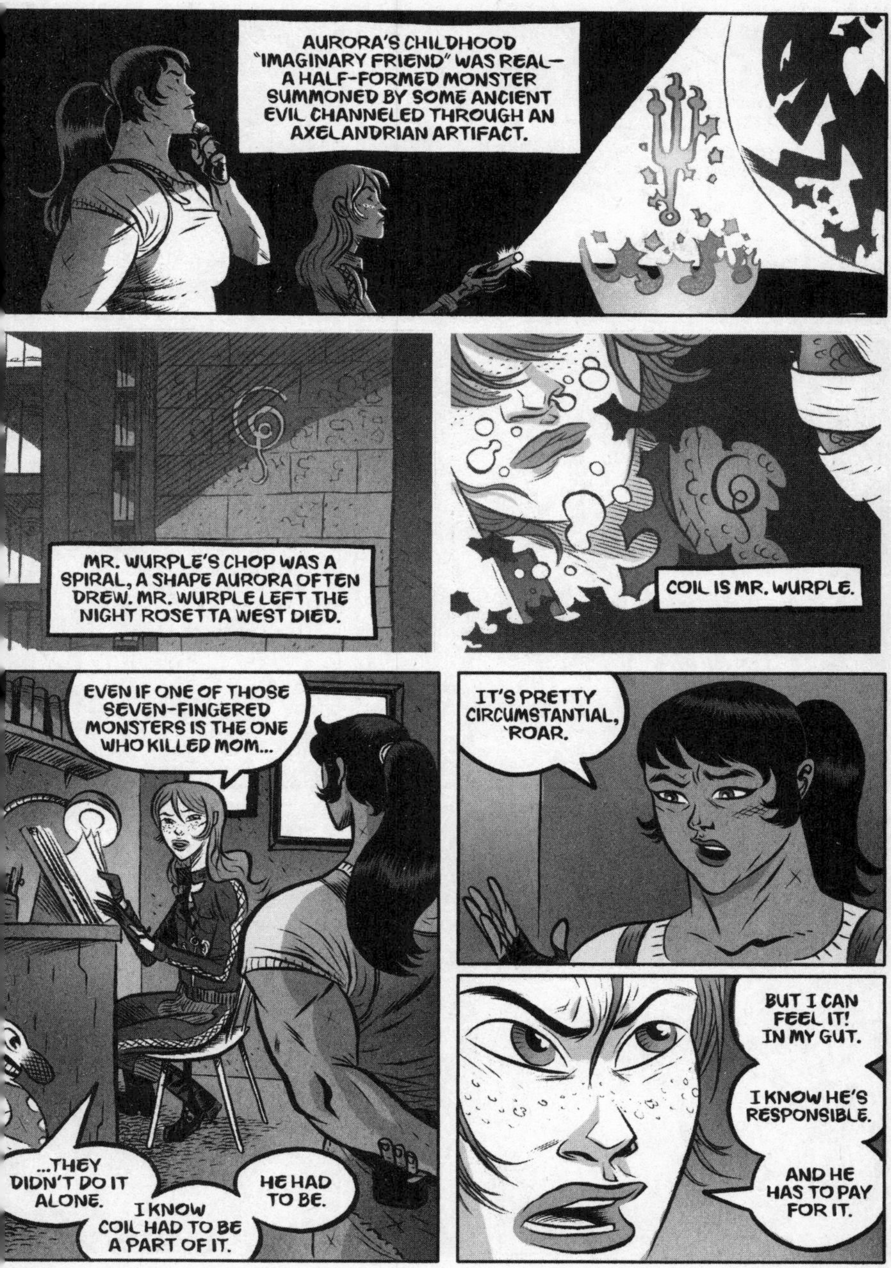
AURORA'S CHILDHOOD "IMAGINARY FRIEND" WAS REAL— A HALF-FORMED MONSTER SUMMONED BY SOME ANCIENT EVIL CHANNELED THROUGH AN AXELANDRIAN ARTIFACT.
MR. WURPLE'S CHOP WAS A SPIRAL, A SHAPE AURORA OFTEN DREW. MR. WURPLE LEFT THE NIGHT ROSETTA WEST DIED.
COIL IS MR. WURPLE.
EVEN IF ONE OF THOSE SEVEN-FINGERED MONSTERS IS THE ONE WHO KILLED MOM...
...THEY DIDN'T DO IT ALONE.
I KNOW COIL HAD TO BE A PART OF IT.
HE HAD TO BE.
IT'S PRETTY CIRCUMSTANTIAL, 'ROAR.
BUT I CAN FEEL IT! IN MY GUT.
I KNOW HE'S RESPONSIBLE.
AND HE HAS TO PAY FOR IT.

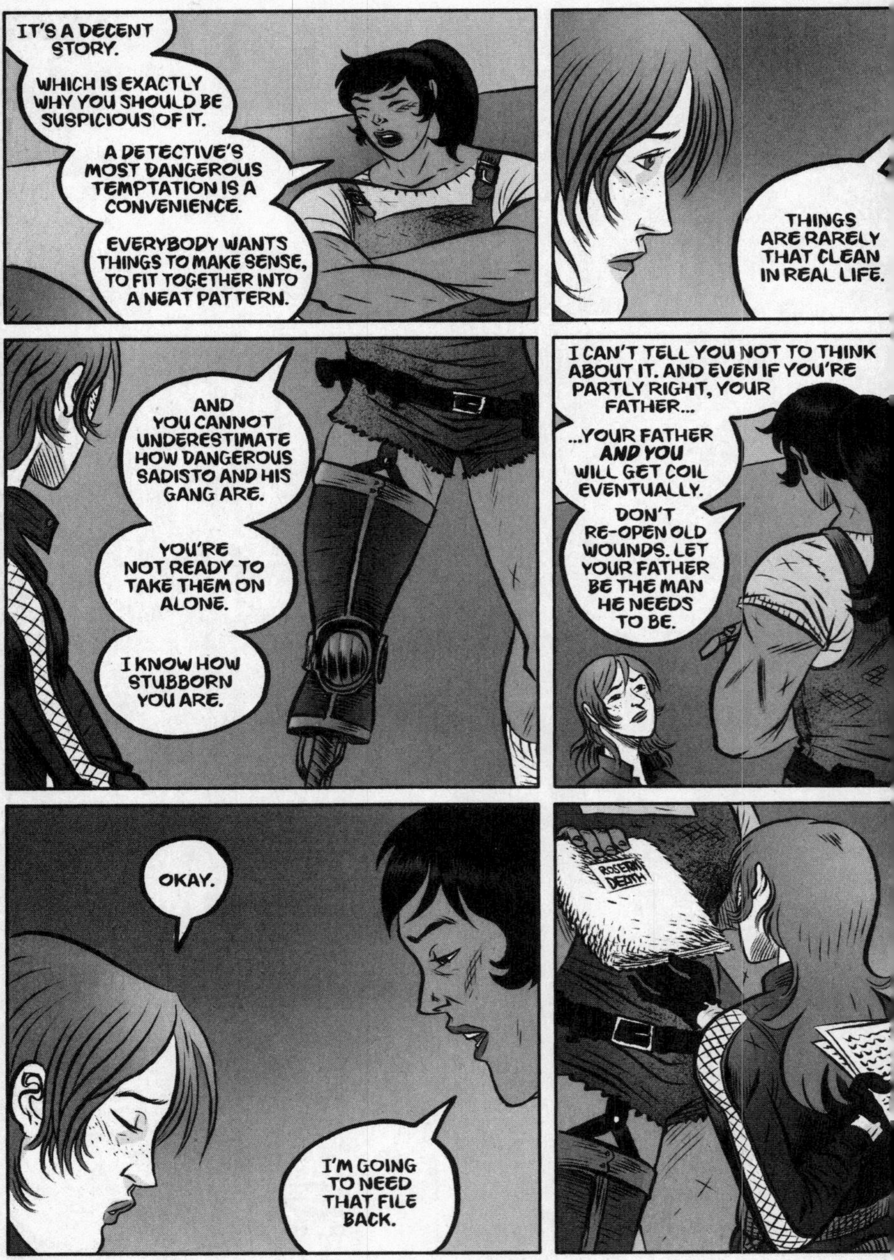
IT'S A DECENT STORY.
WHICH IS EXACTLY WHY YOU SHOULD BE SUSPICIOUS OF IT.
A DETECTIVE'S MOST DANGEROUS TEMPTATION IS A CONVENIENCE.
EVERYBODY WANTS THINGS TO MAKE SENSE, TO FIT TOGETHER INTO A NEAT PATTERN.
THINGS ARE RARELY THAT CLEAN IN REAL LIFE.
AND YOU CANNOT UNDERESTIMATE HOW DANGEROUS SADISTO AND HIS GANG ARE.
YOU'RE NOT READY TO TAKE THEM ON ALONE.
I KNOW HOW STUBBORN YOU ARE.
I CAN'T TELL YOU NOT TO THINK ABOUT IT. AND EVEN IF YOU'RE PARTLY RIGHT, YOUR FATHER...
...YOUR FATHER ***AND YOU*** WILL GET COIL EVENTUALLY.
DON'T RE-OPEN OLD WOUNDS. LET YOUR FATHER BE THE MAN HE NEEDS TO BE.
OKAY.
I'M GOING TO NEED THAT FILE BACK.
ROSEMARY DEDITH

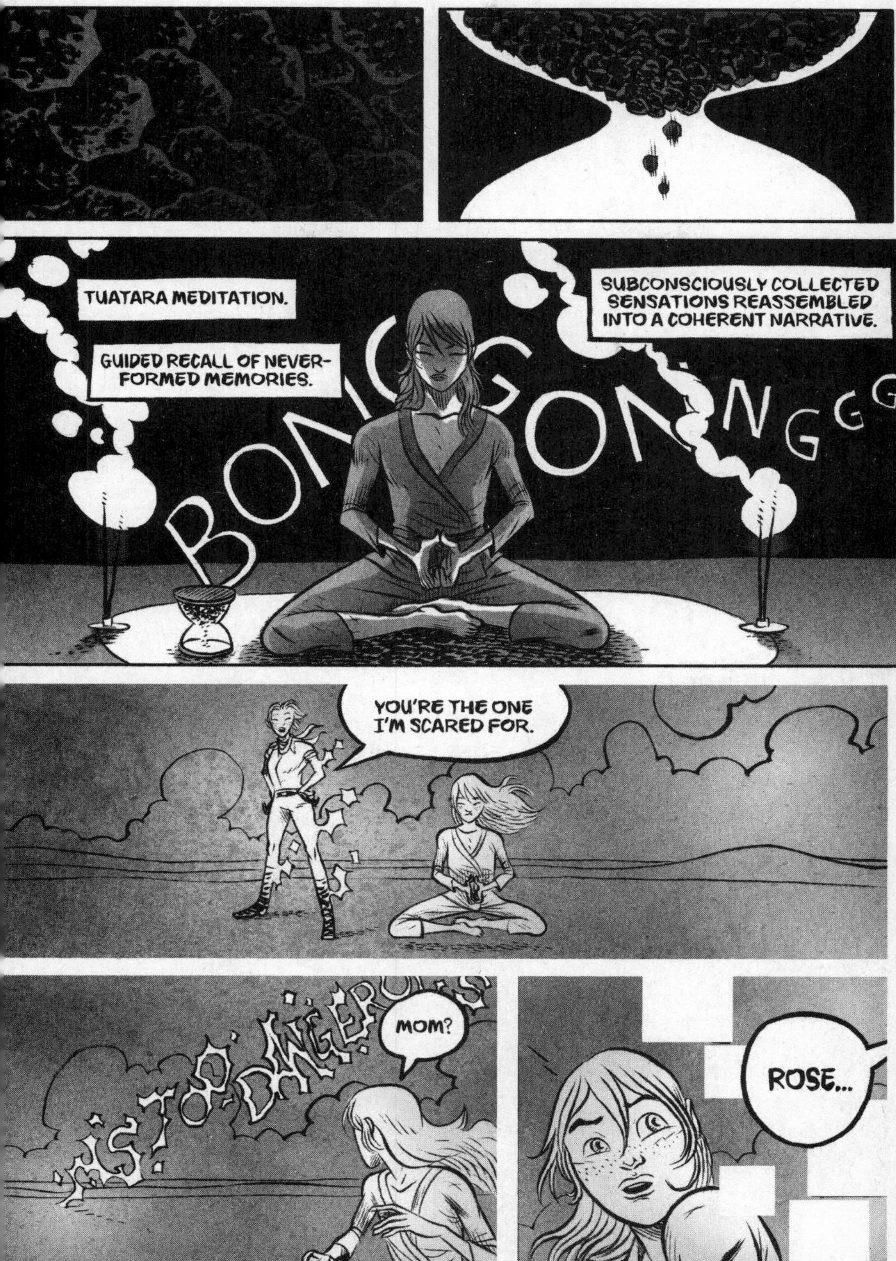
TUATARA MEDITATION.
GUIDED RECALL OF NEVER-FORMED MEMORIES.
SUBCONSCIOUSLY COLLECTED SENSATIONS REASSEMBLED INTO A COHERENT NARRATIVE.
BONG GONNGGG
YOU'RE THE ONE I'M SCARED FOR.
IS TOO DANGEROUS!
MOM?
ROSE...

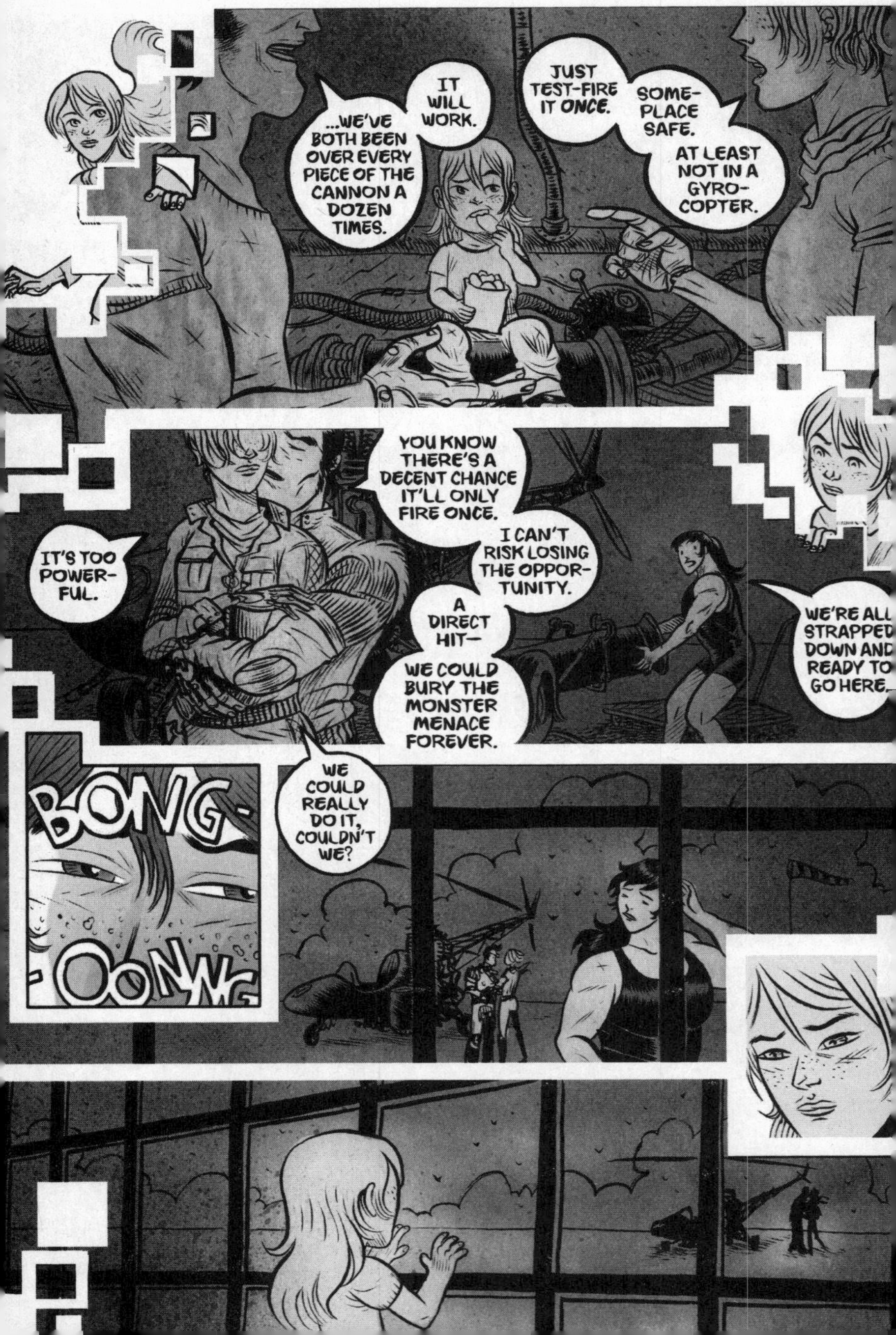
...WE'VE BOTH BEEN OVER EVERY PIECE OF THE CANNON A DOZEN TIMES.
IT WILL WORK.
JUST TEST-FIRE IT ONCE.
SOME-PLACE SAFE.
AT LEAST NOT IN A GYRO-COPTER.
YOU KNOW THERE'S A DECENT CHANCE IT'LL ONLY FIRE ONCE.
IT'S TOO POWER-FUL.
I CAN'T RISK LOSING THE OPPOR-TUNITY.
A DIRECT HIT—
WE COULD BURY THE MONSTER MENACE FOREVER.
WE'RE ALL STRAPPED DOWN AND READY TO GO HERE.
WE COULD REALLY DO IT, COULDN'T WE?
BONG-OONNNG

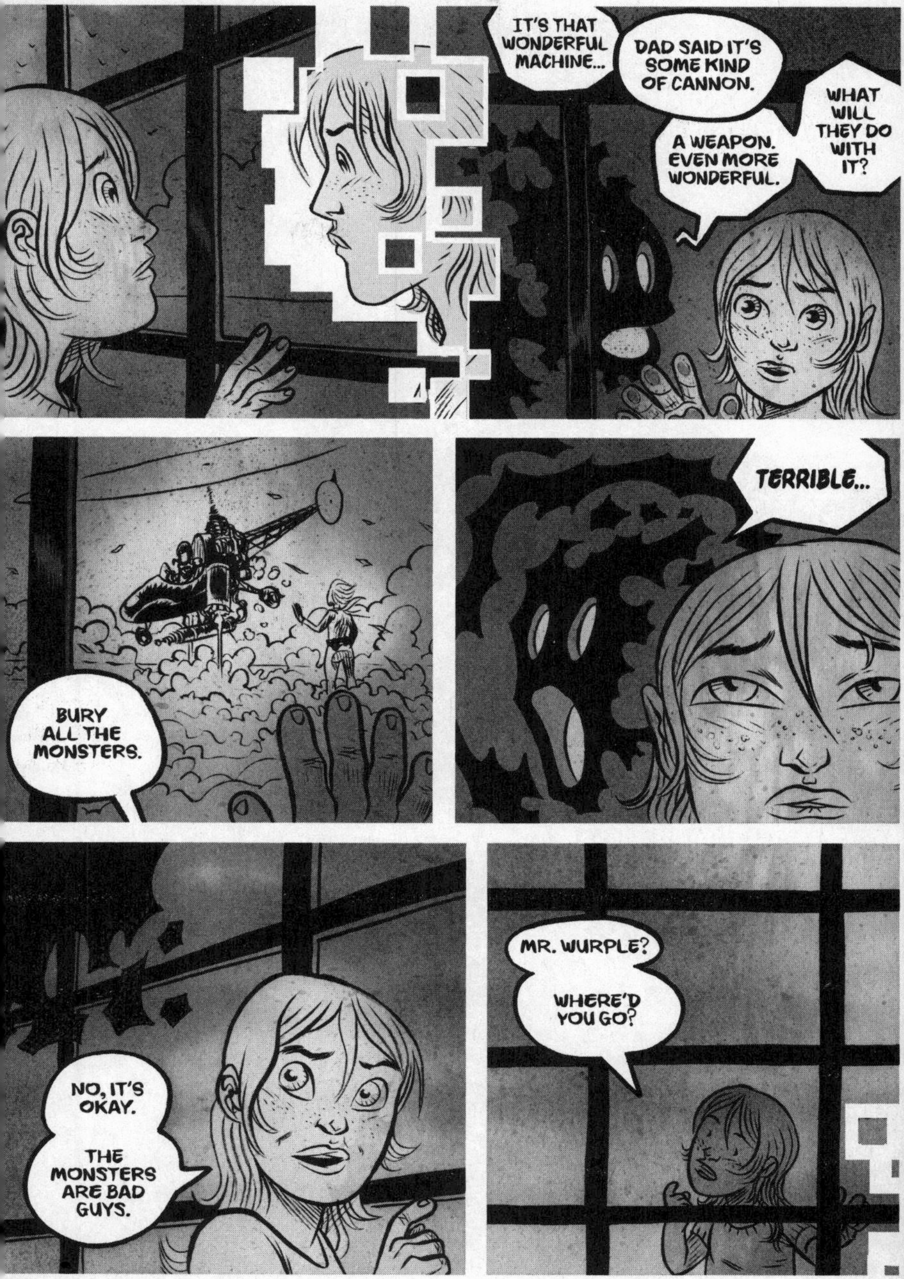
IT'S THAT WONDERFUL MACHINE...
DAD SAID IT'S SOME KIND OF CANNON.
A WEAPON. EVEN MORE WONDERFUL.
WHAT WILL THEY DO WITH IT?
BURY ALL THE MONSTERS.
TERRIBLE...
NO, IT'S OKAY.
THE MONSTERS ARE BAD GUYS.
MR. WURPLE?
WHERE'D YOU GO?

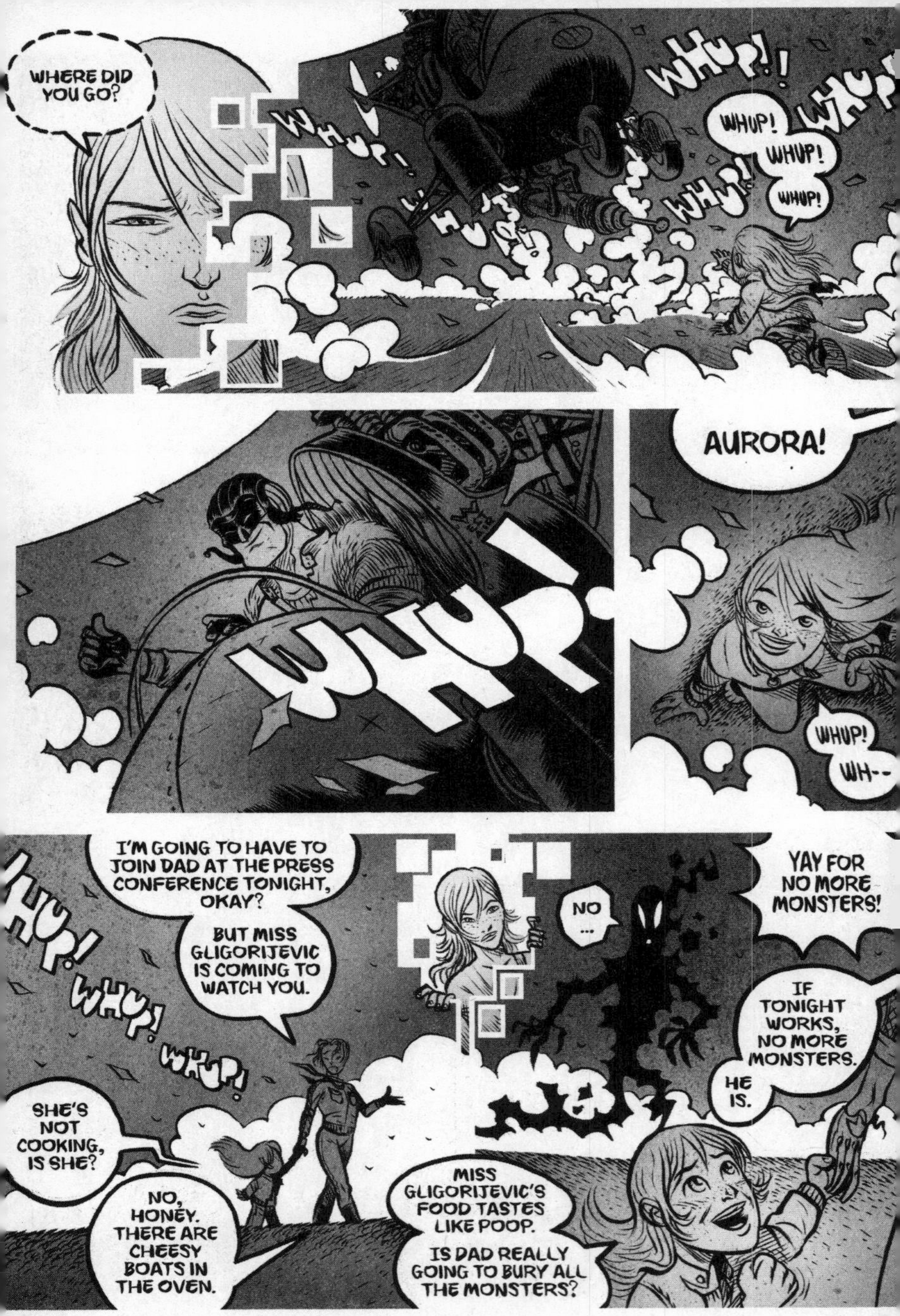
WHERE DID YOU GO?
WHUP!
WHUP!
WHUP!
WHUP!
WHUP!
WHUP!
WHUP!
AURORA!
WHUP!
WHUP!
WH--
WHUP!
WHUP!
WHUP!
I'M GOING TO HAVE TO JOIN DAD AT THE PRESS CONFERENCE TONIGHT, OKAY?
BUT MISS GLIGORIJEVIC IS COMING TO WATCH YOU.
SHE'S NOT COOKING, IS SHE?
NO, HONEY. THERE ARE CHEESY BOATS IN THE OVEN.
NO ...
YAY FOR NO MORE MONSTERS!
IF TONIGHT WORKS, NO MORE MONSTERS.
HE IS.
MISS GLIGORIJEVIC'S FOOD TASTES LIKE POOP.
IS DAD REALLY GOING TO BURY ALL THE MONSTERS?

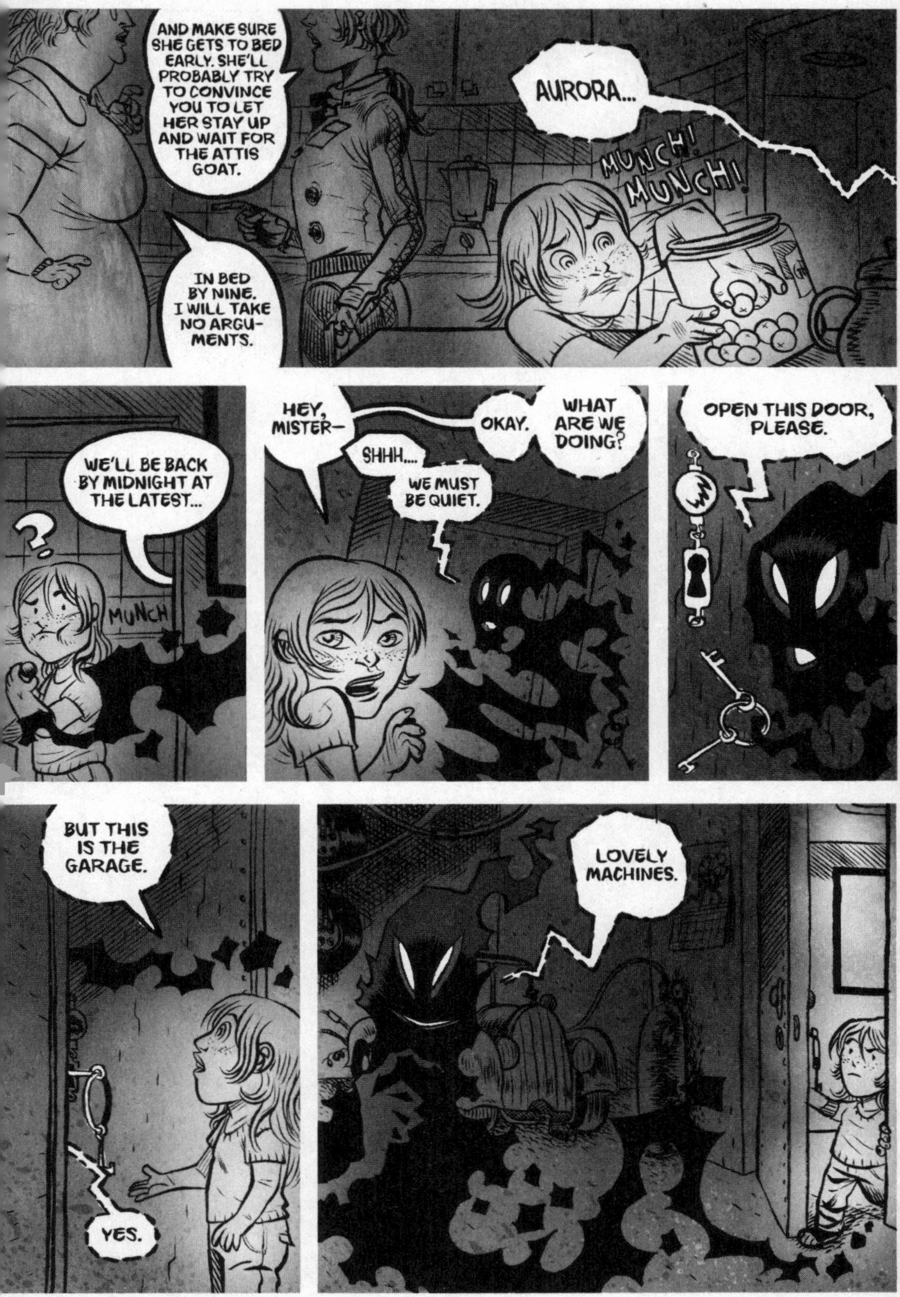
AND MAKE SURE SHE GETS TO BED EARLY. SHE'LL PROBABLY TRY TO CONVINCE YOU TO LET HER STAY UP AND WAIT FOR THE ATTIS GOAT.
IN BED BY NINE. I WILL TAKE NO ARGU-MENTS.
AURORA...
MUNCH! MUNCH!
WE'LL BE BACK BY MIDNIGHT AT THE LATEST...
?
MUNCH
HEY, MISTER—
OKAY.
WHAT ARE WE DOING?
SHHH....
WE MUST BE QUIET.
OPEN THIS DOOR, PLEASE.
BUT THIS IS THE GARAGE.
YES.
LOVELY MACHINES.

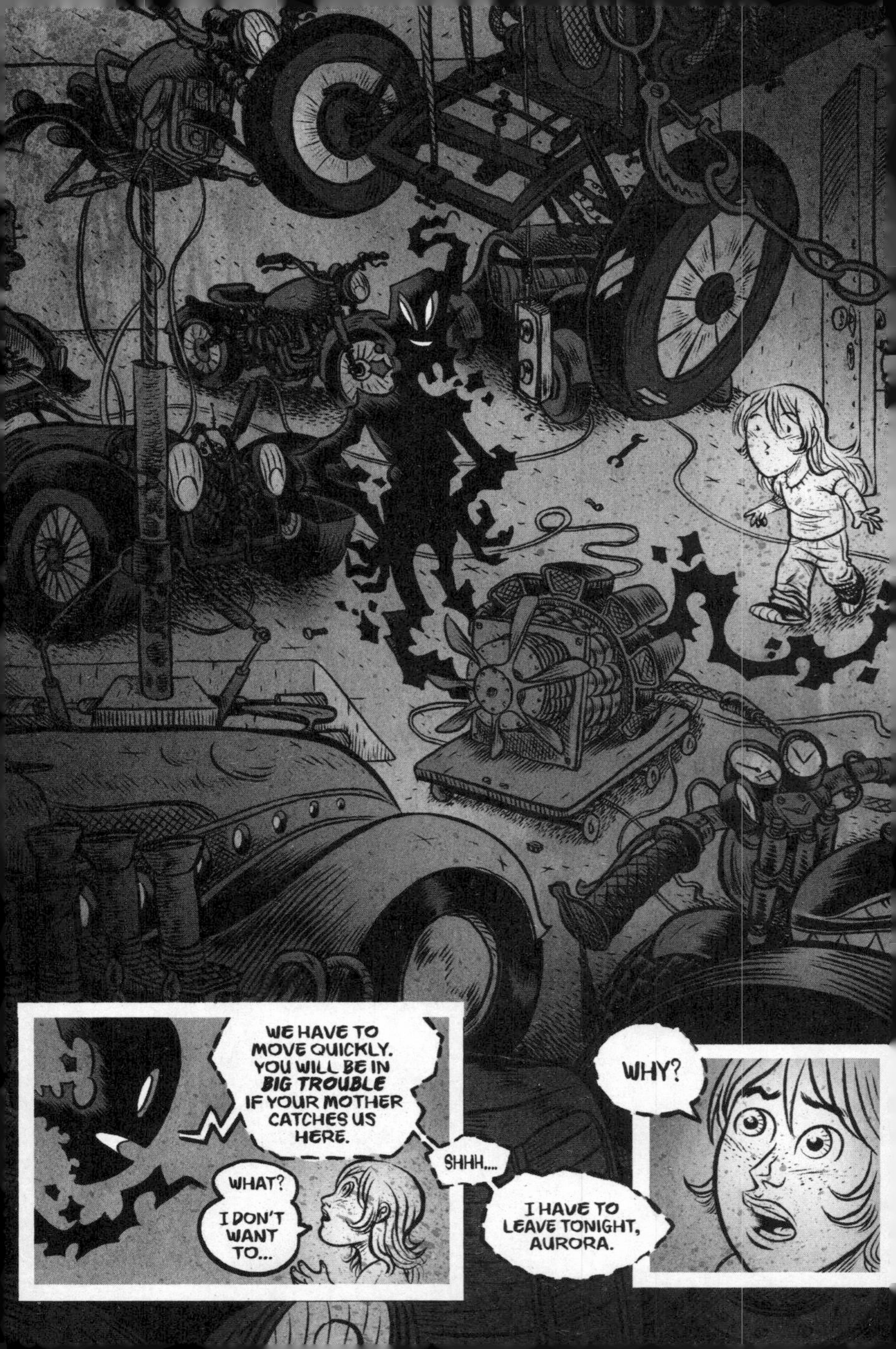
WE HAVE TO MOVE QUICKLY. YOU WILL BE IN BIG TROUBLE IF YOUR MOTHER CATCHES US HERE.
WHAT?
I DON'T WANT TO...
SHHH....
I HAVE TO LEAVE TONIGHT, AURORA.
WHY?

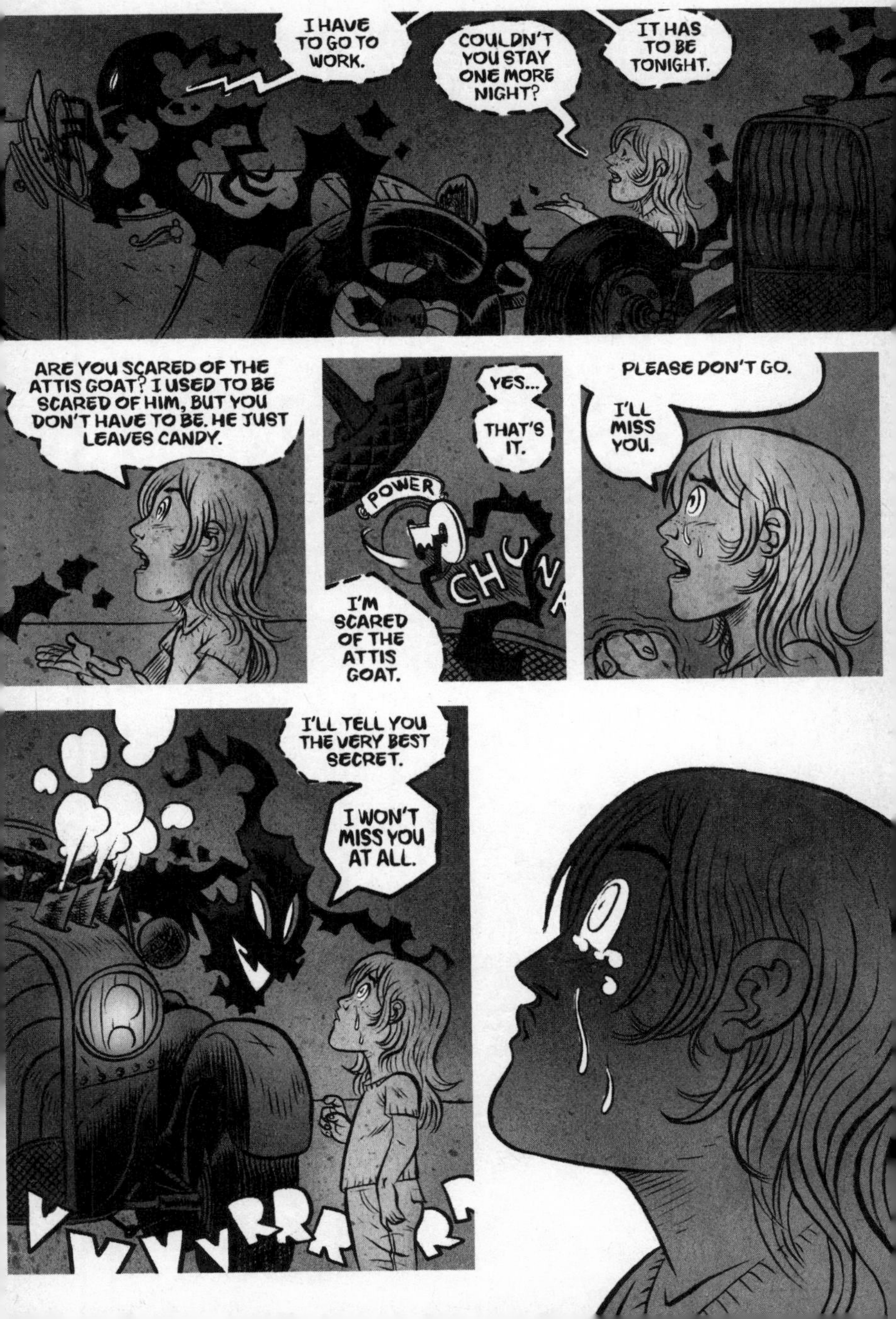

I HAVE TO GO TO WORK.
COULDN'T YOU STAY ONE MORE NIGHT?
IT HAS TO BE TONIGHT.
ARE YOU SCARED OF THE ATTIS GOAT? I USED TO BE SCARED OF HIM, BUT YOU DON'T HAVE TO BE. HE JUST LEAVES CANDY.
YES...
THAT'S IT.
POWER
CHUNK
I'M SCARED OF THE ATTIS GOAT.
PLEASE DON'T GO.
I'LL MISS YOU.
I'LL TELL YOU THE VERY BEST SECRET.
I WON'T MISS YOU AT ALL.
VWVVRRARR

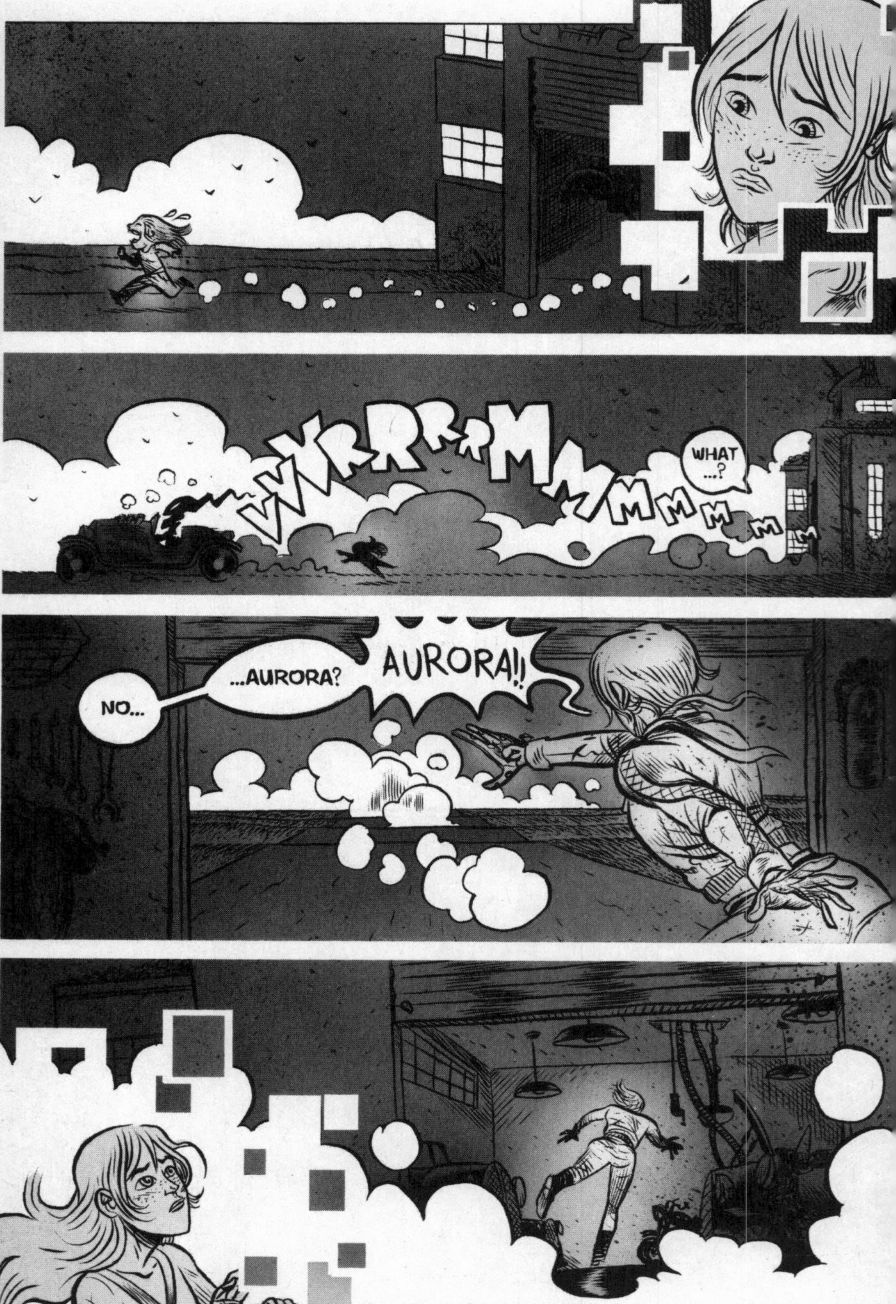
VVVRRRRMMMMMMMM
WHAT ...?
NO...
...AURORA?
AURORA!!

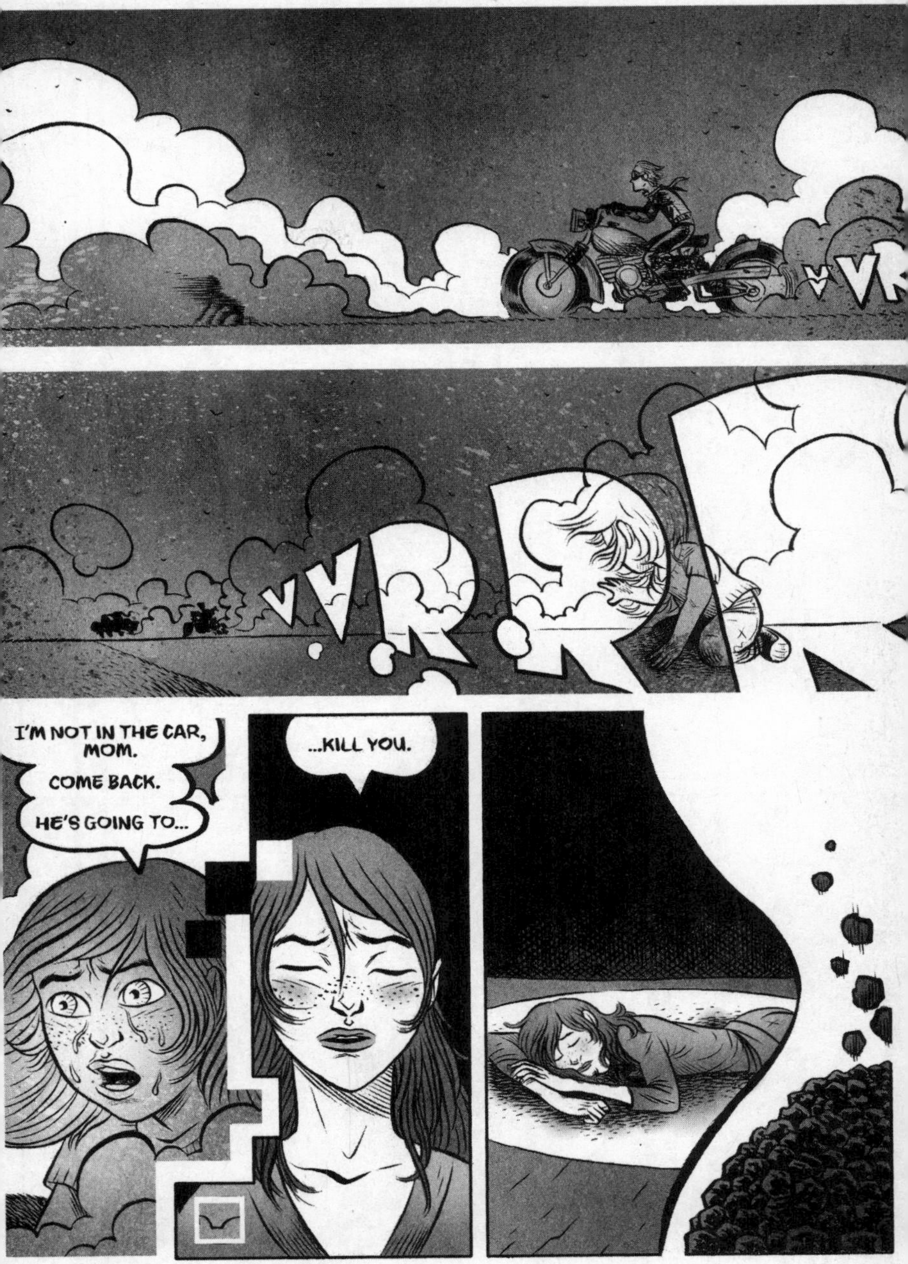
VVR
VVRR
I'M NOT IN THE CAR, MOM.
COME BACK.
HE'S GOING TO...
...KILL YOU.

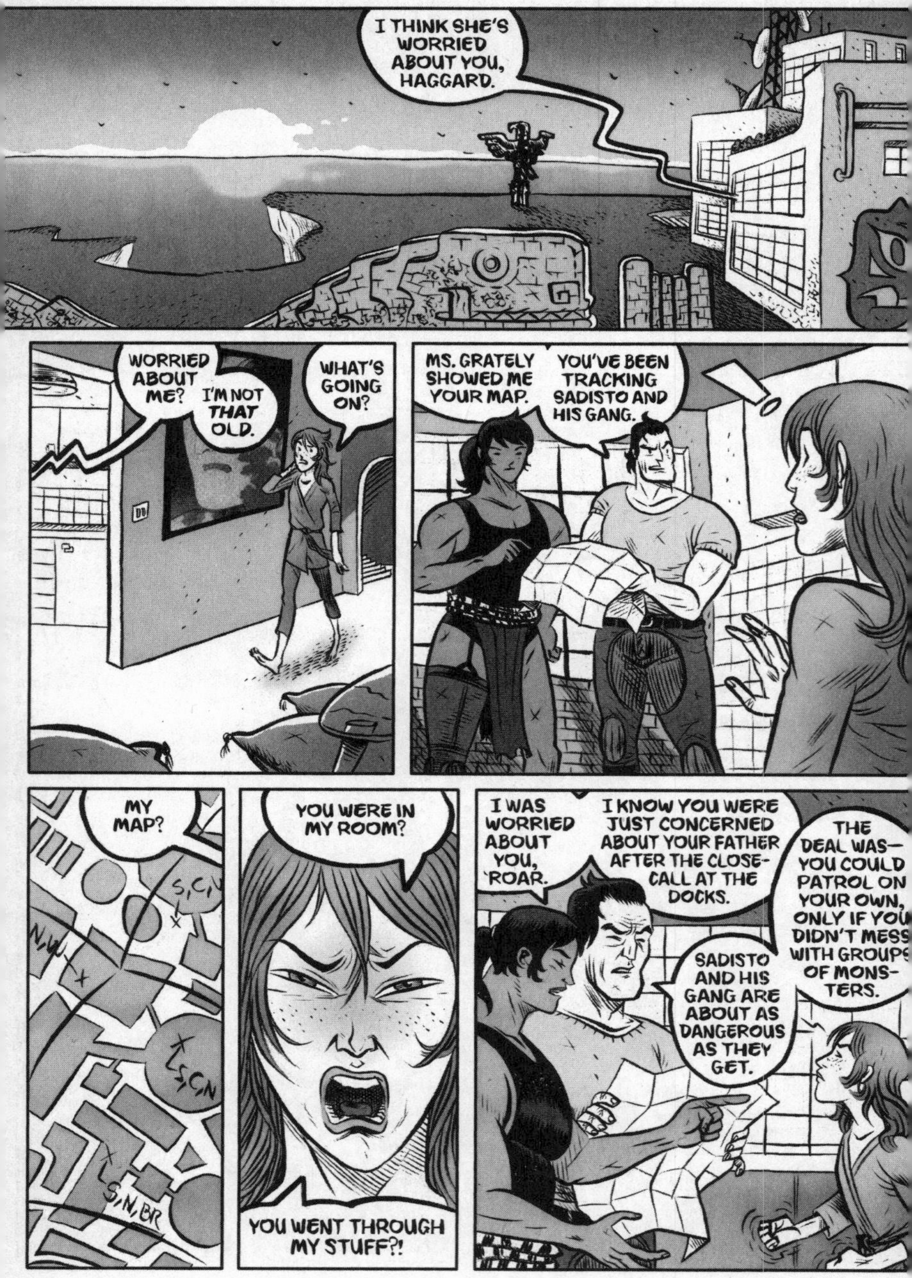

I THINK SHE'S WORRIED ABOUT YOU, HAGGARD.
WORRIED ABOUT ME?
I'M NOT *THAT* OLD.
WHAT'S GOING ON?
MS. GRATELY SHOWED ME YOUR MAP.
YOU'VE BEEN TRACKING SADISTO AND HIS GANG.
!
MY MAP?
S,C,N
N,W
S,C,N
S,N,BR
YOU WERE IN MY ROOM?
YOU WENT THROUGH MY STUFF?!
I WAS WORRIED ABOUT YOU, 'ROAR.
I KNOW YOU WERE JUST CONCERNED ABOUT YOUR FATHER AFTER THE CLOSE-CALL AT THE DOCKS.
THE DEAL WAS—YOU COULD PATROL ON YOUR OWN, ONLY IF YOU DIDN'T MESS WITH GROUPS OF MONSTERS.
SADISTO AND HIS GANG ARE ABOUT AS DANGEROUS AS THEY GET.

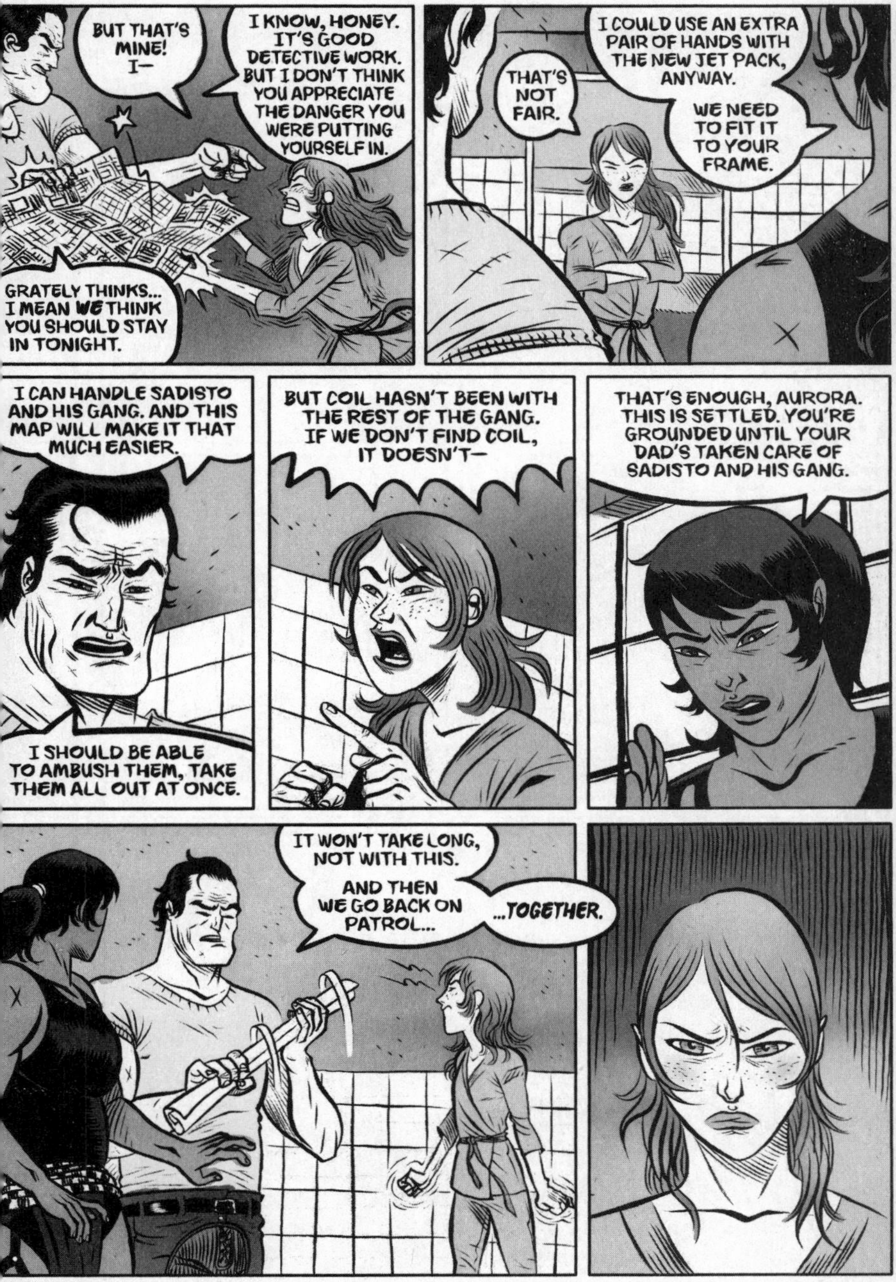
BUT THAT'S MINE! I—
I KNOW, HONEY. IT'S GOOD DETECTIVE WORK. BUT I DON'T THINK YOU APPRECIATE THE DANGER YOU WERE PUTTING YOURSELF IN.
GRATELY THINKS... I MEAN WE THINK YOU SHOULD STAY IN TONIGHT.
THAT'S NOT FAIR.
I COULD USE AN EXTRA PAIR OF HANDS WITH THE NEW JET PACK, ANYWAY.
WE NEED TO FIT IT TO YOUR FRAME.
I CAN HANDLE SADISTO AND HIS GANG. AND THIS MAP WILL MAKE IT THAT MUCH EASIER.
I SHOULD BE ABLE TO AMBUSH THEM, TAKE THEM ALL OUT AT ONCE.
BUT COIL HASN'T BEEN WITH THE REST OF THE GANG. IF WE DON'T FIND COIL, IT DOESN'T—
THAT'S ENOUGH, AURORA. THIS IS SETTLED. YOU'RE GROUNDED UNTIL YOUR DAD'S TAKEN CARE OF SADISTO AND HIS GANG.
IT WON'T TAKE LONG, NOT WITH THIS.
AND THEN WE GO BACK ON PATROL...
...TOGETHER.

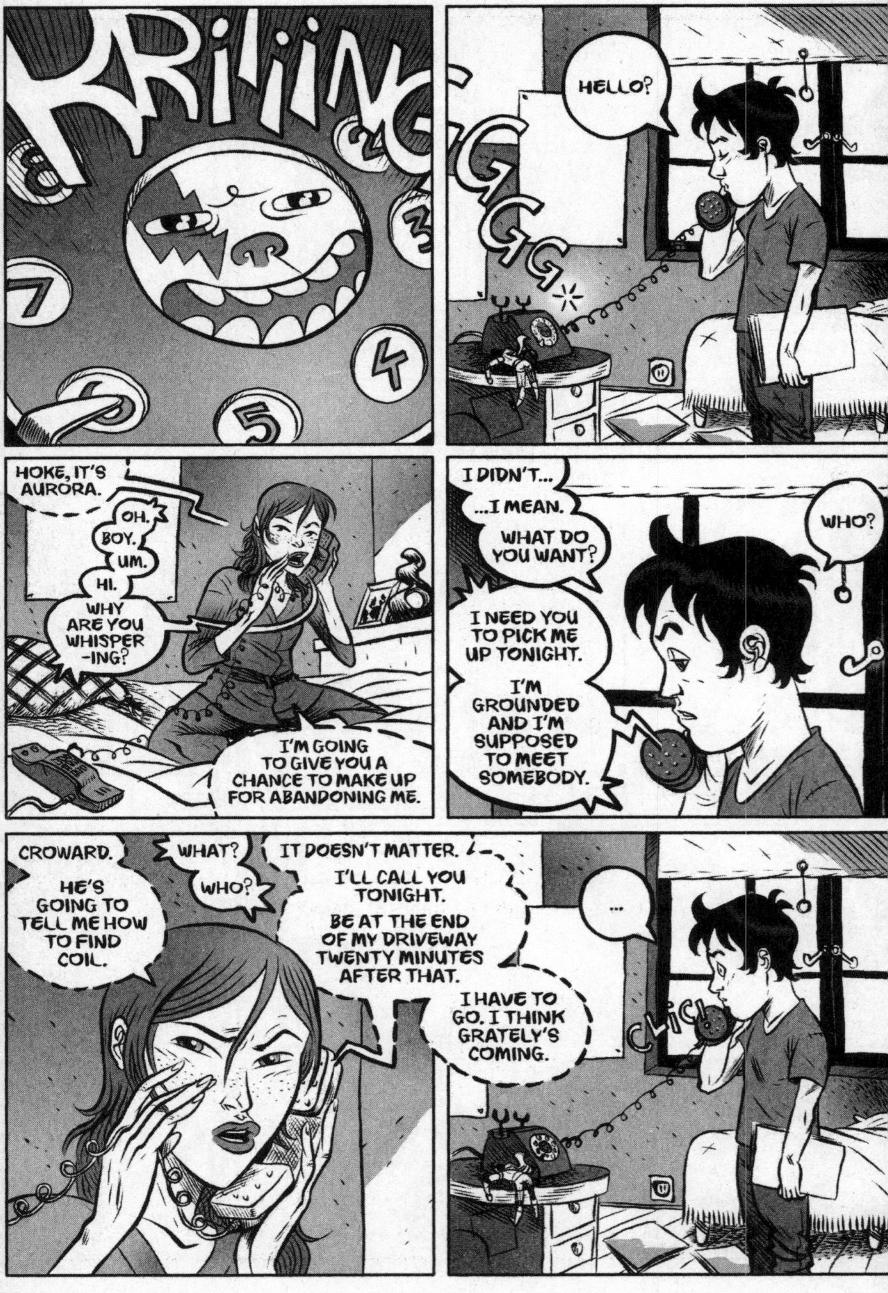
KRIIIING
GGGG
HELLO?
HOKE, IT'S AURORA.
OH.
BOY.
UM.
HI.
WHY ARE YOU WHISPER -ING?
I'M GOING TO GIVE YOU A CHANCE TO MAKE UP FOR ABANDONING ME.
I DIDN'T...
...I MEAN.
WHAT DO YOU WANT?
WHO?
I NEED YOU TO PICK ME UP TONIGHT.
I'M GROUNDED AND I'M SUPPOSED TO MEET SOMEBODY.
CROWARD.
HE'S GOING TO TELL ME HOW TO FIND COIL.
WHAT?
WHO?
IT DOESN'T MATTER.
I'LL CALL YOU TONIGHT.
BE AT THE END OF MY DRIVEWAY TWENTY MINUTES AFTER THAT.
I HAVE TO GO. I THINK GRATELY'S COMING.
...
CLICK

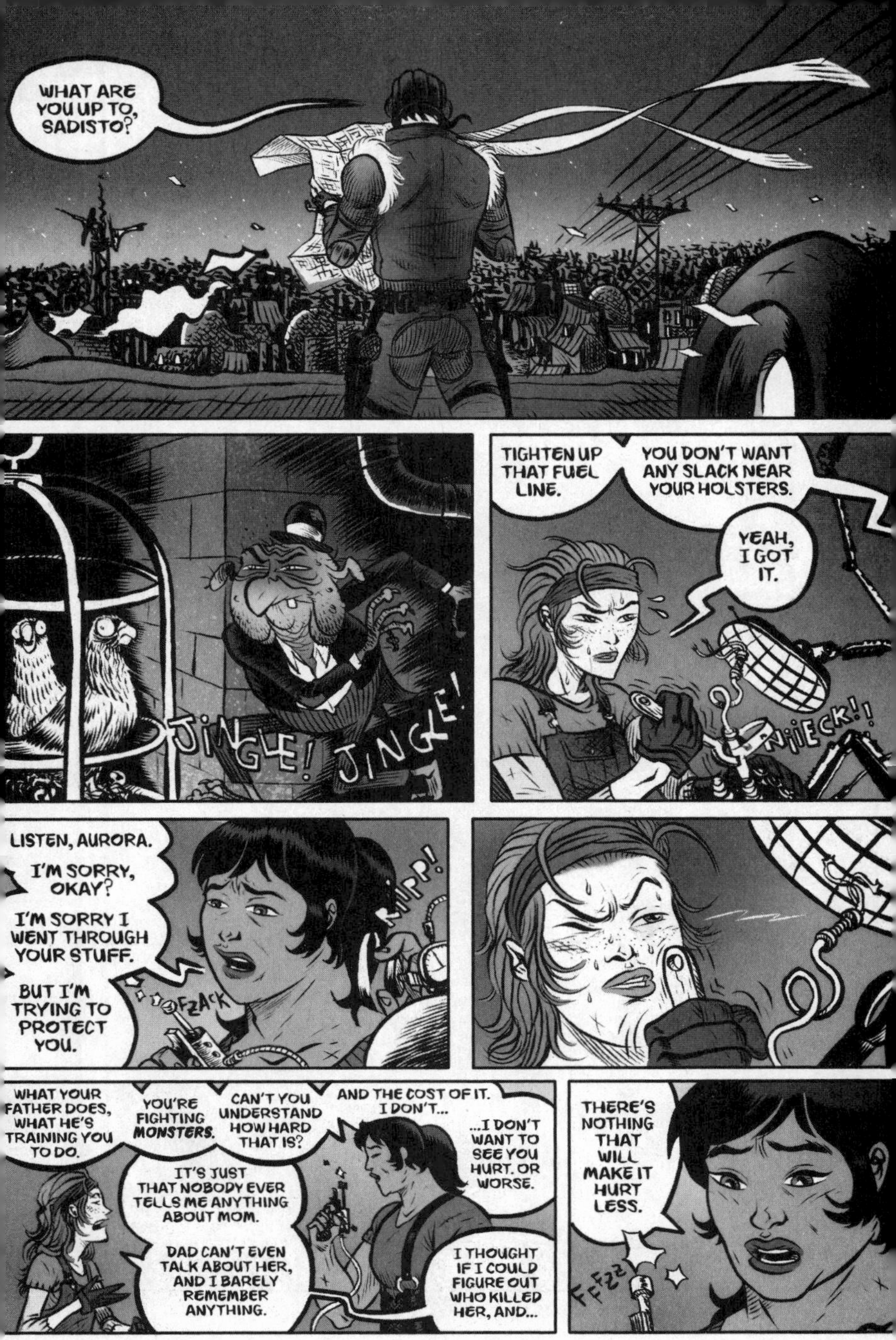

WHAT ARE YOU UP TO, SADISTO?
JINGLE! JINGLE!
TIGHTEN UP THAT FUEL LINE.
YOU DON'T WANT ANY SLACK NEAR YOUR HOLSTERS.
YEAH, I GOT IT.
NIIECK!!
LISTEN, AURORA.
I'M SORRY, OKAY?
I'M SORRY I WENT THROUGH YOUR STUFF.
BUT I'M TRYING TO PROTECT YOU.
FZACK
WHAT YOUR FATHER DOES, WHAT HE'S TRAINING YOU TO DO.
YOU'RE FIGHTING *MONSTERS.*
CAN'T YOU UNDERSTAND HOW HARD THAT IS?
AND THE COST OF IT. I DON'T...
...I DON'T WANT TO SEE YOU HURT. OR WORSE.
IT'S JUST THAT NOBODY EVER TELLS ME ANYTHING ABOUT MOM.
DAD CAN'T EVEN TALK ABOUT HER, AND I BARELY REMEMBER ANYTHING.
I THOUGHT IF I COULD FIGURE OUT WHO KILLED HER, AND...
THERE'S NOTHING THAT WILL MAKE IT HURT LESS.
FFZZZ

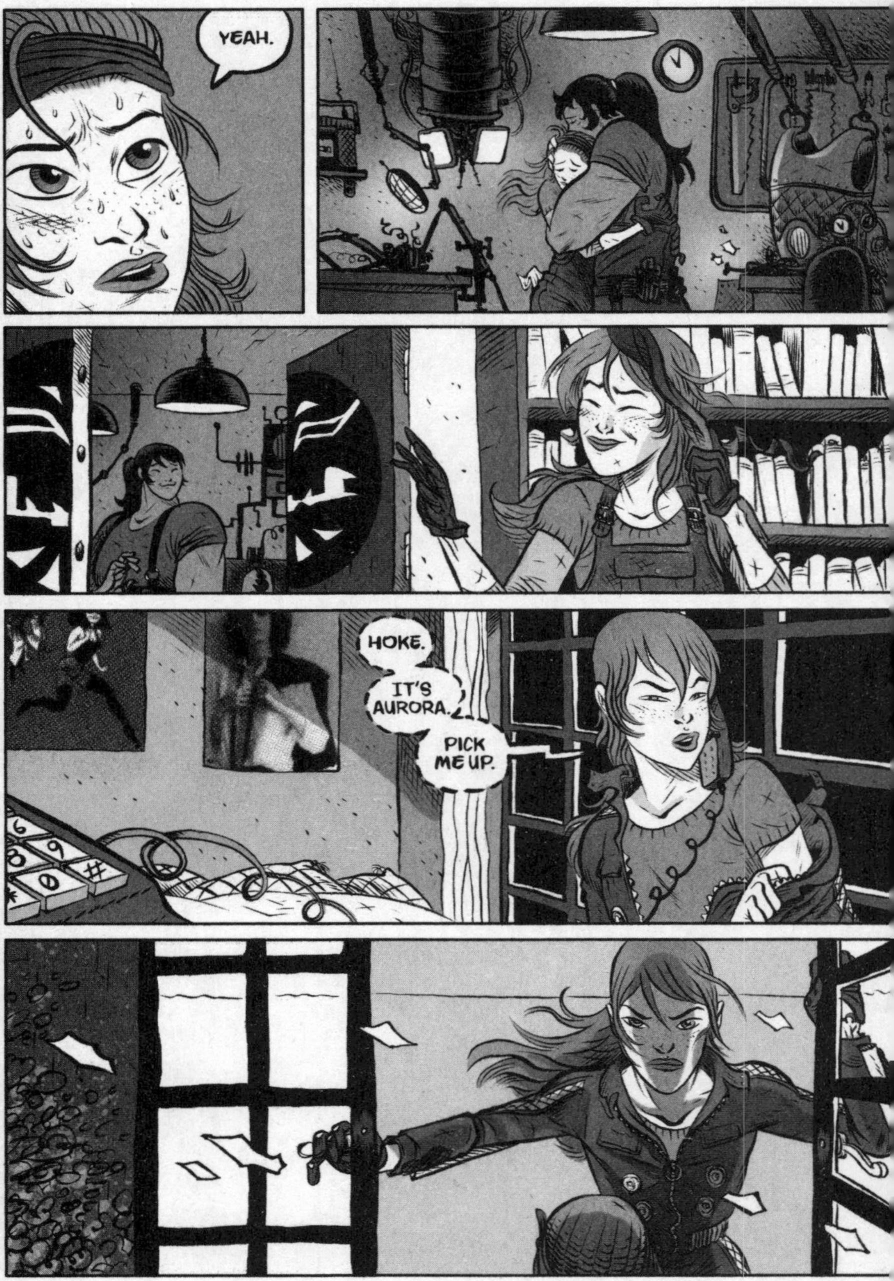
YEAH.
HOKE.
IT'S AURORA.
PICK ME UP.

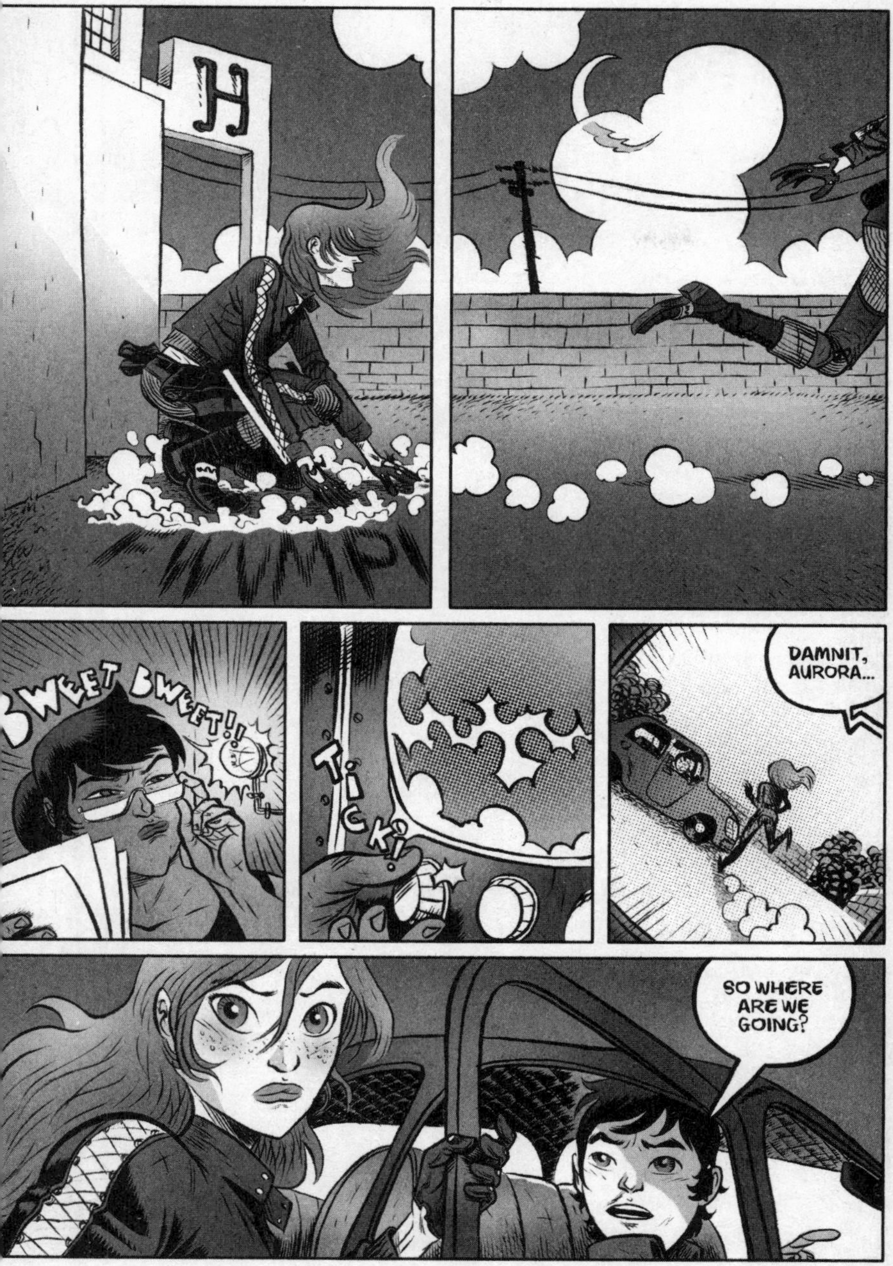
WUMP!
BWEET BWEET!!
TICK!
DAMNIT, AURORA...
SO WHERE ARE WE GOING?

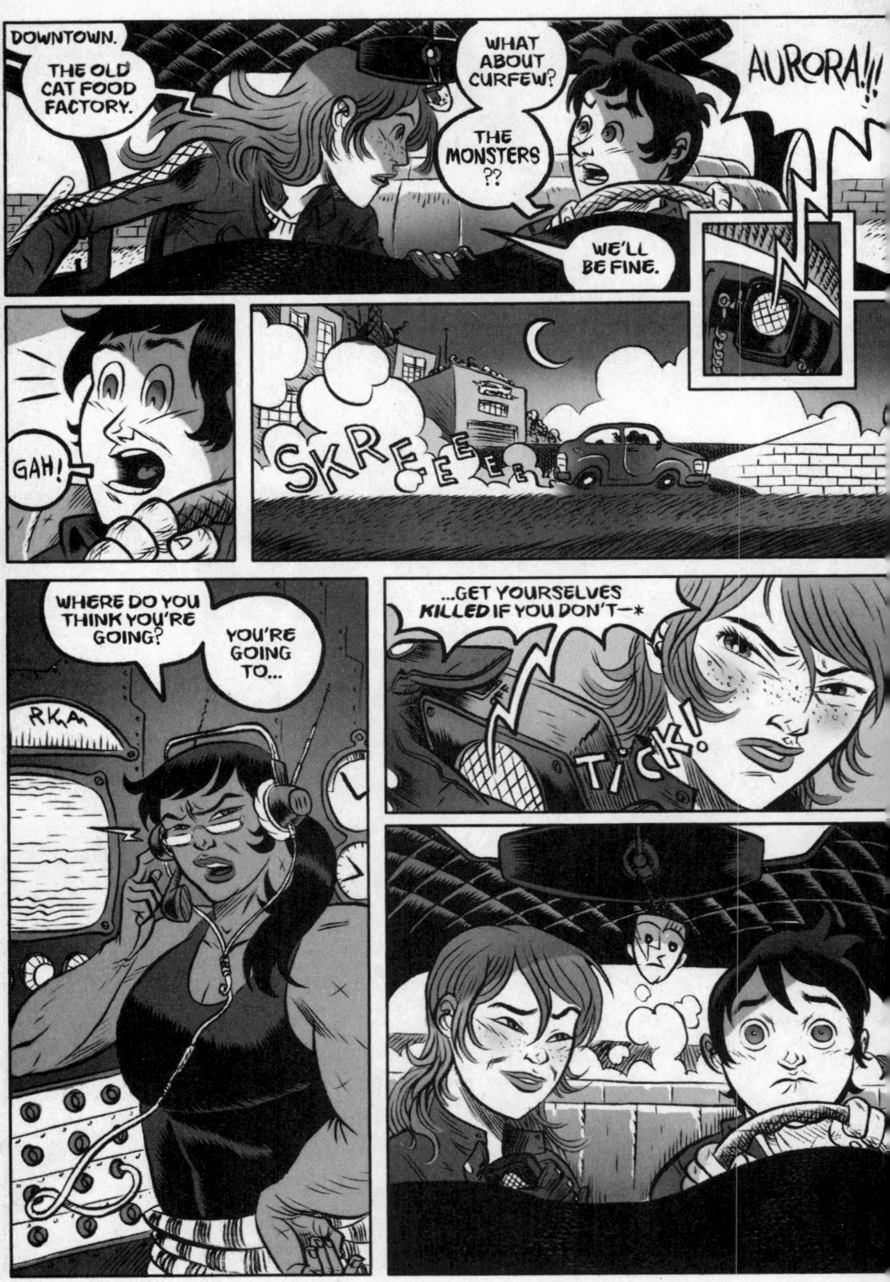
DOWNTOWN.
THE OLD CAT FOOD FACTORY.
WHAT ABOUT CURFEW?
THE MONSTERS ??
WE'LL BE FINE.
AURORA!!!
GAH!
SKREEEEEE
WHERE DO YOU THINK YOU'RE GOING?
YOU'RE GOING TO...
...GET YOURSELVES KILLED IF YOU DON'T—*
TICK!

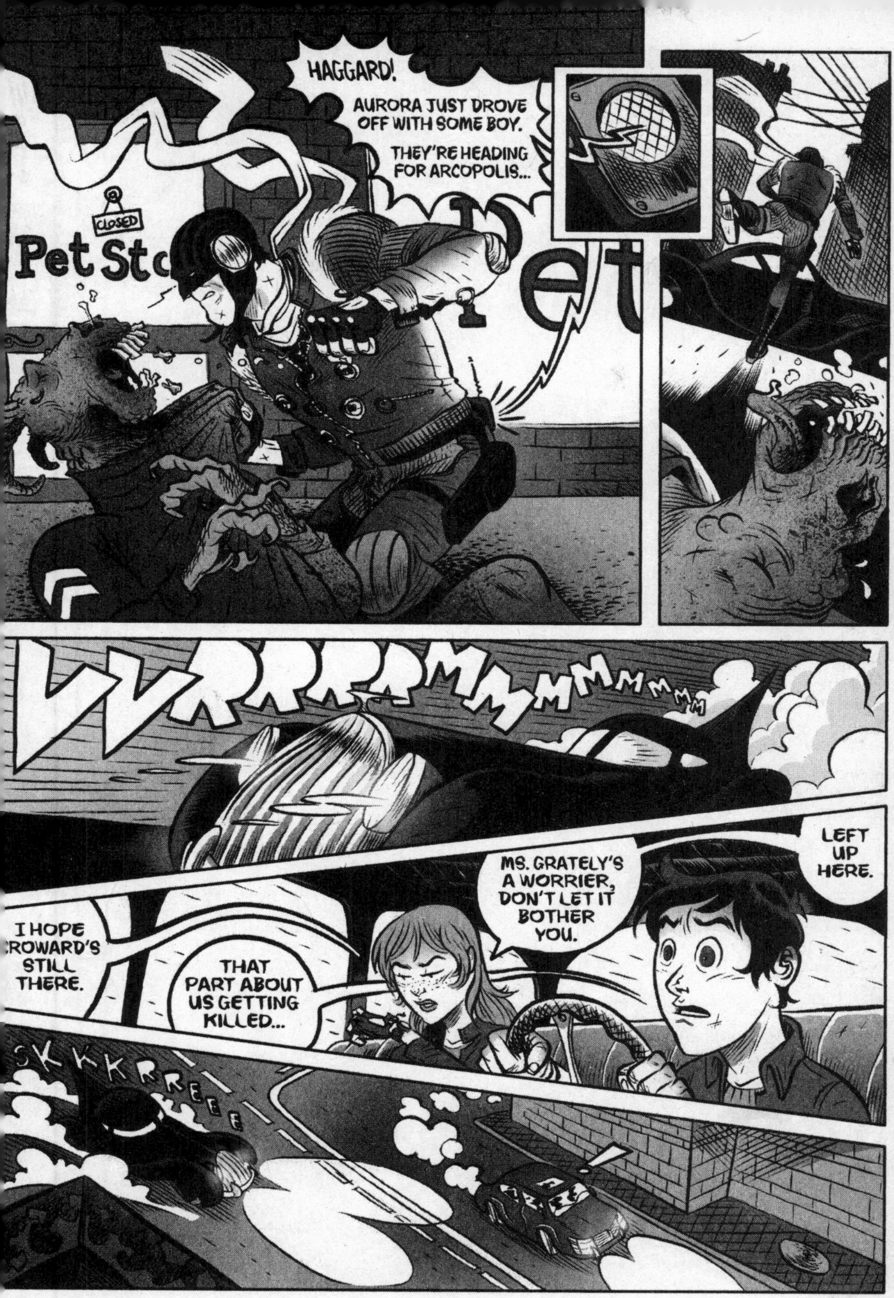
Pet St
CLOSED
HAGGARD!
AURORA JUST DROVE OFF WITH SOME BOY.
THEY'RE HEADING FOR ARCOPOLIS...
VVRRRRRRMMMMMMMMMM
MS. GRATELY'S A WORRIER, DON'T LET IT BOTHER YOU.
LEFT UP HERE.
THAT PART ABOUT US GETTING KILLED...
I HOPE CROWARD'S STILL THERE.
SKKKRREEEE

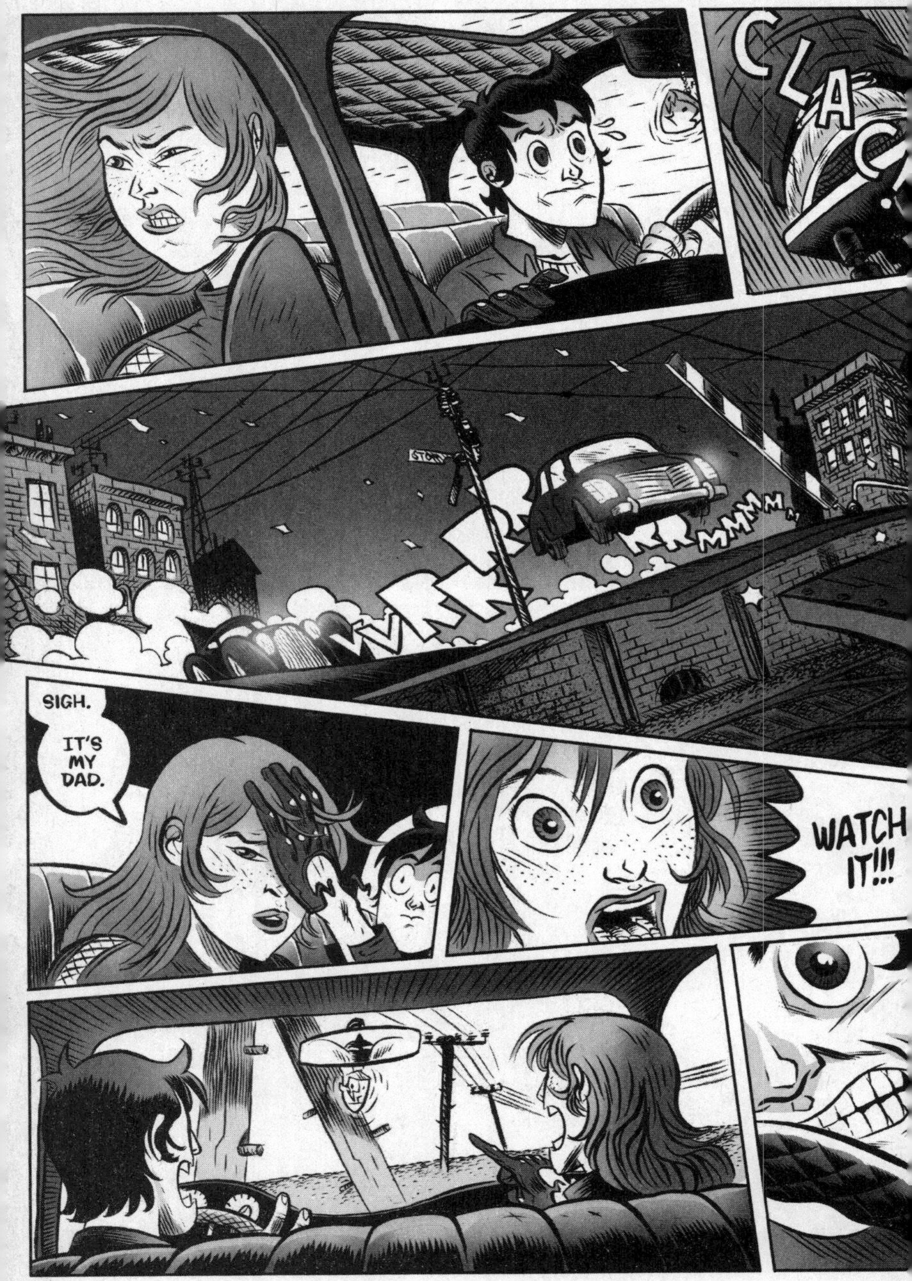
CLACK
VVRRRRMMMM
SIGH.
IT'S MY DAD.
WATCH IT!!!

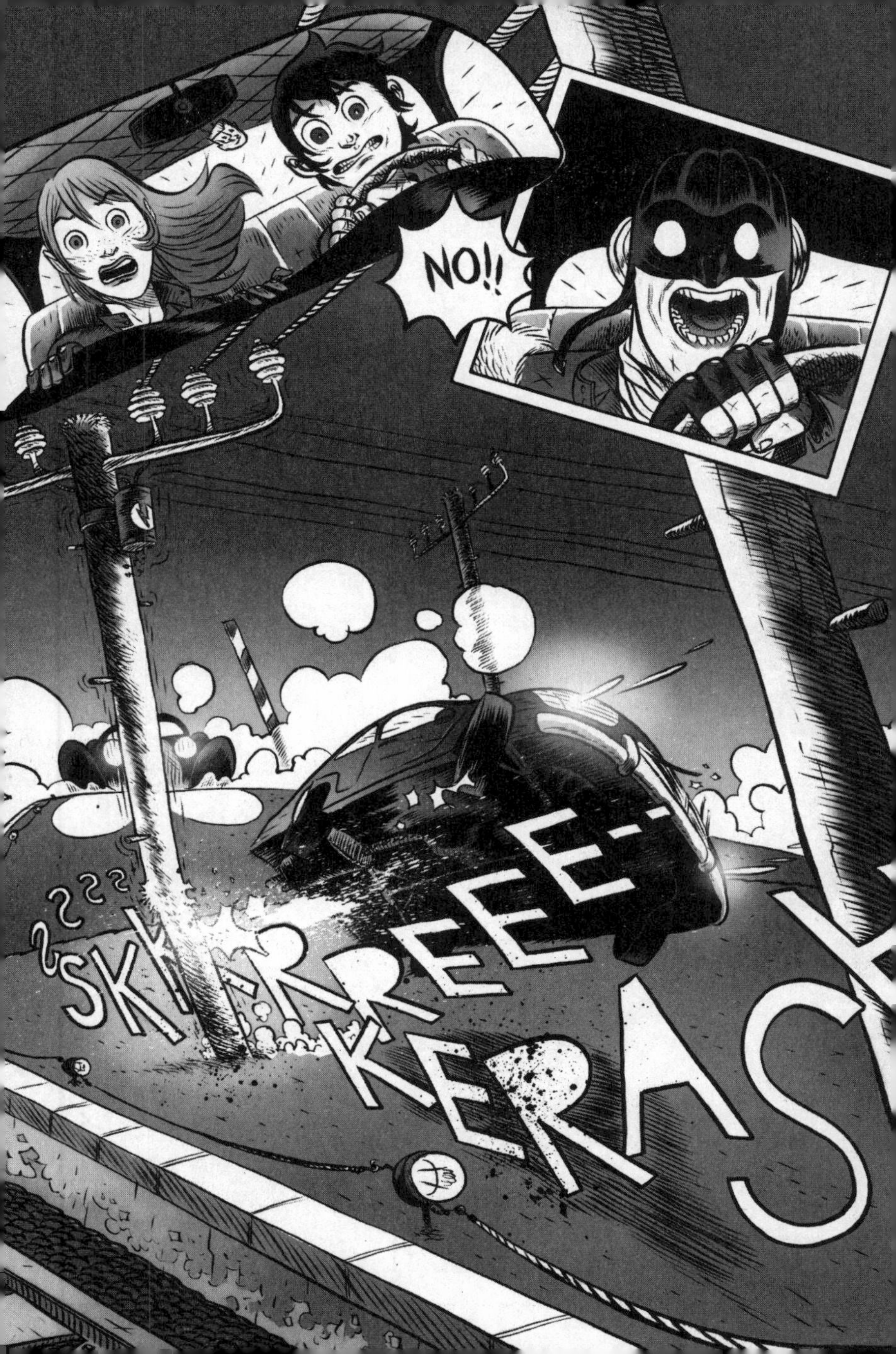
NO!!
SKIRREEE--
KERASH

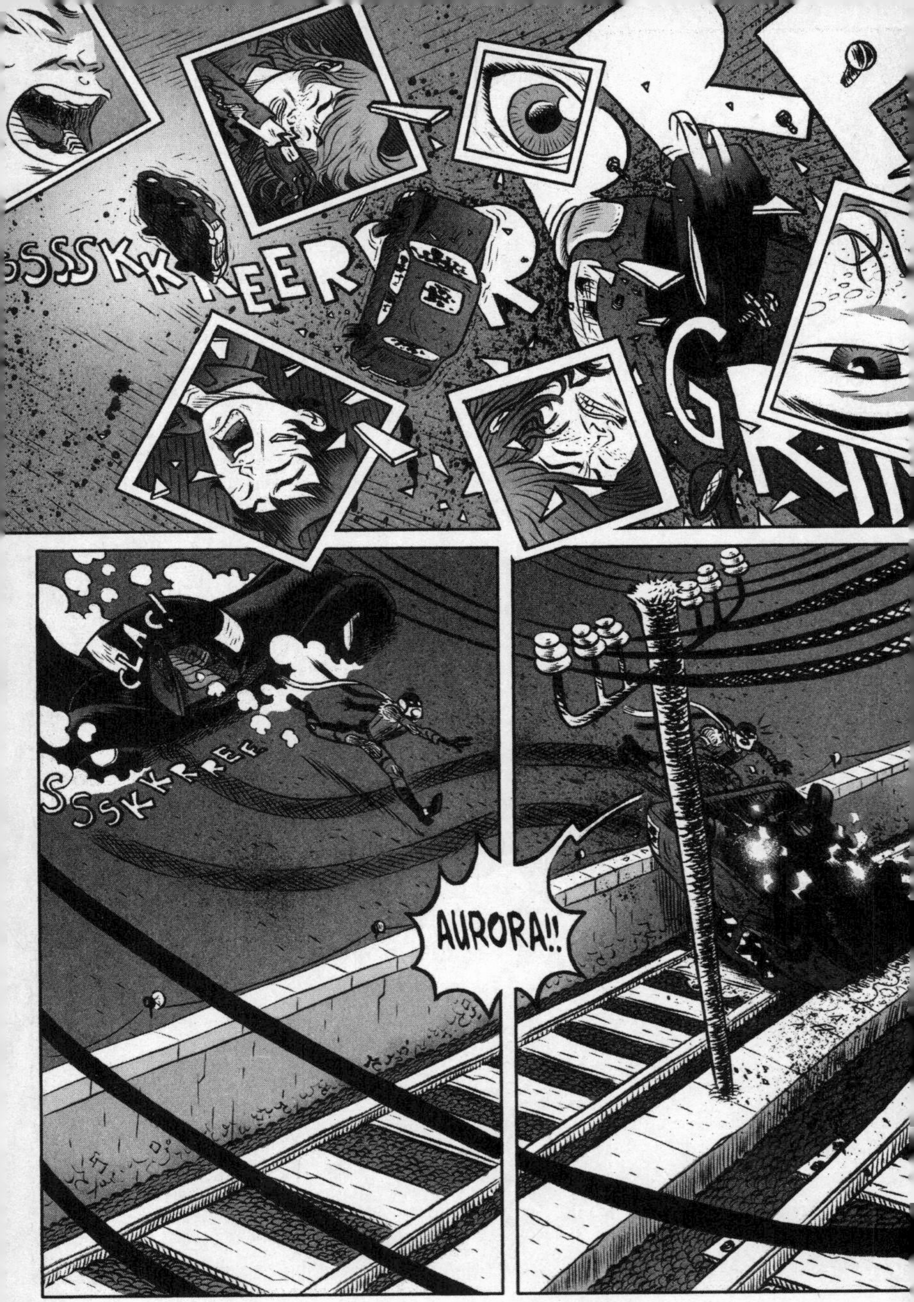
SSSSKKREER
CLAC!
SSSKKRREE
AURORA!!

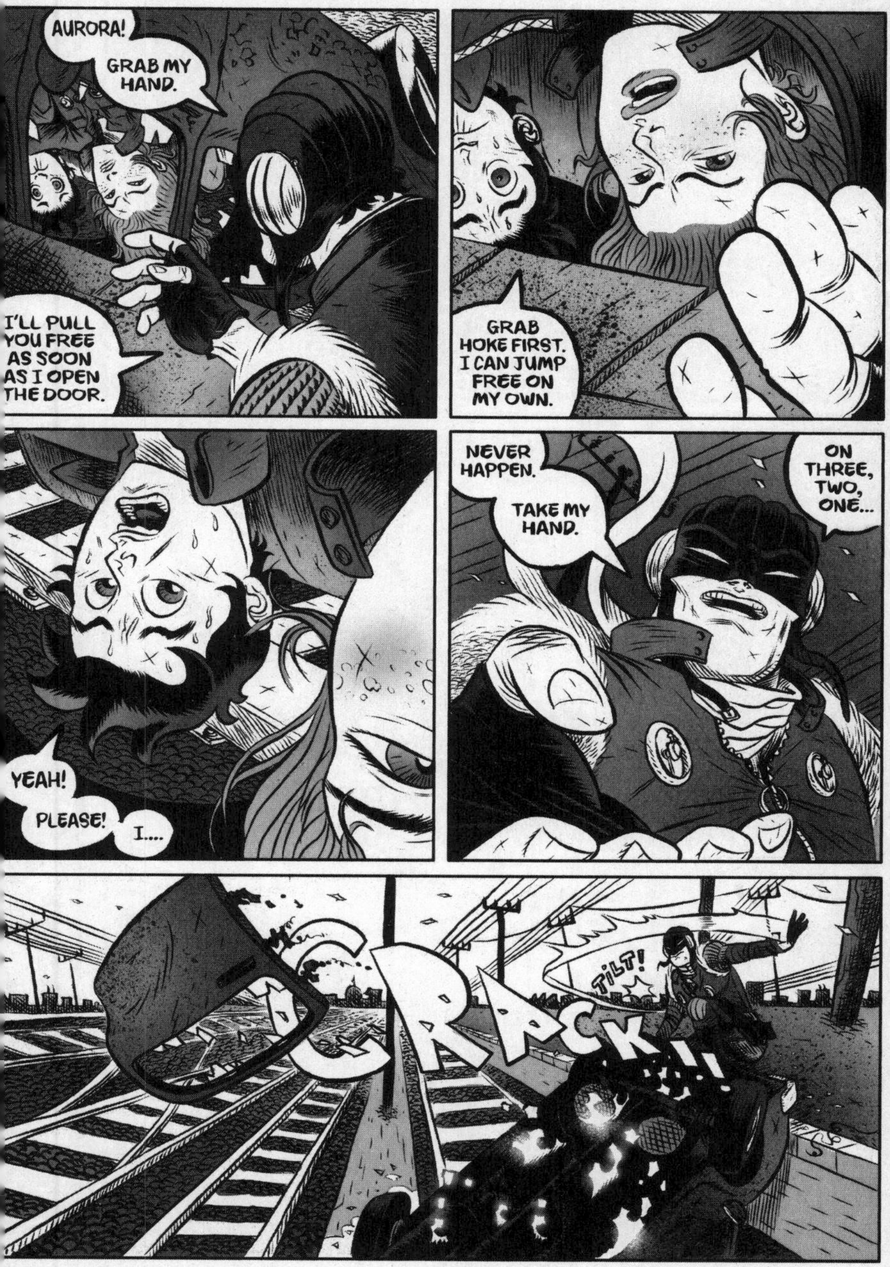
AURORA!
GRAB MY HAND.
I'LL PULL YOU FREE AS SOON AS I OPEN THE DOOR.
GRAB HOKE FIRST. I CAN JUMP FREE ON MY OWN.
YEAH!
PLEASE!
I....
NEVER HAPPEN.
TAKE MY HAND.
ON THREE, TWO, ONE...
CRACK!!
TILT!

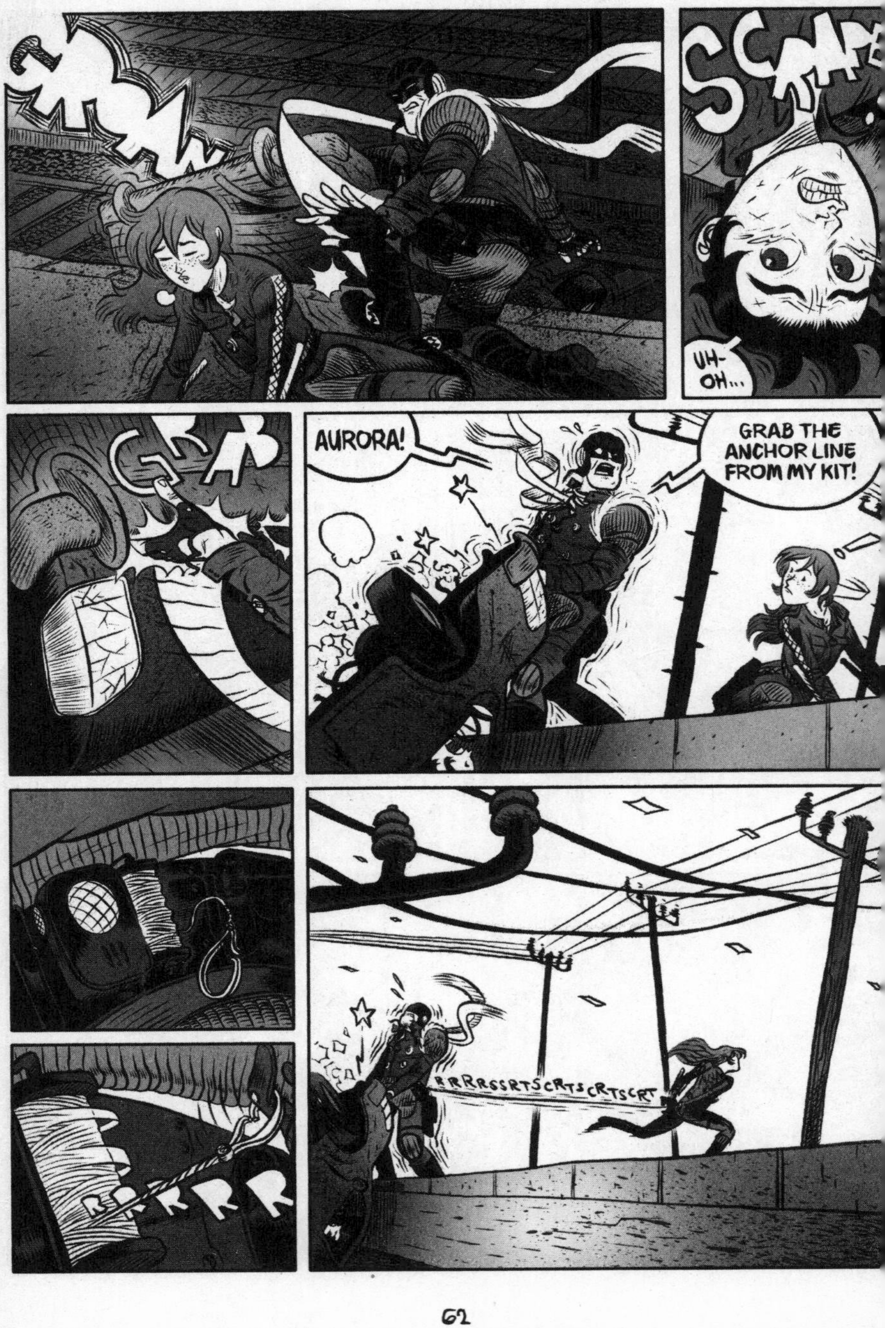
UH-OH...
AURORA!
GRAB THE ANCHOR LINE FROM MY KIT!
RRRRSSRTSCRTSCRTSCRT
RRRRR

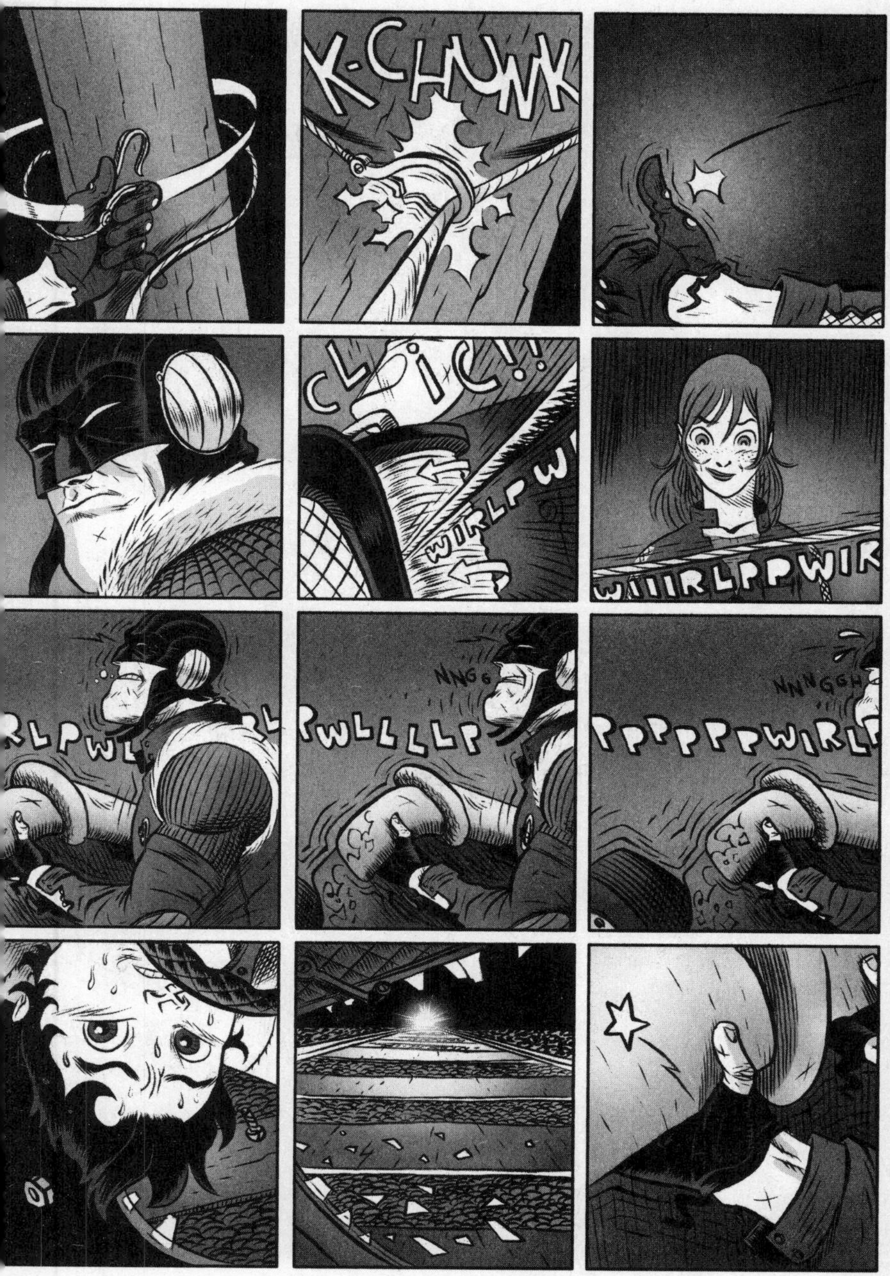
K-CHUNK
CLIC!!
WIRLPWI
WIRLP
WIIIRLPPWIR
RLPWL
RL
PWLLLLLP
NNGG
NNNGGH
PPPPPPWIRLP

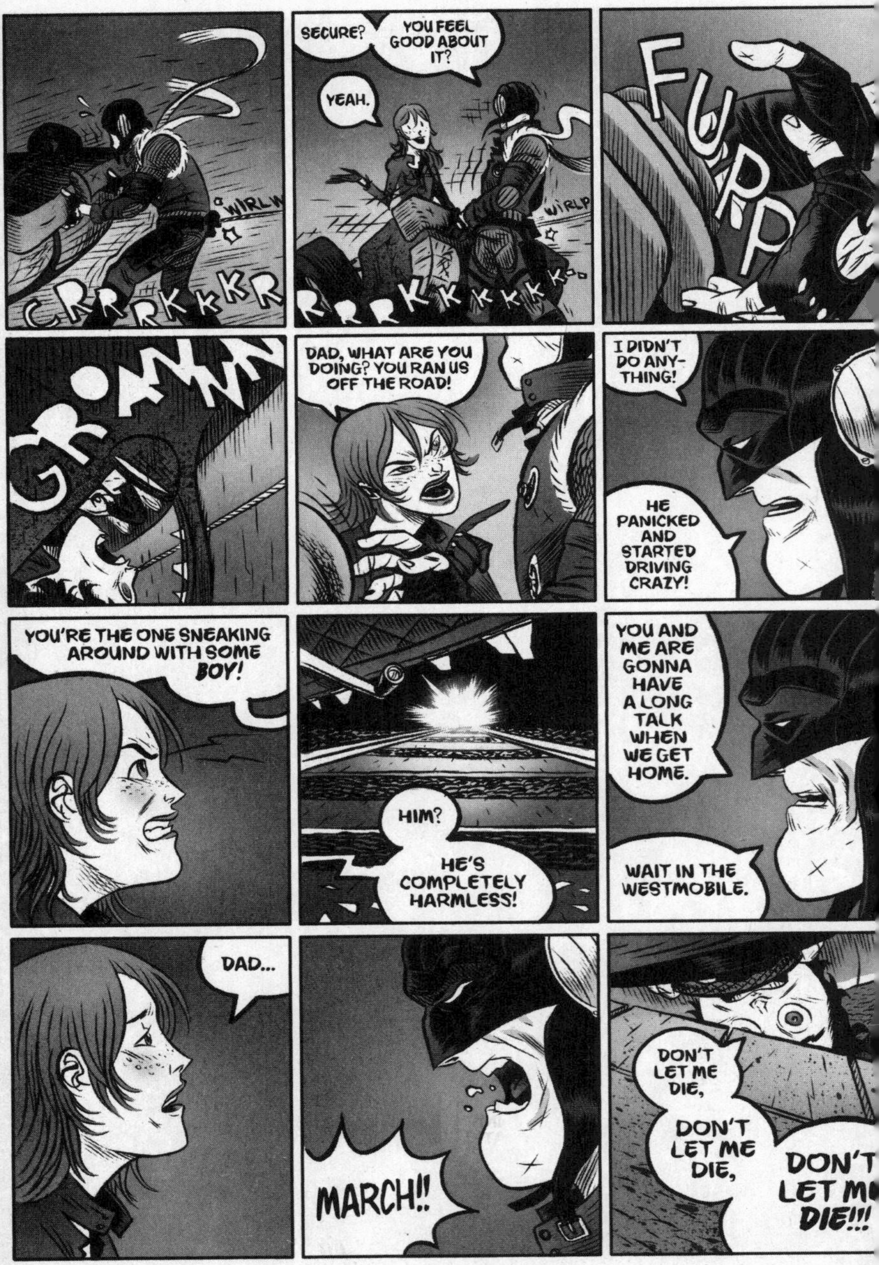
WIRLW
CRRRKKKR
SECURE?
YOU FEEL GOOD ABOUT IT?
YEAH.
WIRLP
RRRRKKKKKK
FUPP
GROAMM
DAD, WHAT ARE YOU DOING? YOU RAN US OFF THE ROAD!
I DIDN'T DO ANYTHING!
HE PANICKED AND STARTED DRIVING CRAZY!
YOU'RE THE ONE SNEAKING AROUND WITH SOME BOY!
HIM?
HE'S COMPLETELY HARMLESS!
YOU AND ME ARE GONNA HAVE A LONG TALK WHEN WE GET HOME.
WAIT IN THE WESTMOBILE.
DAD...
MARCH!!
DON'T LET ME DIE,
DON'T LET ME DIE,
DON'T LET M DIE!!!

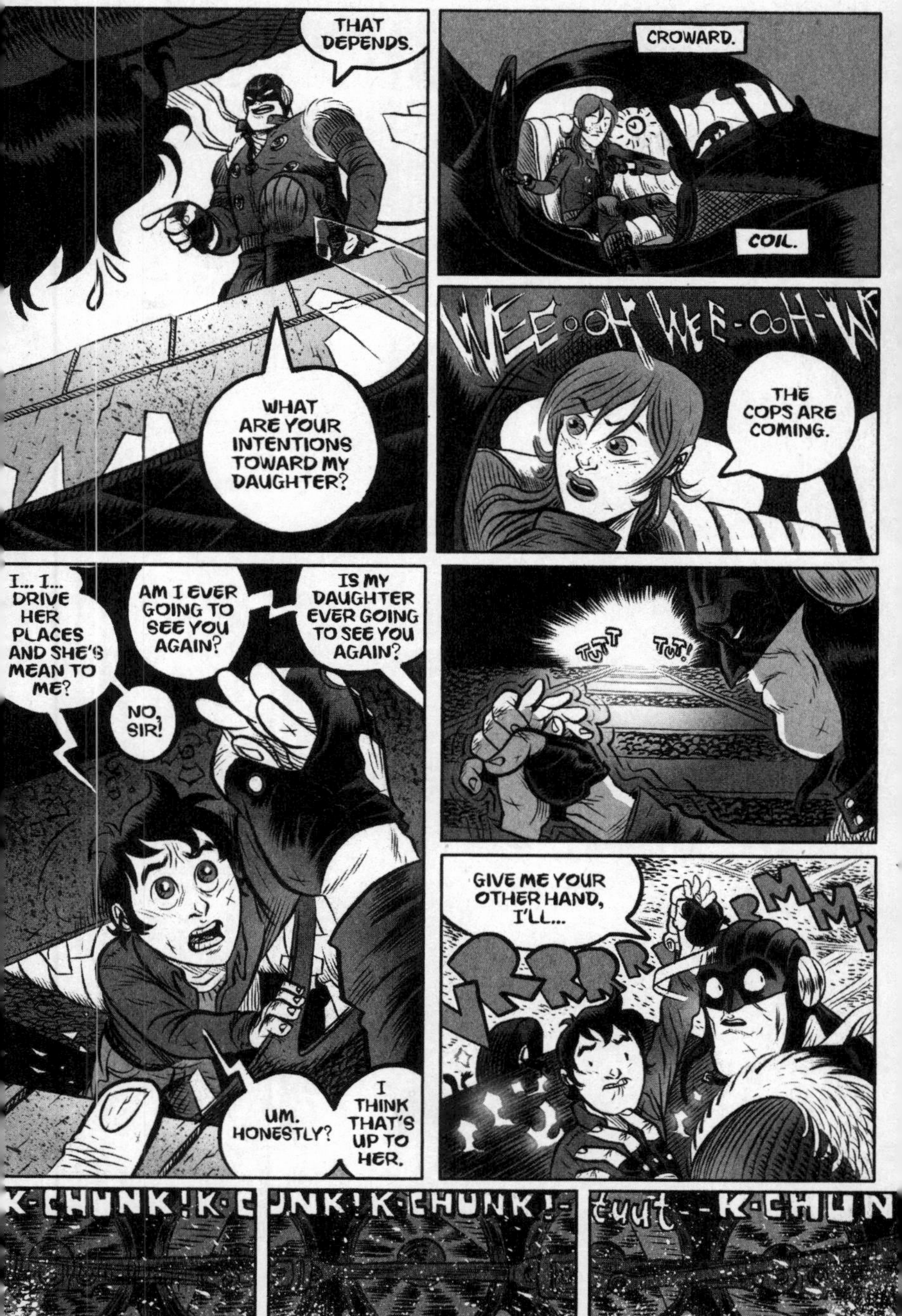
THAT DEPENDS.
WHAT ARE YOUR INTENTIONS TOWARD MY DAUGHTER?
CROWARD.
COIL.
WEE-OOH WEE-OOH-W
THE COPS ARE COMING.
I... I... DRIVE HER PLACES AND SHE'S MEAN TO ME?
AM I EVER GOING TO SEE YOU AGAIN?
NO, SIR!
IS MY DAUGHTER EVER GOING TO SEE YOU AGAIN?
UM. HONESTLY?
I THINK THAT'S UP TO HER.
TUT TUT!
GIVE ME YOUR OTHER HAND, I'LL...
VRRRR
K-CHUNK! K-CHUNK! K-CHUNK! -tuut- -K-CHUN

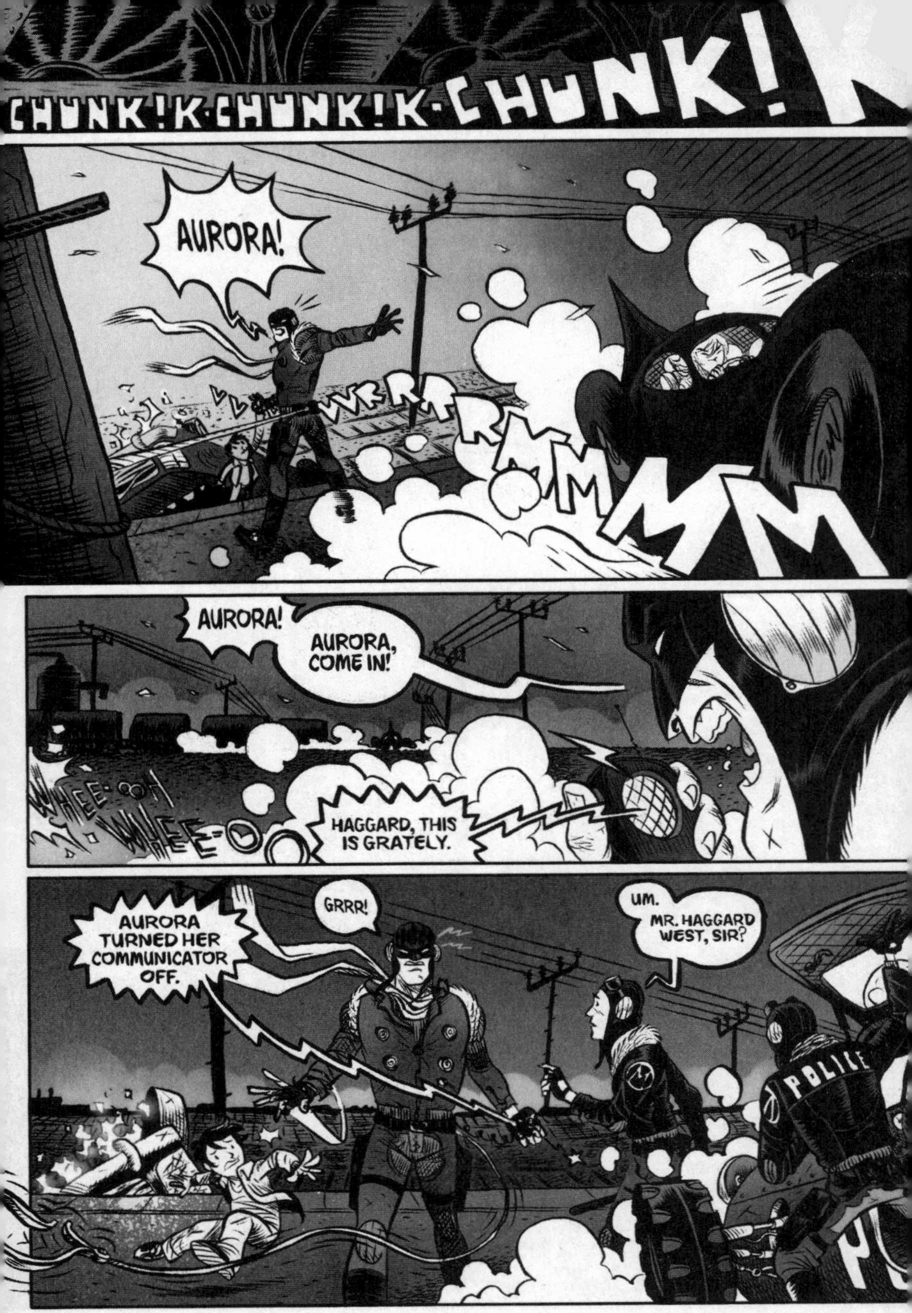
CHUNK! K-CHUNK! K-CHUNK!
AURORA!
VVRRRAMMMM
AURORA!
AURORA, COME IN!
WHEE-OOH WHEE-OO
HAGGARD, THIS IS GRATELY.
AURORA TURNED HER COMMUNICATOR OFF.
GRRR!
UM. MR. HAGGARD WEST, SIR?
POLICE

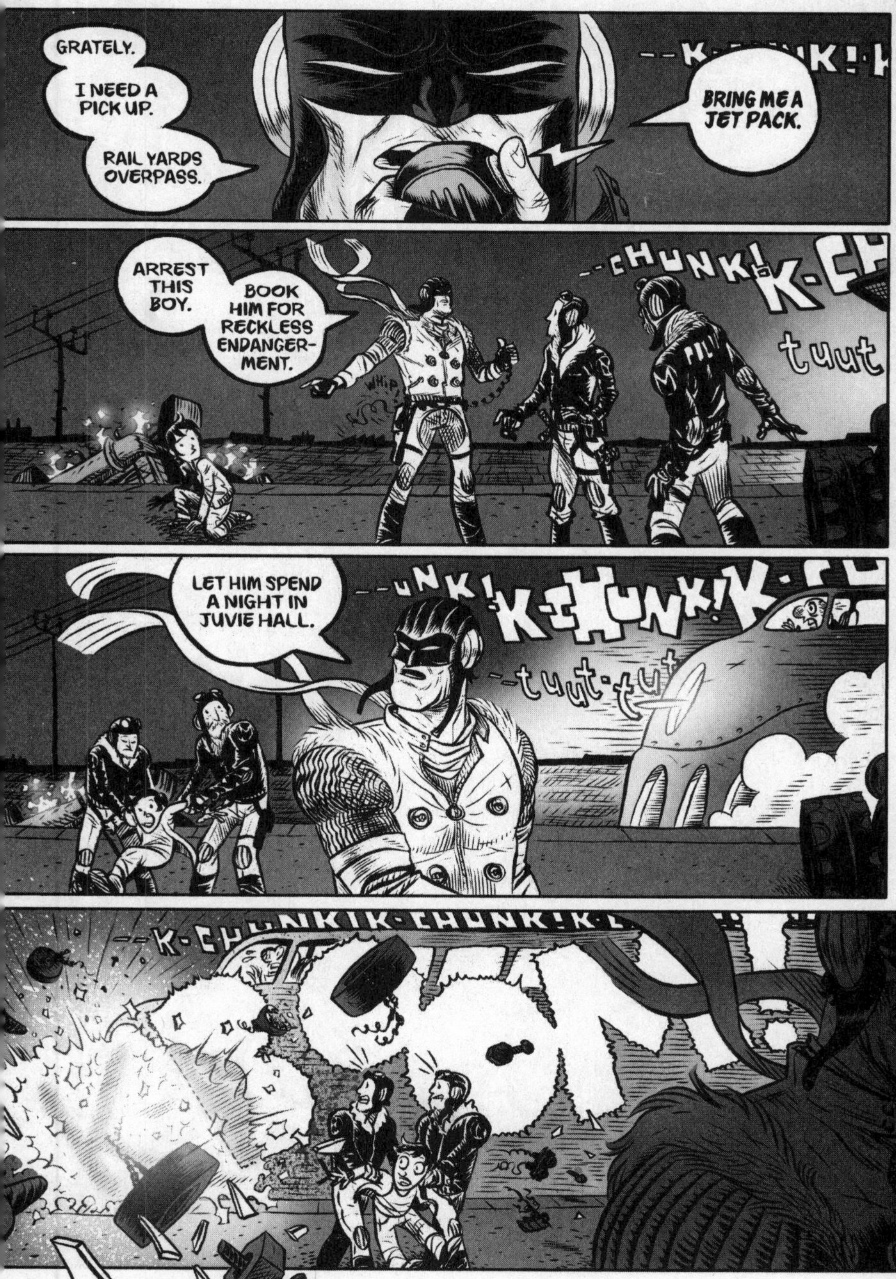
GRATELY.
I NEED A PICK UP.
RAIL YARDS OVERPASS.
BRING ME A JET PACK.
--K-CHUNK!-K
ARREST THIS BOY.
BOOK HIM FOR RECKLESS ENDANGERMENT.
WHIP
--CHUNK! K-CH
tuut
LET HIM SPEND A NIGHT IN JUVIE HALL.
--UNK! K-CHUNK! K-CH
--tuut-tut
--K-CHUNK! K-CHUNK! K-C

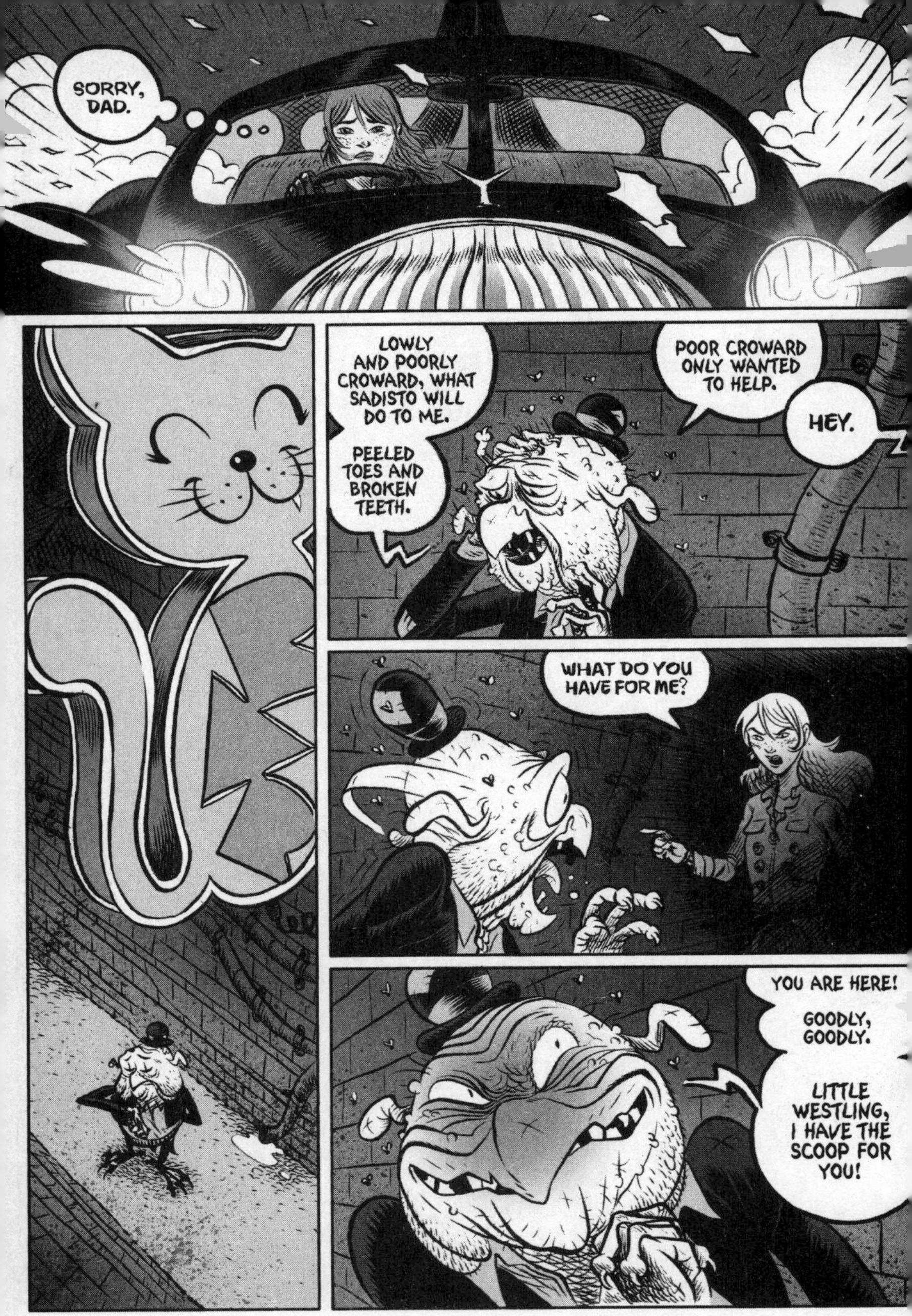
SORRY, DAD.
LOWLY AND POORLY CROWARD, WHAT SADISTO WILL DO TO ME.
PEELED TOES AND BROKEN TEETH.
POOR CROWARD ONLY WANTED TO HELP.
HEY.
WHAT DO YOU HAVE FOR ME?
YOU ARE HERE!
GOODLY, GOODLY.
LITTLE WESTLING, I HAVE THE SCOOP FOR YOU!

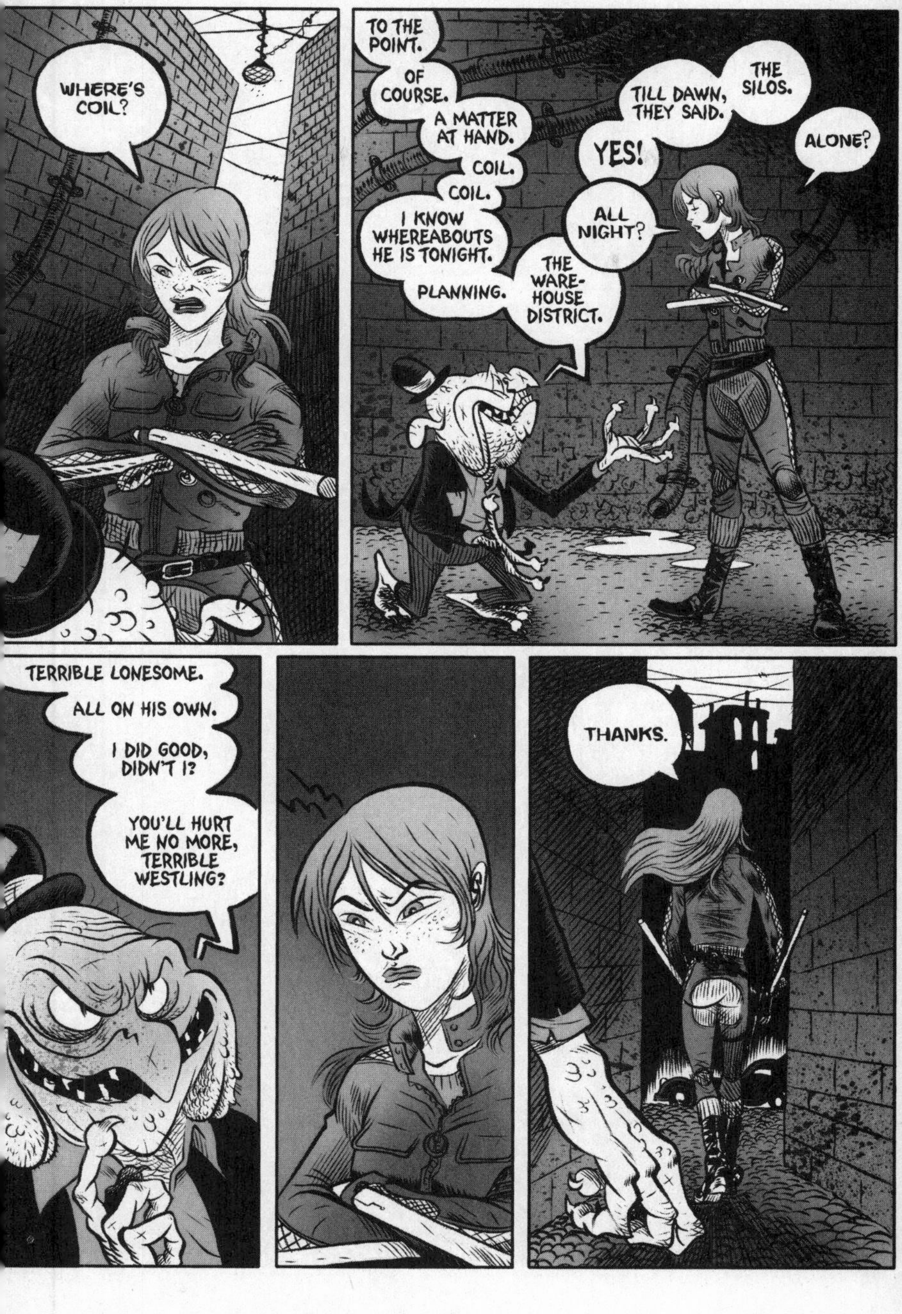
WHERE'S COIL?
TO THE POINT.
OF COURSE.
A MATTER AT HAND.
COIL.
COIL.
I KNOW WHEREABOUTS HE IS TONIGHT.
PLANNING.
THE WARE-HOUSE DISTRICT.
ALL NIGHT?
YES!
TILL DAWN, THEY SAID.
THE SILOS.
ALONE?
TERRIBLE LONESOME.
ALL ON HIS OWN.
I DID GOOD, DIDN'T I?
YOU'LL HURT ME NO MORE, TERRIBLE WESTLING?
THANKS.

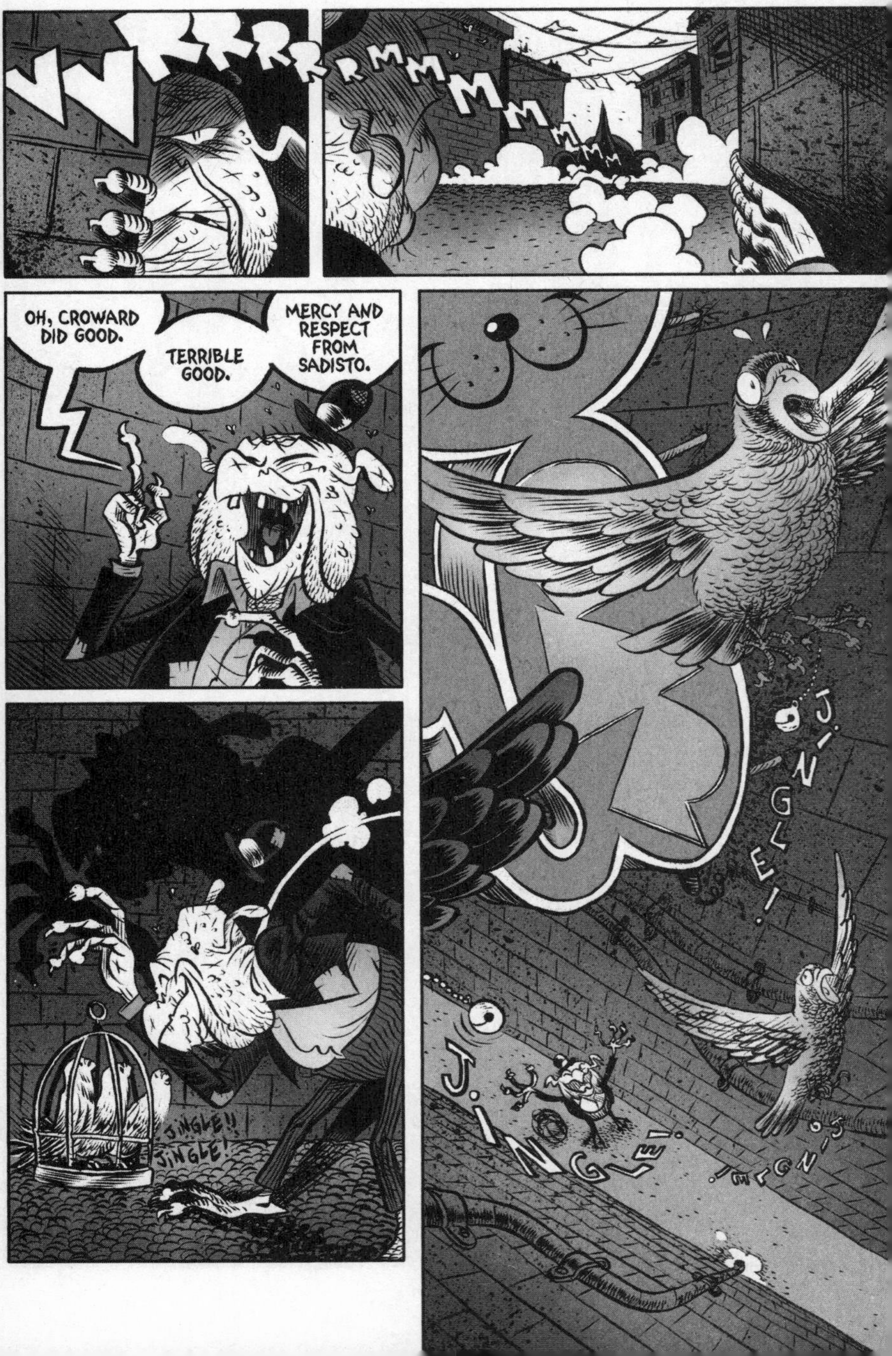
VVRRRRRRRMMMMMMMM
OH, CROWARD DID GOOD.
TERRIBLE GOOD.
MERCY AND RESPECT FROM SADISTO.
JINGLE!! JINGLE!
JINGLE!
JINGLE!
JINGLE!

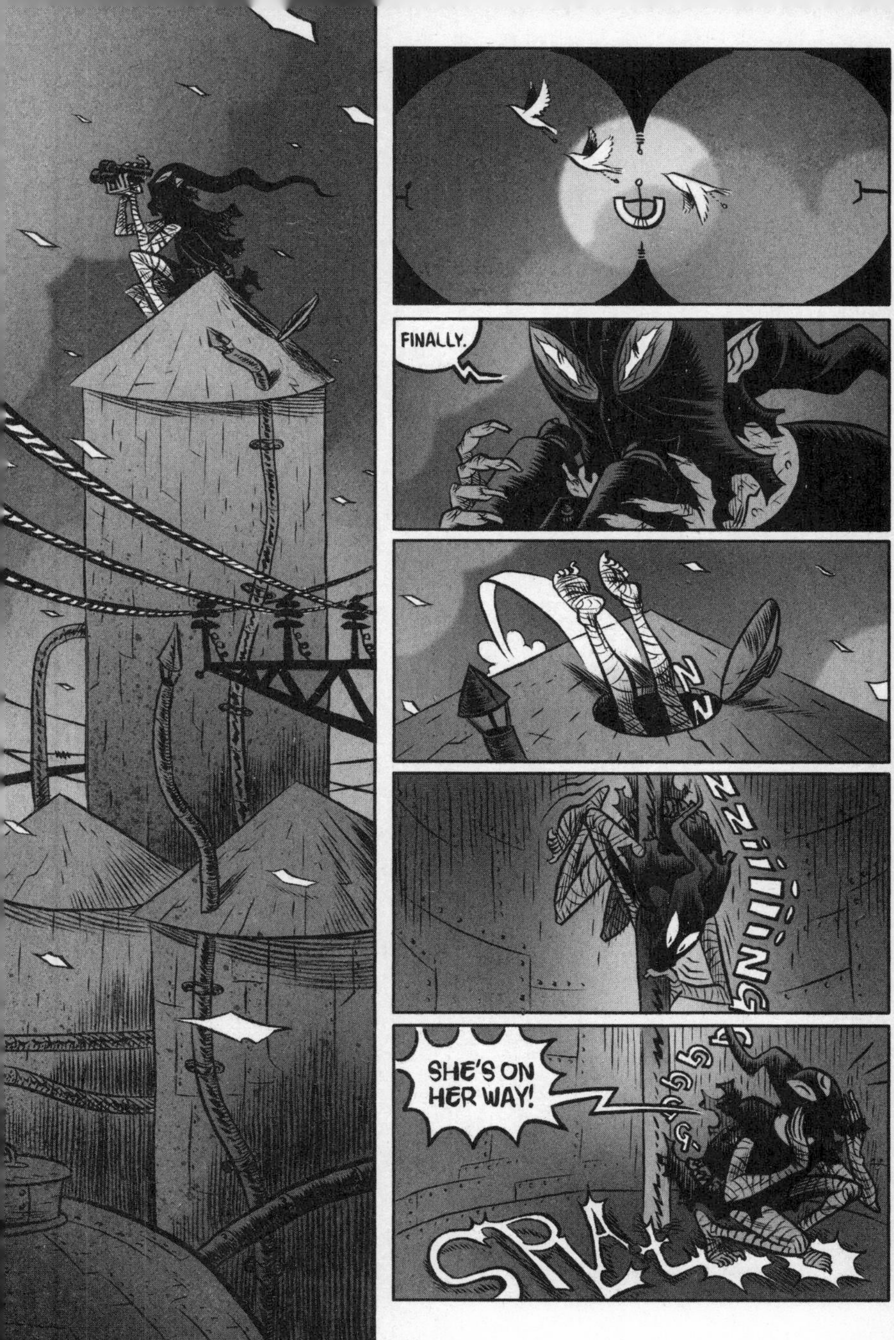
FINALLY.
SHE'S ON HER WAY!

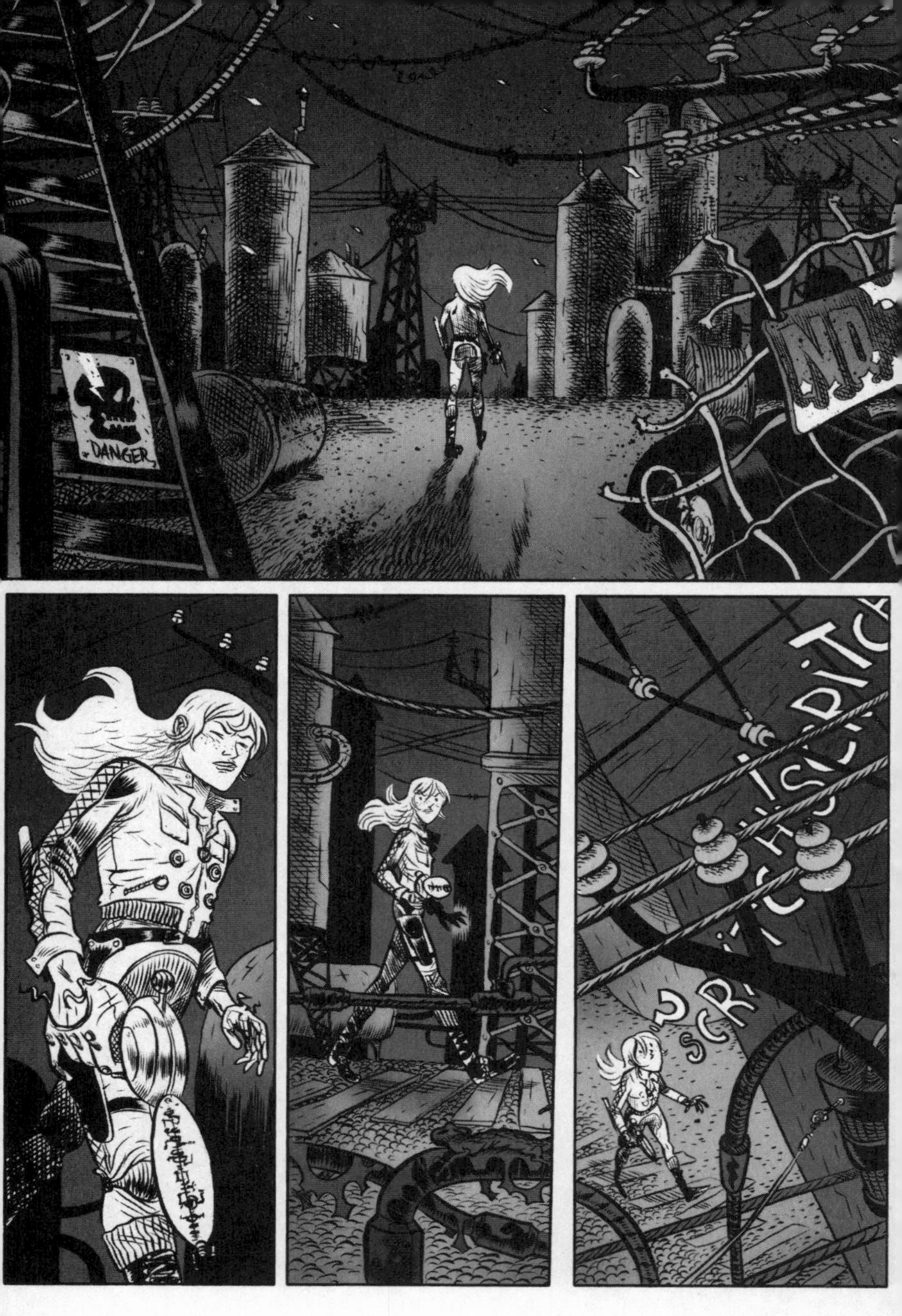
DANGER

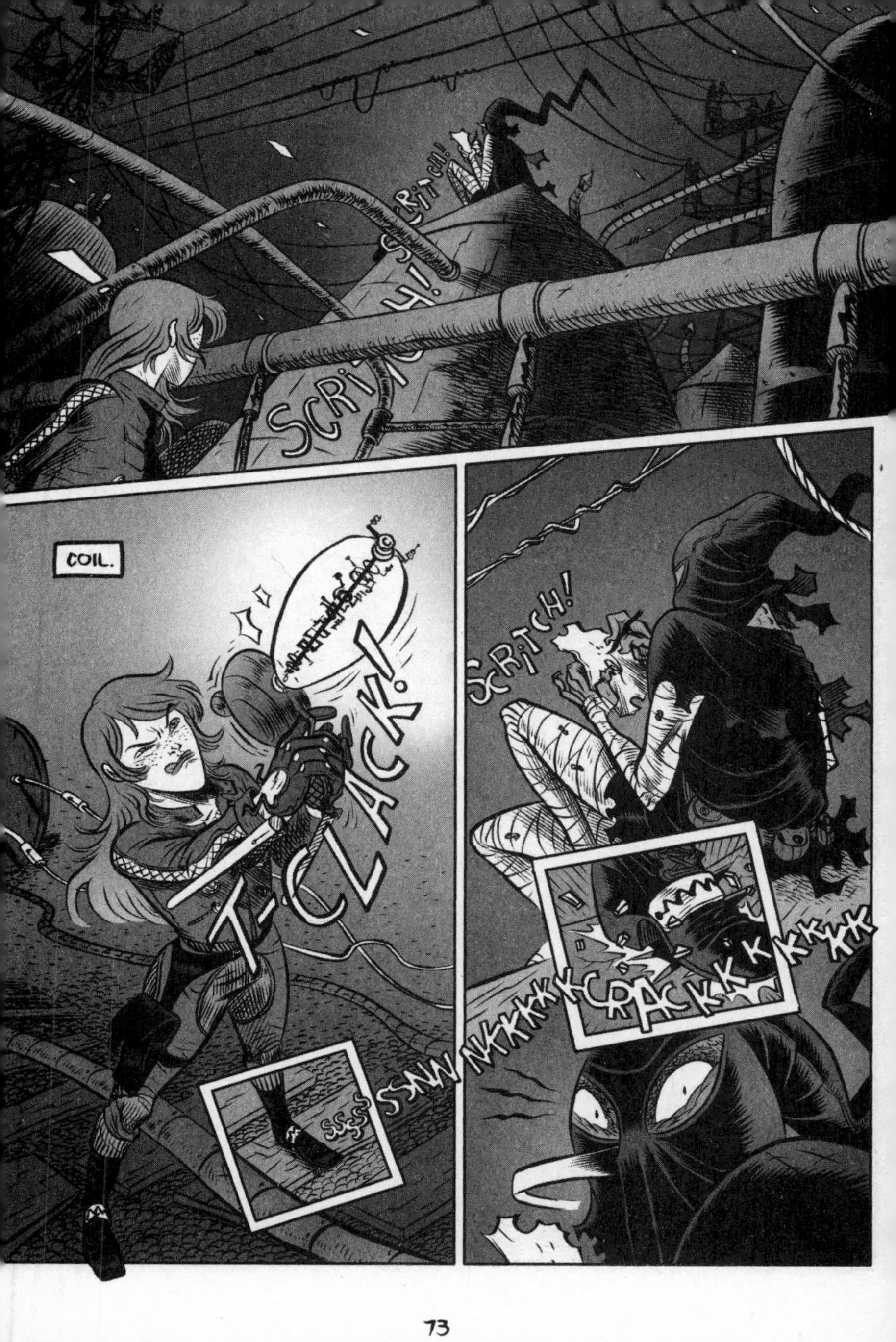
SCRITCH!
SCRiTCH!
COIL.
T-CLACK!
SCRiTCH!
SSSSNNNKKKKCRACKKKKKK

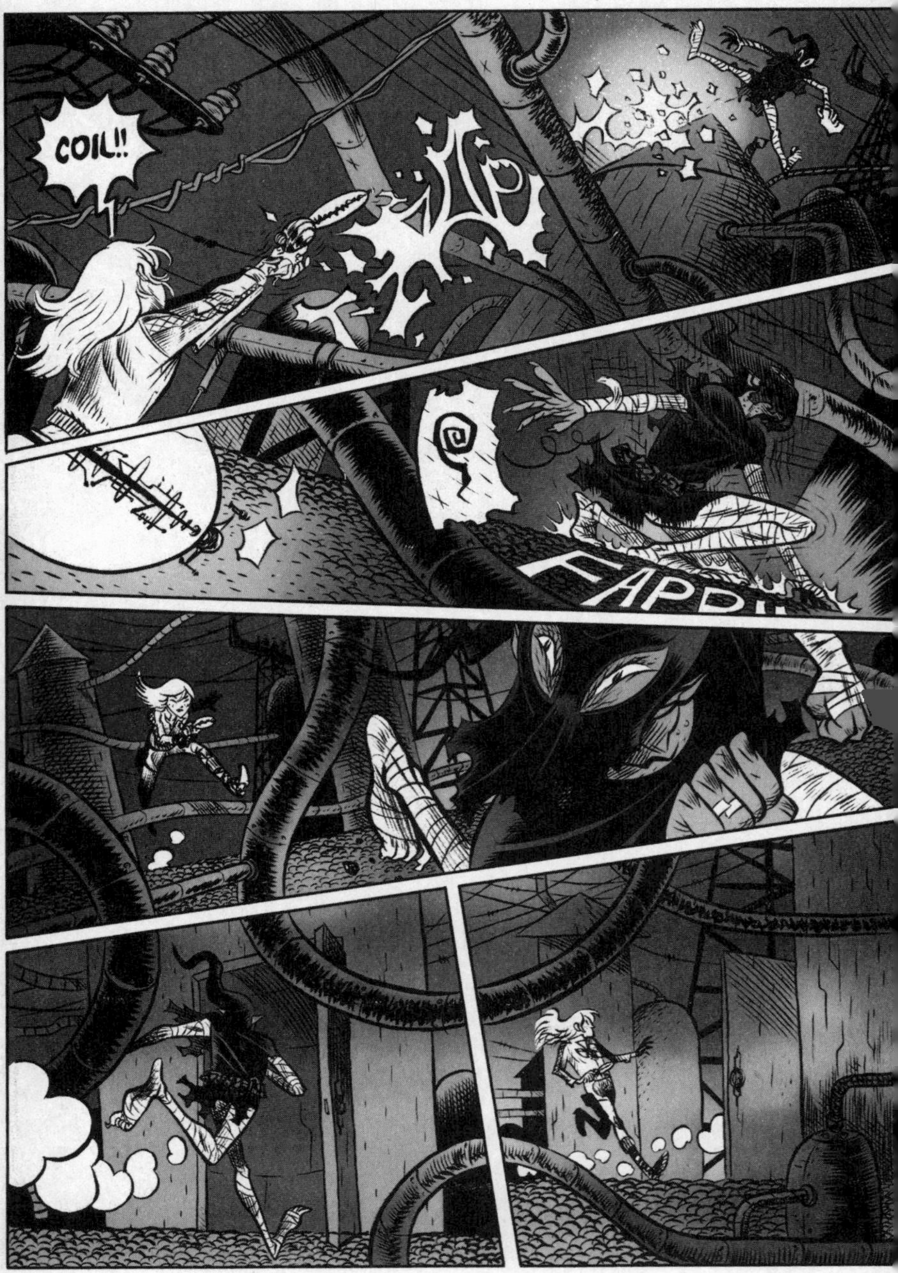
COIL!!
FAPP!!

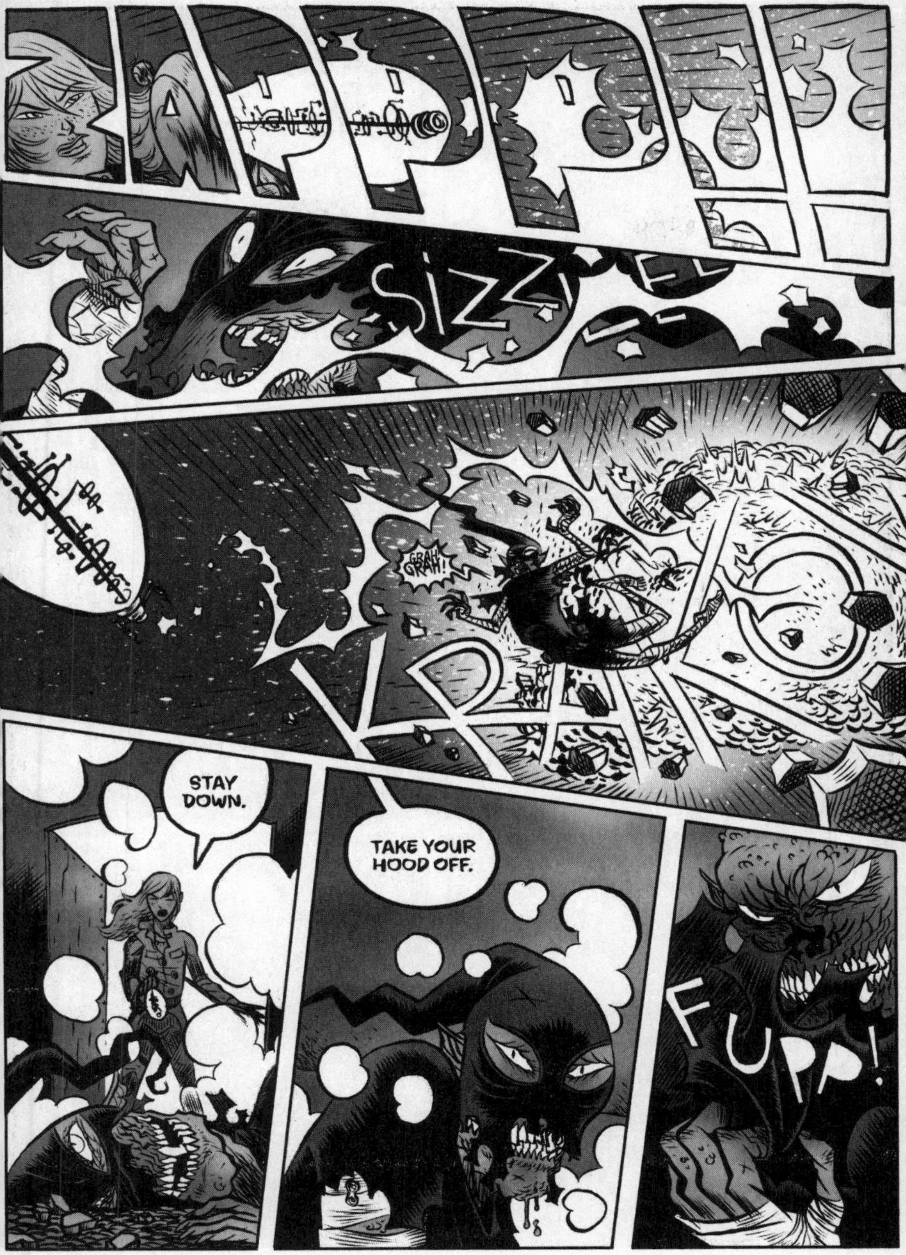
GRAH GRAH!
STAY DOWN.
TAKE YOUR HOOD OFF.
FUPP!

WHY WERE YOU LOOKING FOR ME?

YOU KILLED MY MOTHER.

I DID NOT.

WHAT WAS HER NAME? ROSE...

ROSETTA.

YES.

THINGS ARE SO HAZY FROM THAT TIME. I WAS ONLY A WISP, LITTLE MORE THAN A NIGHTMARE.

BUT I DID NOT KILL YOUR MOTHER.

THEN WHO DID? THE SEVEN-FINGERED MONSTER?

THE SEVEN-FINGERED...?

I HAVE NO IDEA WHAT YOU'RE TALKING ABOUT.

YOU KNOW.

IF YOU DON'T TALK I'LL KILL YOU.

YOU'LL KILL ME ANYWAY.

YES.

CHIK!!

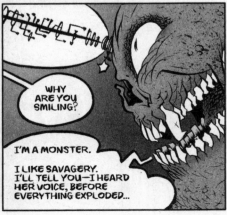

WHY ARE YOU SMILING?

I'M A MONSTER.

I LIKE SAVAGERY. I'LL TELL YOU—I HEARD HER VOICE, BEFORE EVERYTHING EXPLODED...

...YOUR MOTHER WAS CALLING YOUR NAME.

WHAT?

WHAT DO YOU MEAN SHE WAS CALLING MY NAME?

LOOK AT ME!

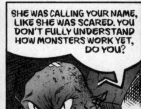

SHE WAS CALLING YOUR NAME, LIKE SHE WAS SCARED. YOU DON'T FULLY UNDERSTAND HOW MONSTERS WORK YET, DO YOU?

IT WOULD BE EASIER TO SHOW YOU.

STOP!

STAY DOWN!

SHOOT ME IF THAT'S WHAT YOU NEED TO DO.

JUMP!

BUT THEN YOU'LL NEVER KNOW.

WAIT...

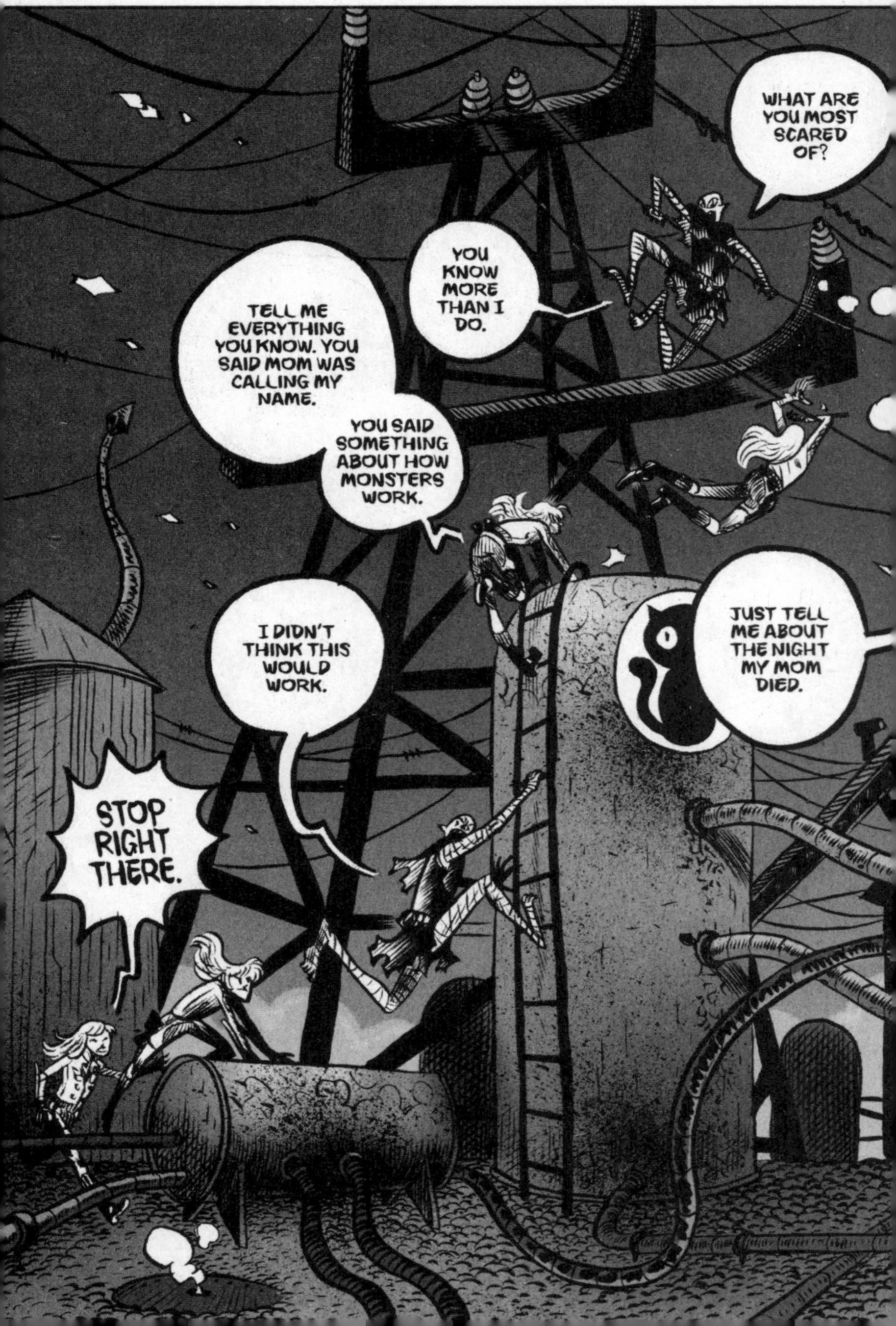
WHAT ARE YOU MOST SCARED OF?
YOU KNOW MORE THAN I DO.
TELL ME EVERYTHING YOU KNOW. YOU SAID MOM WAS CALLING MY NAME.
YOU SAID SOMETHING ABOUT HOW MONSTERS WORK.
JUST TELL ME ABOUT THE NIGHT MY MOM DIED.
I DIDN'T THINK THIS WOULD WORK.
STOP RIGHT THERE.

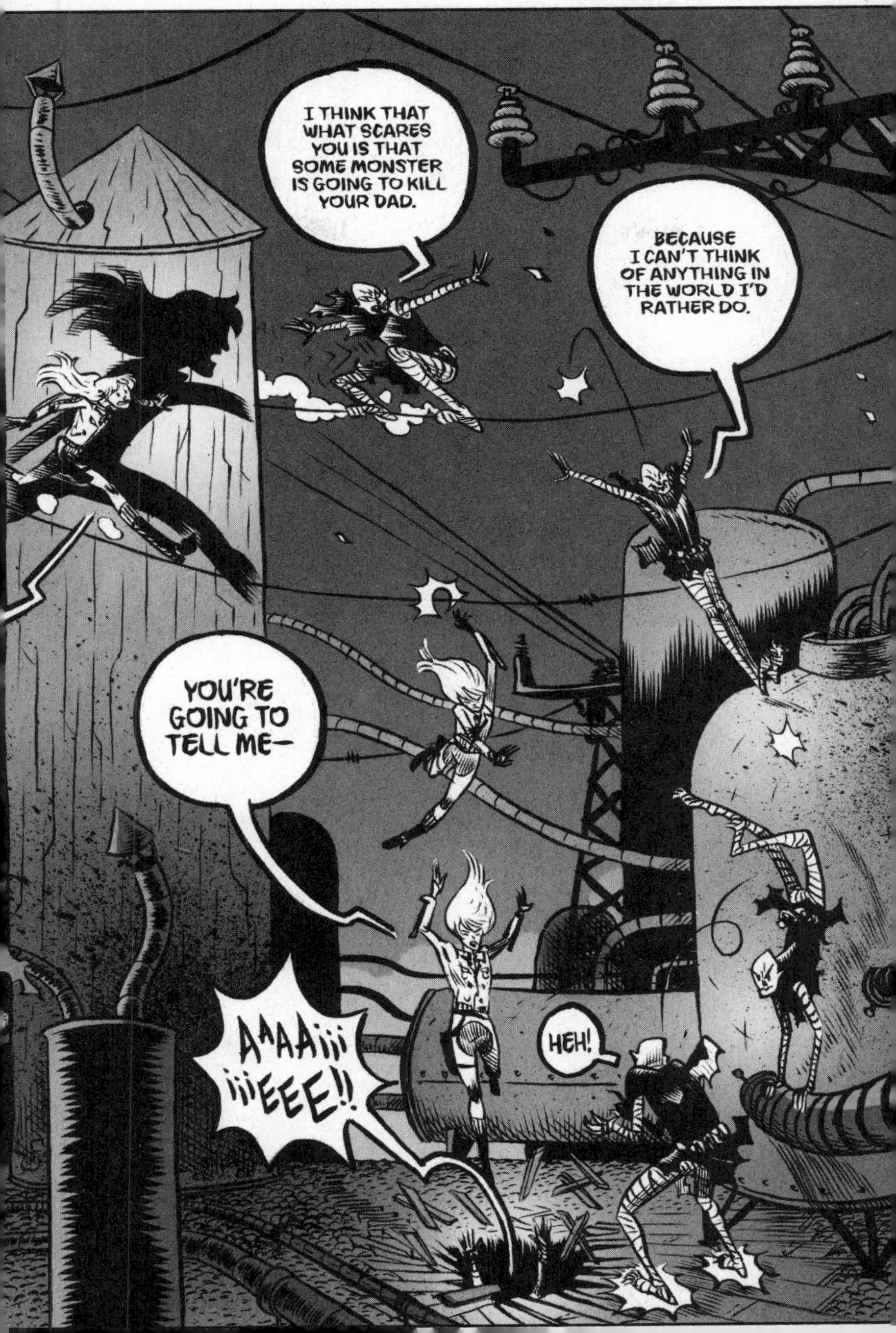
I THINK THAT WHAT SCARES YOU IS THAT SOME MONSTER IS GOING TO KILL YOUR DAD.
BECAUSE I CAN'T THINK OF ANYTHING IN THE WORLD I'D RATHER DO.
YOU'RE GOING TO TELL ME—
AAAAiiii iiiEEE!!
HEH!

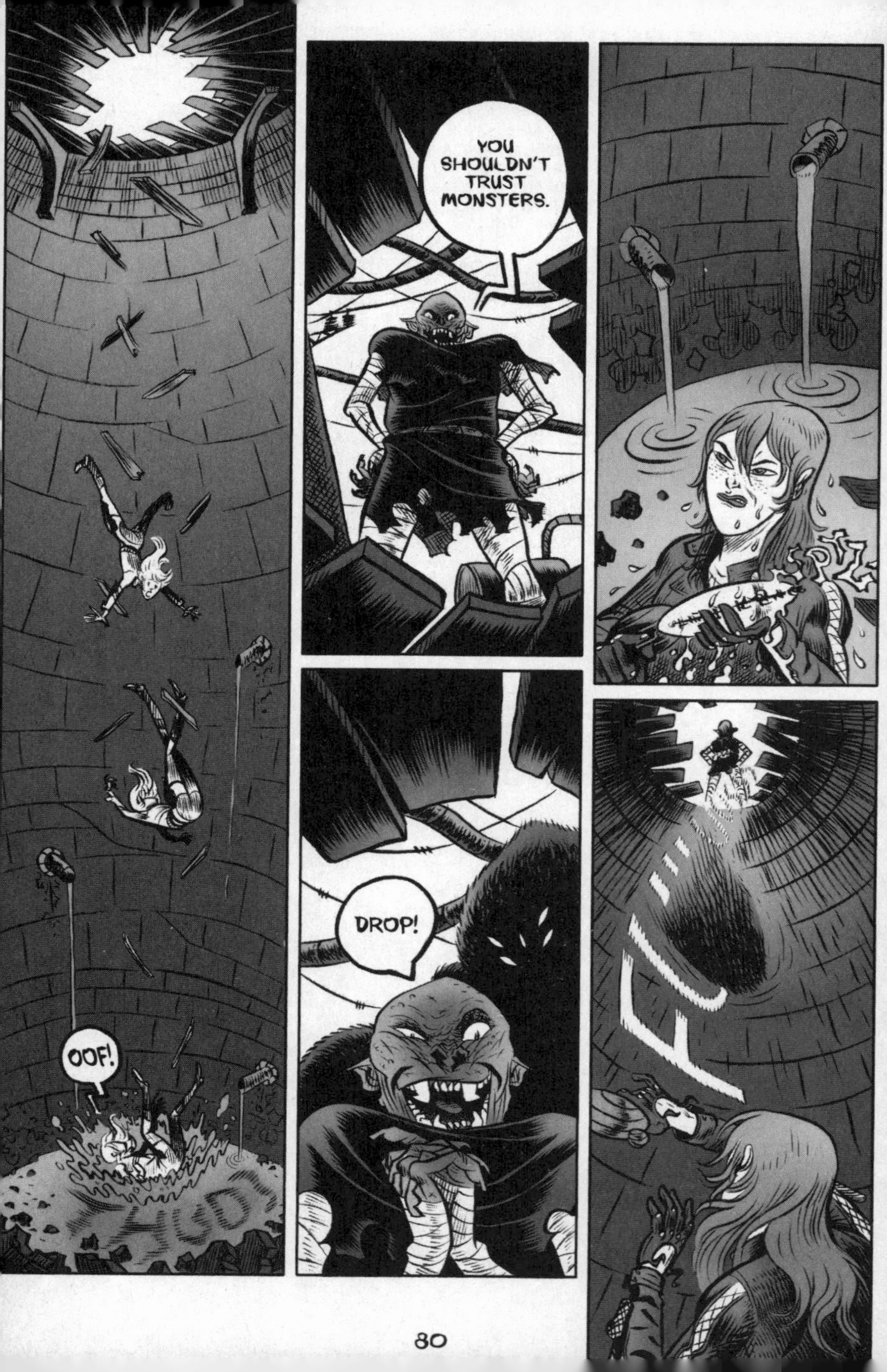
OOF!
YOU SHOULDN'T TRUST MONSTERS.
DROP!

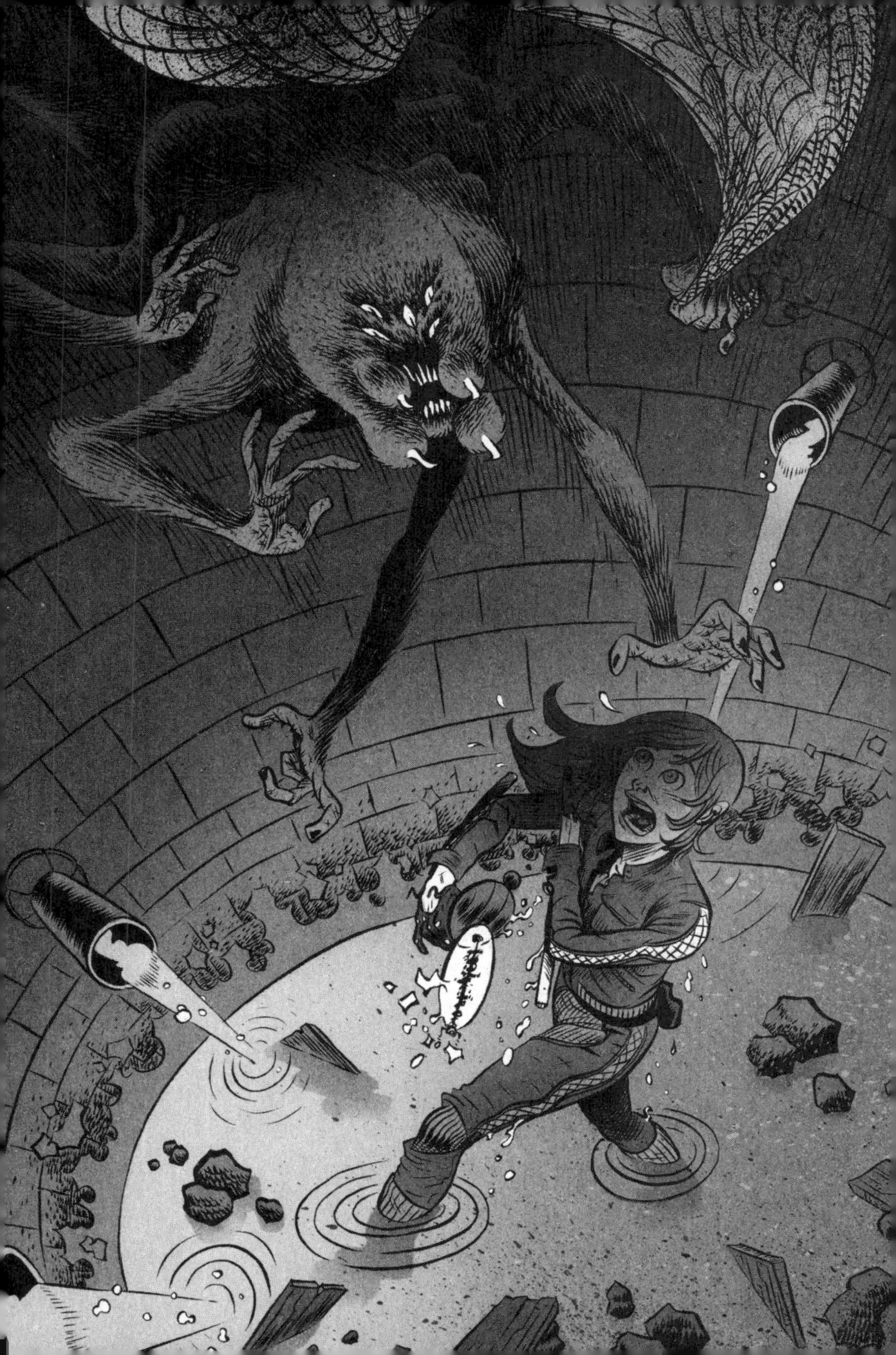

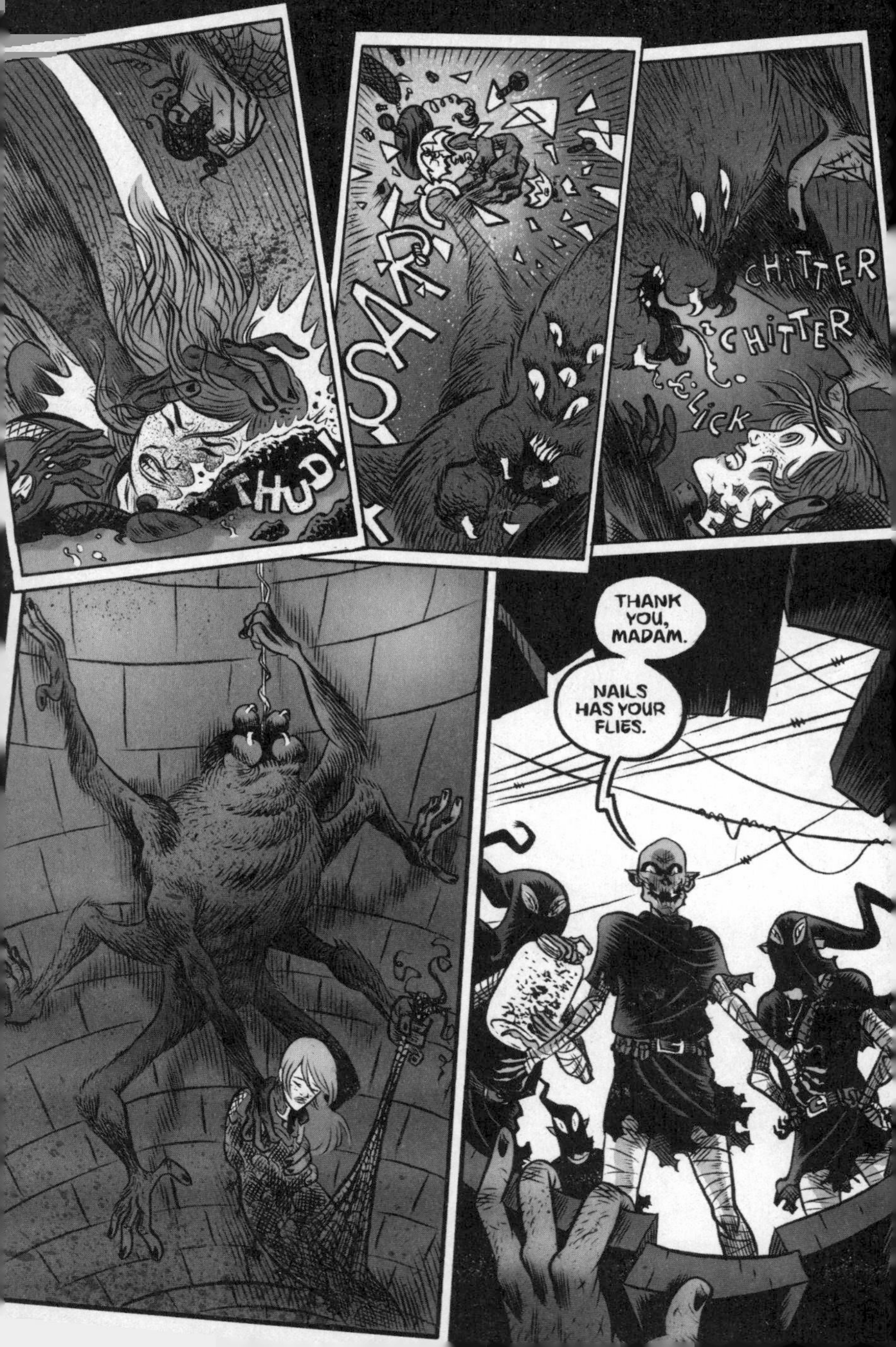
THUD!
SMASH
CHITTER
CHITTER
CLICK
THANK YOU, MADAM.
NAILS HAS YOUR FLIES.

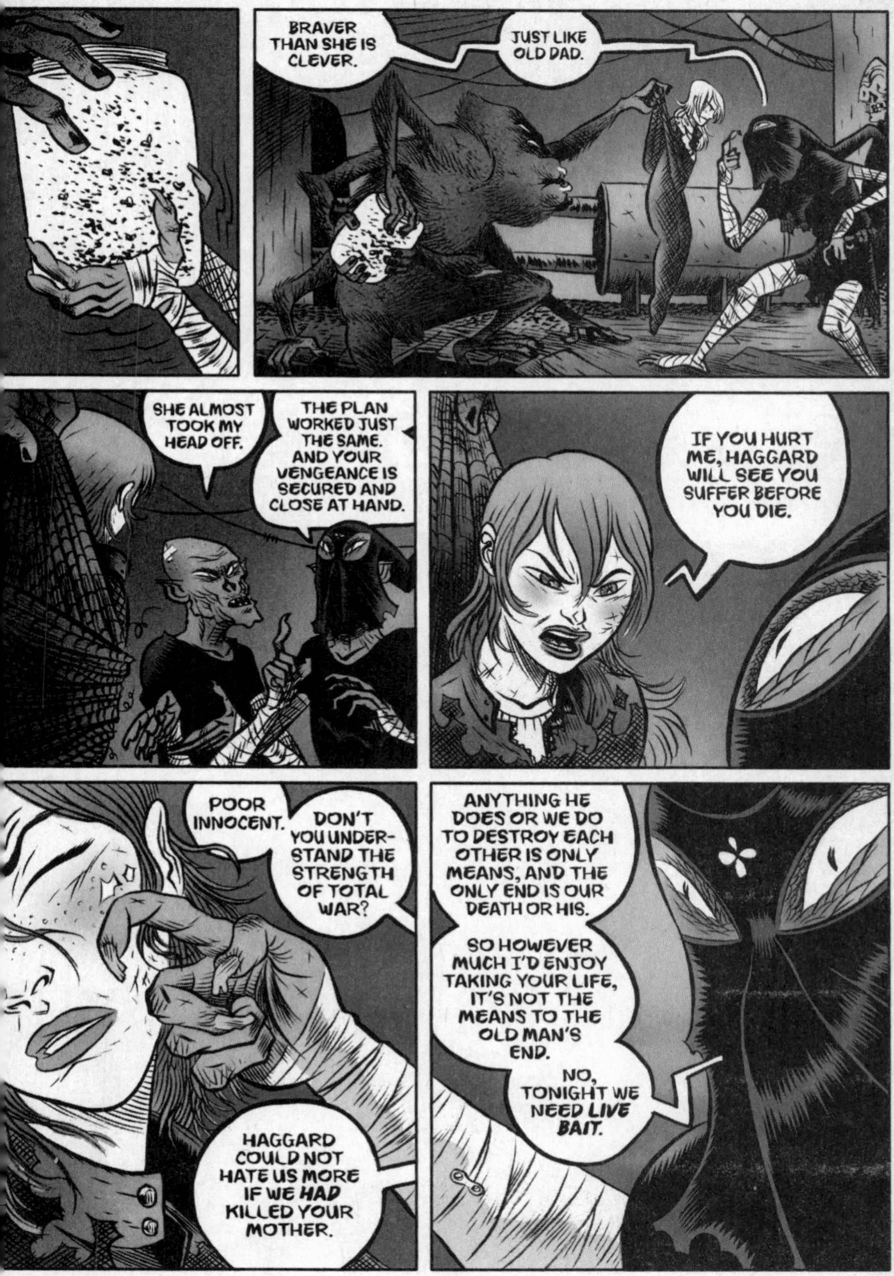
BRAVER THAN SHE IS CLEVER.
JUST LIKE OLD DAD.
SHE ALMOST TOOK MY HEAD OFF.
THE PLAN WORKED JUST THE SAME. AND YOUR VENGEANCE IS SECURED AND CLOSE AT HAND.
IF YOU HURT ME, HAGGARD WILL SEE YOU SUFFER BEFORE YOU DIE.
POOR INNOCENT.
DON'T YOU UNDER-STAND THE STRENGTH OF TOTAL WAR?
HAGGARD COULD NOT HATE US MORE IF WE *HAD* KILLED YOUR MOTHER.
ANYTHING HE DOES OR WE DO TO DESTROY EACH OTHER IS ONLY MEANS, AND THE ONLY END IS OUR DEATH OR HIS.
SO HOWEVER MUCH I'D ENJOY TAKING YOUR LIFE, IT'S NOT THE MEANS TO THE OLD MAN'S END.
NO, TONIGHT WE NEED *LIVE BAIT*.

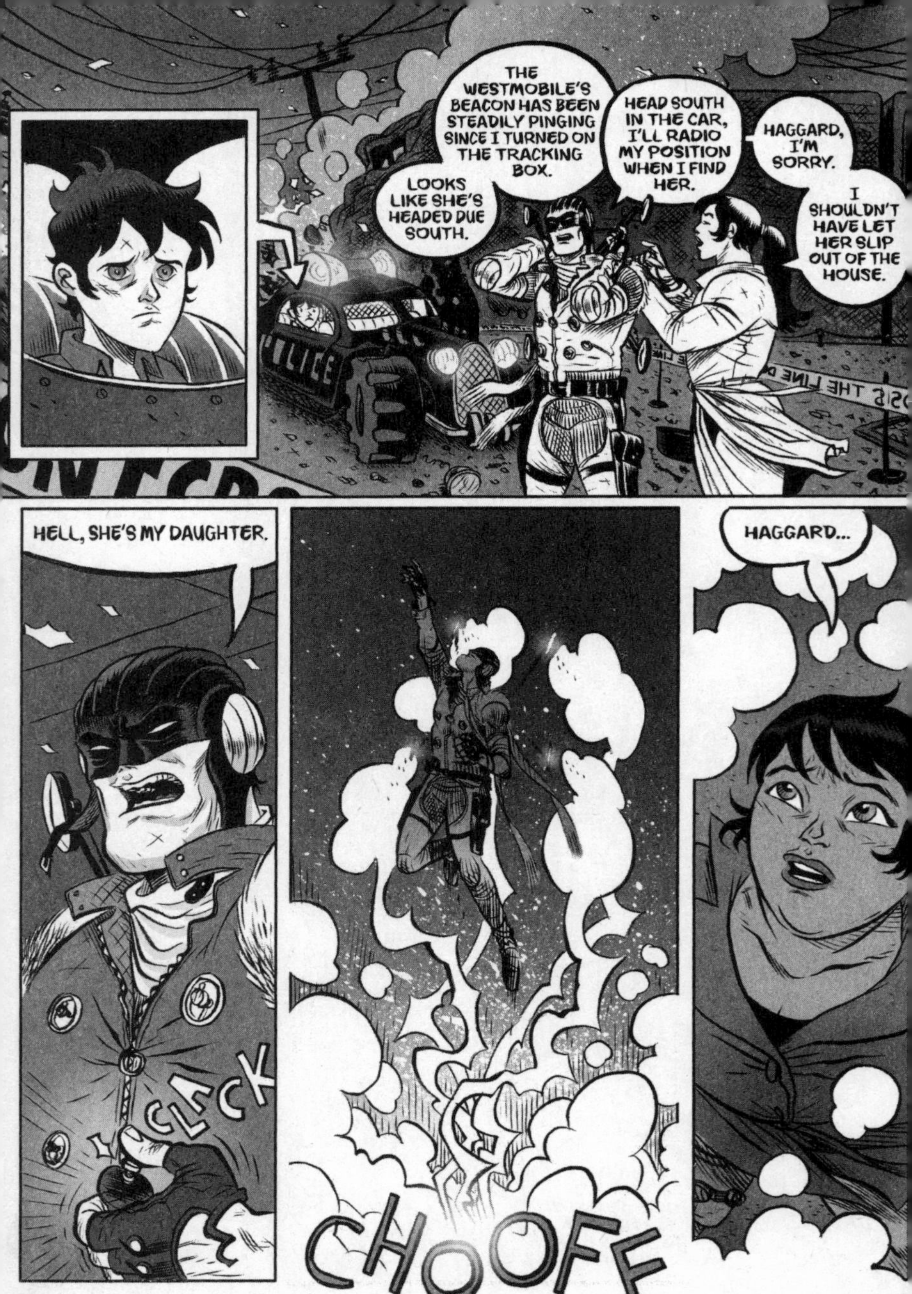
THE WESTMOBILE'S BEACON HAS BEEN STEADILY PINGING SINCE I TURNED ON THE TRACKING BOX.
LOOKS LIKE SHE'S HEADED DUE SOUTH.
HEAD SOUTH IN THE CAR, I'LL RADIO MY POSITION WHEN I FIND HER.
HAGGARD, I'M SORRY.
I SHOULDN'T HAVE LET HER SLIP OUT OF THE HOUSE.
HELL, SHE'S MY DAUGHTER.
CLACK
CHOOFF
HAGGARD...

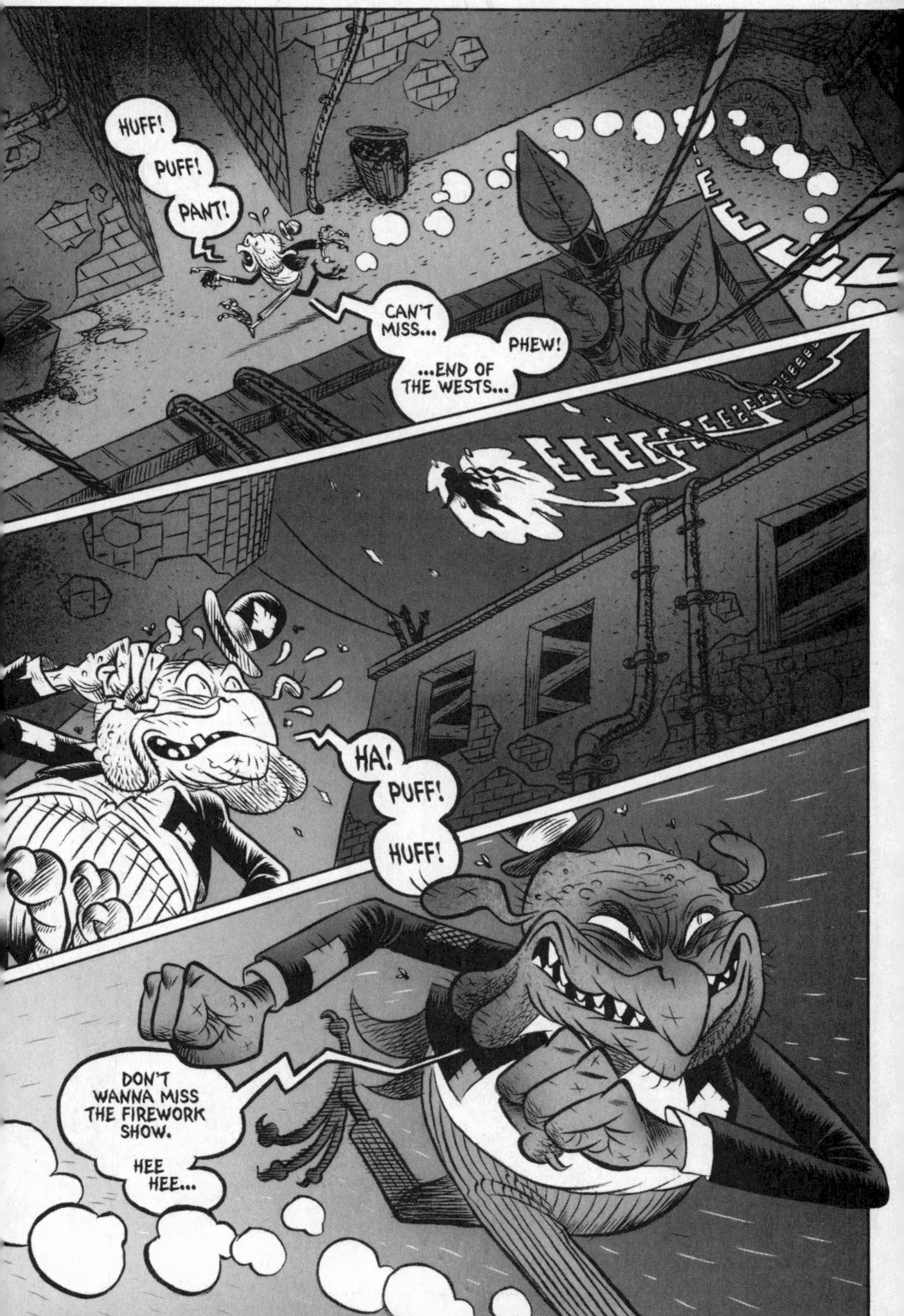
HUFF!
PUFF!
PANT!
CAN'T MISS...
PHEW!
...END OF THE WESTS...
HA!
PUFF!
HUFF!
DON'T WANNA MISS THE FIREWORK SHOW.
HEE HEE...

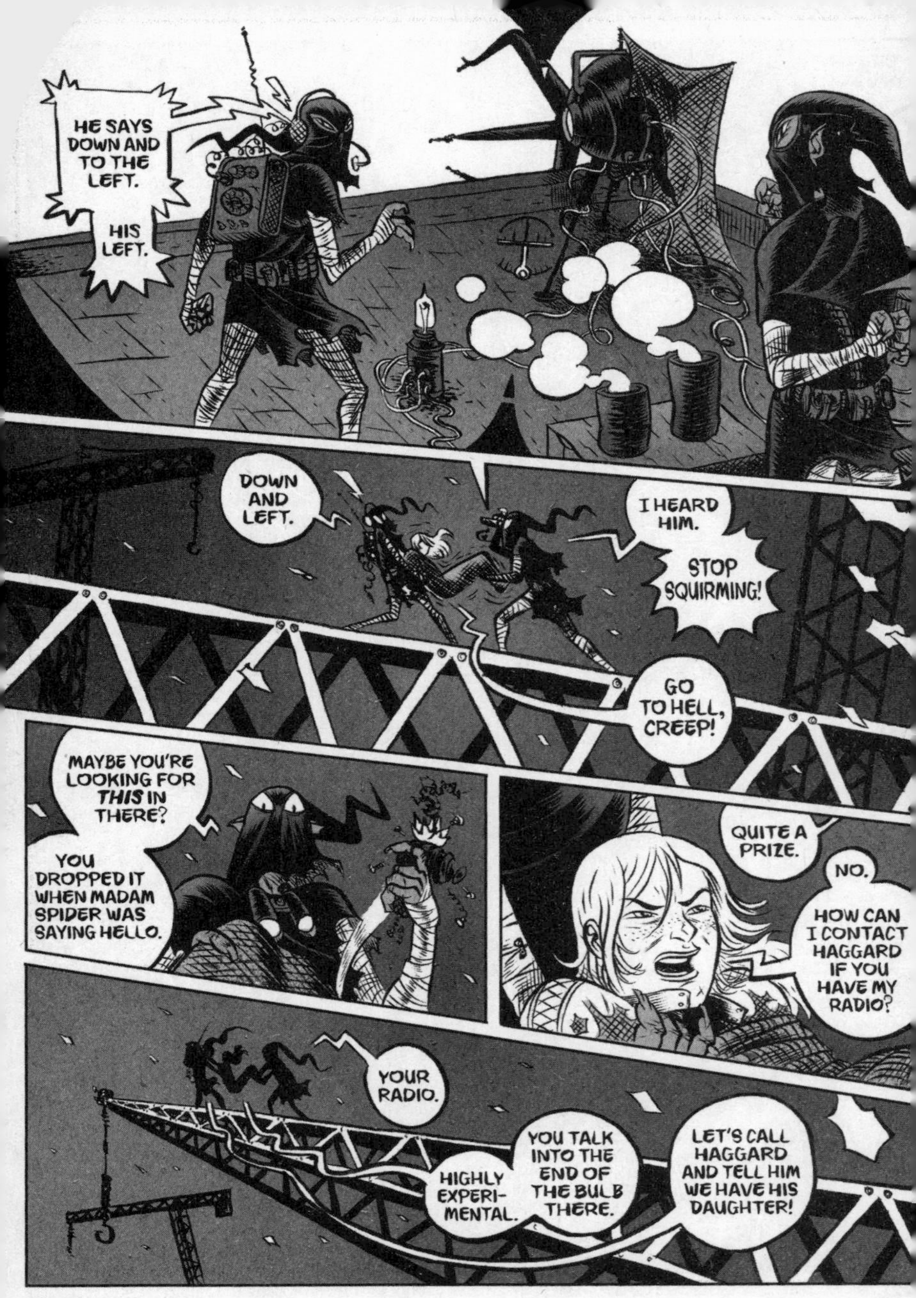
HE SAYS DOWN AND TO THE LEFT.
HIS LEFT.
DOWN AND LEFT.
I HEARD HIM.
STOP SQUIRMING!
GO TO HELL, CREEP!
MAYBE YOU'RE LOOKING FOR *THIS* IN THERE?
YOU DROPPED IT WHEN MADAM SPIDER WAS SAYING HELLO.
QUITE A PRIZE.
NO.
HOW CAN I CONTACT HAGGARD IF YOU HAVE MY RADIO?
YOUR RADIO.
HIGHLY EXPERI-MENTAL.
YOU TALK INTO THE END OF THE BULB THERE.
LET'S CALL HAGGARD AND TELL HIM WE HAVE HIS DAUGHTER!

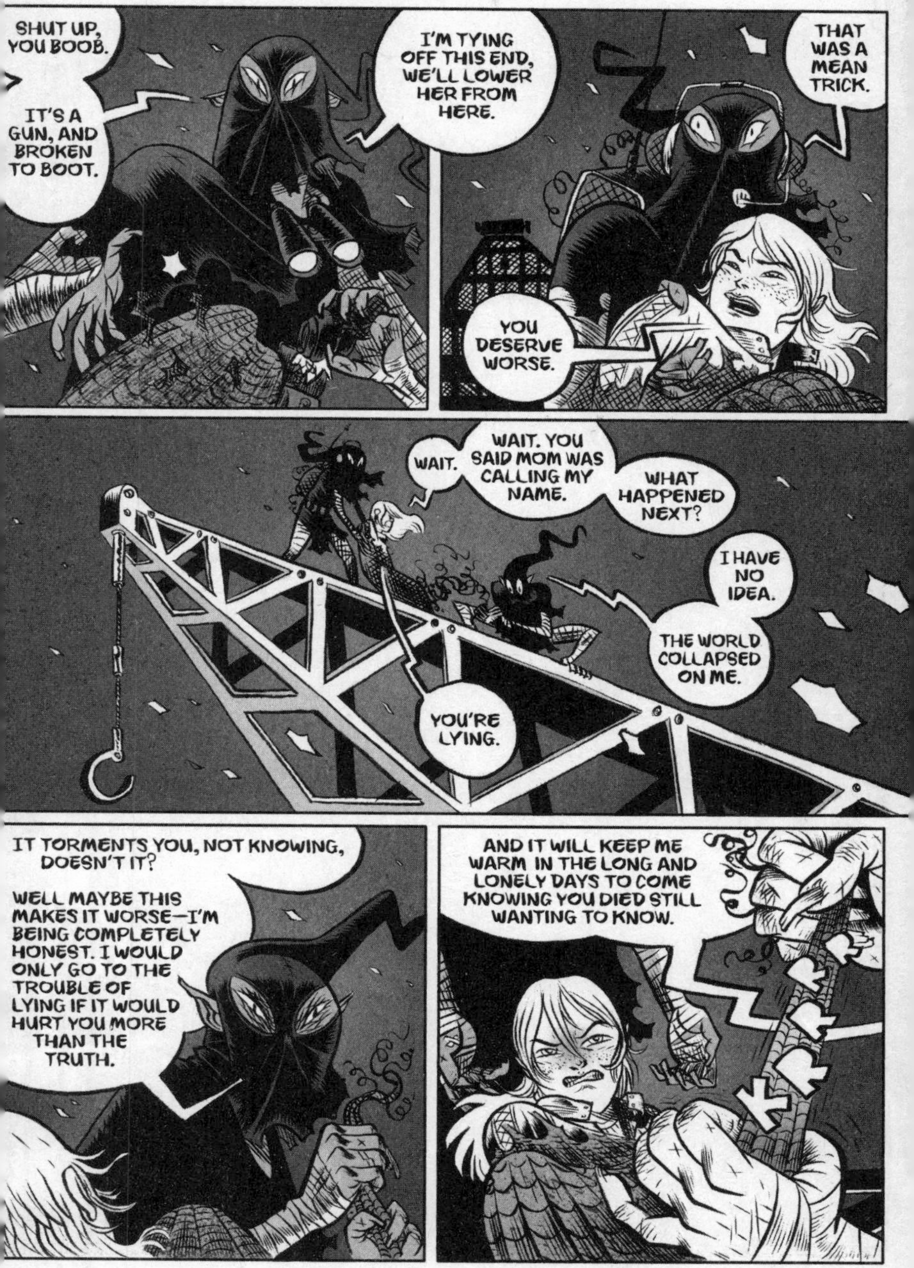
SHUT UP, YOU BOOB.
IT'S A GUN, AND BROKEN TO BOOT.
I'M TYING OFF THIS END, WE'LL LOWER HER FROM HERE.
THAT WAS A MEAN TRICK.
YOU DESERVE WORSE.
WAIT.
WAIT. YOU SAID MOM WAS CALLING MY NAME.
WHAT HAPPENED NEXT?
I HAVE NO IDEA.
THE WORLD COLLAPSED ON ME.
YOU'RE LYING.
IT TORMENTS YOU, NOT KNOWING, DOESN'T IT?
WELL MAYBE THIS MAKES IT WORSE—I'M BEING COMPLETELY HONEST. I WOULD ONLY GO TO THE TROUBLE OF LYING IF IT WOULD HURT YOU MORE THAN THE TRUTH.
AND IT WILL KEEP ME WARM IN THE LONG AND LONELY DAYS TO COME KNOWING YOU DIED STILL WANTING TO KNOW.
KRRRK

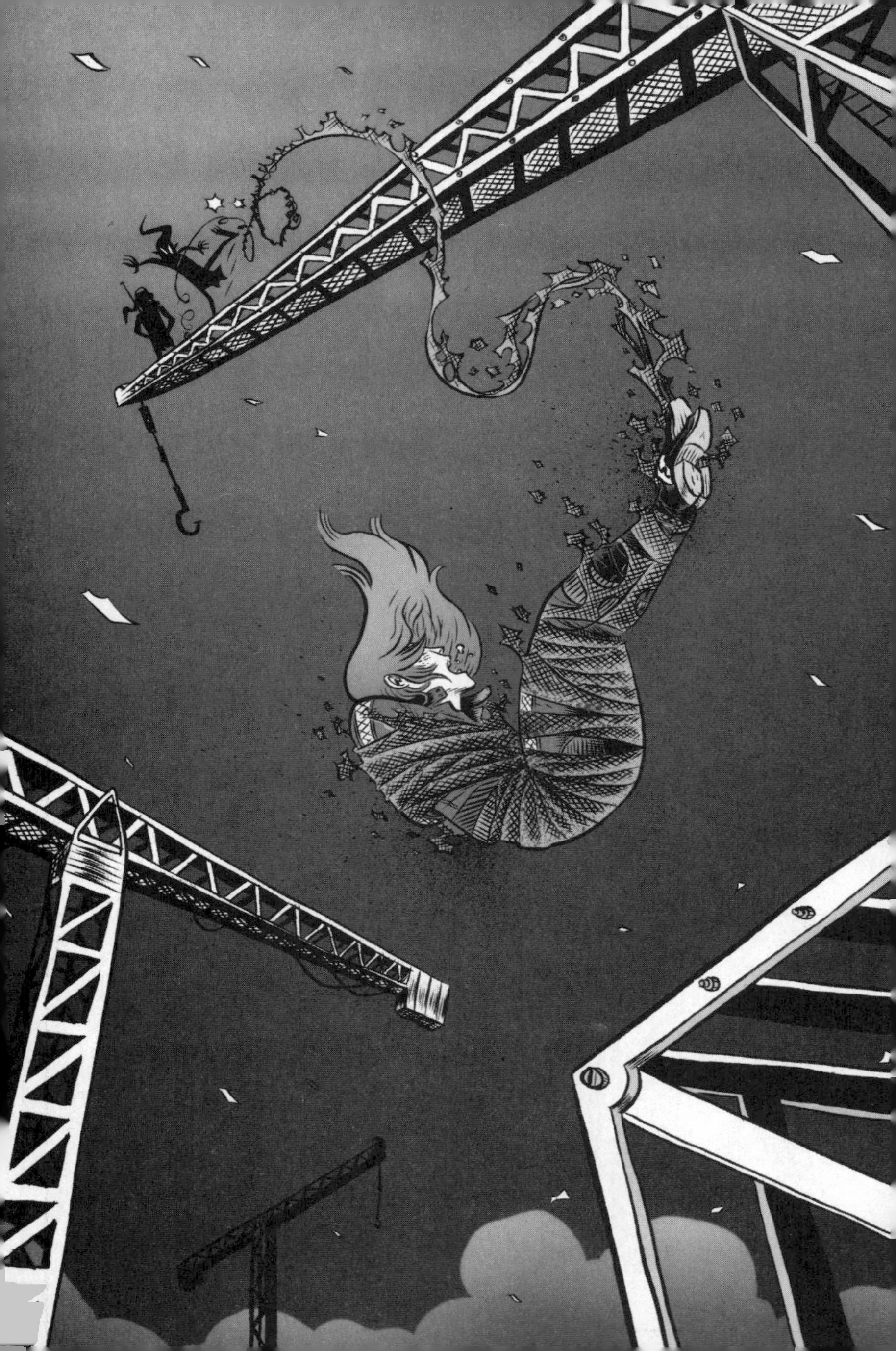

GASP!!

TOING

AN-NNG!!!

ASK HIM.

HOW WE LOOKING, BOSS?

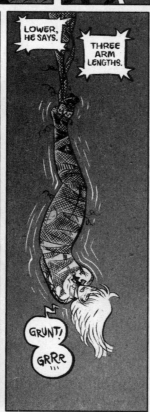

LOWER, HE SAYS.

THREE ARM LENGTHS.

GRUNT! GRRR

RIGHT THERE!

STOP HER THERE!

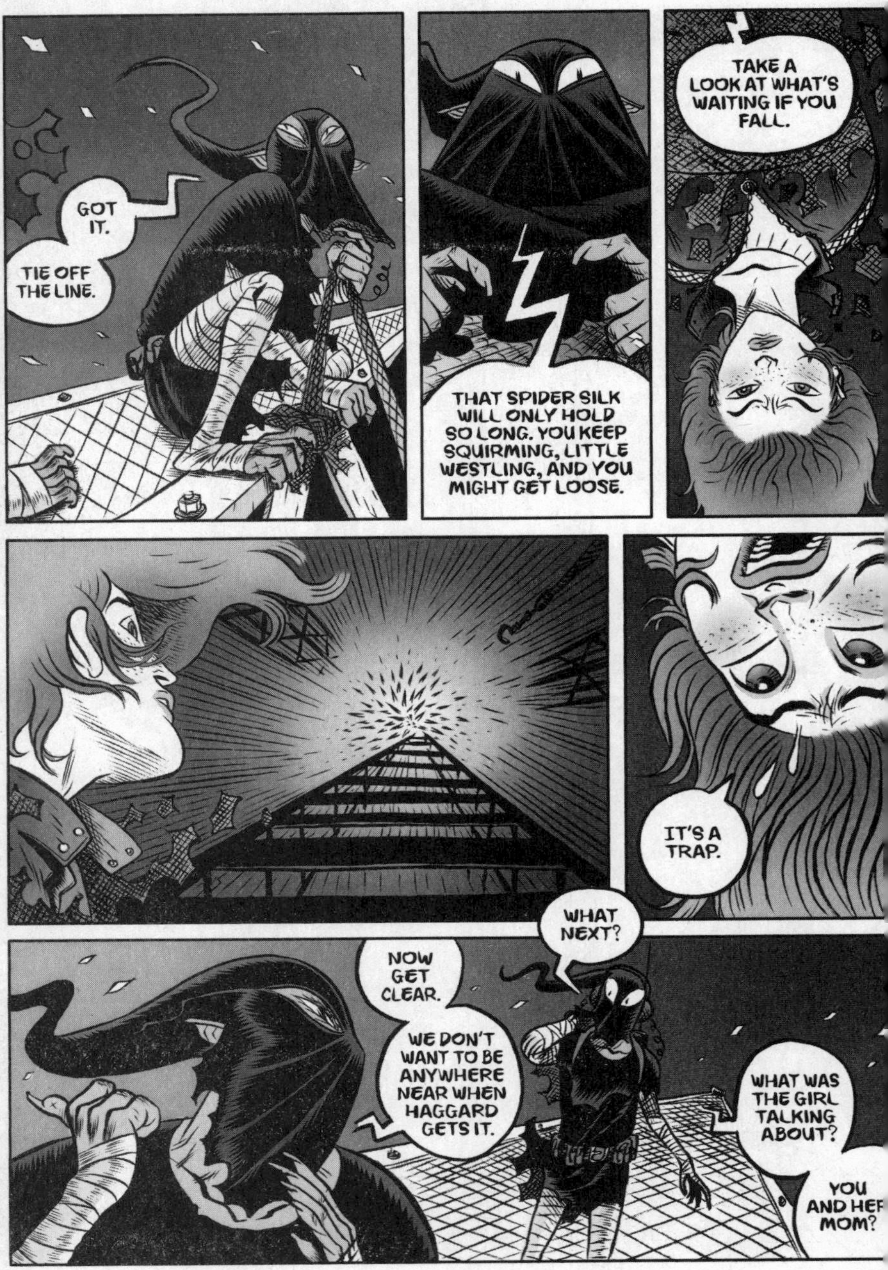
GOT IT.
TIE OFF THE LINE.
THAT SPIDER SILK WILL ONLY HOLD SO LONG. YOU KEEP SQUIRMING, LITTLE WESTLING, AND YOU MIGHT GET LOOSE.
TAKE A LOOK AT WHAT'S WAITING IF YOU FALL.
IT'S A TRAP.
WHAT NEXT?
NOW GET CLEAR.
WE DON'T WANT TO BE ANYWHERE NEAR WHEN HAGGARD GETS IT.
WHAT WAS THE GIRL TALKING ABOUT?
YOU AND HER MOM?

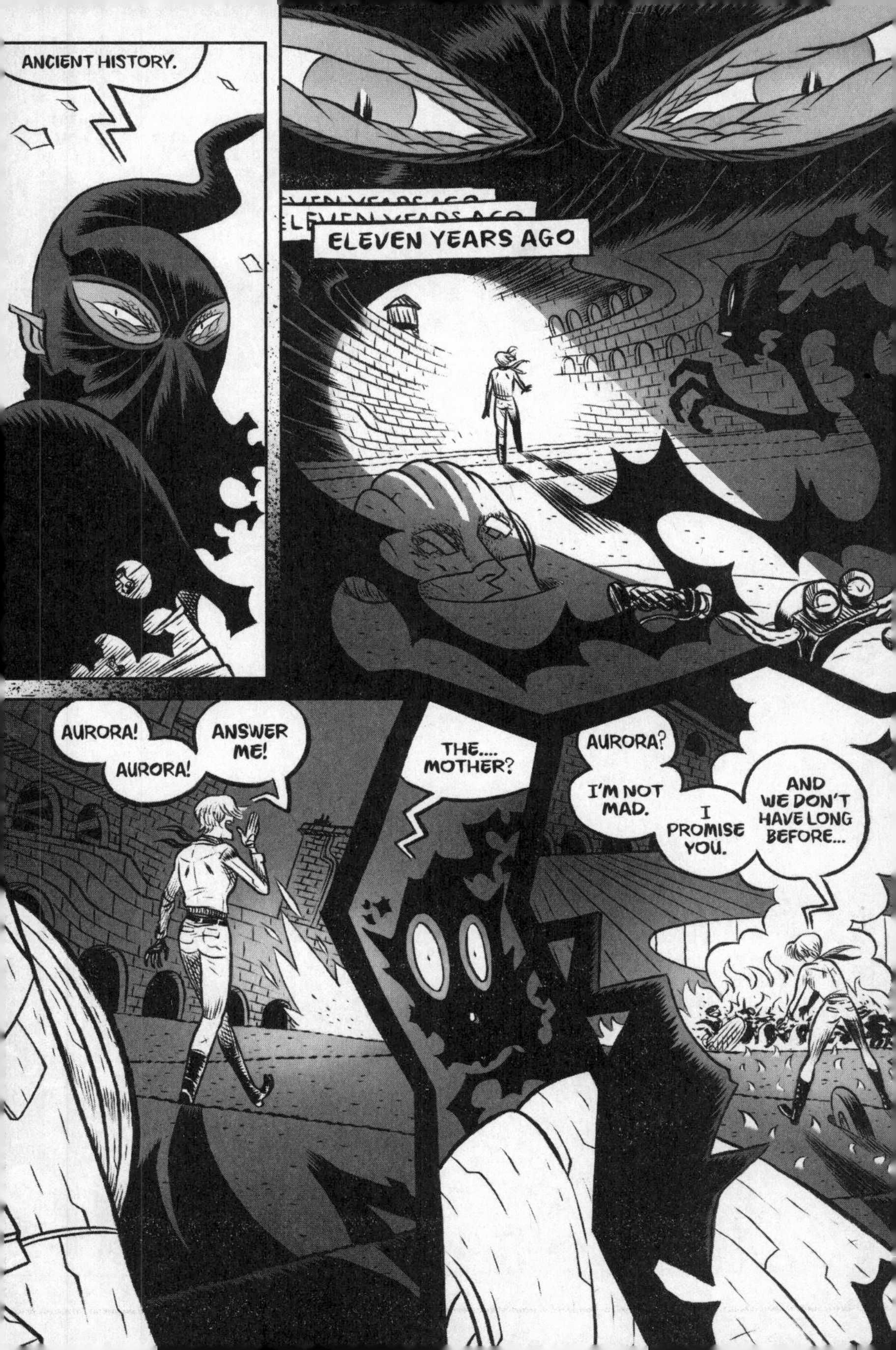
ANCIENT HISTORY.
ELEVEN YEARS AGO
AURORA!
AURORA!
ANSWER ME!
THE.... MOTHER?
AURORA?
I'M NOT MAD.
I PROMISE YOU.
AND WE DON'T HAVE LONG BEFORE...

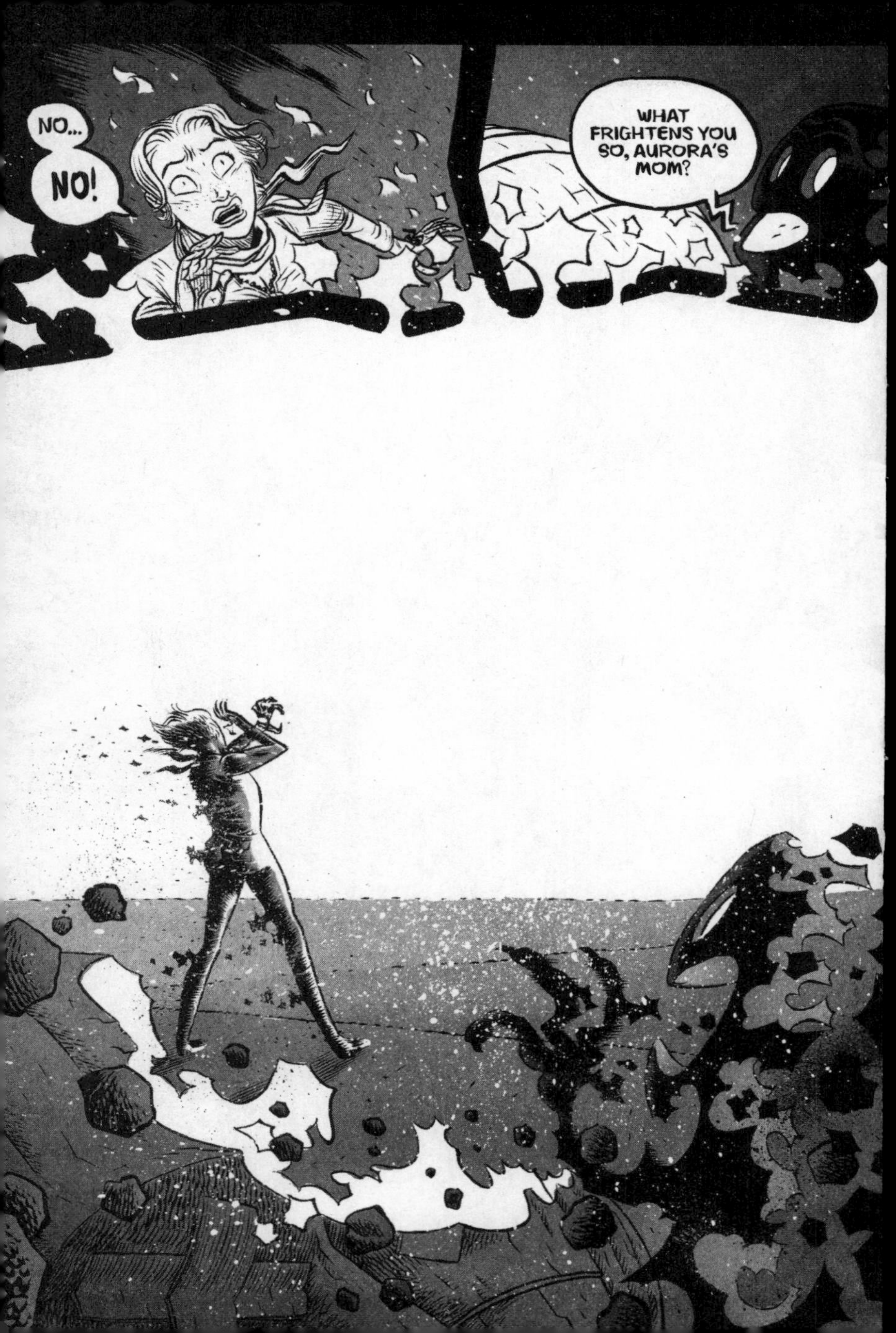
NO...
NO!
WHAT FRIGHTENS YOU SO, AURORA'S MOM?

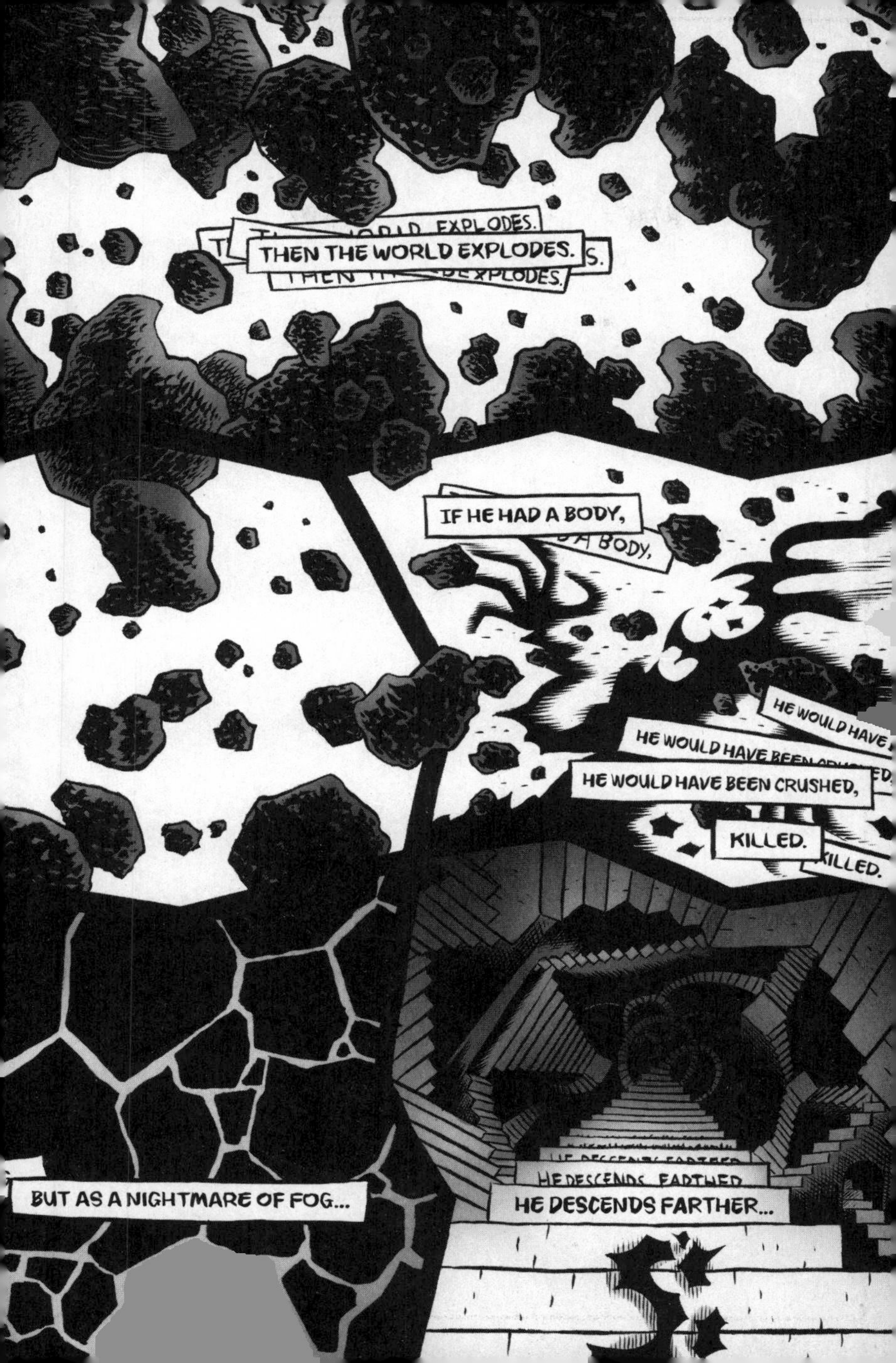
THEN THE WORLD EXPLODES.
IF HE HAD A BODY,
HE WOULD HAVE BEEN CRUSHED,
KILLED.
BUT AS A NIGHTMARE OF FOG...
HE DESCENDS FARTHER...

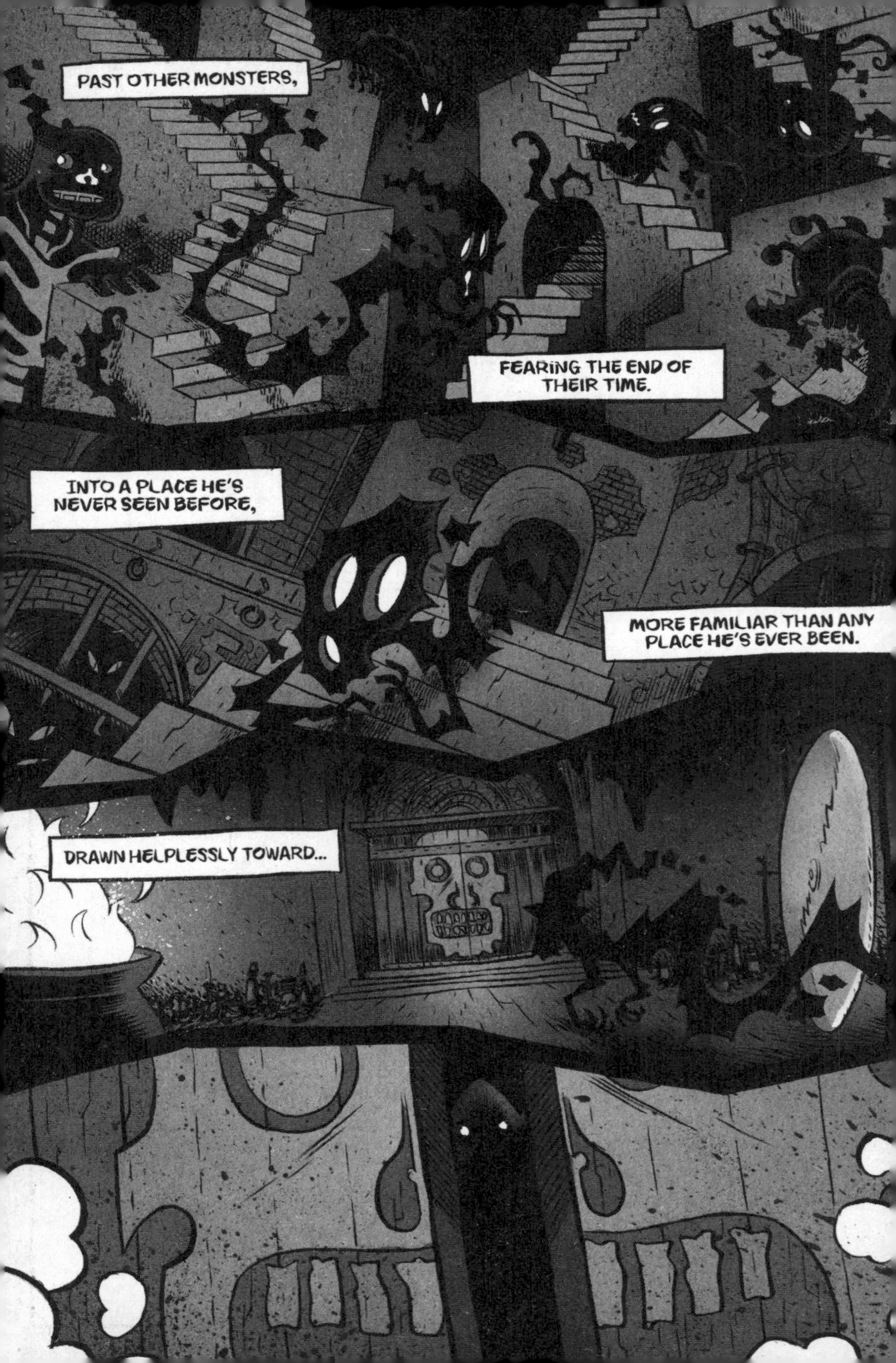
PAST OTHER MONSTERS,
FEARING THE END OF THEIR TIME.
INTO A PLACE HE'S NEVER SEEN BEFORE,
MORE FAMILIAR THAN ANY PLACE HE'S EVER BEEN.
DRAWN HELPLESSLY TOWARD...

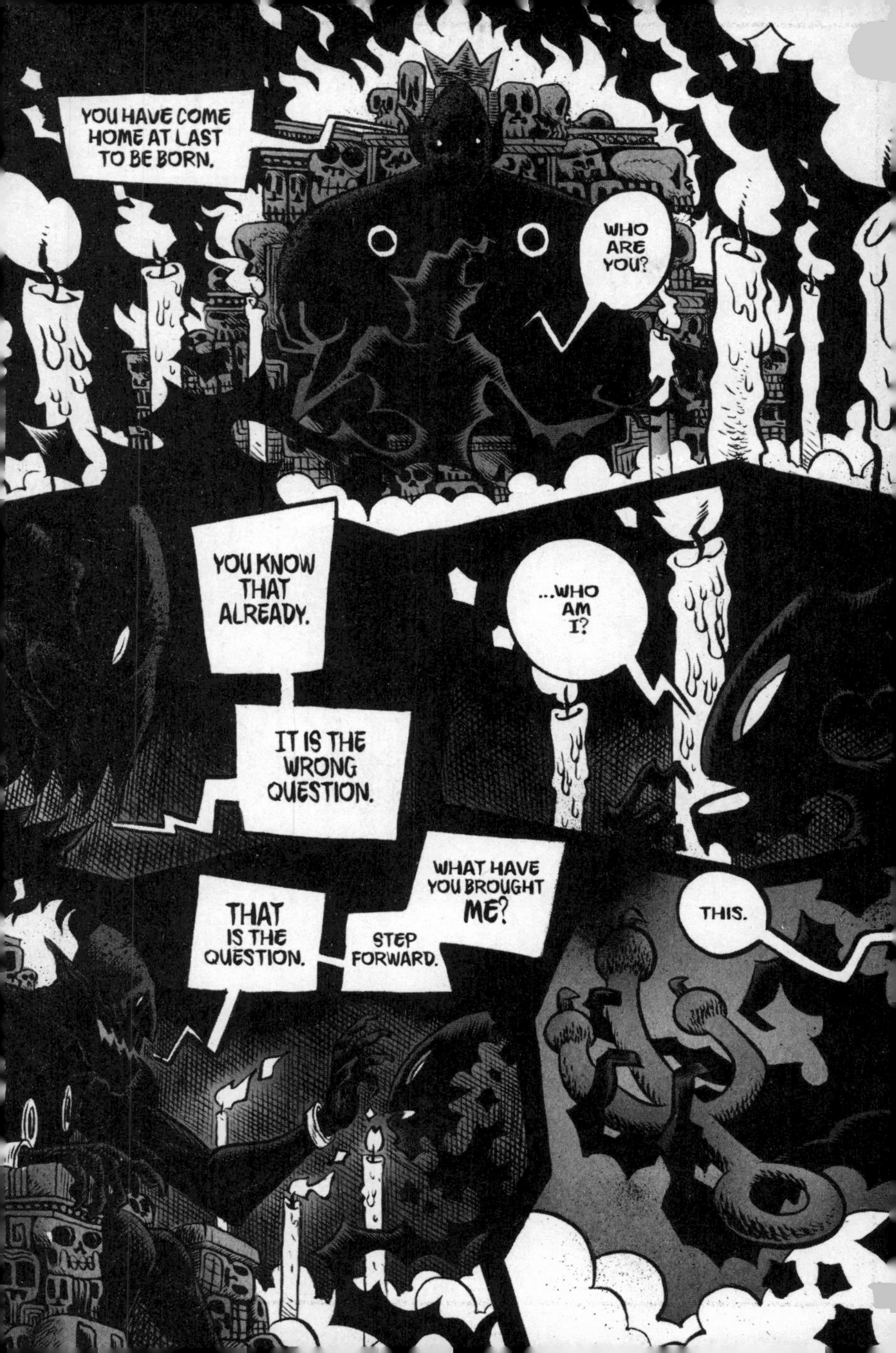
YOU HAVE COME HOME AT LAST TO BE BORN.
WHO ARE YOU?
YOU KNOW THAT ALREADY.
IT IS THE WRONG QUESTION.
...WHO AM I?
THAT IS THE QUESTION.
STEP FORWARD.
WHAT HAVE YOU BROUGHT ME?
THIS.

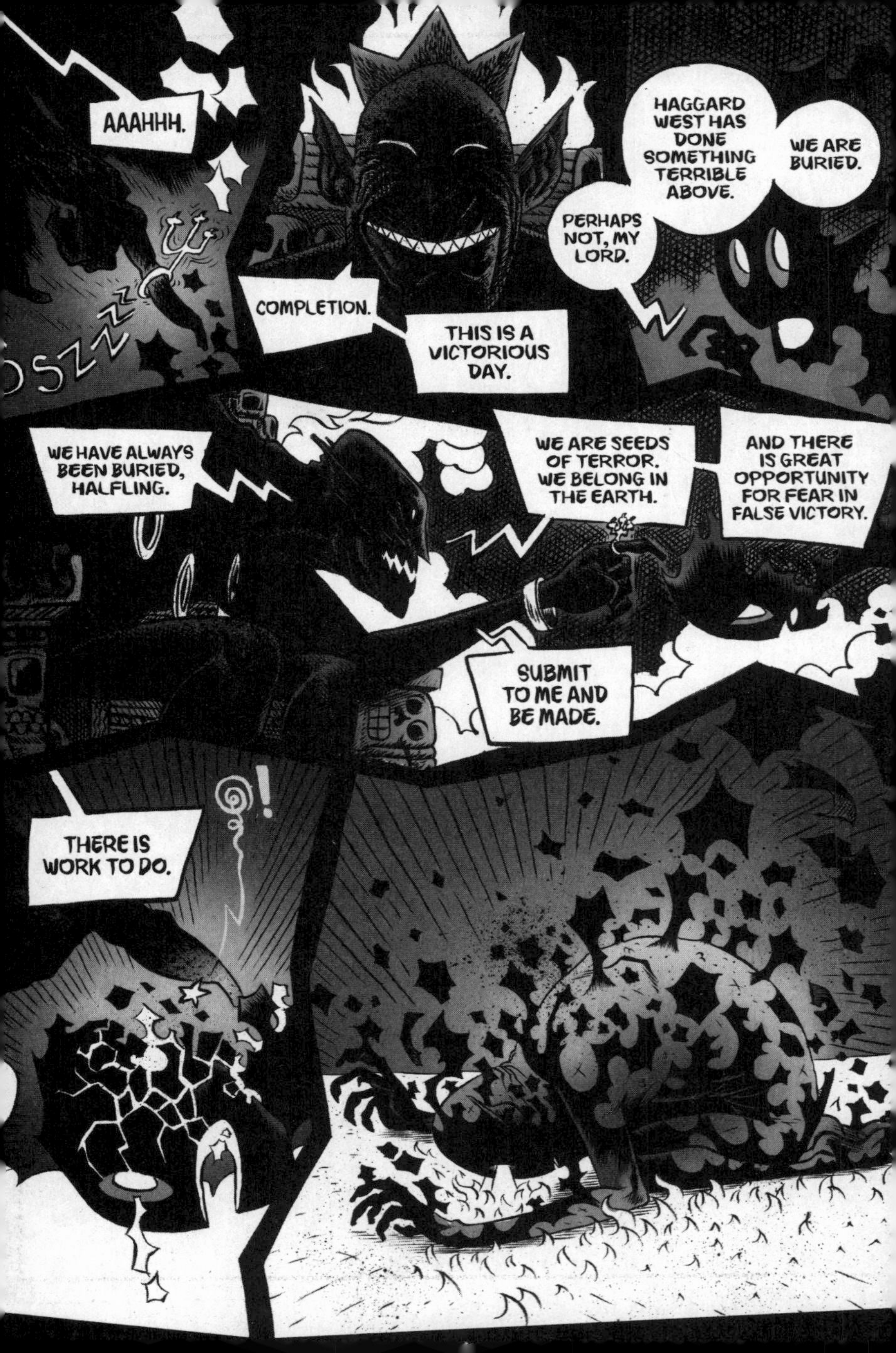
AAAHHH.
DSZZZZZ
COMPLETION.
THIS IS A VICTORIOUS DAY.
HAGGARD WEST HAS DONE SOMETHING TERRIBLE ABOVE.
WE ARE BURIED.
PERHAPS NOT, MY LORD.
WE HAVE ALWAYS BEEN BURIED, HALFLING.
WE ARE SEEDS OF TERROR. WE BELONG IN THE EARTH.
AND THERE IS GREAT OPPORTUNITY FOR FEAR IN FALSE VICTORY.
SUBMIT TO ME AND BE MADE.
!
THERE IS WORK TO DO.

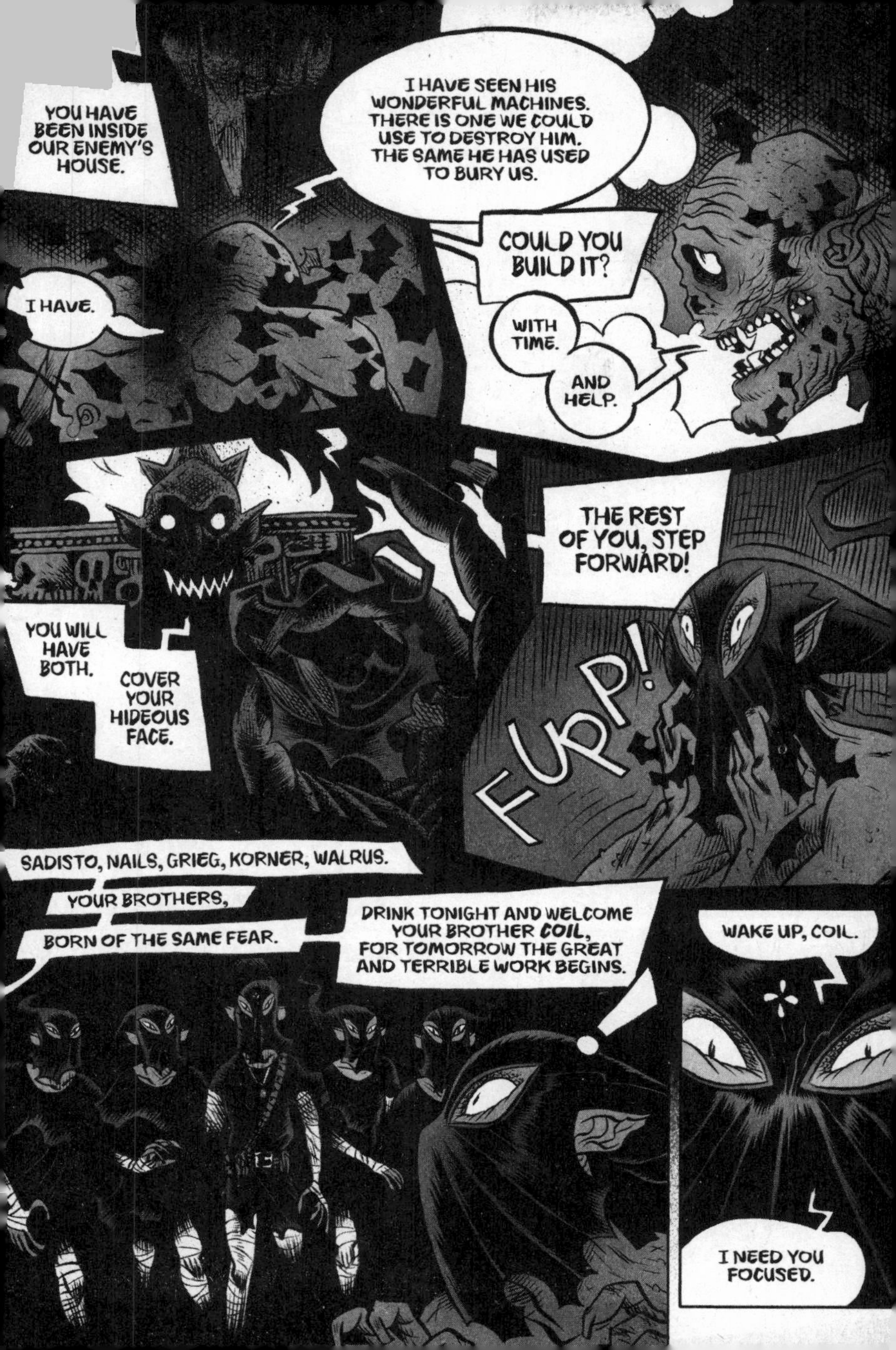
YOU HAVE BEEN INSIDE OUR ENEMY'S HOUSE.
I HAVE.
I HAVE SEEN HIS WONDERFUL MACHINES. THERE IS ONE WE COULD USE TO DESTROY HIM. THE SAME HE HAS USED TO BURY US.
COULD YOU BUILD IT?
WITH TIME.
AND HELP.
YOU WILL HAVE BOTH.
COVER YOUR HIDEOUS FACE.
THE REST OF YOU, STEP FORWARD!
FUP!
SADISTO, NAILS, GRIEG, KORNER, WALRUS.
YOUR BROTHERS,
BORN OF THE SAME FEAR.
DRINK TONIGHT AND WELCOME YOUR BROTHER COIL, FOR TOMORROW THE GREAT AND TERRIBLE WORK BEGINS.
WAKE UP, COIL.
I NEED YOU FOCUSED.

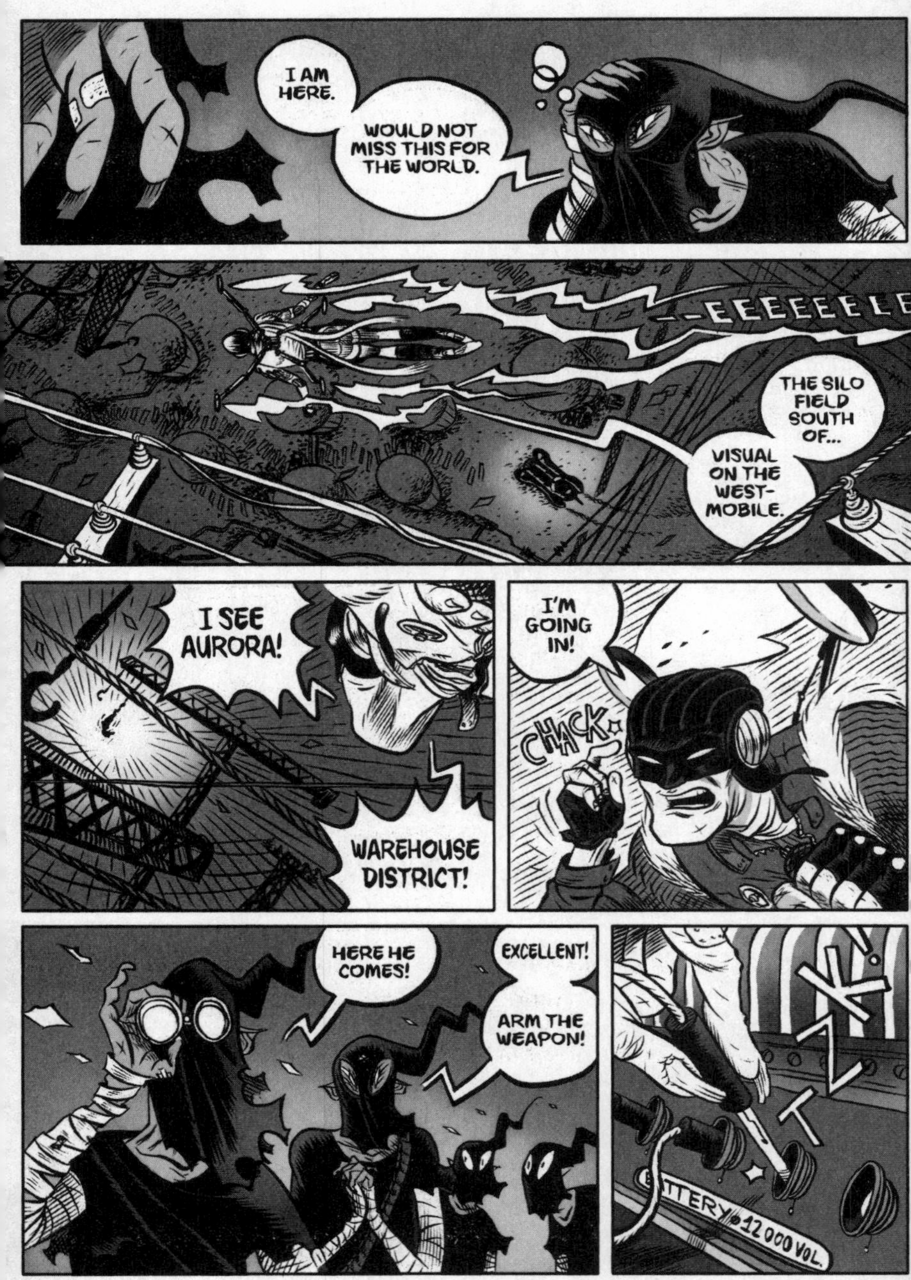
I AM HERE.
WOULD NOT MISS THIS FOR THE WORLD.
--EEEEEEEEE
THE SILO FIELD SOUTH OF...
VISUAL ON THE WEST-MOBILE.
I SEE AURORA!
WAREHOUSE DISTRICT!
I'M GOING IN!
CHACK
HERE HE COMES!
EXCELLENT!
ARM THE WEAPON!
KZZT
TTERY 12 000 VOL.

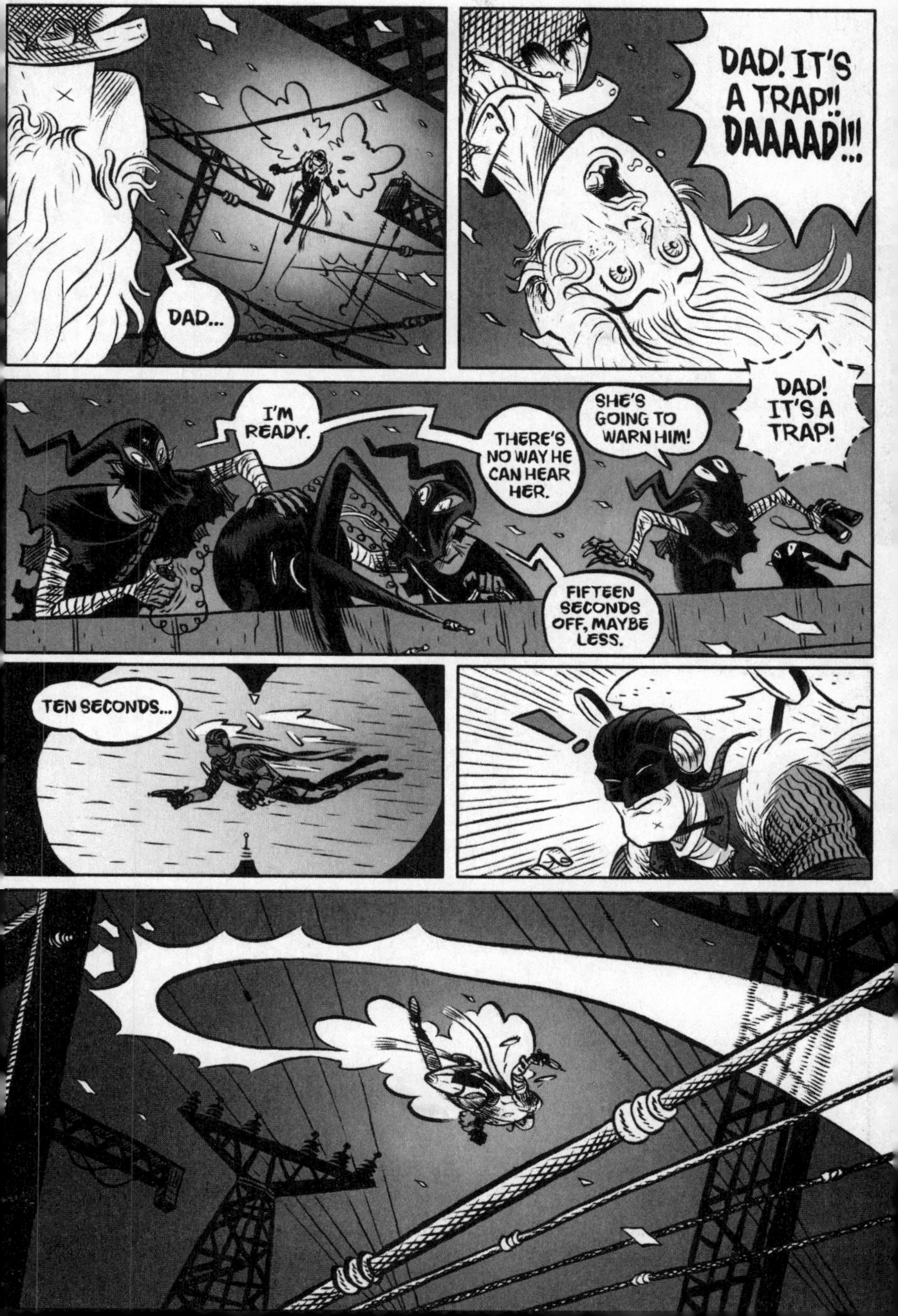
DAD...
DAD! IT'S A TRAP!! DAAAAD!!!...
DAD! IT'S A TRAP!
I'M READY.
SHE'S GOING TO WARN HIM!
THERE'S NO WAY HE CAN HEAR HER.
FIFTEEN SECONDS OFF, MAYBE LESS.
TEN SECONDS...
!

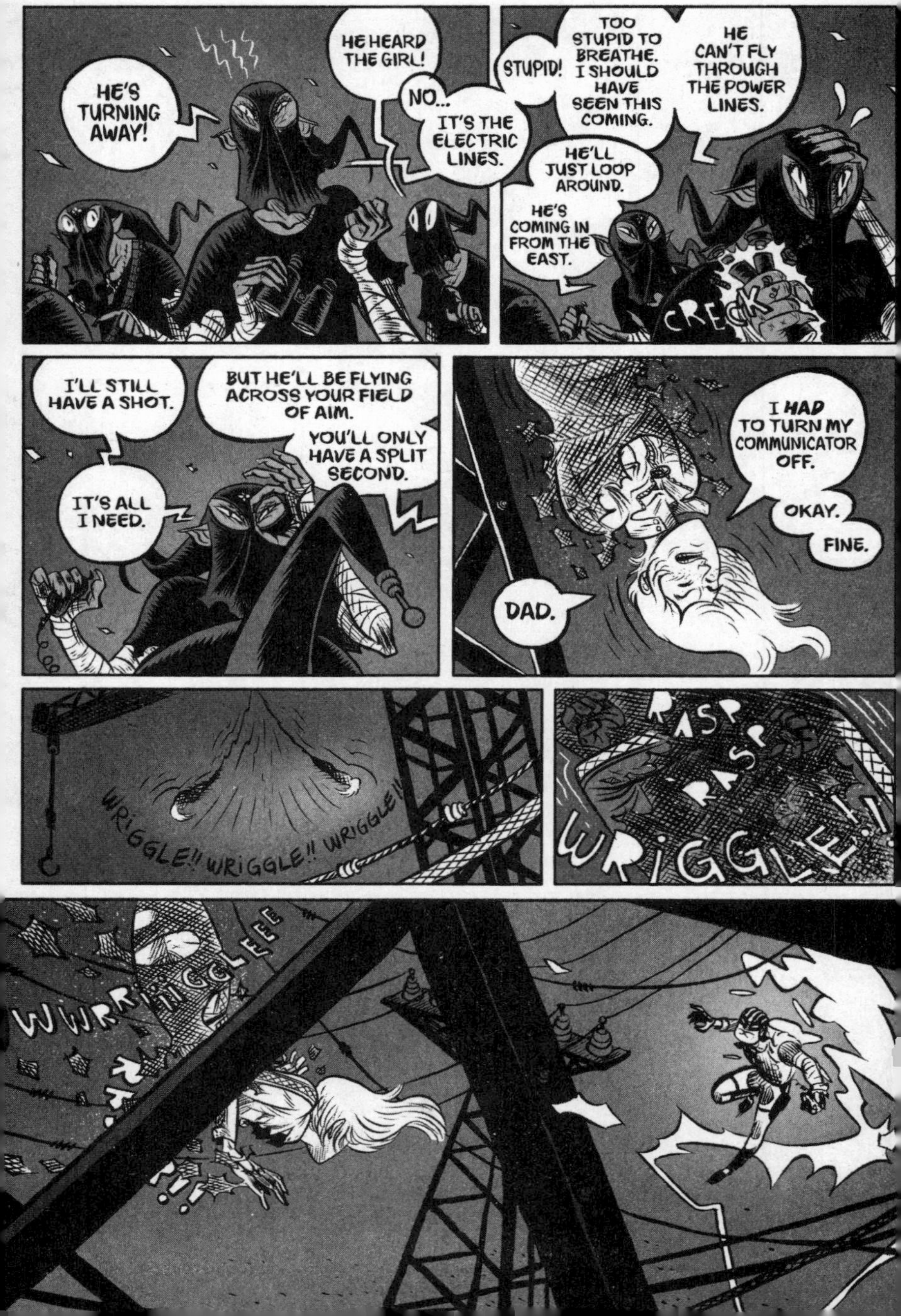
HE'S TURNING AWAY!
HE HEARD THE GIRL!
NO... IT'S THE ELECTRIC LINES.
STUPID!
TOO STUPID TO BREATHE. I SHOULD HAVE SEEN THIS COMING.
HE CAN'T FLY THROUGH THE POWER LINES.
HE'LL JUST LOOP AROUND.
HE'S COMING IN FROM THE EAST.
CRECK
I'LL STILL HAVE A SHOT.
BUT HE'LL BE FLYING ACROSS YOUR FIELD OF AIM.
YOU'LL ONLY HAVE A SPLIT SECOND.
IT'S ALL I NEED.
I HAD TO TURN MY COMMUNICATOR OFF.
OKAY.
FINE.
DAD.
WRIGGLE!! WRIGGLE!! WRIGGLE!!
RASP RASP RASP
WRIGGLE!!
WWRRIIGGLEEE

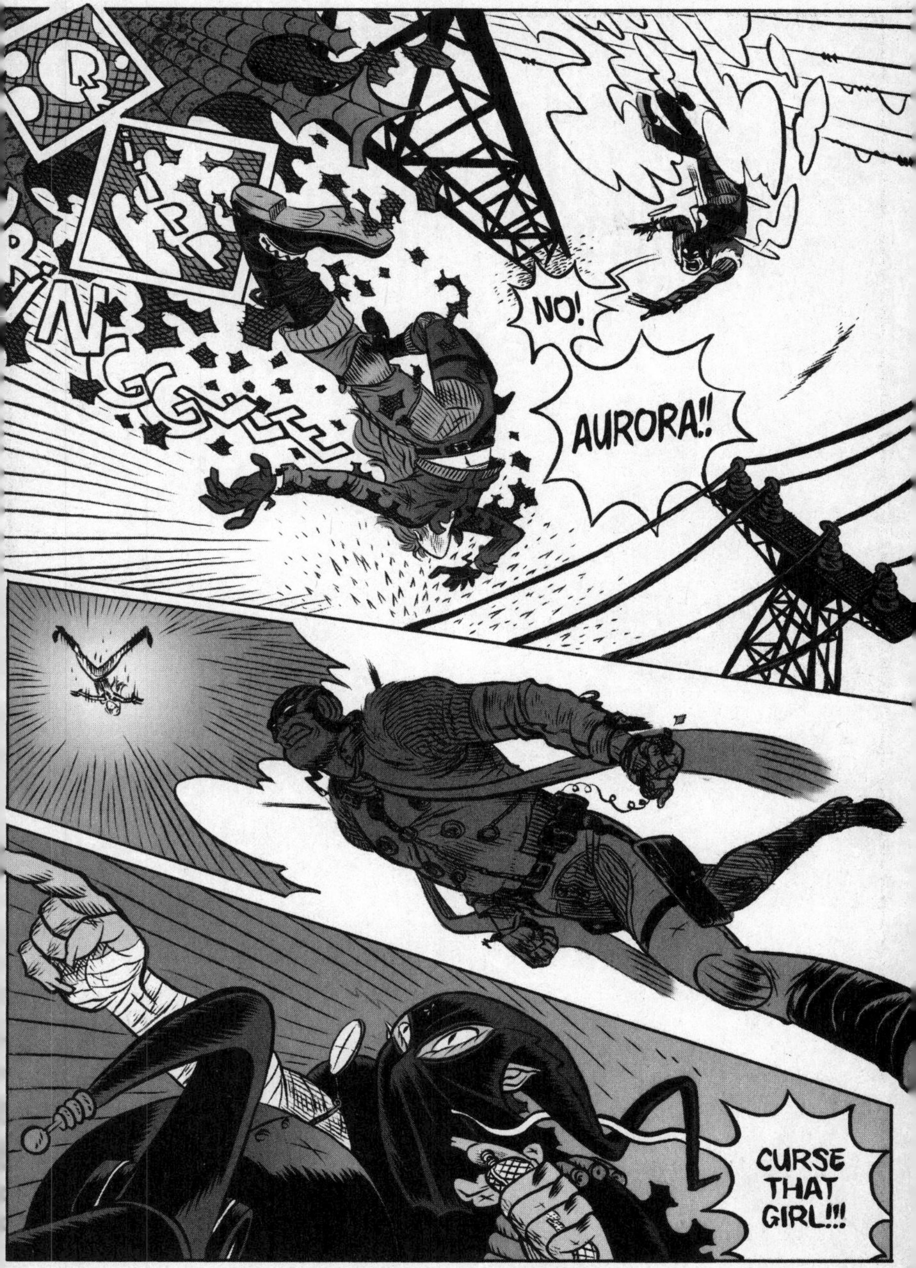
RIIPP
NO!
AURORA!!
CURSE THAT GIRL!!!

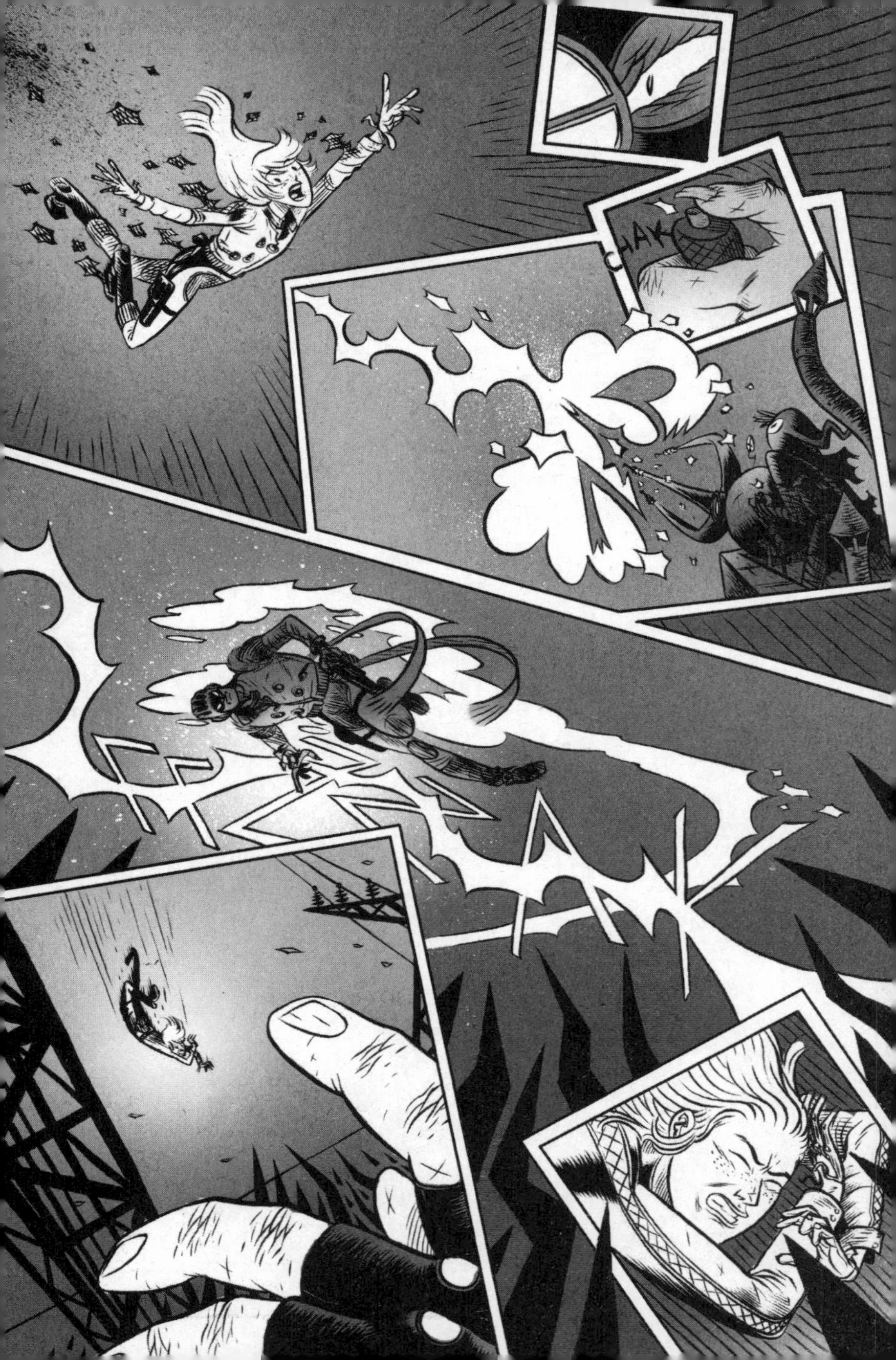
CHAK

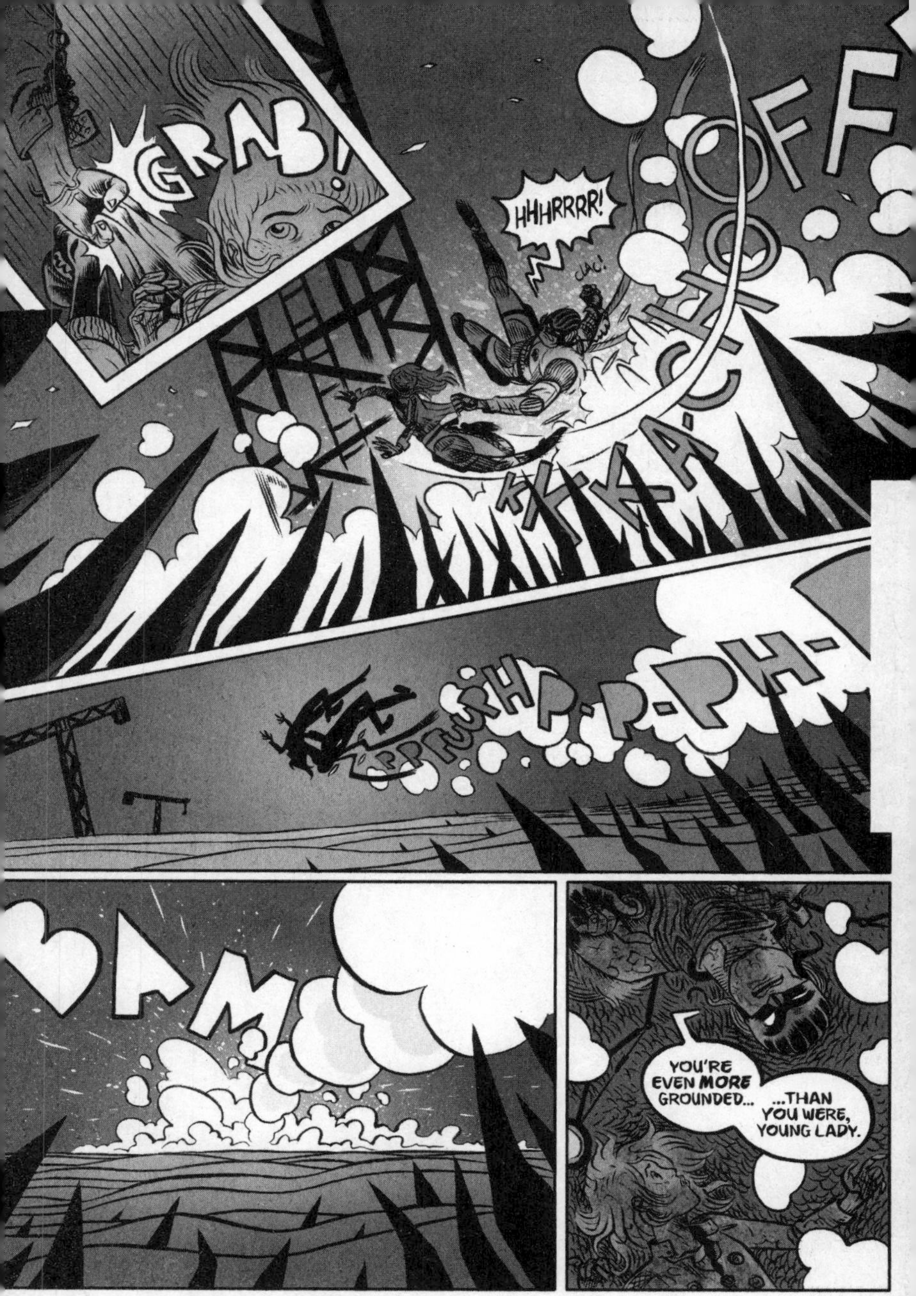
GRAB!
HHHRRRR!
KKKA-CH-OOOFF
PPFFURHP-P-PH-
AM
YOU'RE EVEN **MORE** GROUNDED...
...THAN YOU WERE, YOUNG LADY.

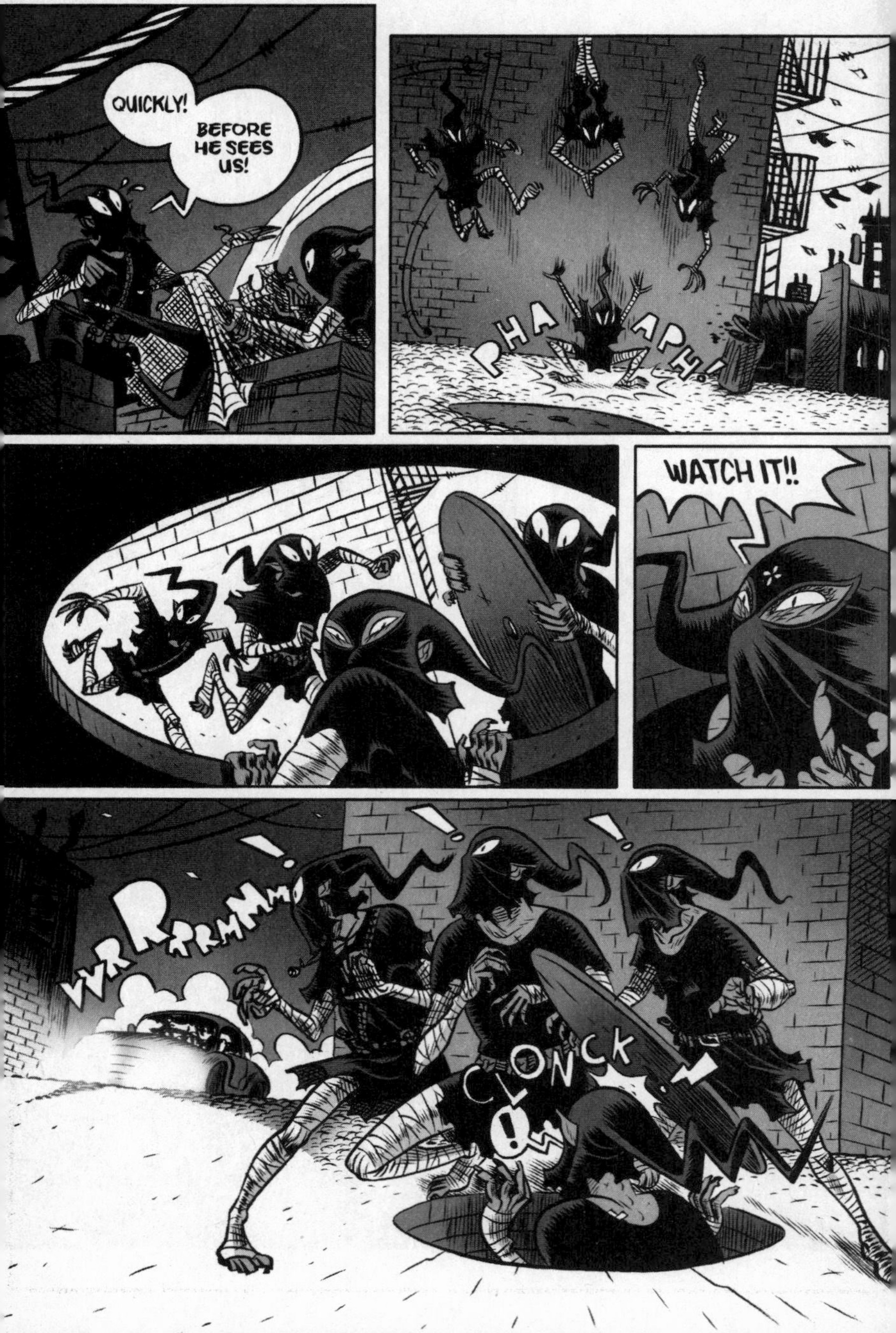
QUICKLY!
BEFORE HE SEES US!
PHAAPH!
WATCH IT!!
!
!
!
VVRRRRMMMM
CLONCK
!

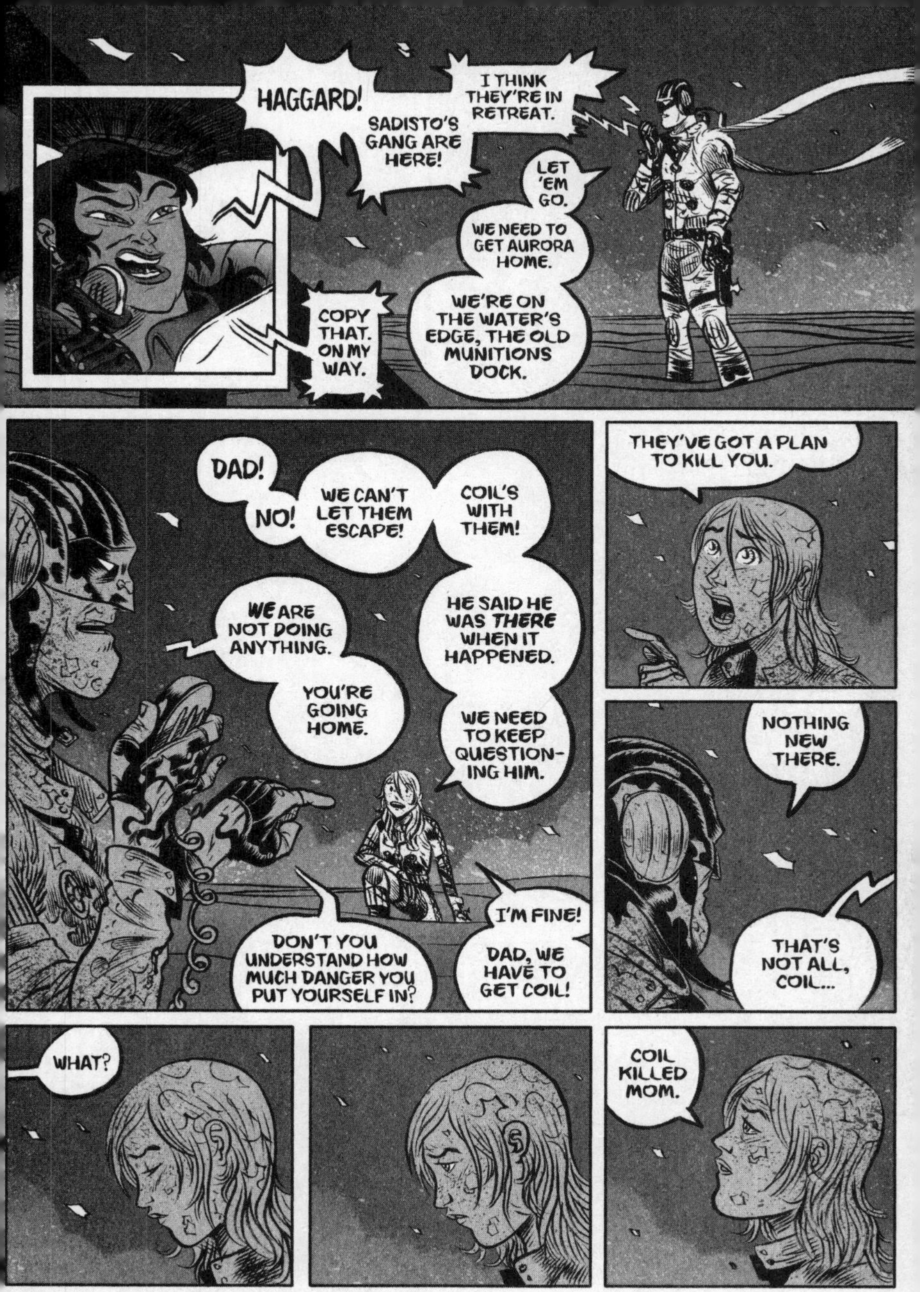
HAGGARD!
SADISTO'S GANG ARE HERE!
I THINK THEY'RE IN RETREAT.
LET 'EM GO.
WE NEED TO GET AURORA HOME.
WE'RE ON THE WATER'S EDGE, THE OLD MUNITIONS DOCK.
COPY THAT. ON MY WAY.
DAD!
NO!
WE CAN'T LET THEM ESCAPE!
COIL'S WITH THEM!
HE SAID HE WAS THERE WHEN IT HAPPENED.
WE NEED TO KEEP QUESTIONING HIM.
WE ARE NOT DOING ANYTHING.
YOU'RE GOING HOME.
DON'T YOU UNDERSTAND HOW MUCH DANGER YOU PUT YOURSELF IN?
I'M FINE!
DAD, WE HAVE TO GET COIL!
THEY'VE GOT A PLAN TO KILL YOU.
NOTHING NEW THERE.
THAT'S NOT ALL, COIL...
WHAT?
COIL KILLED MOM.

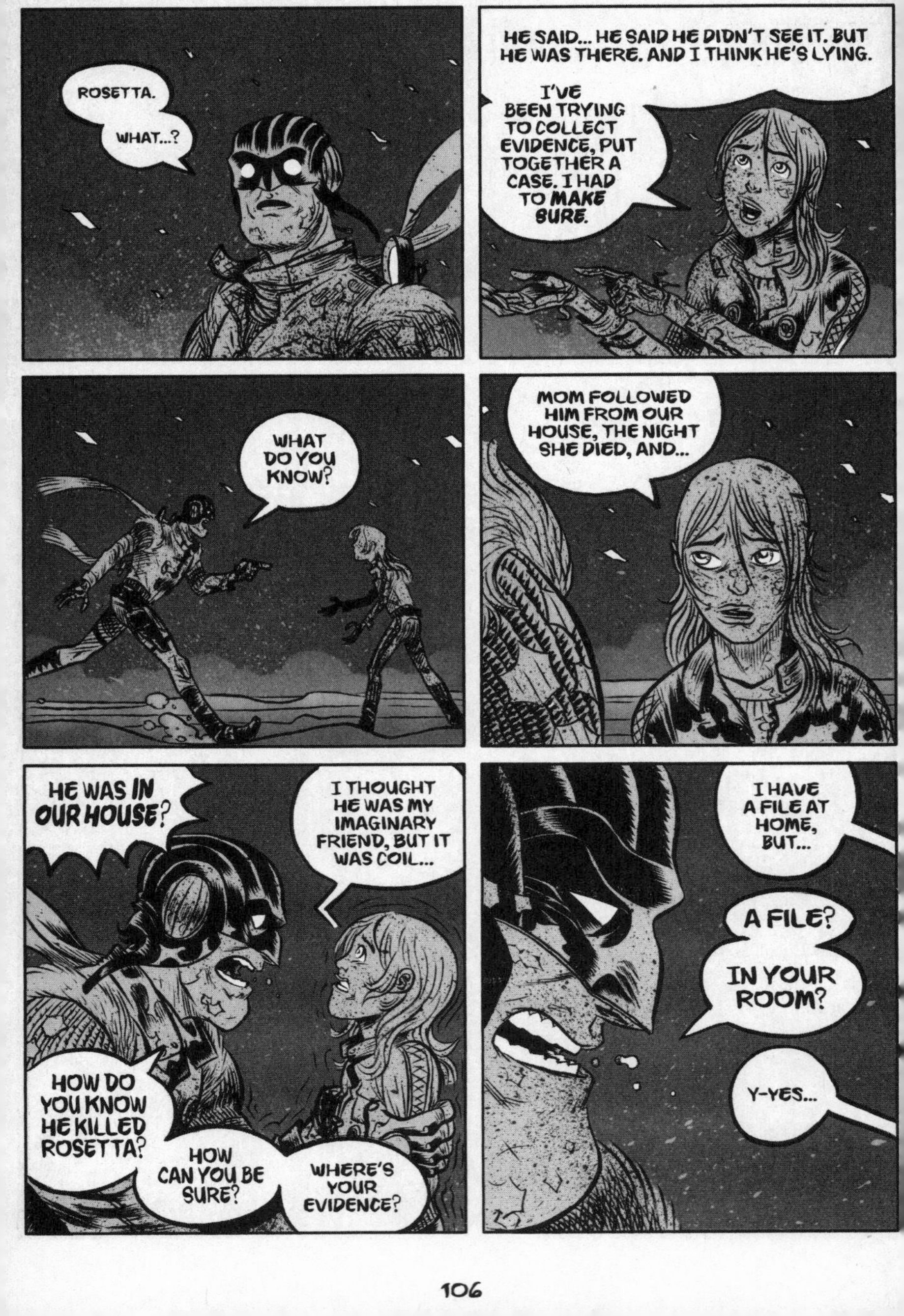
ROSETTA.
WHAT...?
HE SAID... HE SAID HE DIDN'T SEE IT. BUT HE WAS THERE. AND I THINK HE'S LYING.
I'VE BEEN TRYING TO COLLECT EVIDENCE, PUT TOGETHER A CASE. I HAD TO MAKE SURE.
WHAT DO YOU KNOW?
MOM FOLLOWED HIM FROM OUR HOUSE, THE NIGHT SHE DIED, AND...
HE WAS IN OUR HOUSE?
I THOUGHT HE WAS MY IMAGINARY FRIEND, BUT IT WAS COIL...
HOW DO YOU KNOW HE KILLED ROSETTA?
HOW CAN YOU BE SURE?
WHERE'S YOUR EVIDENCE?
I HAVE A FILE AT HOME, BUT...
A FILE?
IN YOUR ROOM?
Y-YES...

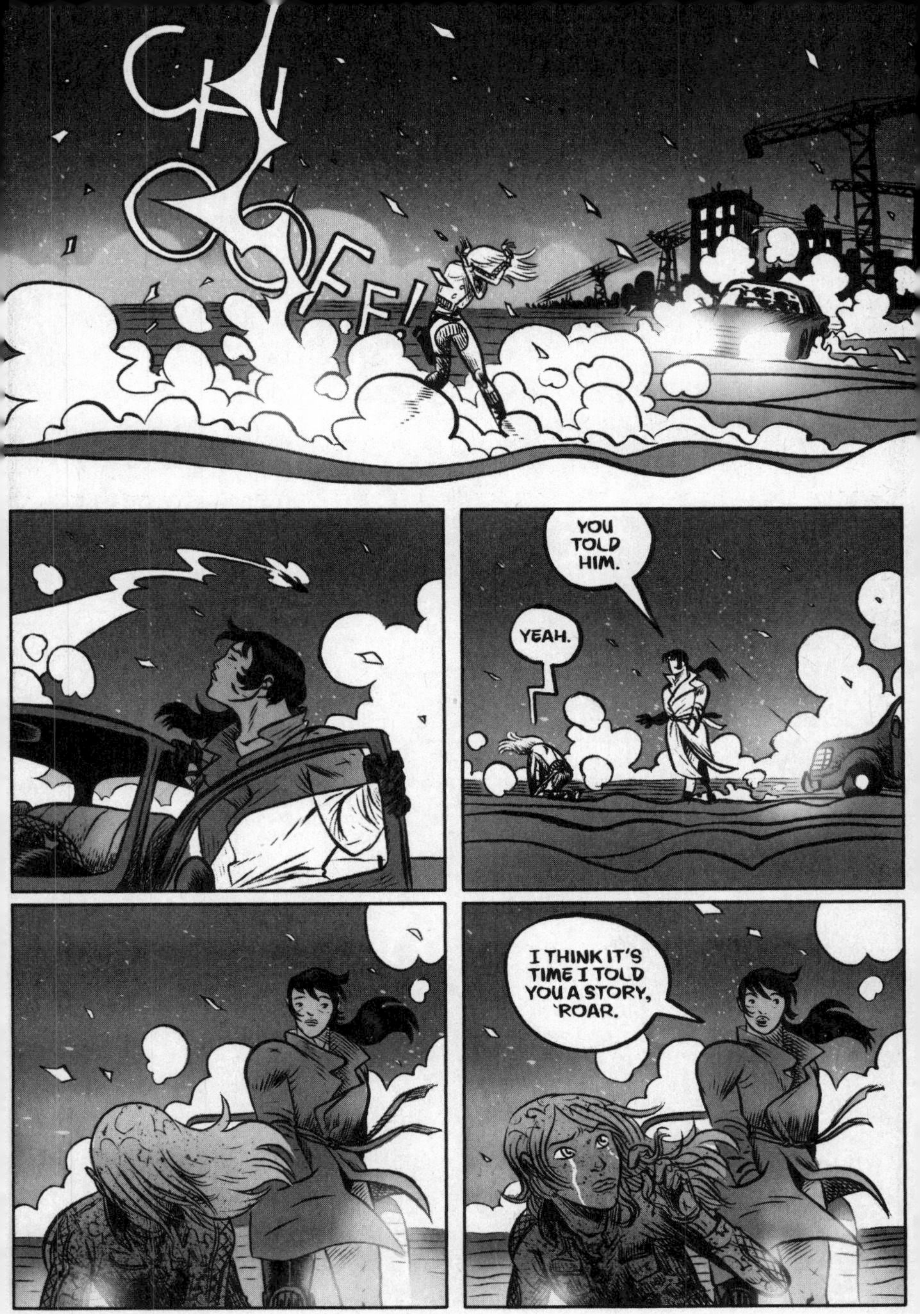
CHOOFF!
YOU TOLD HIM.
YEAH.
I THINK IT'S TIME I TOLD YOU A STORY, 'ROAR.

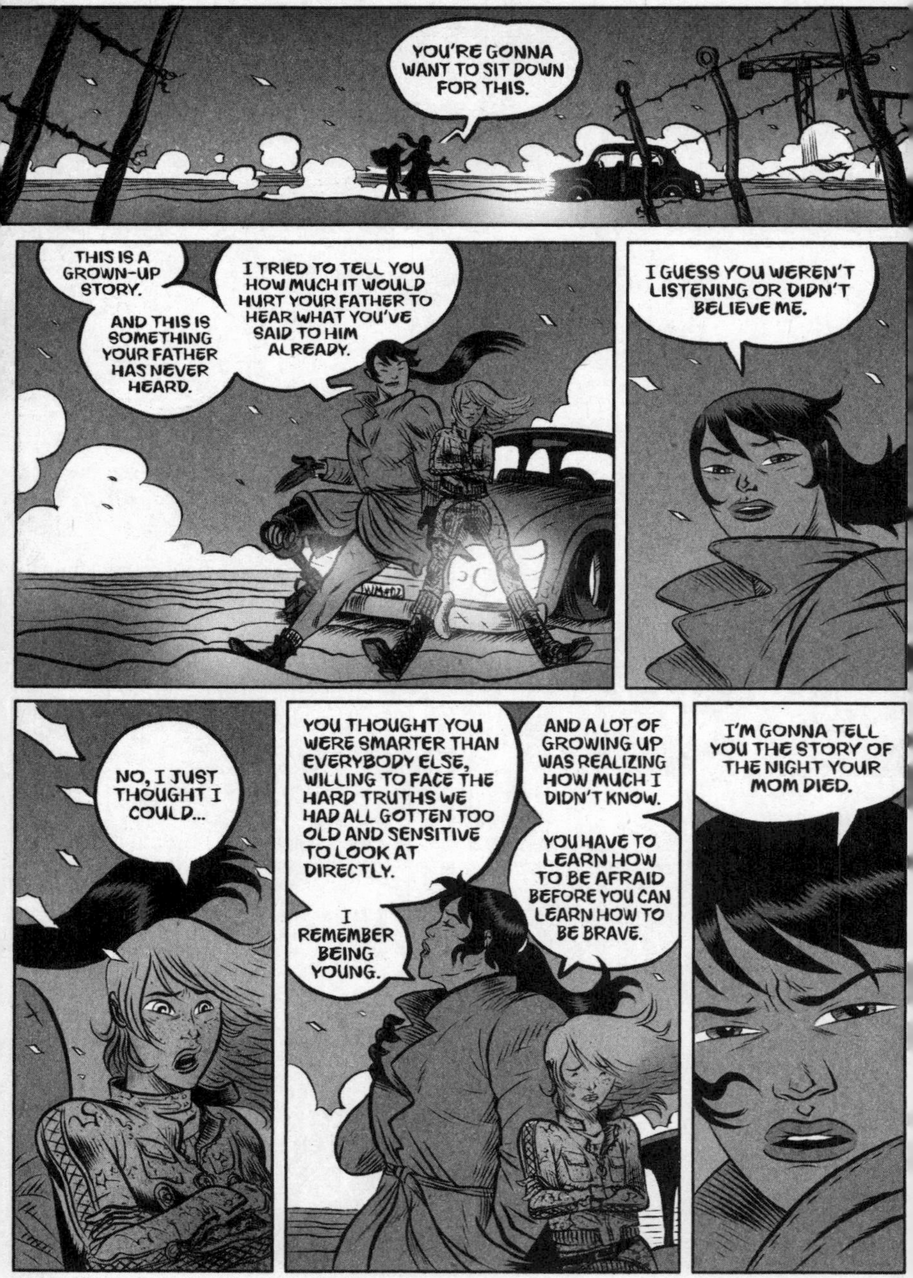

YOU'RE GONNA WANT TO SIT DOWN FOR THIS.
THIS IS A GROWN-UP STORY.
AND THIS IS SOMETHING YOUR FATHER HAS NEVER HEARD.
I TRIED TO TELL YOU HOW MUCH IT WOULD HURT YOUR FATHER TO HEAR WHAT YOU'VE SAID TO HIM ALREADY.
I GUESS YOU WEREN'T LISTENING OR DIDN'T BELIEVE ME.
NO, I JUST THOUGHT I COULD...
YOU THOUGHT YOU WERE SMARTER THAN EVERYBODY ELSE, WILLING TO FACE THE HARD TRUTHS WE HAD ALL GOTTEN TOO OLD AND SENSITIVE TO LOOK AT DIRECTLY.
I REMEMBER BEING YOUNG.
AND A LOT OF GROWING UP WAS REALIZING HOW MUCH I DIDN'T KNOW.
YOU HAVE TO LEARN HOW TO BE AFRAID BEFORE YOU CAN LEARN HOW TO BE BRAVE.
I'M GONNA TELL YOU THE STORY OF THE NIGHT YOUR MOM DIED.

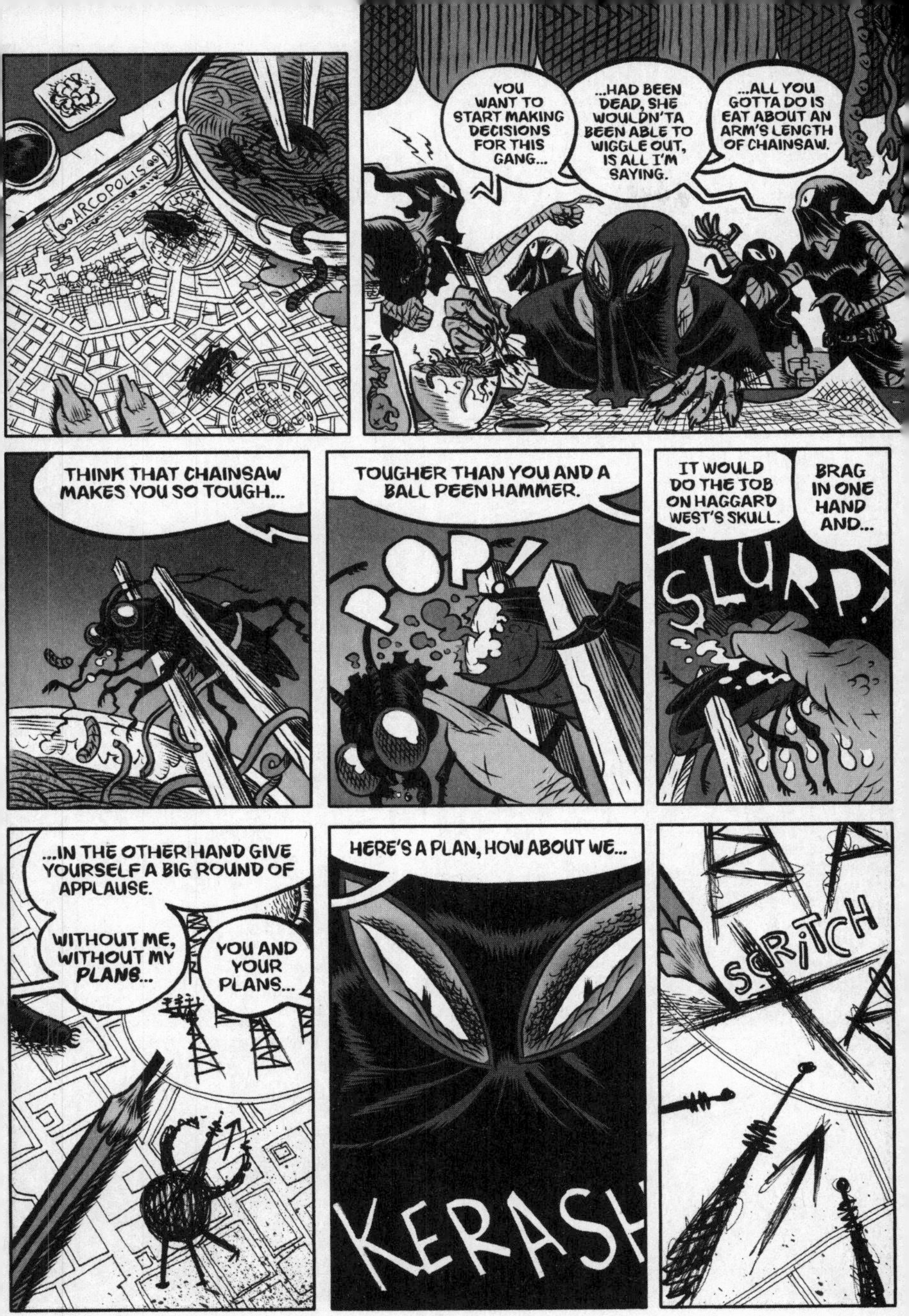
ARCOPOLIS
YOU WANT TO START MAKING DECISIONS FOR THIS GANG...
...HAD BEEN DEAD, SHE WOULDN'TA BEEN ABLE TO WIGGLE OUT, IS ALL I'M SAYING.
...ALL YOU GOTTA DO IS EAT ABOUT AN ARM'S LENGTH OF CHAINSAW.
THINK THAT CHAINSAW MAKES YOU SO TOUGH...
TOUGHER THAN YOU AND A BALL PEEN HAMMER.
POP!
IT WOULD DO THE JOB ON HAGGARD WEST'S SKULL.
BRAG IN ONE HAND AND...
SLURP
...IN THE OTHER HAND GIVE YOURSELF A BIG ROUND OF APPLAUSE.
WITHOUT ME, WITHOUT MY PLANS...
YOU AND YOUR PLANS...
HERE'S A PLAN, HOW ABOUT WE...
KERASH
SCRITCH

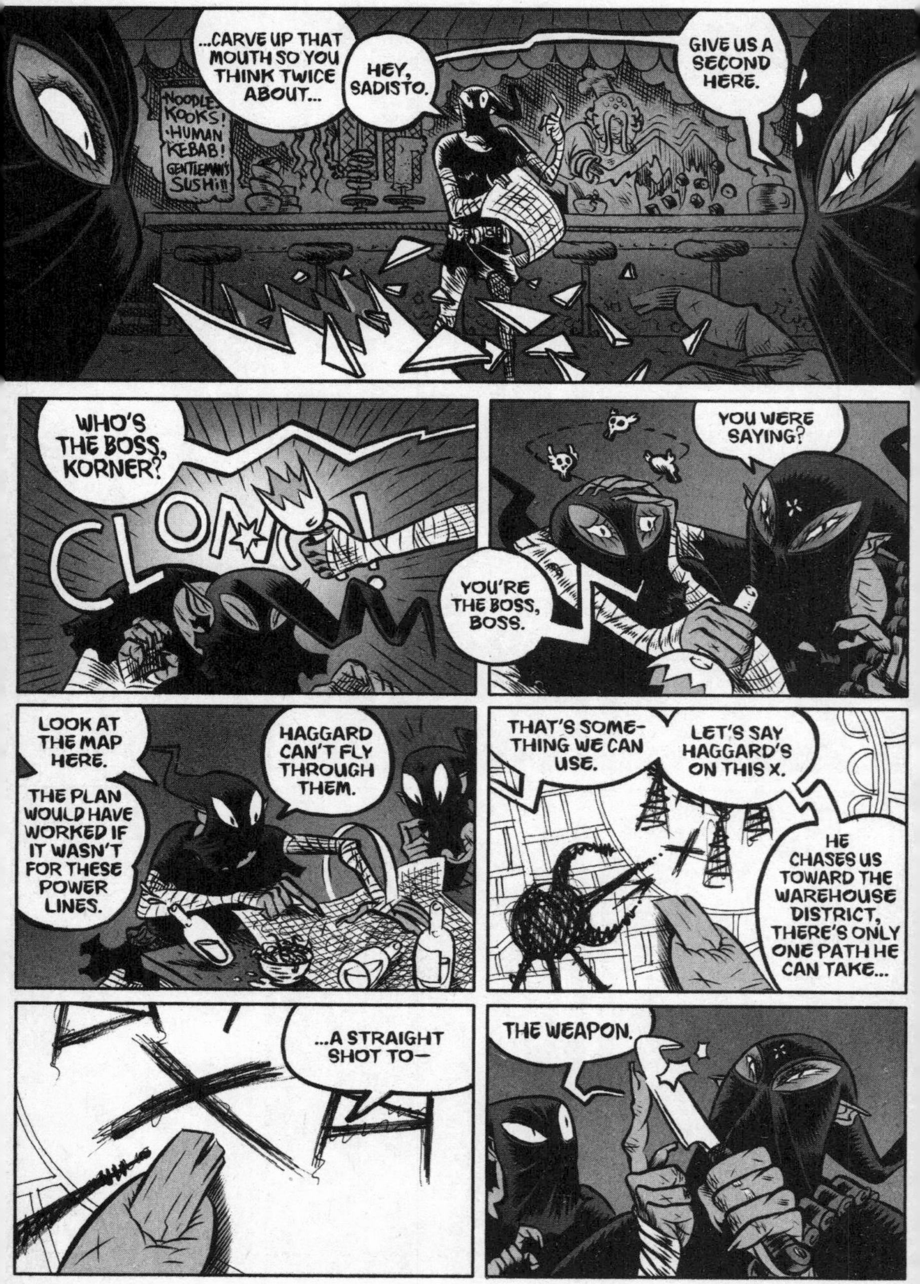
NOODLE KOOKS! HUMAN KEBAB! GENTLEMAN'S SUSHI!!
...CARVE UP THAT MOUTH SO YOU THINK TWICE ABOUT...
HEY, SADISTO.
GIVE US A SECOND HERE.
WHO'S THE BOSS, KORNER?
CLOMP!
YOU WERE SAYING?
YOU'RE THE BOSS, BOSS.
LOOK AT THE MAP HERE.
THE PLAN WOULD HAVE WORKED IF IT WASN'T FOR THESE POWER LINES.
HAGGARD CAN'T FLY THROUGH THEM.
THAT'S SOMETHING WE CAN USE.
LET'S SAY HAGGARD'S ON THIS X.
HE CHASES US TOWARD THE WAREHOUSE DISTRICT, THERE'S ONLY ONE PATH HE CAN TAKE...
...A STRAIGHT SHOT TO—
THE WEAPON.

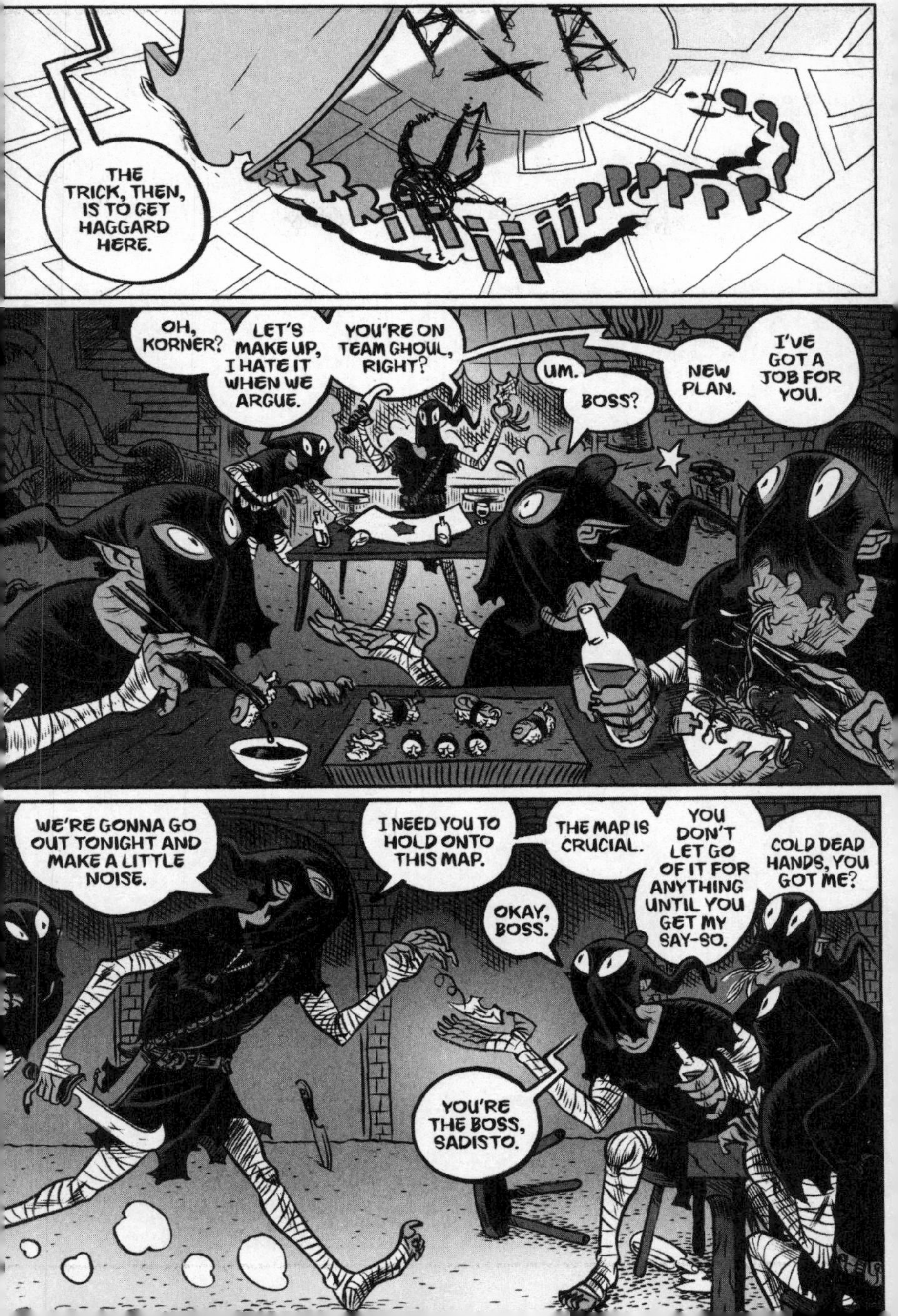
THE TRICK, THEN, IS TO GET HAGGARD HERE.
RRRiiiiiiiPPPPPPPP!
OH, KORNER?
LET'S MAKE UP, I HATE IT WHEN WE ARGUE.
YOU'RE ON TEAM GHOUL, RIGHT?
UM.
BOSS?
NEW PLAN.
I'VE GOT A JOB FOR YOU.
WE'RE GONNA GO OUT TONIGHT AND MAKE A LITTLE NOISE.
I NEED YOU TO HOLD ONTO THIS MAP.
THE MAP IS CRUCIAL.
YOU DON'T LET GO OF IT FOR ANYTHING UNTIL YOU GET MY SAY-SO.
COLD DEAD HANDS, YOU GOT ME?
OKAY, BOSS.
YOU'RE THE BOSS, SADISTO.

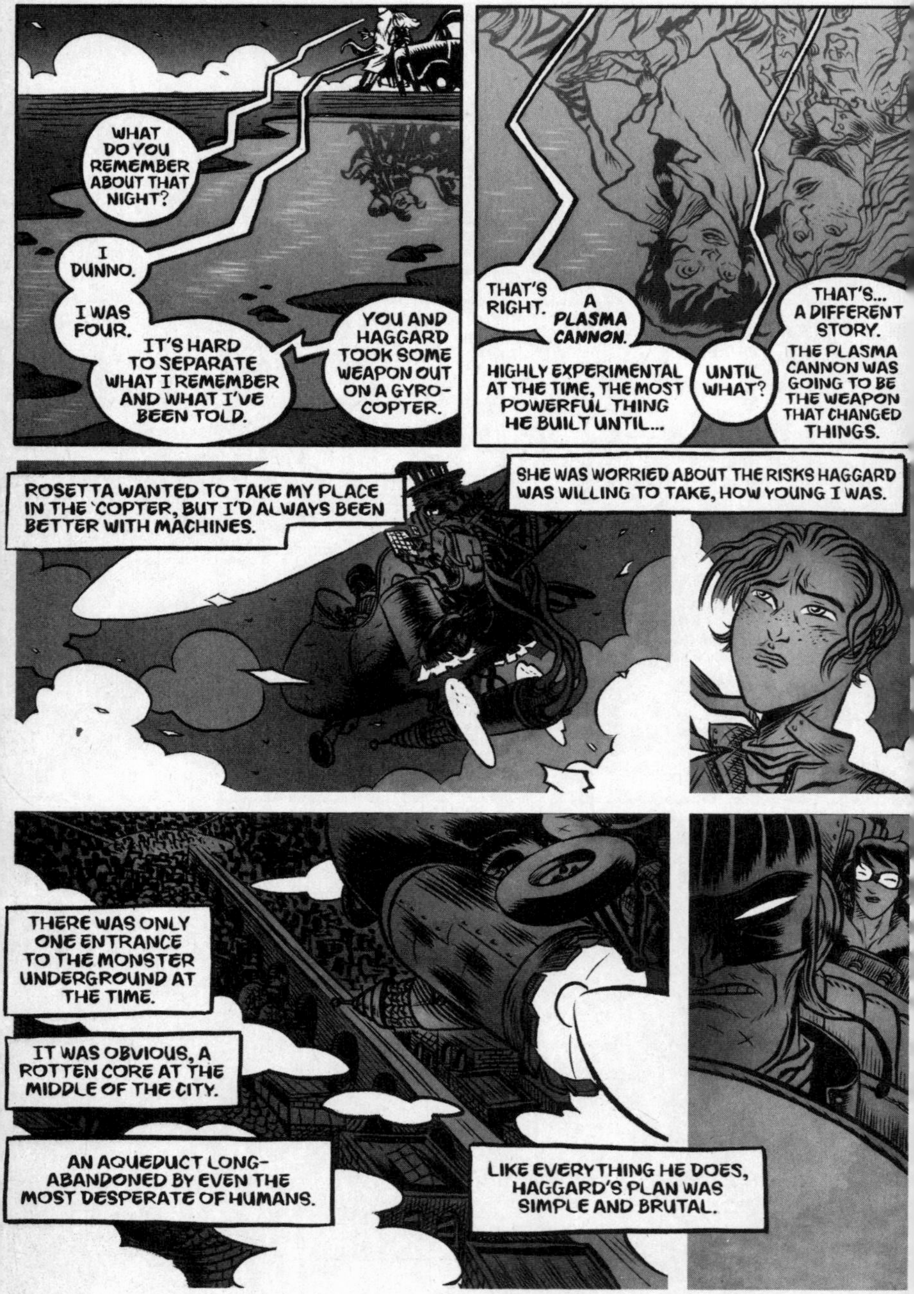
WHAT DO YOU REMEMBER ABOUT THAT NIGHT?
I DUNNO.
I WAS FOUR.
IT'S HARD TO SEPARATE WHAT I REMEMBER AND WHAT I'VE BEEN TOLD.
YOU AND HAGGARD TOOK SOME WEAPON OUT ON A GYRO-COPTER.
THAT'S RIGHT.
A PLASMA CANNON.
HIGHLY EXPERIMENTAL AT THE TIME, THE MOST POWERFUL THING HE BUILT UNTIL...
UNTIL WHAT?
THAT'S... A DIFFERENT STORY.
THE PLASMA CANNON WAS GOING TO BE THE WEAPON THAT CHANGED THINGS.
ROSETTA WANTED TO TAKE MY PLACE IN THE 'COPTER, BUT I'D ALWAYS BEEN BETTER WITH MACHINES.
SHE WAS WORRIED ABOUT THE RISKS HAGGARD WAS WILLING TO TAKE, HOW YOUNG I WAS.
THERE WAS ONLY ONE ENTRANCE TO THE MONSTER UNDERGROUND AT THE TIME.
IT WAS OBVIOUS, A ROTTEN CORE AT THE MIDDLE OF THE CITY.
AN AQUEDUCT LONG-ABANDONED BY EVEN THE MOST DESPERATE OF HUMANS.
LIKE EVERYTHING HE DOES, HAGGARD'S PLAN WAS SIMPLE AND BRUTAL.

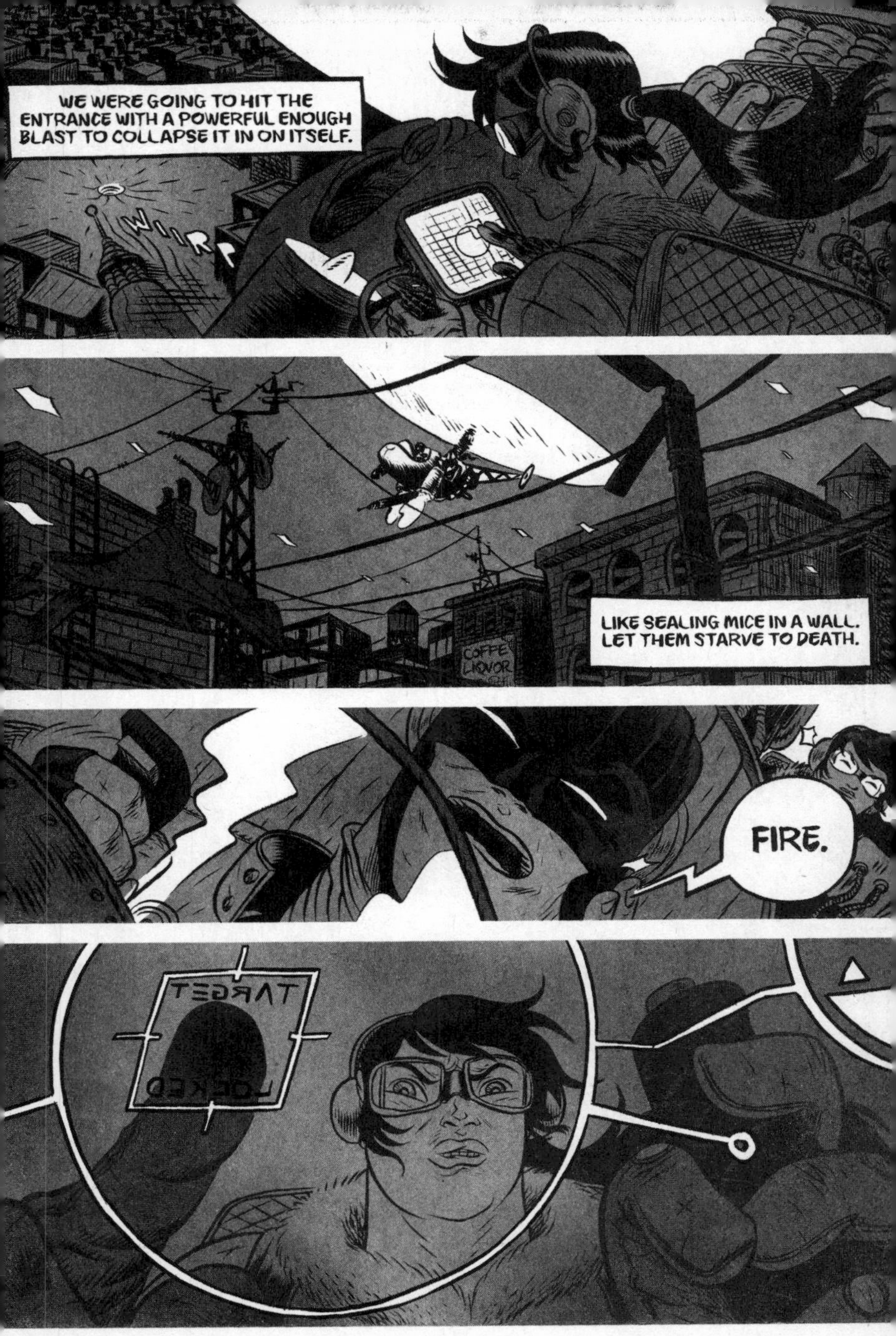
WE WERE GOING TO HIT THE ENTRANCE WITH A POWERFUL ENOUGH BLAST TO COLLAPSE IT IN ON ITSELF.
COFFE
LIQVOR
LIKE SEALING MICE IN A WALL. LET THEM STARVE TO DEATH.
FIRE.

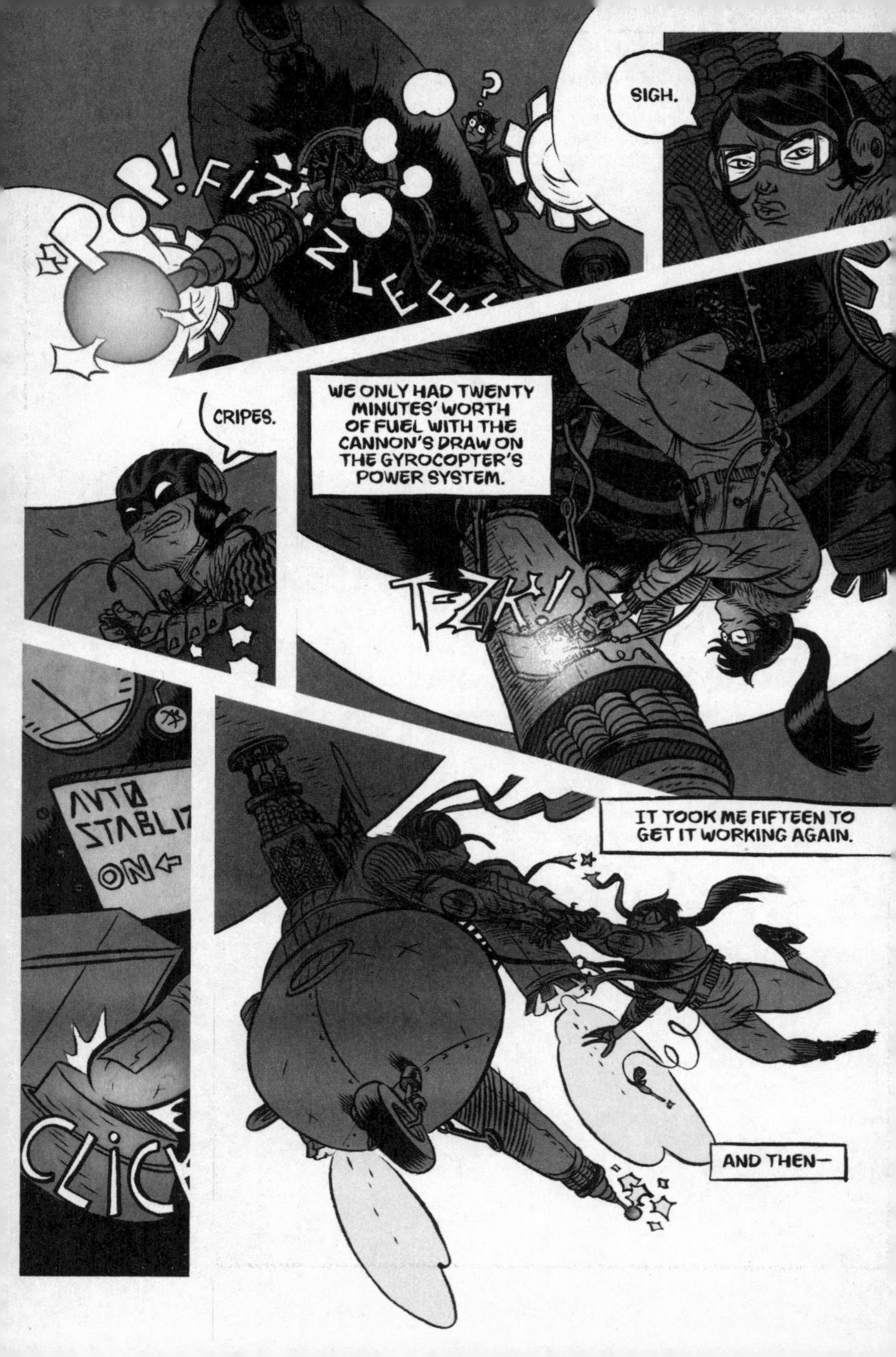
POP!
FIZ
ZLEEE
?
SIGH.
CRIPES.
WE ONLY HAD TWENTY MINUTES' WORTH OF FUEL WITH THE CANNON'S DRAW ON THE GYROCOPTER'S POWER SYSTEM.
T-ZK!
AUTO STABLIZ
ON
CLIC
IT TOOK ME FIFTEEN TO GET IT WORKING AGAIN.
AND THEN—

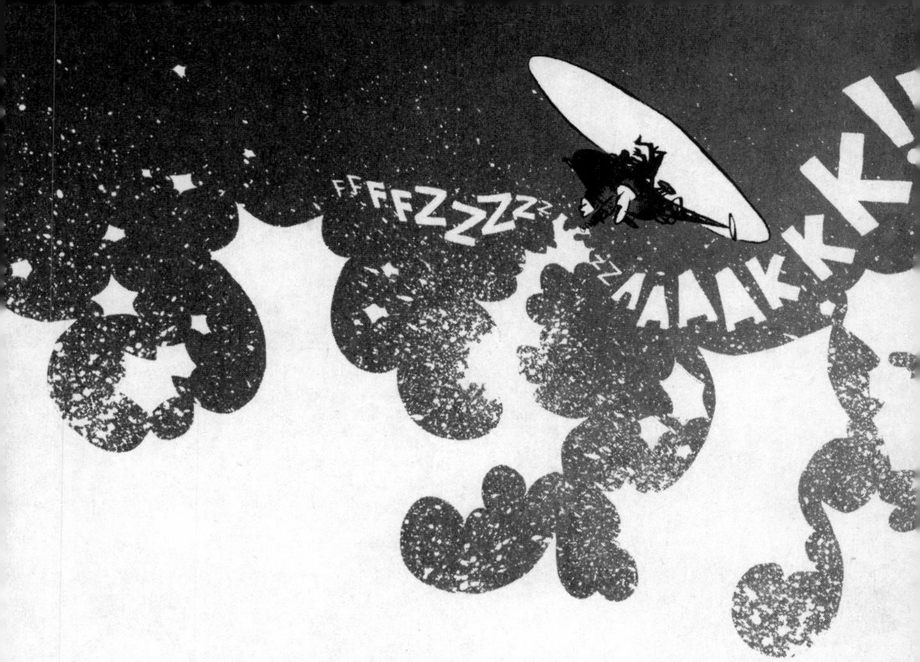
FFFFZZZZZZ
ZZAAAAKK!!

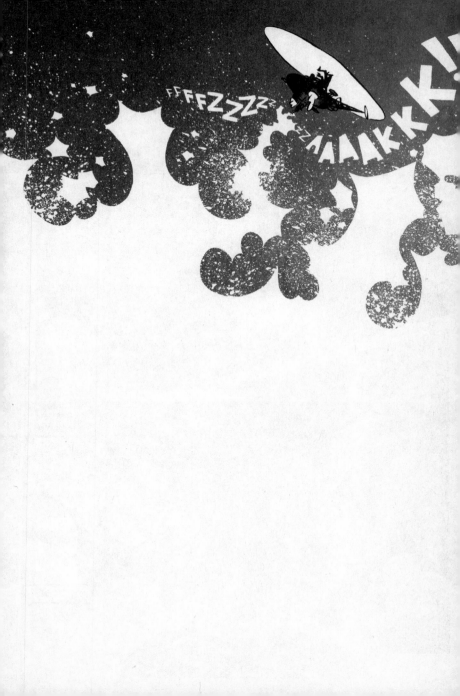

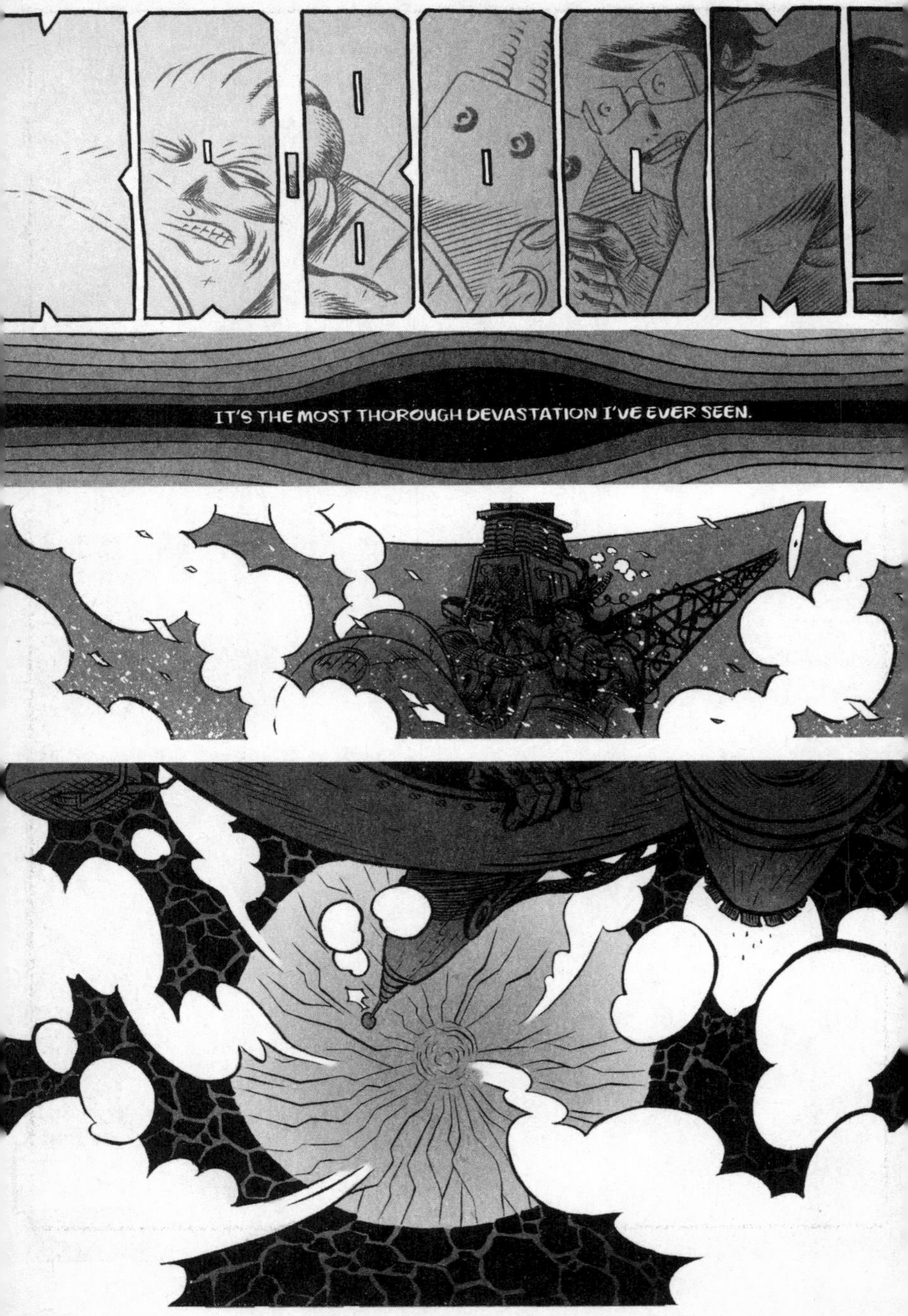
IT'S THE MOST THOROUGH DEVASTATION I'VE EVER SEEN.

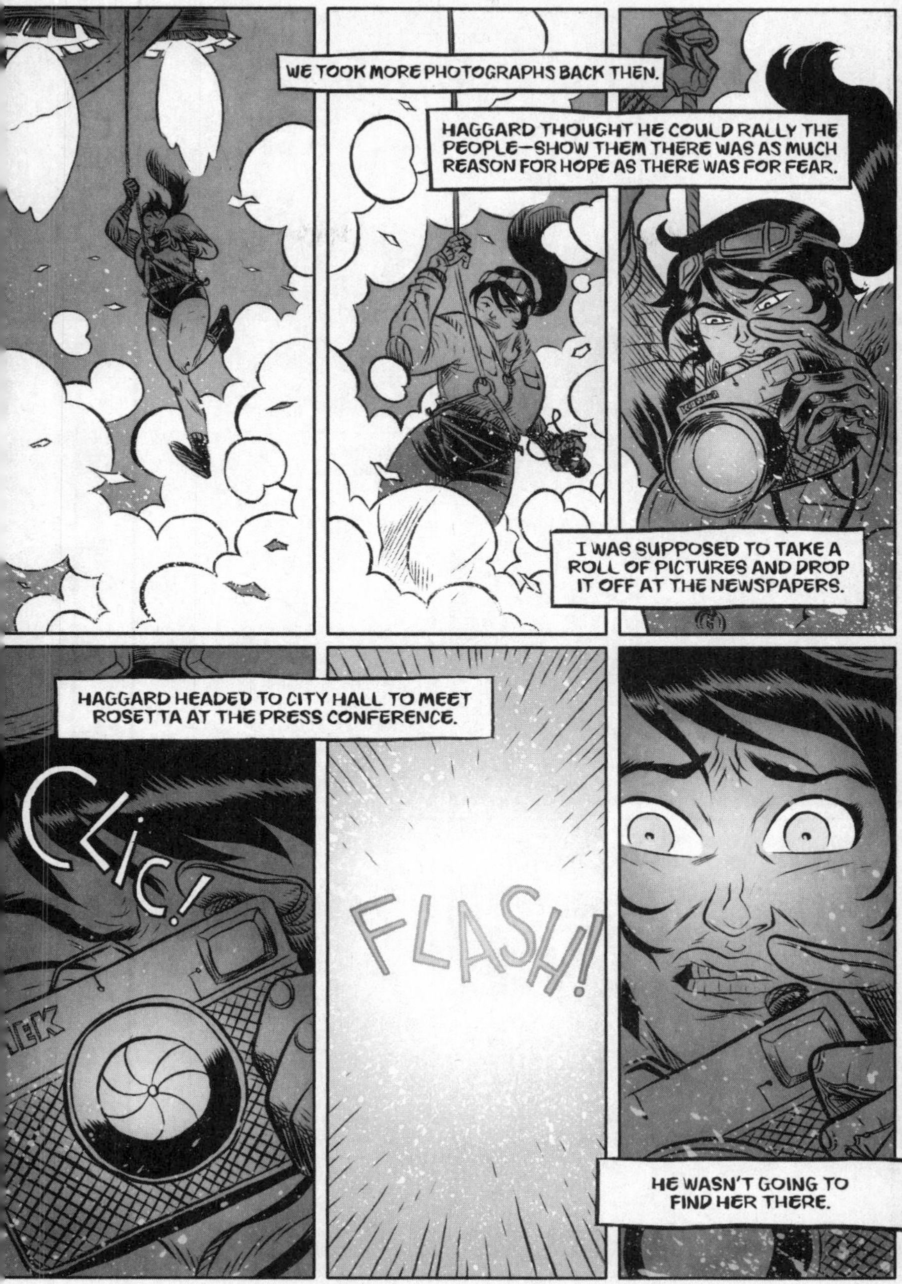
WE TOOK MORE PHOTOGRAPHS BACK THEN.
HAGGARD THOUGHT HE COULD RALLY THE PEOPLE—SHOW THEM THERE WAS AS MUCH REASON FOR HOPE AS THERE WAS FOR FEAR.
I WAS SUPPOSED TO TAKE A ROLL OF PICTURES AND DROP IT OFF AT THE NEWSPAPERS.
HAGGARD HEADED TO CITY HALL TO MEET ROSETTA AT THE PRESS CONFERENCE.
CLIC!
FLASH!
HE WASN'T GOING TO FIND HER THERE.

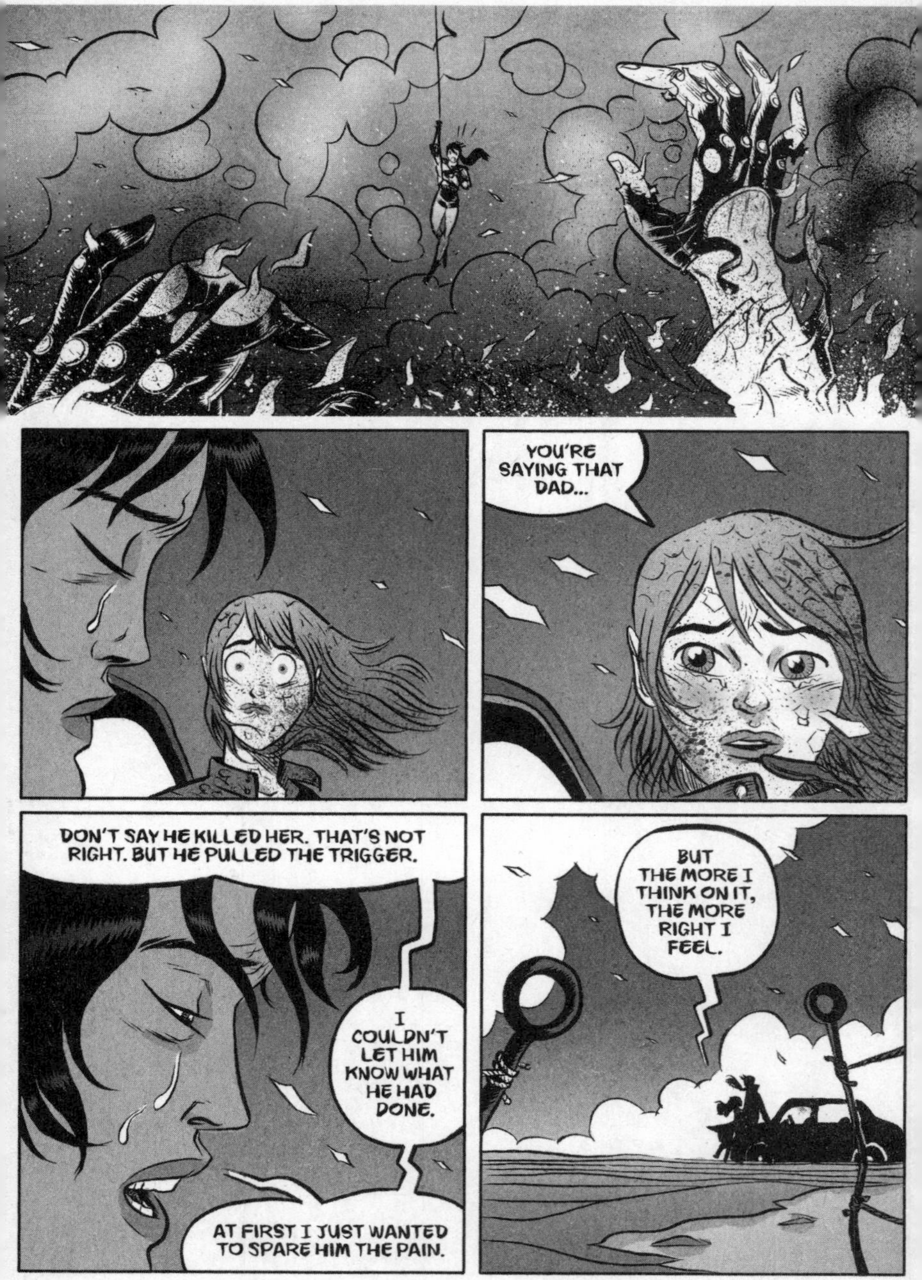
YOU'RE SAYING THAT DAD...
DON'T SAY HE KILLED HER. THAT'S NOT RIGHT. BUT HE PULLED THE TRIGGER.
I COULDN'T LET HIM KNOW WHAT HE HAD DONE.
AT FIRST I JUST WANTED TO SPARE HIM THE PAIN.
BUT THE MORE I THINK ON IT, THE MORE RIGHT I FEEL.

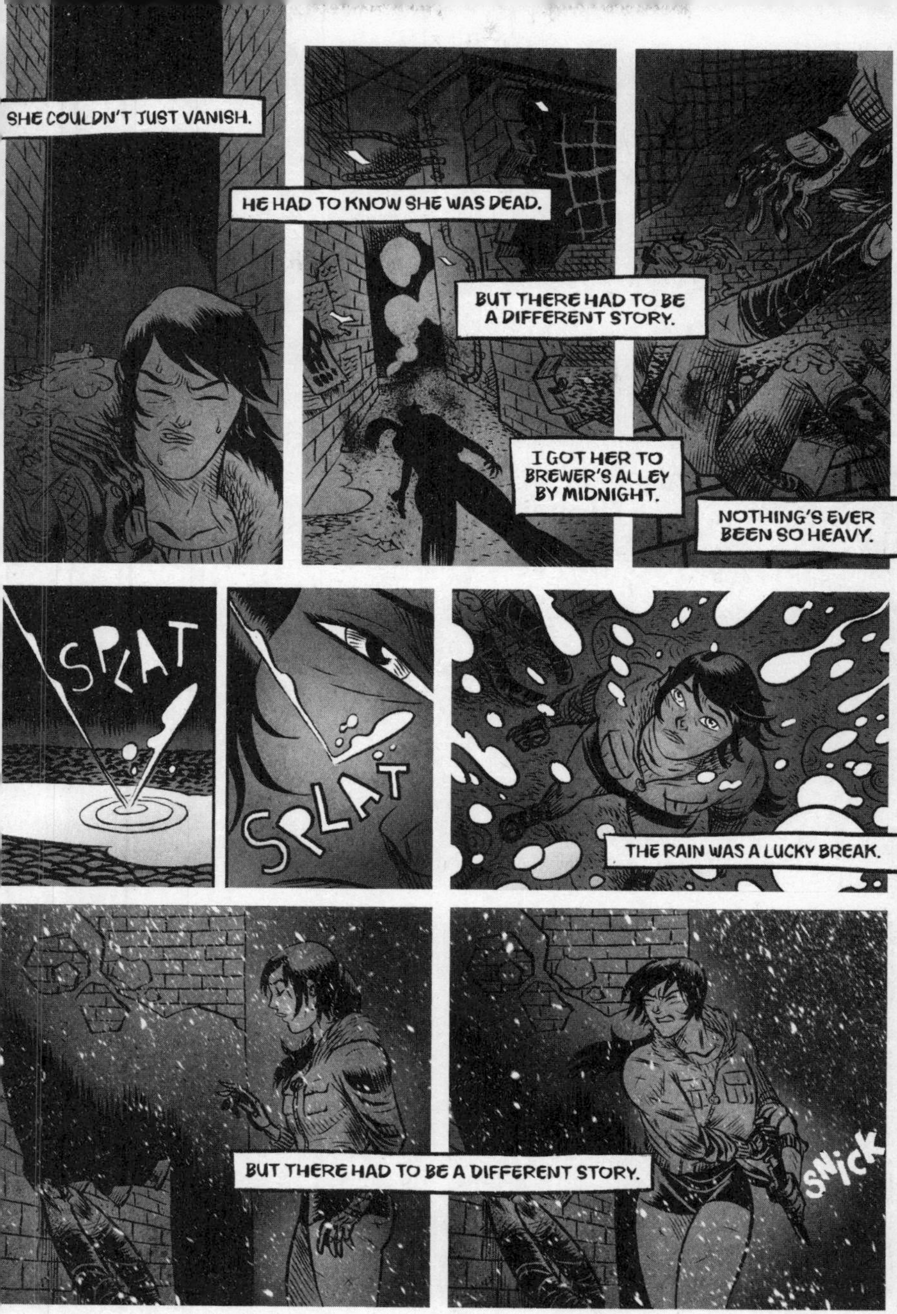
SHE COULDN'T JUST VANISH.
HE HAD TO KNOW SHE WAS DEAD.
BUT THERE HAD TO BE A DIFFERENT STORY.
I GOT HER TO BREWER'S ALLEY BY MIDNIGHT.
NOTHING'S EVER BEEN SO HEAVY.
SPLAT
SPLAT
THE RAIN WAS A LUCKY BREAK.
BUT THERE HAD TO BE A DIFFERENT STORY.
SNICK

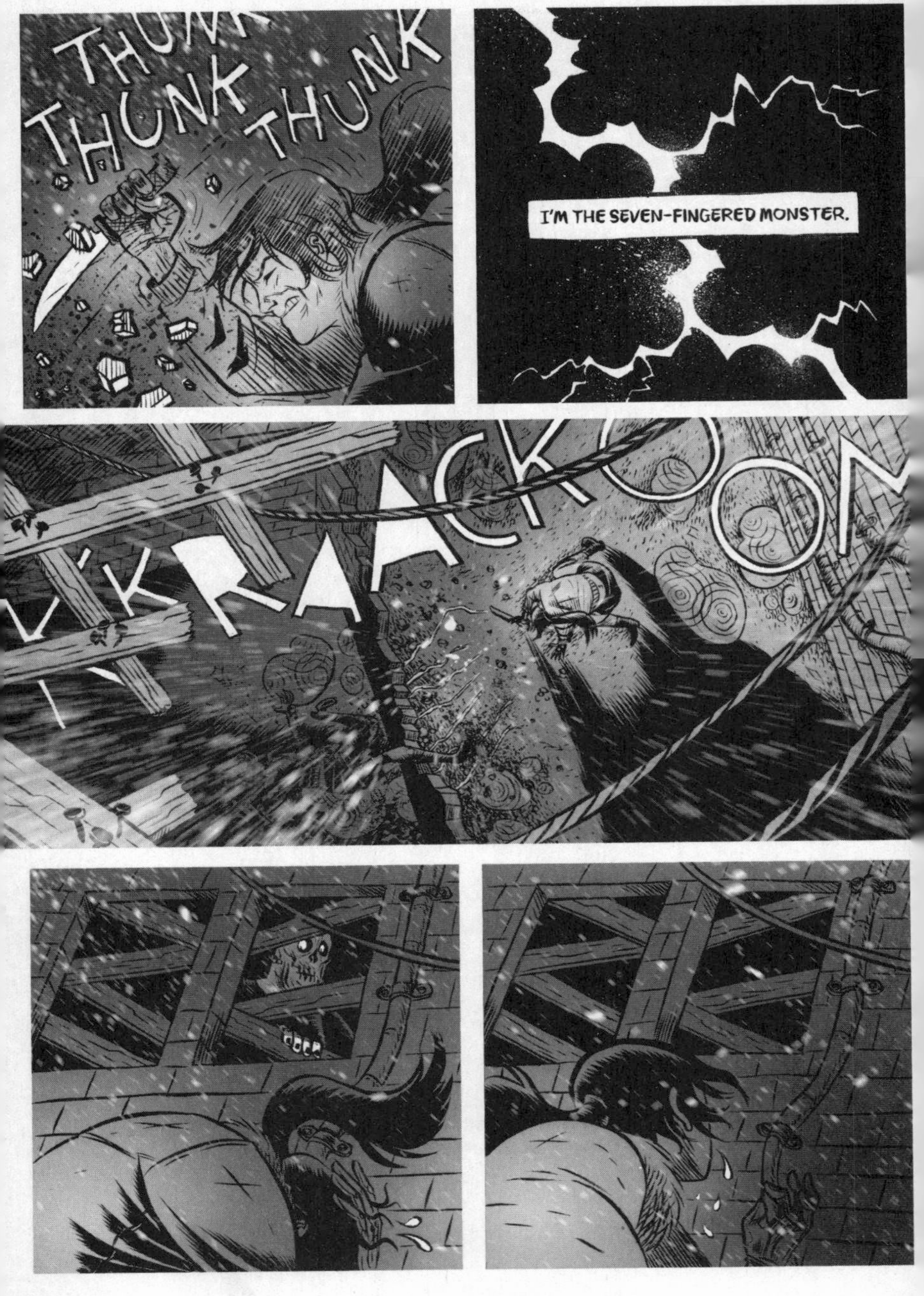
THUNK
THUNK THUNK THUNK
I'M THE SEVEN-FINGERED MONSTER.
K'KRAACKOOM

IT WAS ALL I COULD THINK TO DO.

WE HAD NEVER SEEN A SEVEN-FINGERED MONSTER BEFORE. I THOUGHT...

...IT WOULD DRIVE HAGGARD ON.

GIVE HIM SOMETHING TO LOOK FOR HE COULD NEVER FIND.

MAKE SURE HE WOULD NEVER GIVE UP ON ARCOPOLIS.

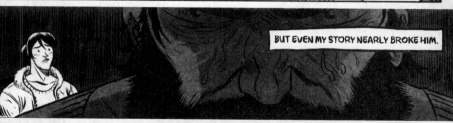

BUT EVEN MY STORY NEARLY BROKE HIM.

I'LL NEVER KNOW IF I DID THE RIGHT THING.

MS. GRATELY...

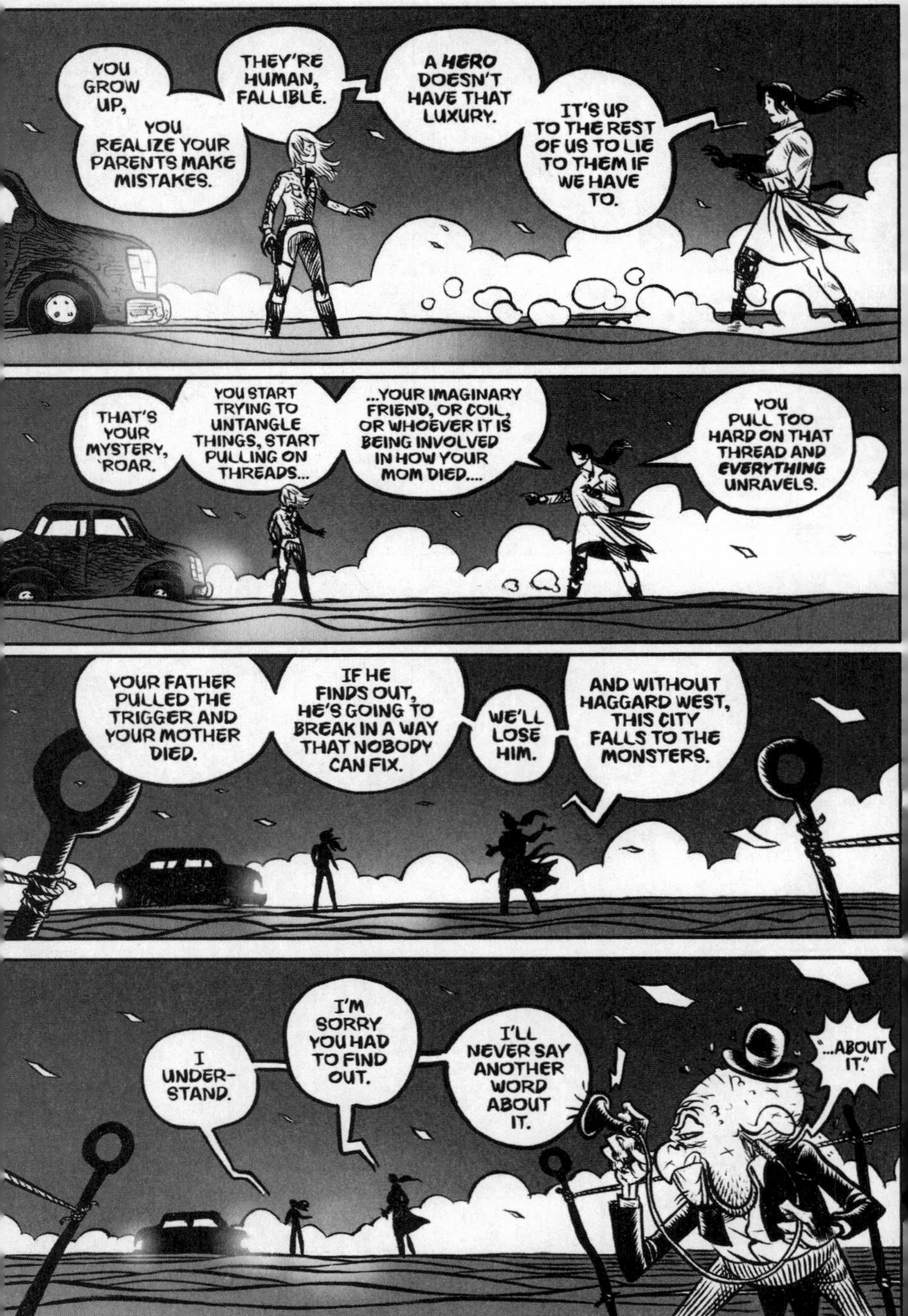
YOU GROW UP,
YOU REALIZE YOUR PARENTS MAKE MISTAKES.
THEY'RE HUMAN, FALLIBLE.
A HERO DOESN'T HAVE THAT LUXURY.
IT'S UP TO THE REST OF US TO LIE TO THEM IF WE HAVE TO.
THAT'S YOUR MYSTERY, 'ROAR.
YOU START TRYING TO UNTANGLE THINGS, START PULLING ON THREADS...
...YOUR IMAGINARY FRIEND, OR COIL, OR WHOEVER IT IS BEING INVOLVED IN HOW YOUR MOM DIED....
YOU PULL TOO HARD ON THAT THREAD AND EVERYTHING UNRAVELS.
YOUR FATHER PULLED THE TRIGGER AND YOUR MOTHER DIED.
IF HE FINDS OUT, HE'S GOING TO BREAK IN A WAY THAT NOBODY CAN FIX.
WE'LL LOSE HIM.
AND WITHOUT HAGGARD WEST, THIS CITY FALLS TO THE MONSTERS.
I UNDER-STAND.
I'M SORRY YOU HAD TO FIND OUT.
I'LL NEVER SAY ANOTHER WORD ABOUT IT.
"...ABOUT IT."

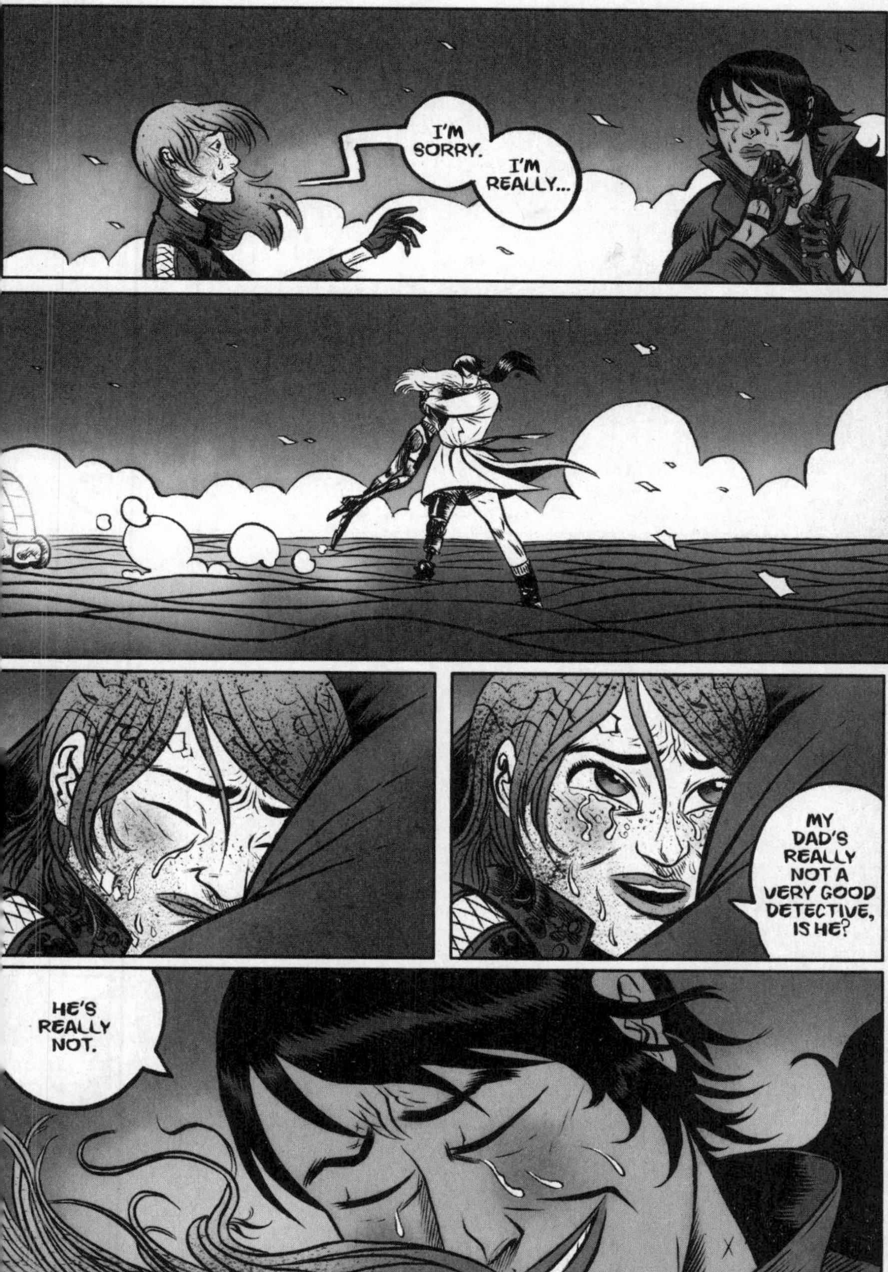
I'M SORRY.
I'M REALLY...
MY DAD'S REALLY NOT A VERY GOOD DETECTIVE, IS HE?
HE'S REALLY NOT.

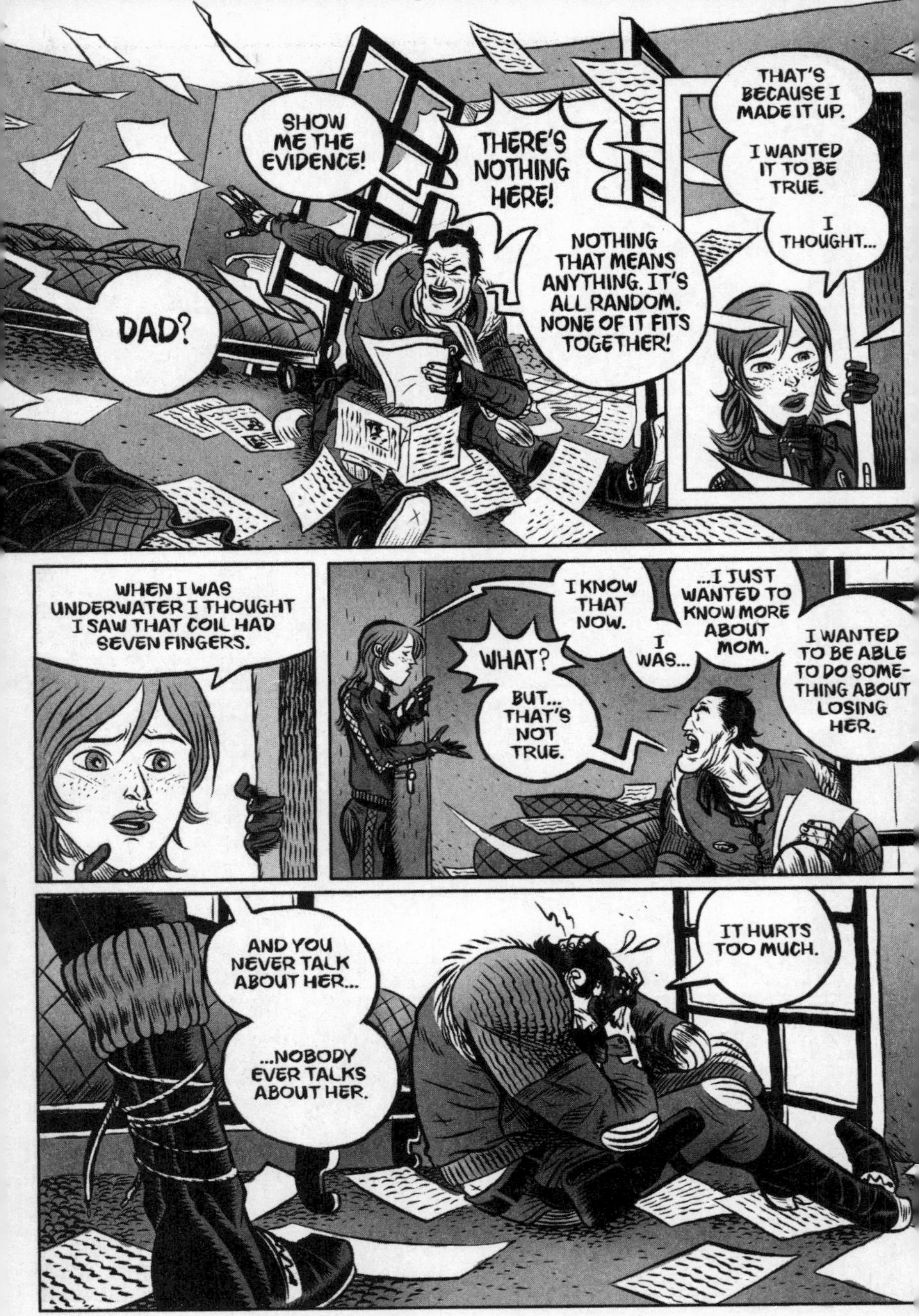
DAD?
SHOW ME THE EVIDENCE!
THERE'S NOTHING HERE!
NOTHING THAT MEANS ANYTHING. IT'S ALL RANDOM. NONE OF IT FITS TOGETHER!
THAT'S BECAUSE I MADE IT UP.
I WANTED IT TO BE TRUE.
I THOUGHT...
WHEN I WAS UNDERWATER I THOUGHT I SAW THAT COIL HAD SEVEN FINGERS.
WHAT?
BUT... THAT'S NOT TRUE.
I KNOW THAT NOW.
I WAS...
...I JUST WANTED TO KNOW MORE ABOUT MOM.
I WANTED TO BE ABLE TO DO SOME-THING ABOUT LOSING HER.
AND YOU NEVER TALK ABOUT HER...
...NOBODY EVER TALKS ABOUT HER.
IT HURTS TOO MUCH.

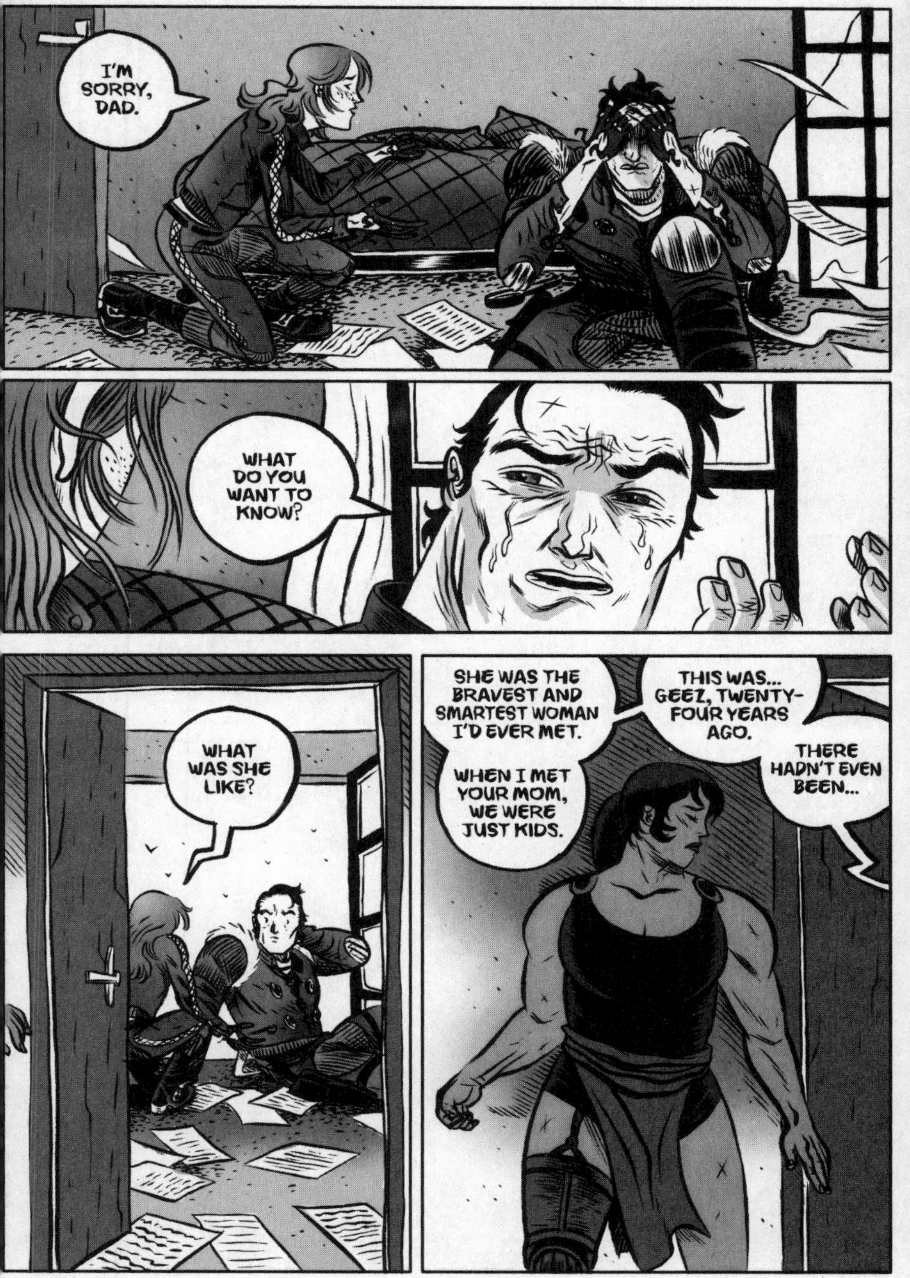
I'M SORRY, DAD.
WHAT DO YOU WANT TO KNOW?
WHAT WAS SHE LIKE?
SHE WAS THE BRAVEST AND SMARTEST WOMAN I'D EVER MET.
WHEN I MET YOUR MOM, WE WERE JUST KIDS.
THIS WAS... GEEZ, TWENTY-FOUR YEARS AGO.
THERE HADN'T EVEN BEEN...

SADISTO!

MUST FIND... SO SWEET.

SUCH A SECRET...

SUCH A DELICIOUS MORSEL OF KNOWLEDGE.

A FEW LITTLE WORDS AND HAGGARD WEST...

DO YOU KNOW WHERE SADISTO IS?

GRMM HRAAAAGH CAT SHNACK.

OKAY, THANKS.

Meao

HISS

JUMPP!!!

OOH-WEE OOH-WEE

SADISTO!!

WEE-O

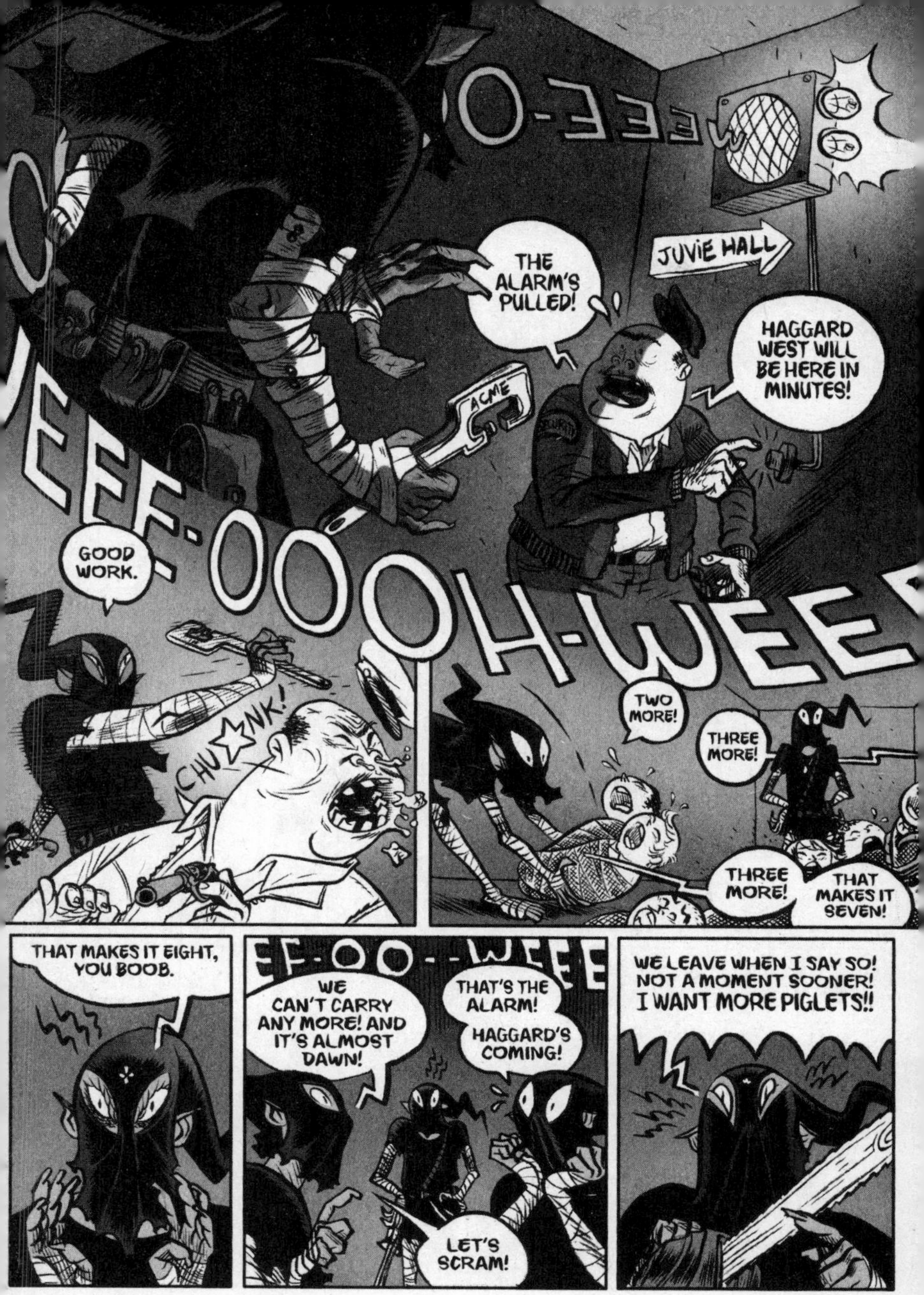
EEE-OOO
JUVIE HALL
THE ALARM'S PULLED!
HAGGARD WEST WILL BE HERE IN MINUTES!
EEE-OOOOH-WEEE
GOOD WORK.
CHU☆NK!
TWO MORE!
THREE MORE!
THREE MORE!
THAT MAKES IT SEVEN!
THAT MAKES IT EIGHT, YOU BOOB.
EE-OO--WEEE
WE CAN'T CARRY ANY MORE! AND IT'S ALMOST DAWN!
THAT'S THE ALARM!
HAGGARD'S COMING!
LET'S SCRAM!
WE LEAVE WHEN I SAY SO! NOT A MOMENT SOONER! I WANT MORE PIGLETS!!

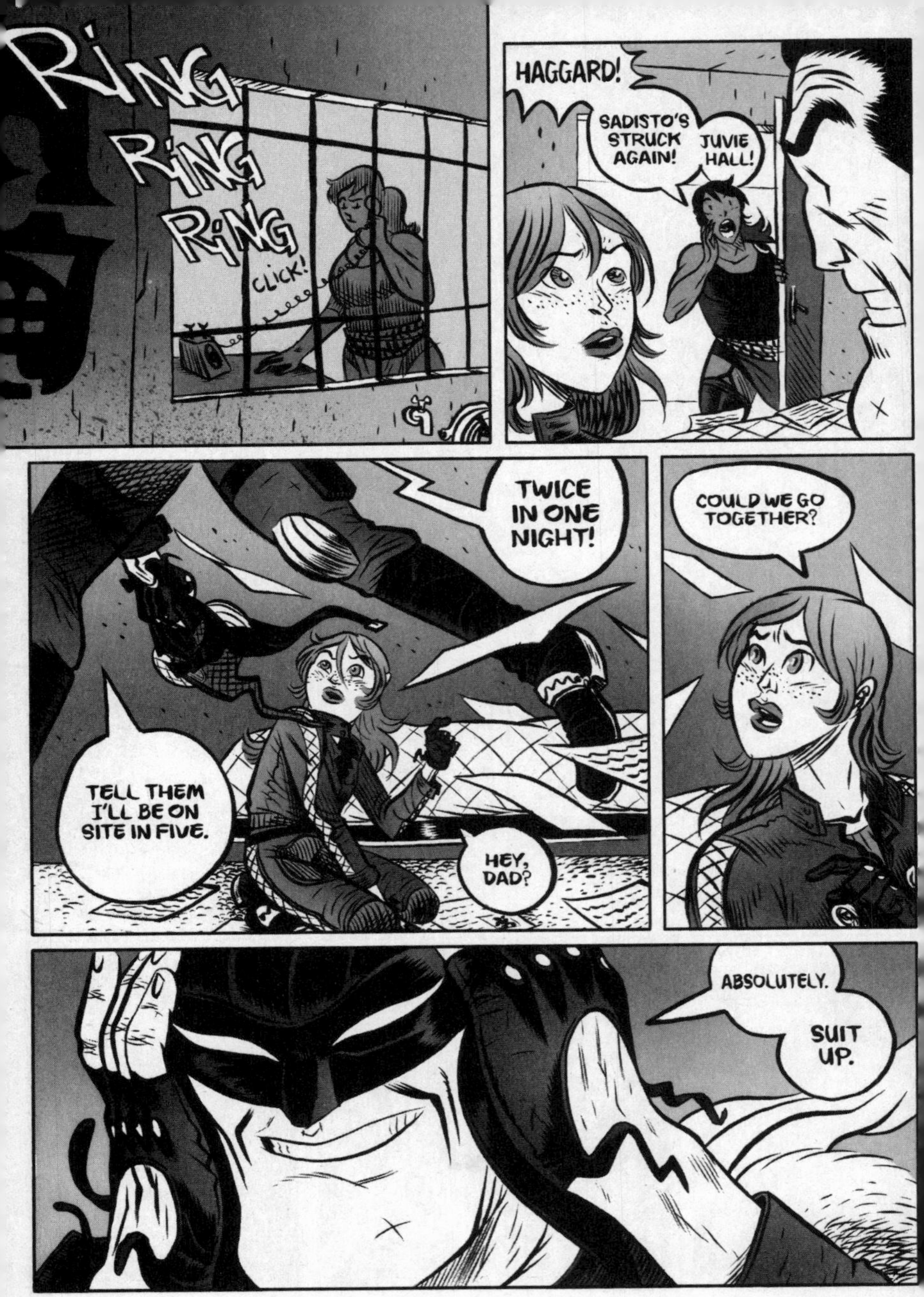
RING
RING
RING
CLICK!
HAGGARD!
SADISTO'S STRUCK AGAIN!
JUVIE HALL!
TWICE IN ONE NIGHT!
TELL THEM I'LL BE ON SITE IN FIVE.
HEY, DAD?
COULD WE GO TOGETHER?
ABSOLUTELY.
SUIT UP.

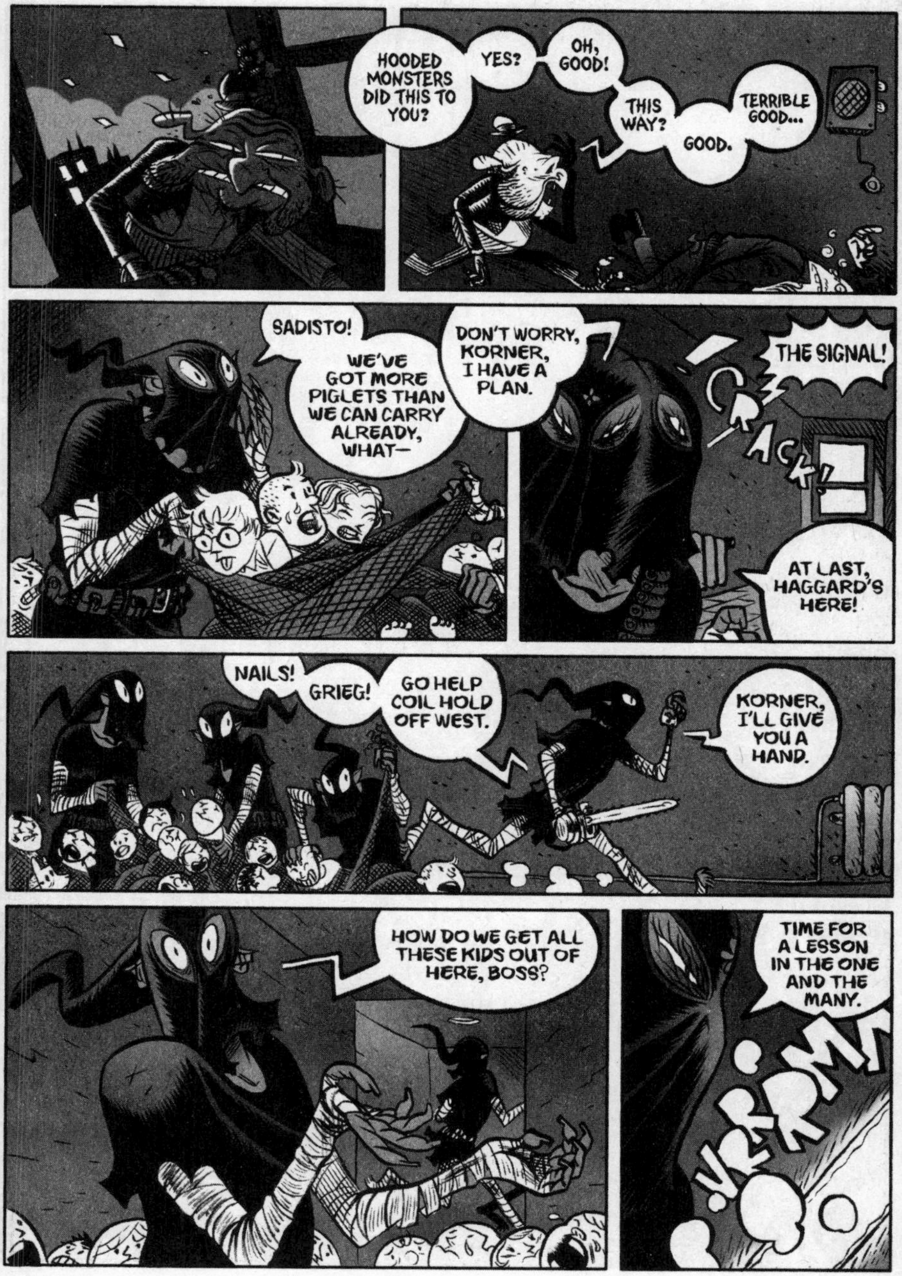
HOODED MONSTERS DID THIS TO YOU?
YES?
OH, GOOD!
THIS WAY?
GOOD.
TERRIBLE GOOD...
SADISTO!
WE'VE GOT MORE PIGLETS THAN WE CAN CARRY ALREADY, WHAT—
DON'T WORRY, KORNER, I HAVE A PLAN.
CRACK!
THE SIGNAL!
AT LAST, HAGGARD'S HERE!
NAILS!
GRIEG!
GO HELP COIL HOLD OFF WEST.
KORNER, I'LL GIVE YOU A HAND.
HOW DO WE GET ALL THESE KIDS OUT OF HERE, BOSS?
TIME FOR A LESSON IN THE ONE AND THE MANY.
VRRRM

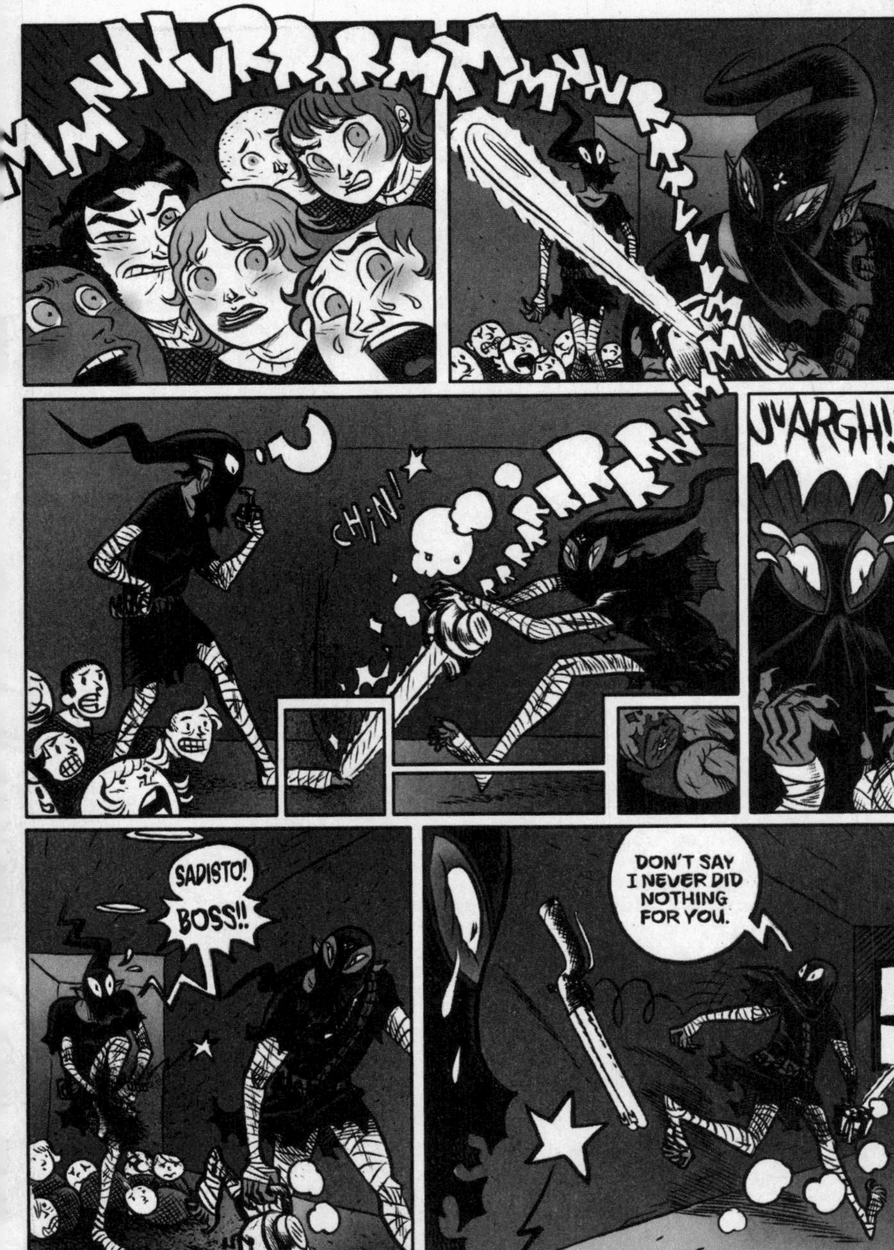
MMNNVRRRRMMMNNVRRRVVMMM
RRRRRRRRRNNN
CHiN!
JUARGH!!
SADISTO!
BOSS!!
DON'T SAY I NEVER DID NOTHING FOR YOU.

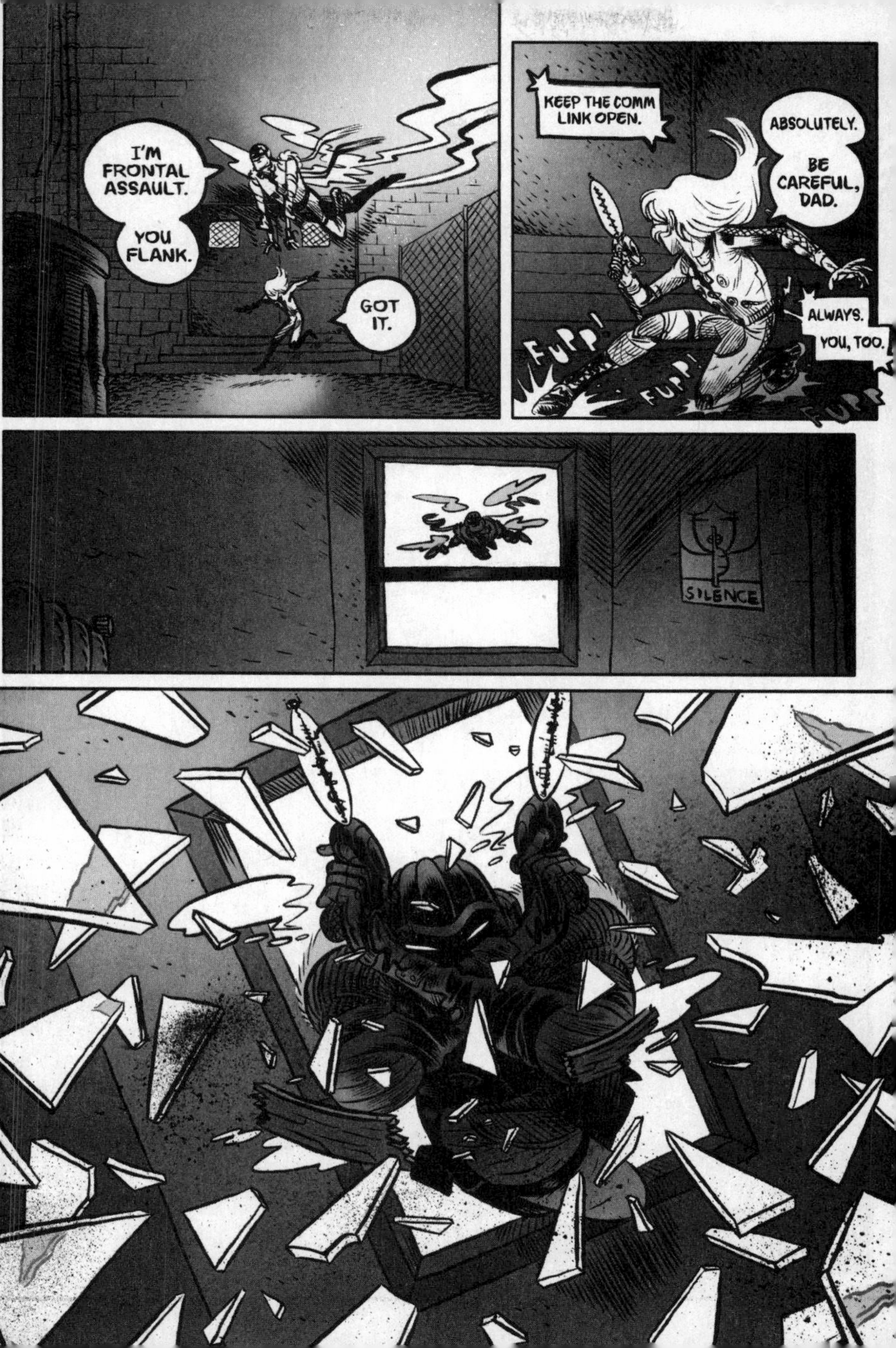
I'M FRONTAL ASSAULT.
YOU FLANK.
GOT IT.
KEEP THE COMM LINK OPEN.
ABSOLUTELY.
BE CAREFUL, DAD.
FUPP!
FUPP!
ALWAYS.
YOU, TOO.
FUPP
SILENCE

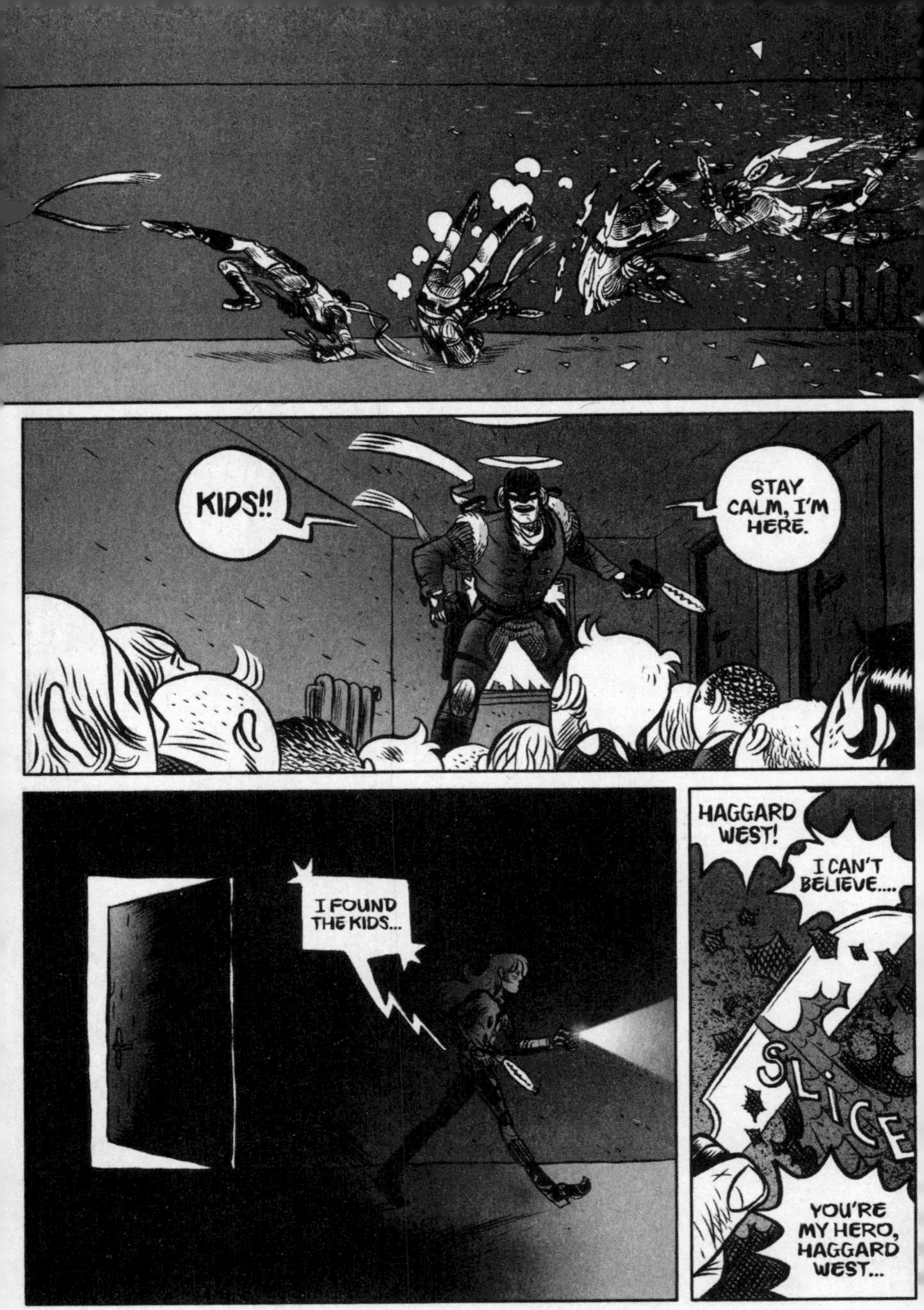
KIDS!!
STAY CALM, I'M HERE.
I FOUND THE KIDS...
HAGGARD WEST!
I CAN'T BELIEVE....
SLICE
YOU'RE MY HERO, HAGGARD WEST...

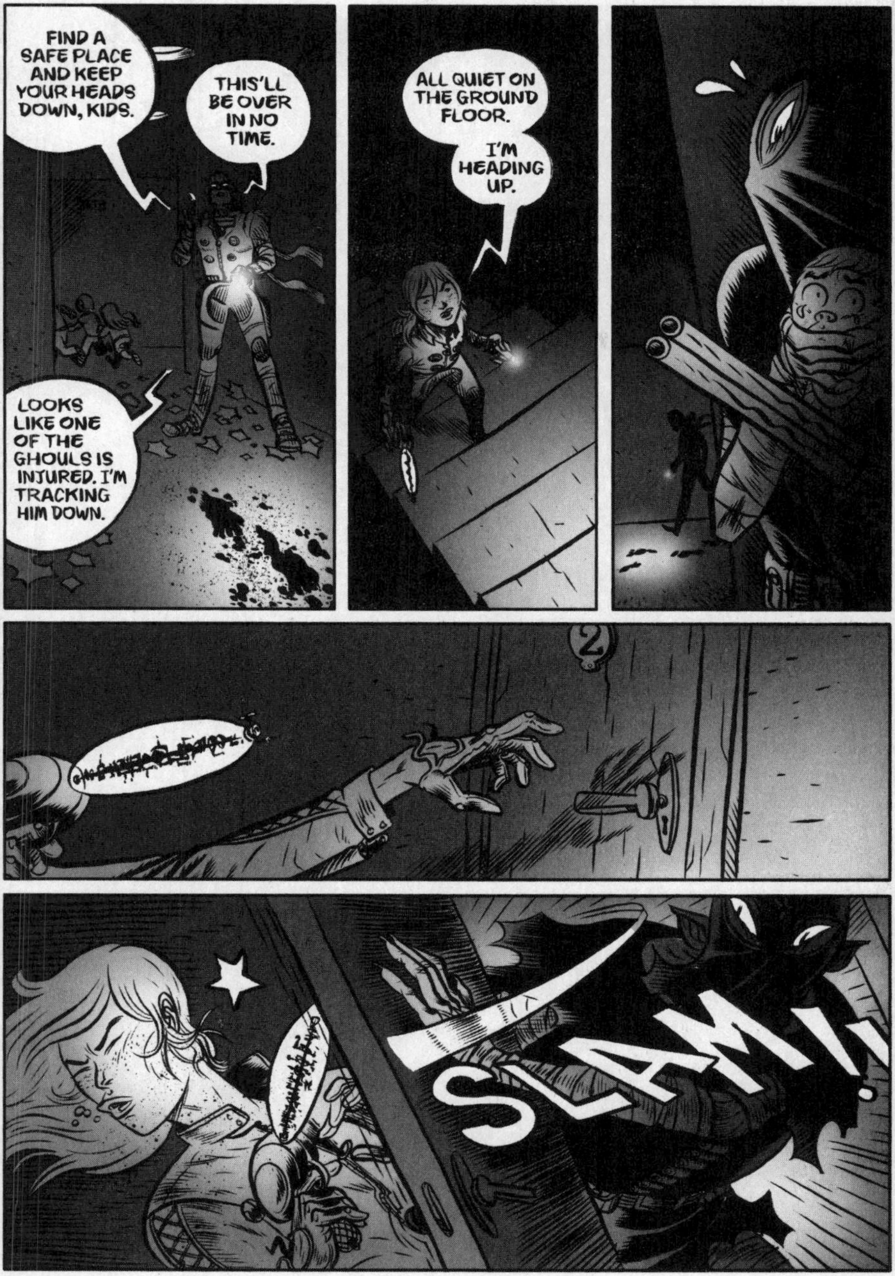
FIND A SAFE PLACE AND KEEP YOUR HEADS DOWN, KIDS.
THIS'LL BE OVER IN NO TIME.
LOOKS LIKE ONE OF THE GHOULS IS INJURED. I'M TRACKING HIM DOWN.
ALL QUIET ON THE GROUND FLOOR.
I'M HEADING UP.
2
SLAM!!

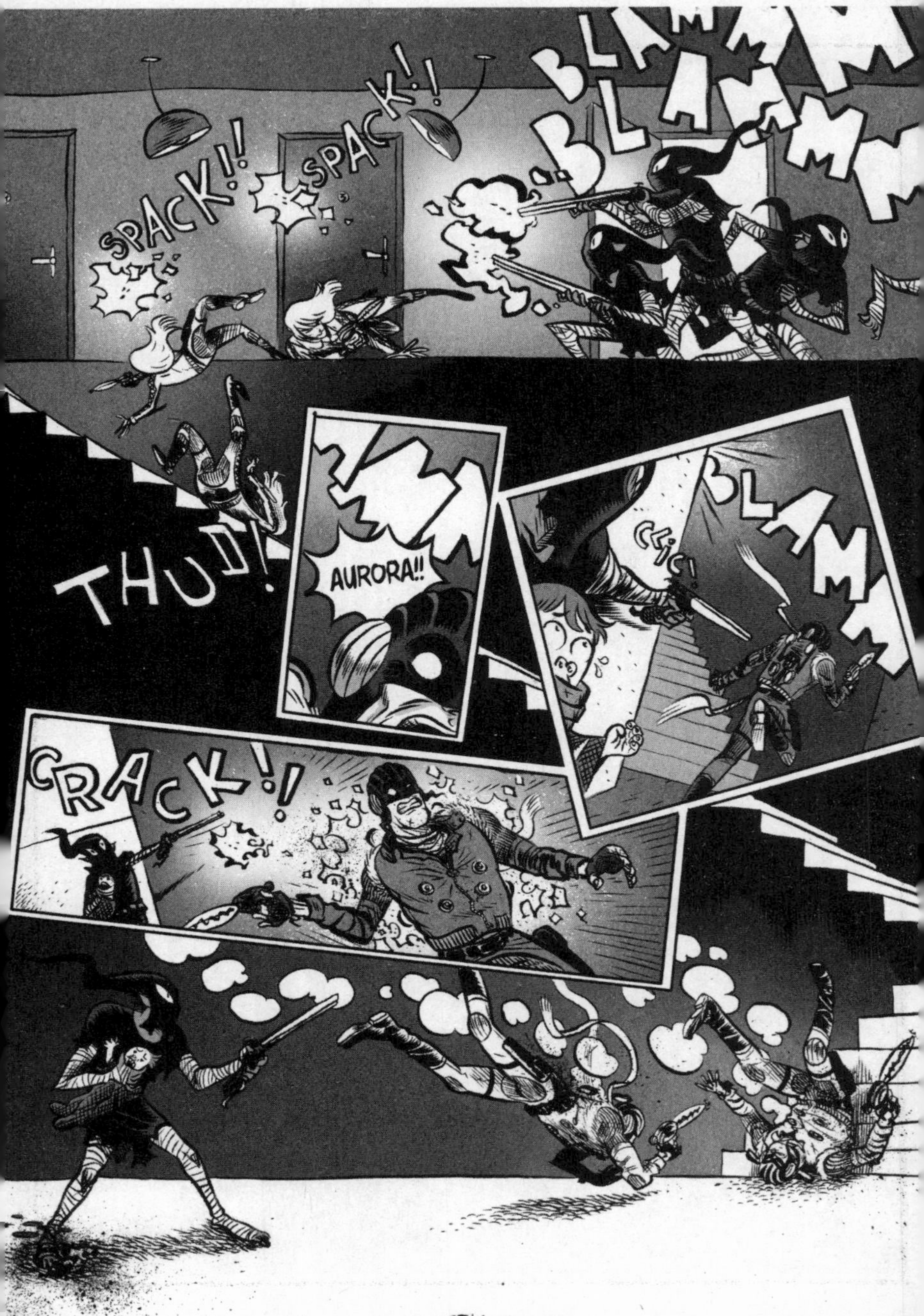
SPACK!!
SPACK!!
BLAMM
BLAMMM
THUD!
AURORA!!
BLAMM
CRACK!!

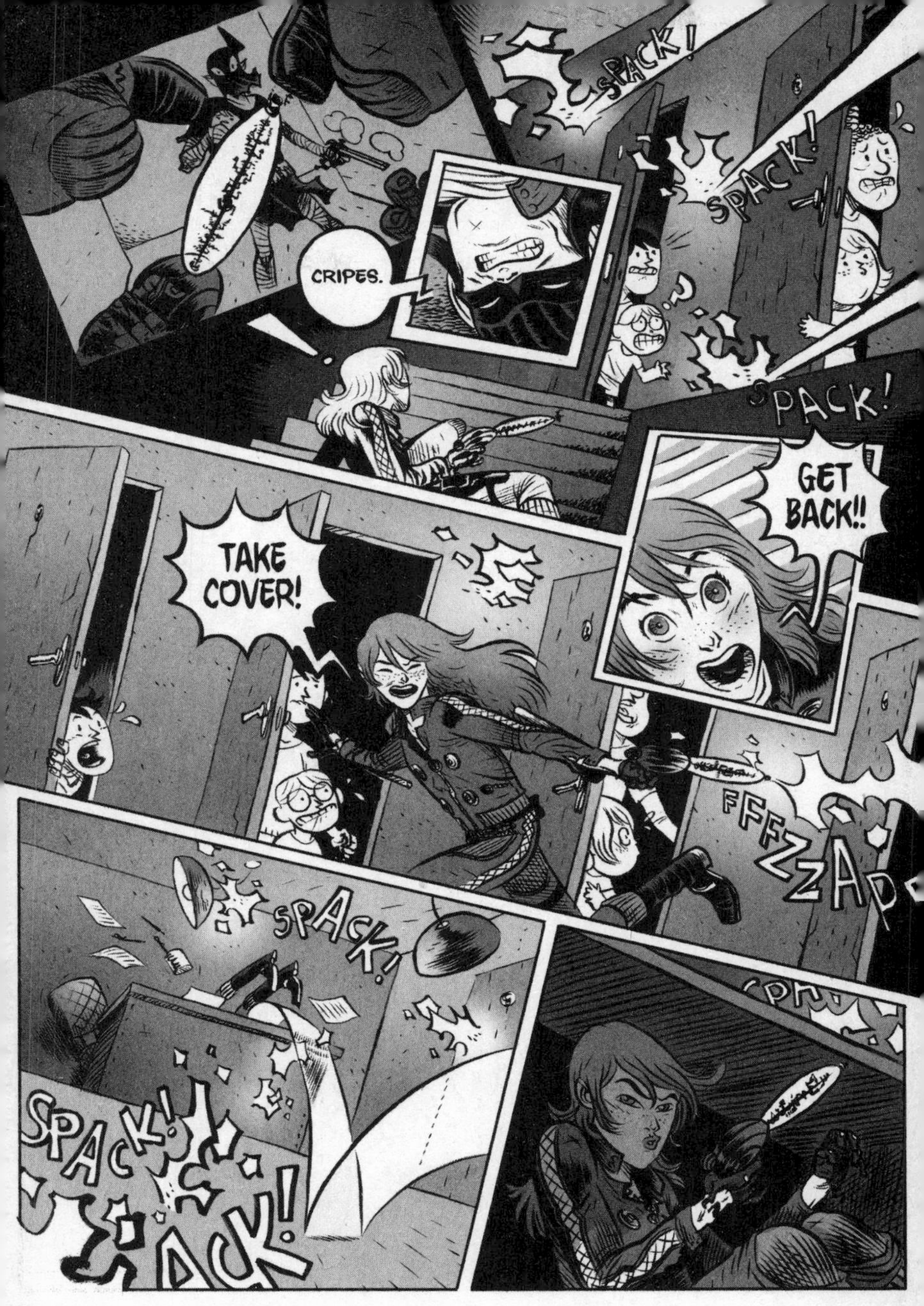
SPACK!
SPACK!
CRIPES.
SPACK!
GET BACK!!
TAKE COVER!
FFFZZAP
SPACK!
SPACK!
ACK!

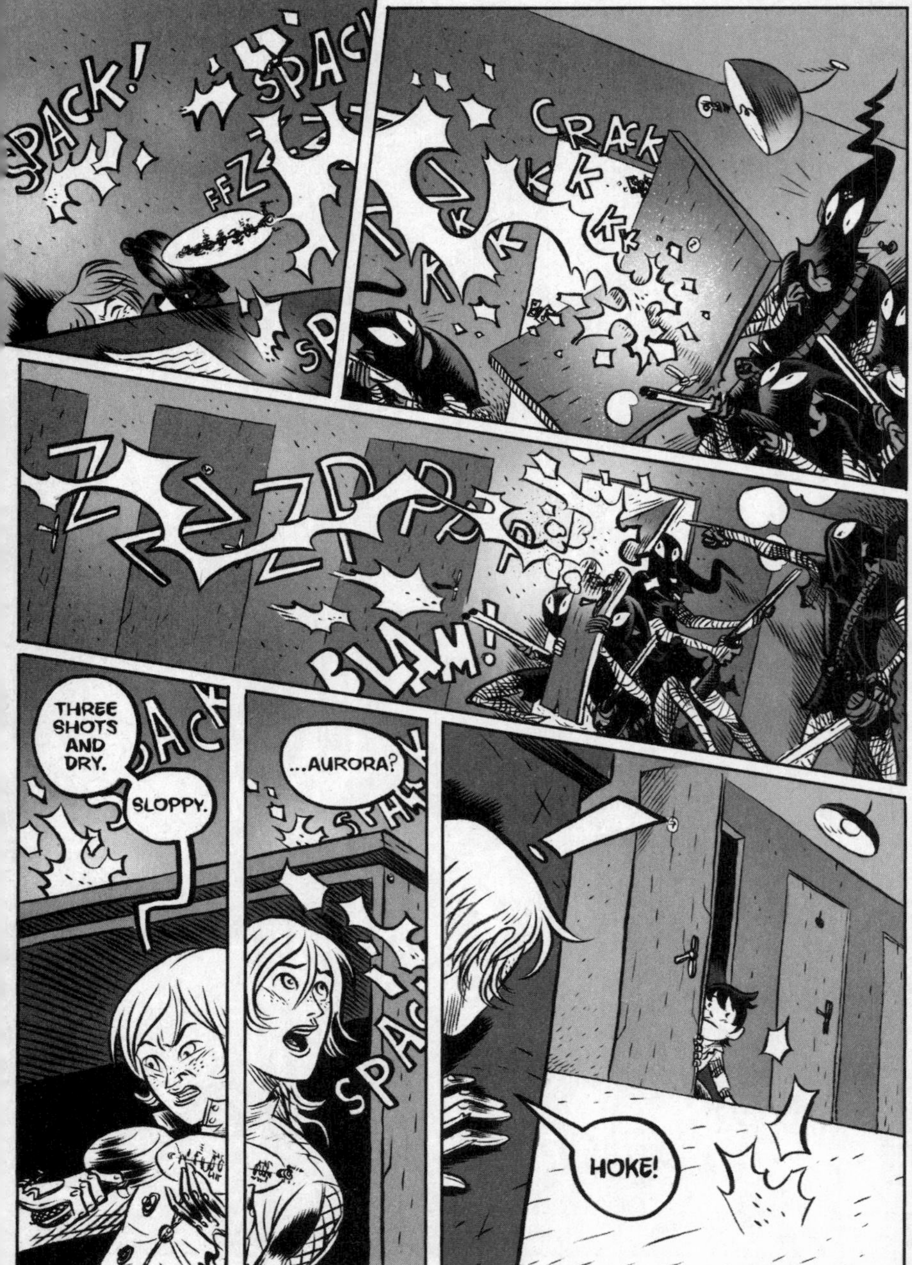

SPACK!
SPACK
FFZZ
CRACK
KKKK
SP
ZZZZPPPP
BLAM!
THREE SHOTS AND DRY.
SLOPPY.
...AURORA?
HOKE!

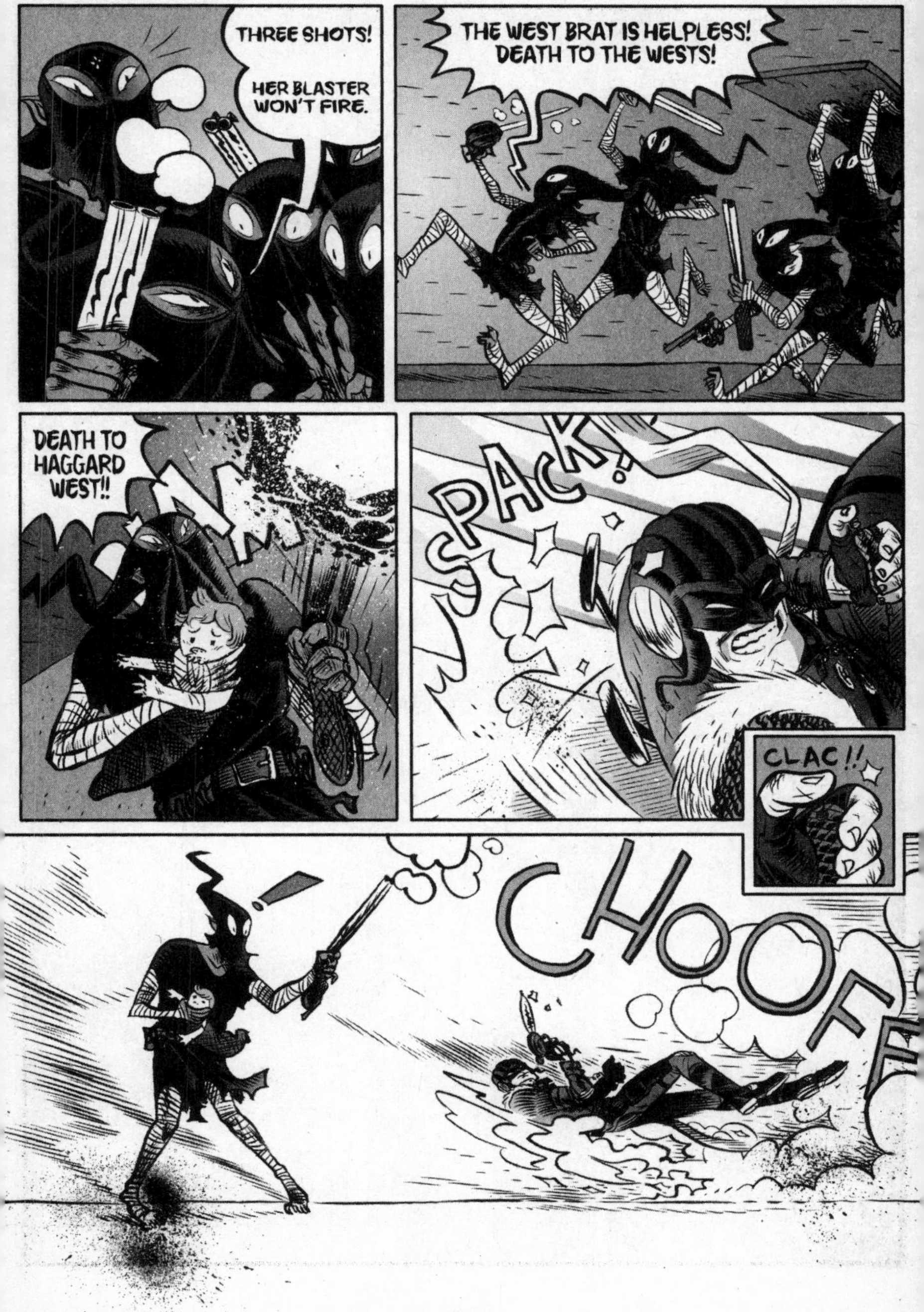
THREE SHOTS!
HER BLASTER WON'T FIRE.
THE WEST BRAT IS HELPLESS! DEATH TO THE WESTS!
DEATH TO HAGGARD WEST!!
SPACK!
CLAC!!
CHOOFF

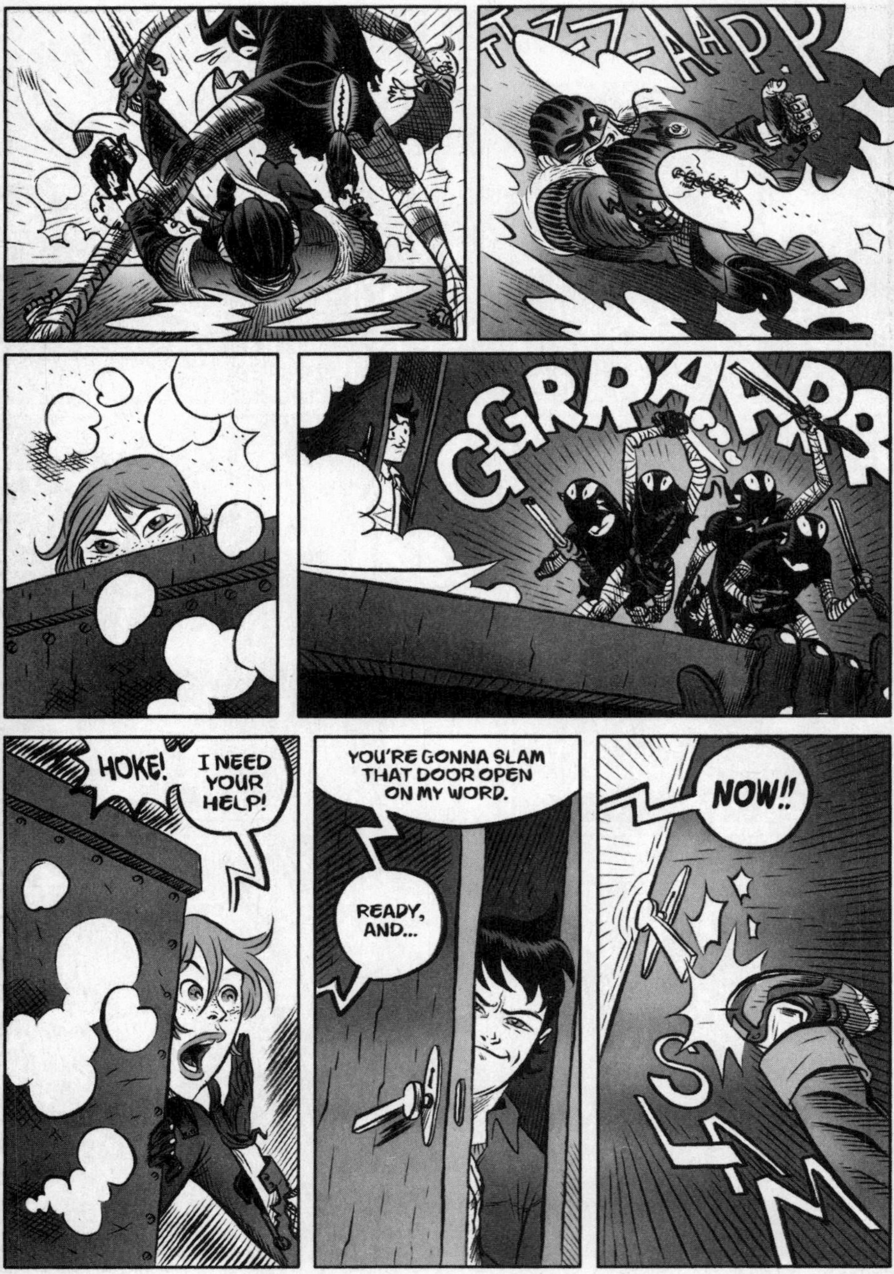
TZZ-AAPR
GGRRAAARR
HOKE!
I NEED YOUR HELP!
YOU'RE GONNA SLAM THAT DOOR OPEN ON MY WORD.
READY, AND...
NOW!!
SLAM

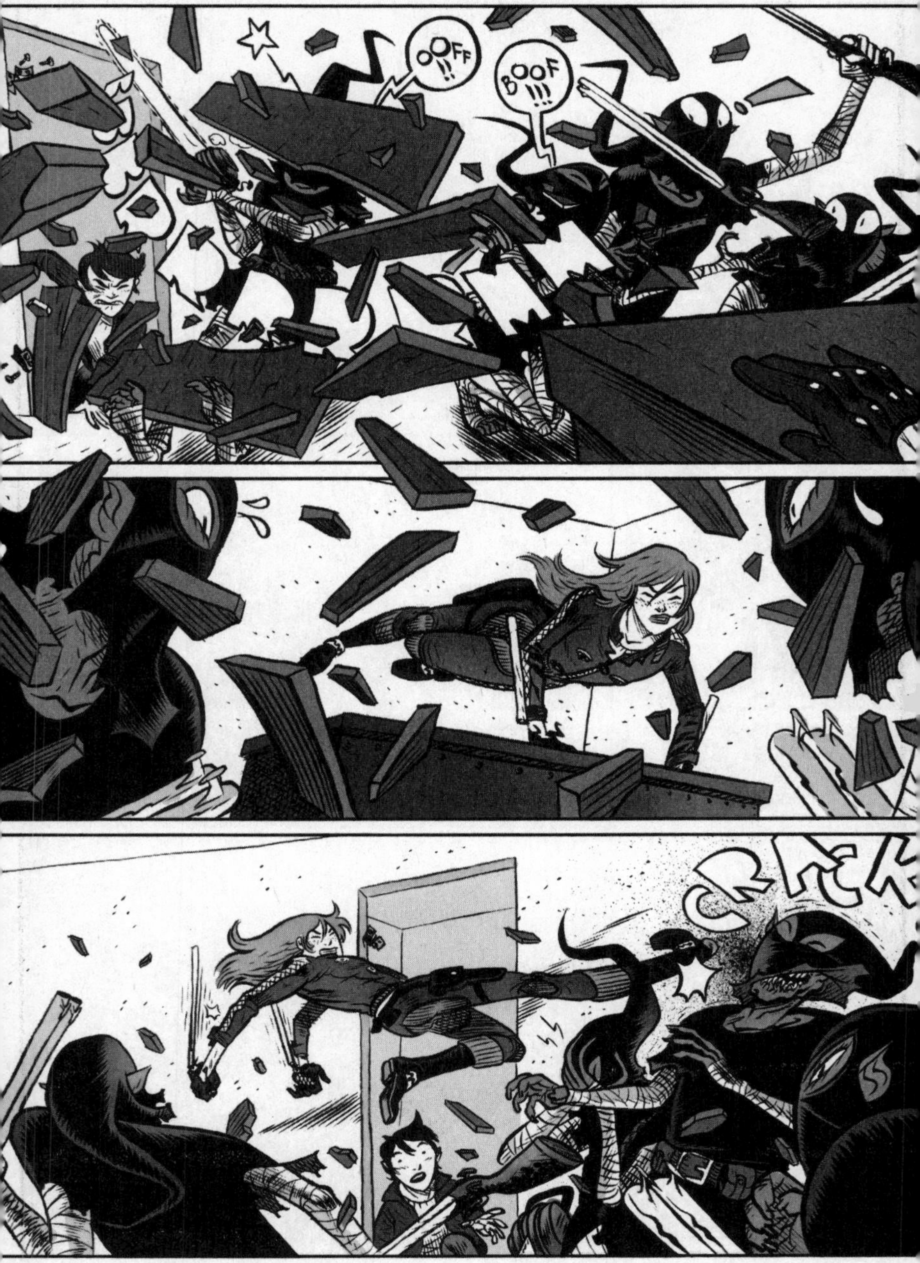

OOFF !!
BOOF !!!

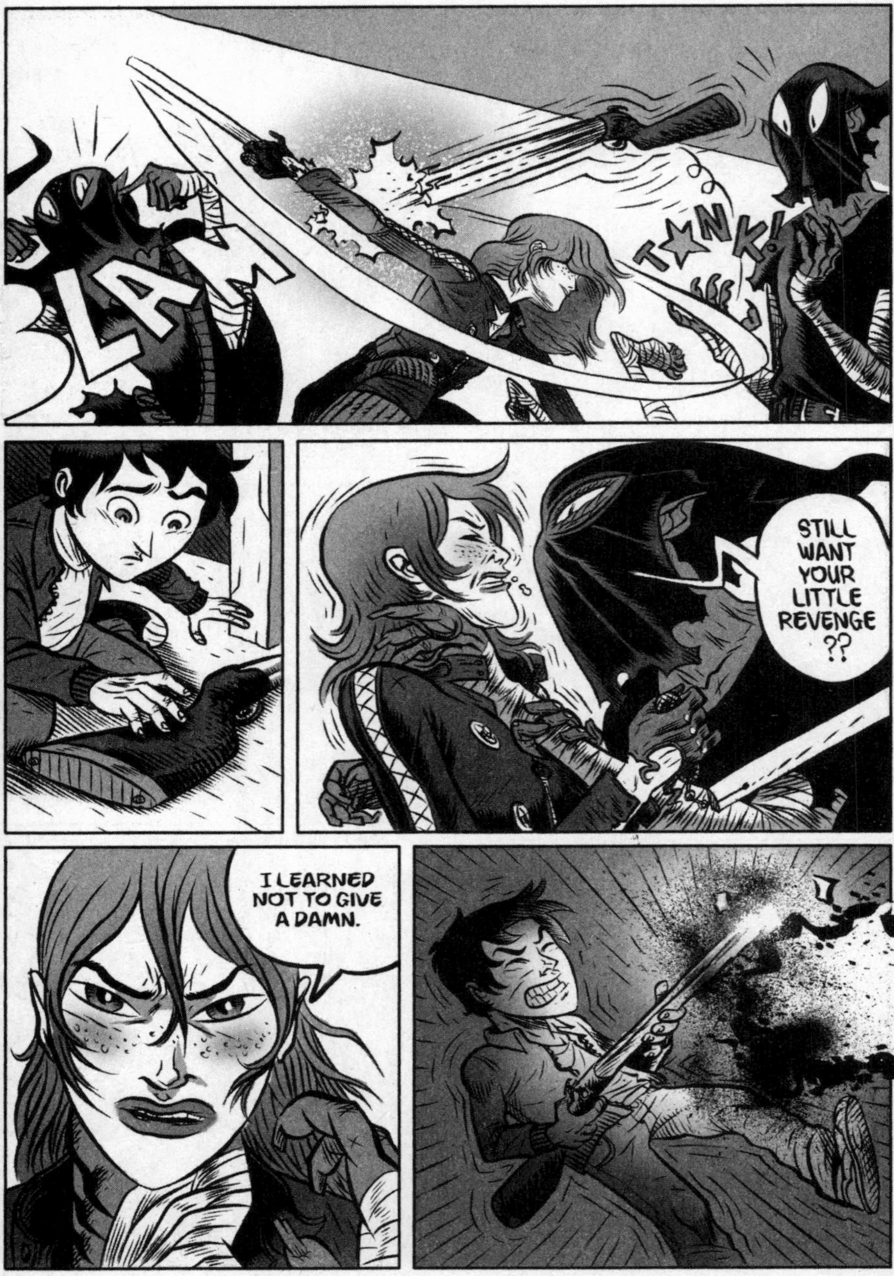

LAM
T★NK!
STILL WANT YOUR LITTLE REVENGE ??
I LEARNED NOT TO GIVE A DAMN.

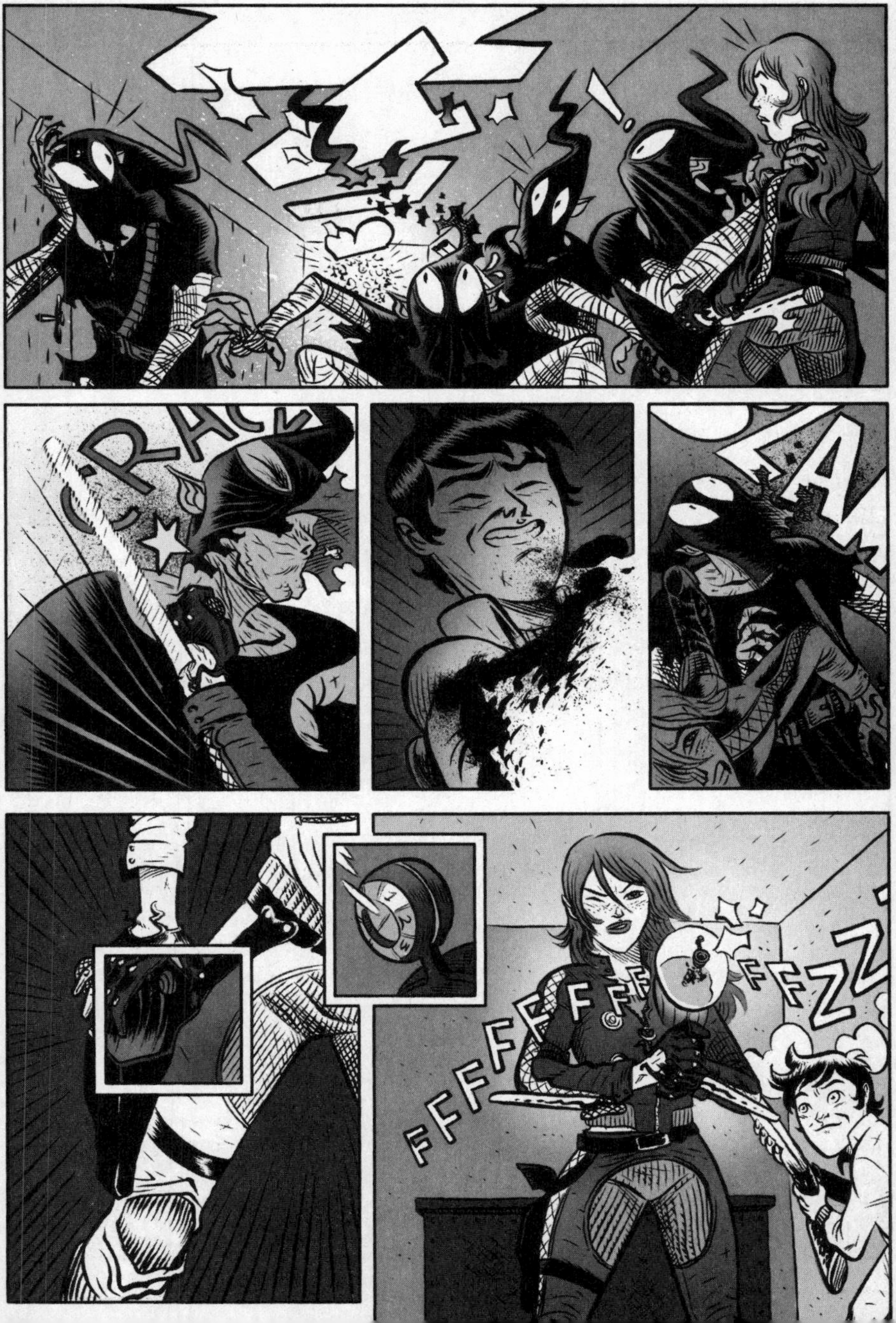

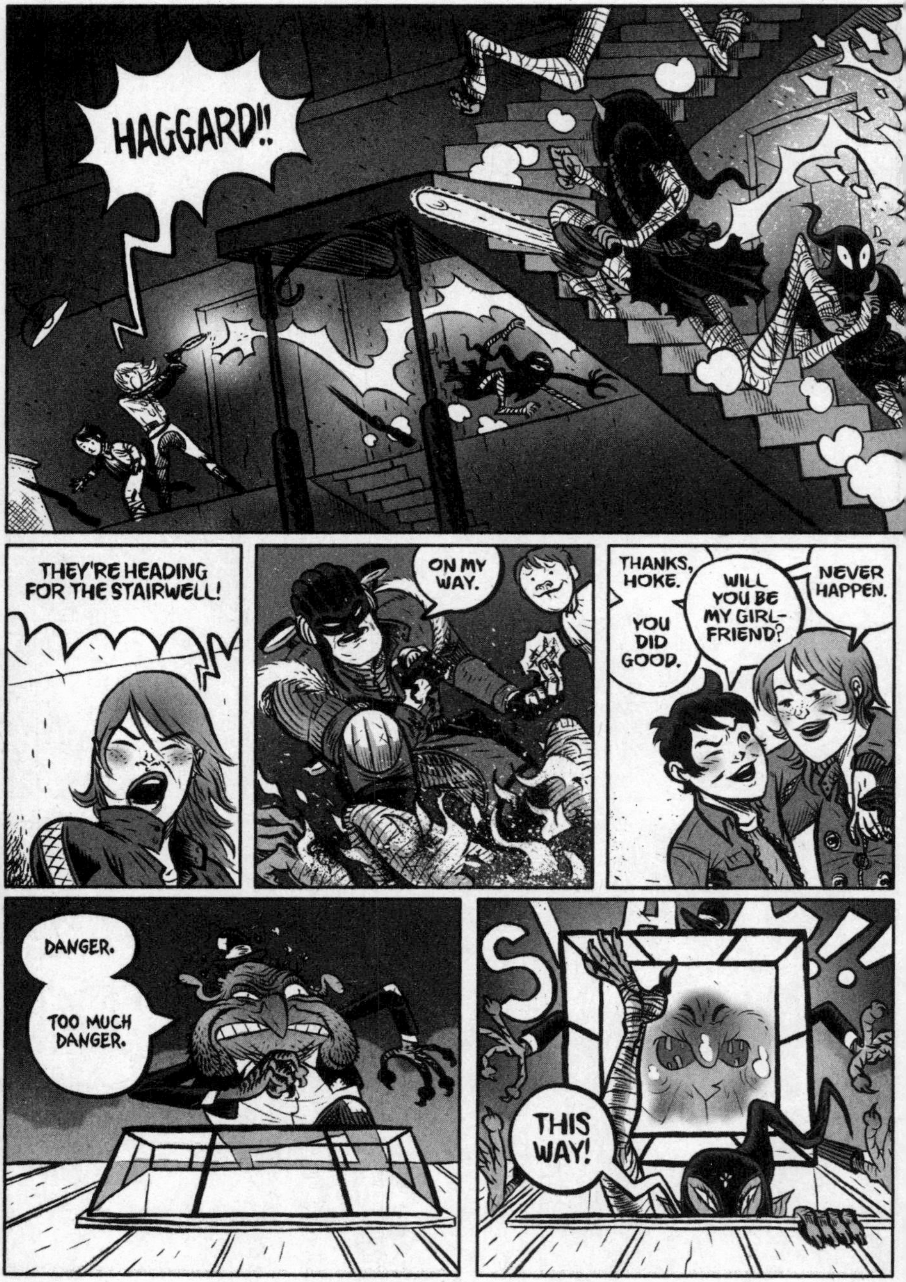
HAGGARD!!
THEY'RE HEADING FOR THE STAIRWELL!
ON MY WAY.
THANKS, HOKE.
YOU DID GOOD.
WILL YOU BE MY GIRL-FRIEND?
NEVER HAPPEN.
DANGER.
TOO MUCH DANGER.
S
!!
THIS WAY!

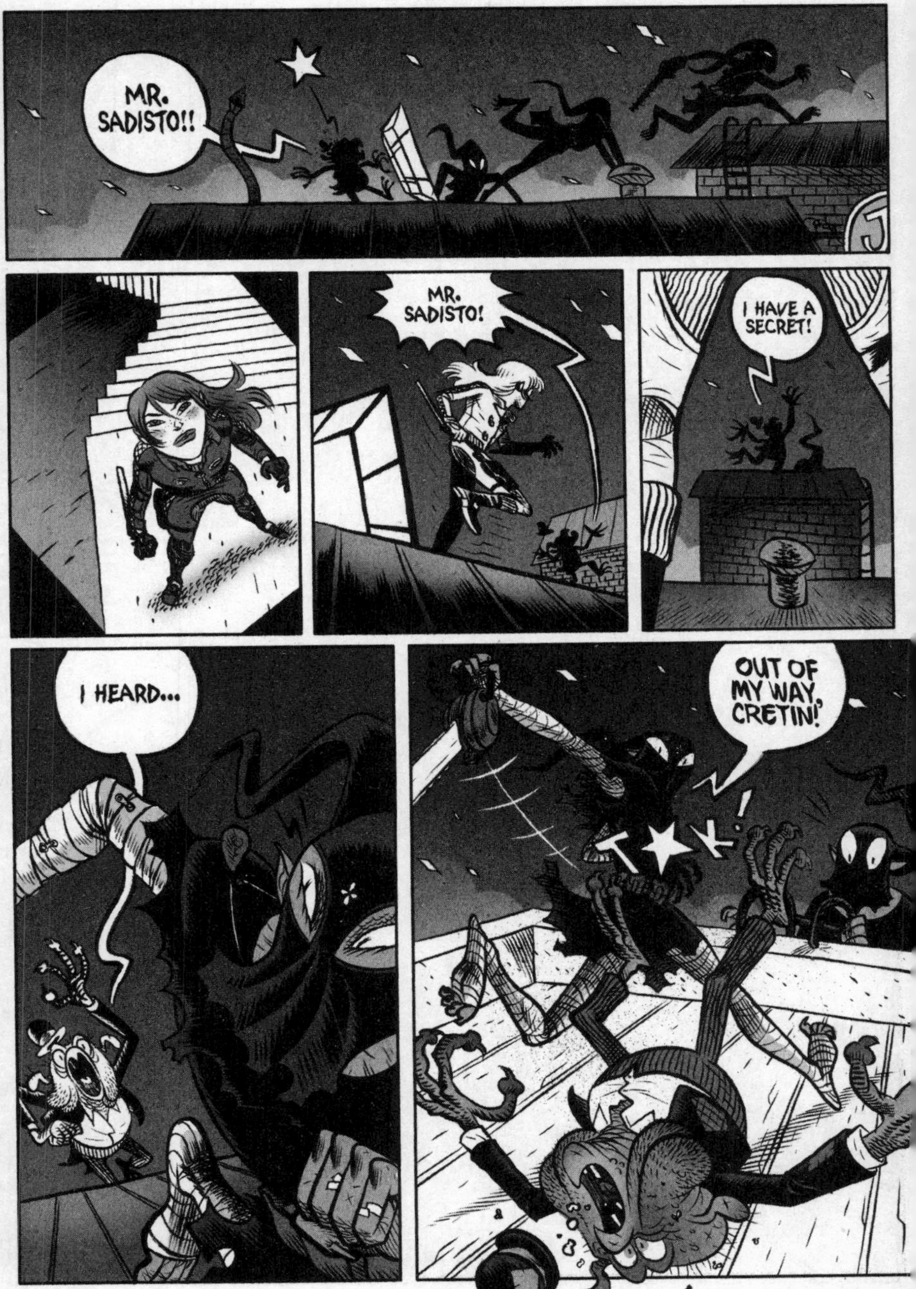
MR. SADISTO!!
MR. SADISTO!
I HAVE A SECRET!
I HEARD...
OUT OF MY WAY, CRETIN!
TOK!

WAIT! SADISTO!! I HAVE A TERRIBLE SECRET!

IT'S HAGGARD!

ARCOPOLIS GARBAGE

HAGGARD WEST!!! HE KILLED HIS—

CR★CK!

WHAT DID YOU HEAR?

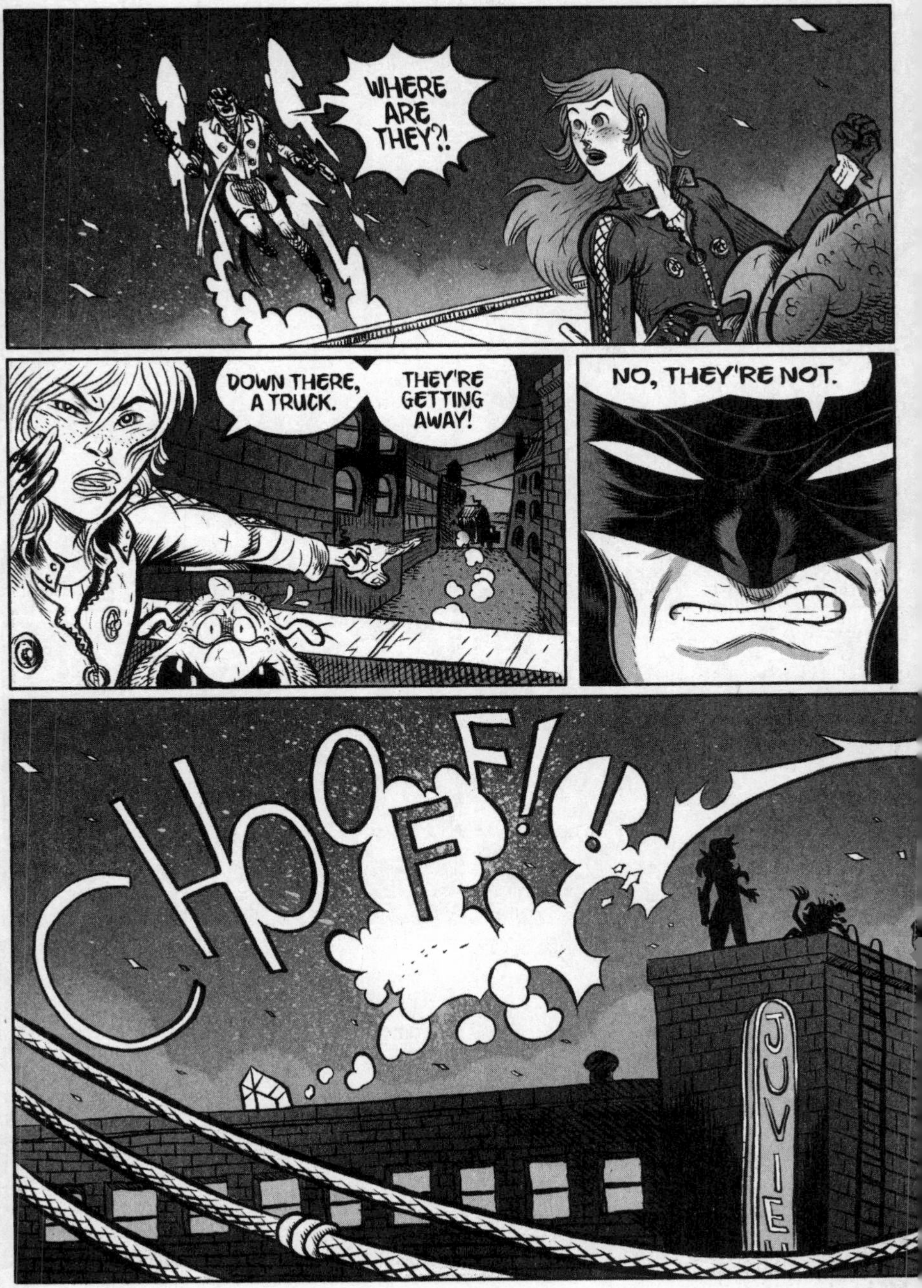
WHERE ARE THEY?!
DOWN THERE, A TRUCK.
THEY'RE GETTING AWAY!
NO, THEY'RE NOT.
CHOOFF!
JUVIE

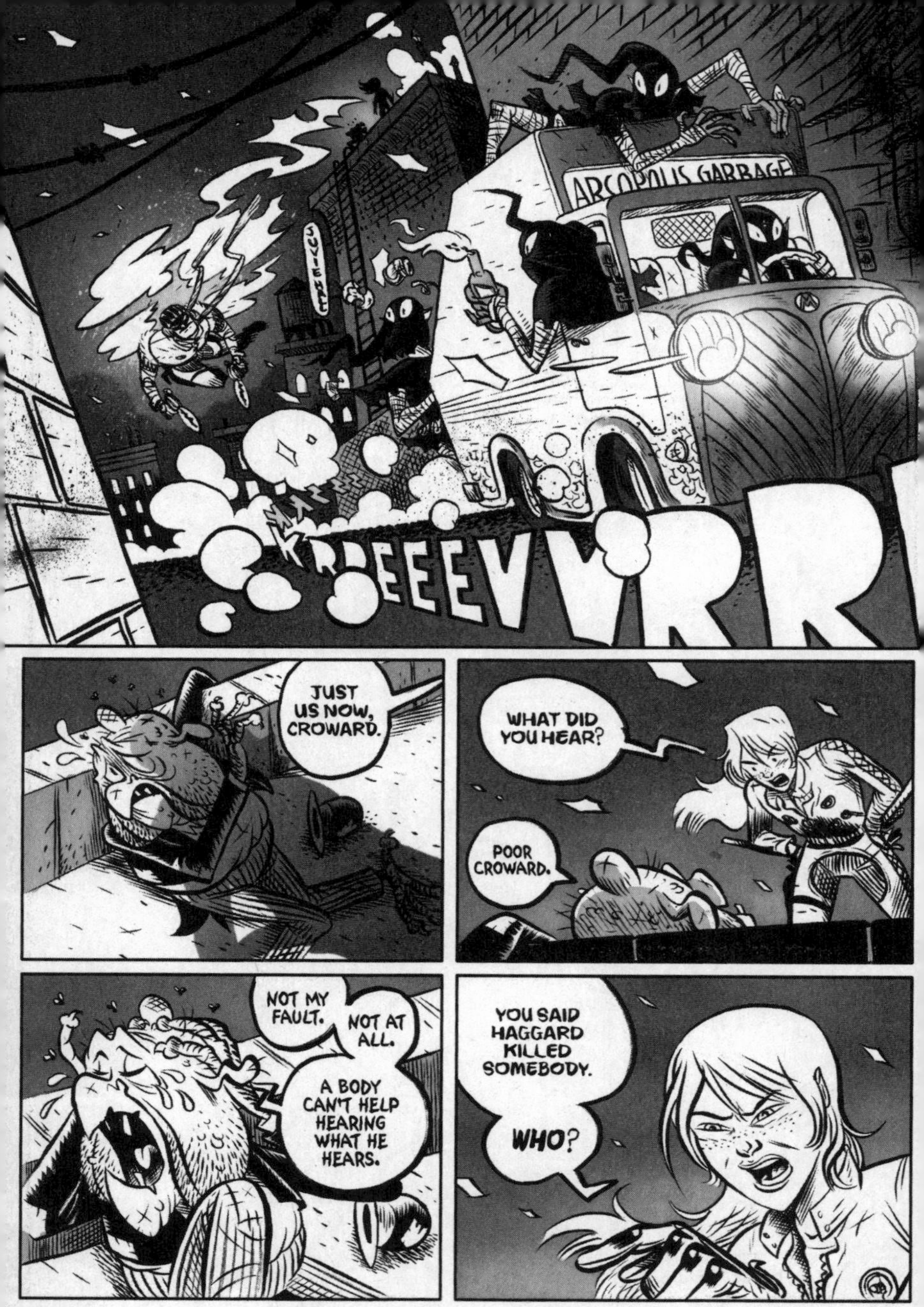
ARCOPOLIS GARBAGE
JUVIE HALL
KRREEEVVRRR
JUST US NOW, CROWARD.
WHAT DID YOU HEAR?
POOR CROWARD.
NOT MY FAULT.
NOT AT ALL.
A BODY CAN'T HELP HEARING WHAT HE HEARS.
YOU SAID HAGGARD KILLED SOMEBODY.
WHO?

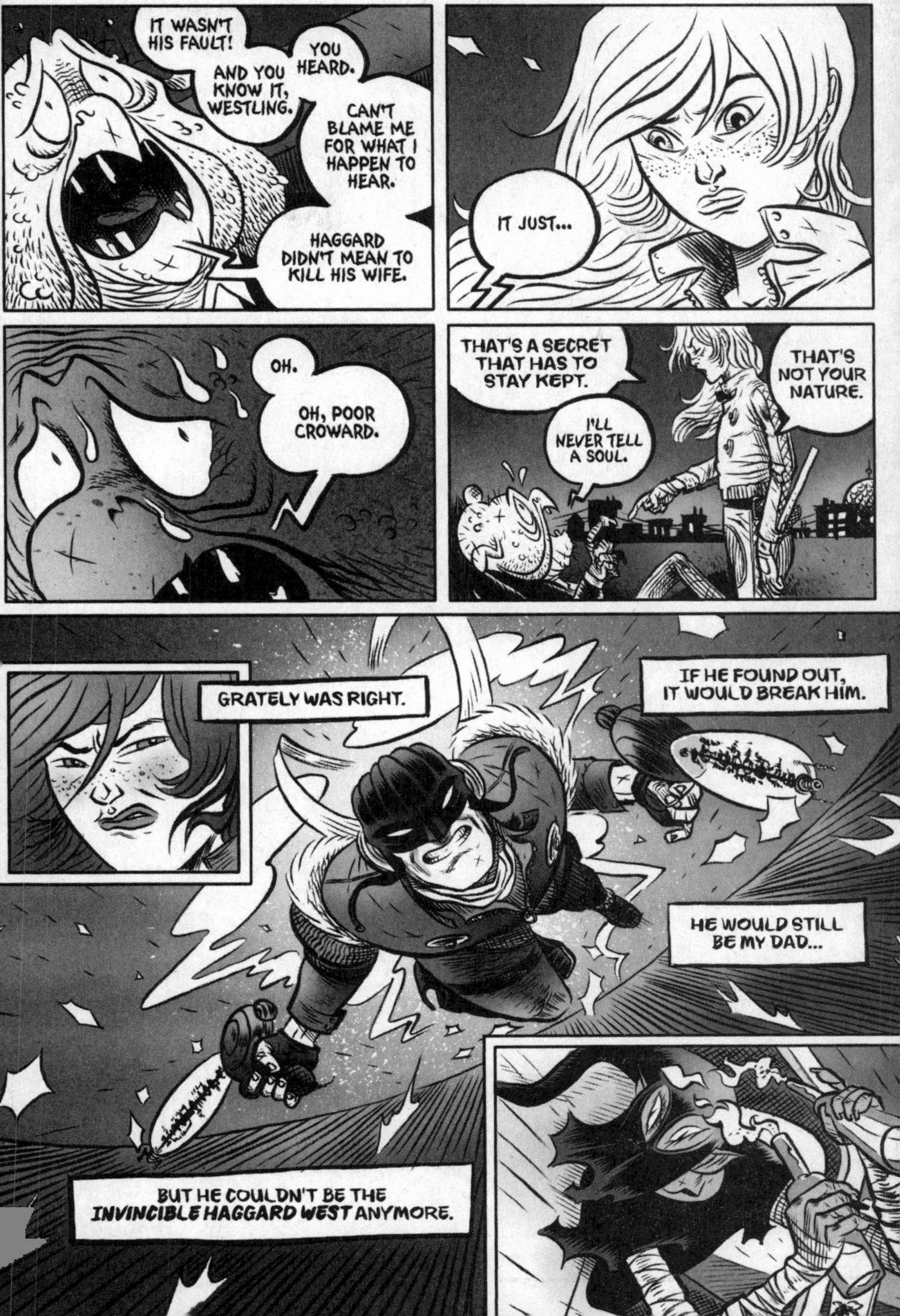
IT WASN'T HIS FAULT!
YOU HEARD.
AND YOU KNOW IT, WESTLING.
CAN'T BLAME ME FOR WHAT I HAPPEN TO HEAR.
HAGGARD DIDN'T MEAN TO KILL HIS WIFE.
IT JUST...
OH.
OH, POOR CROWARD.
THAT'S A SECRET THAT HAS TO STAY KEPT.
I'LL NEVER TELL A SOUL.
THAT'S NOT YOUR NATURE.
GRATELY WAS RIGHT.
IF HE FOUND OUT, IT WOULD BREAK HIM.
HE WOULD STILL BE MY DAD...
BUT HE COULDN'T BE THE INVINCIBLE HAGGARD WEST ANYMORE.

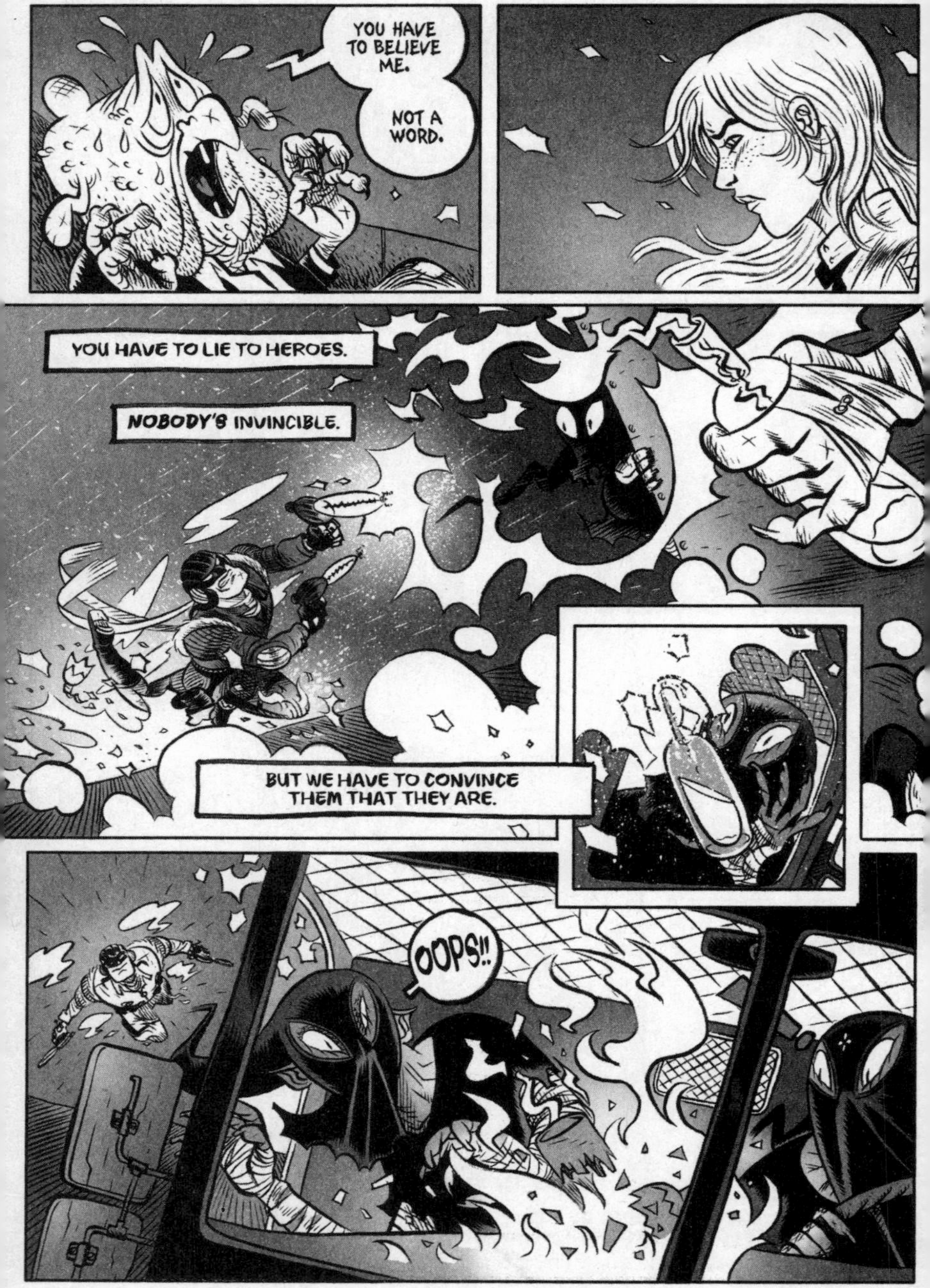
YOU HAVE TO BELIEVE ME.
NOT A WORD.
YOU HAVE TO LIE TO HEROES.
NOBODY'S INVINCIBLE.
BUT WE HAVE TO CONVINCE THEM THAT THEY ARE.
OOPS!!

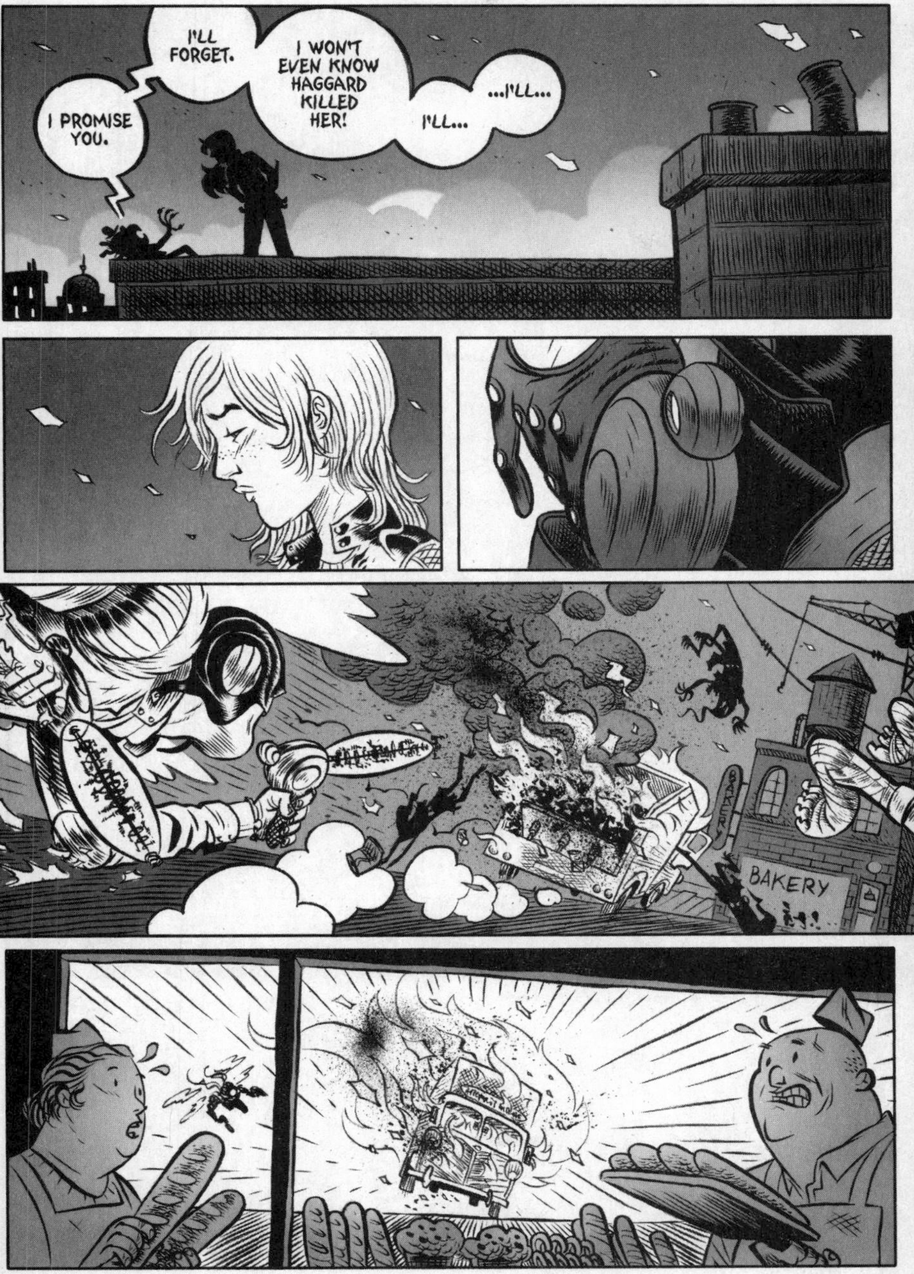
I PROMISE YOU.
I'LL FORGET.
I WON'T EVEN KNOW HAGGARD KILLED HER!
I'LL...
...I'LL...
BAKERY
BAKERY

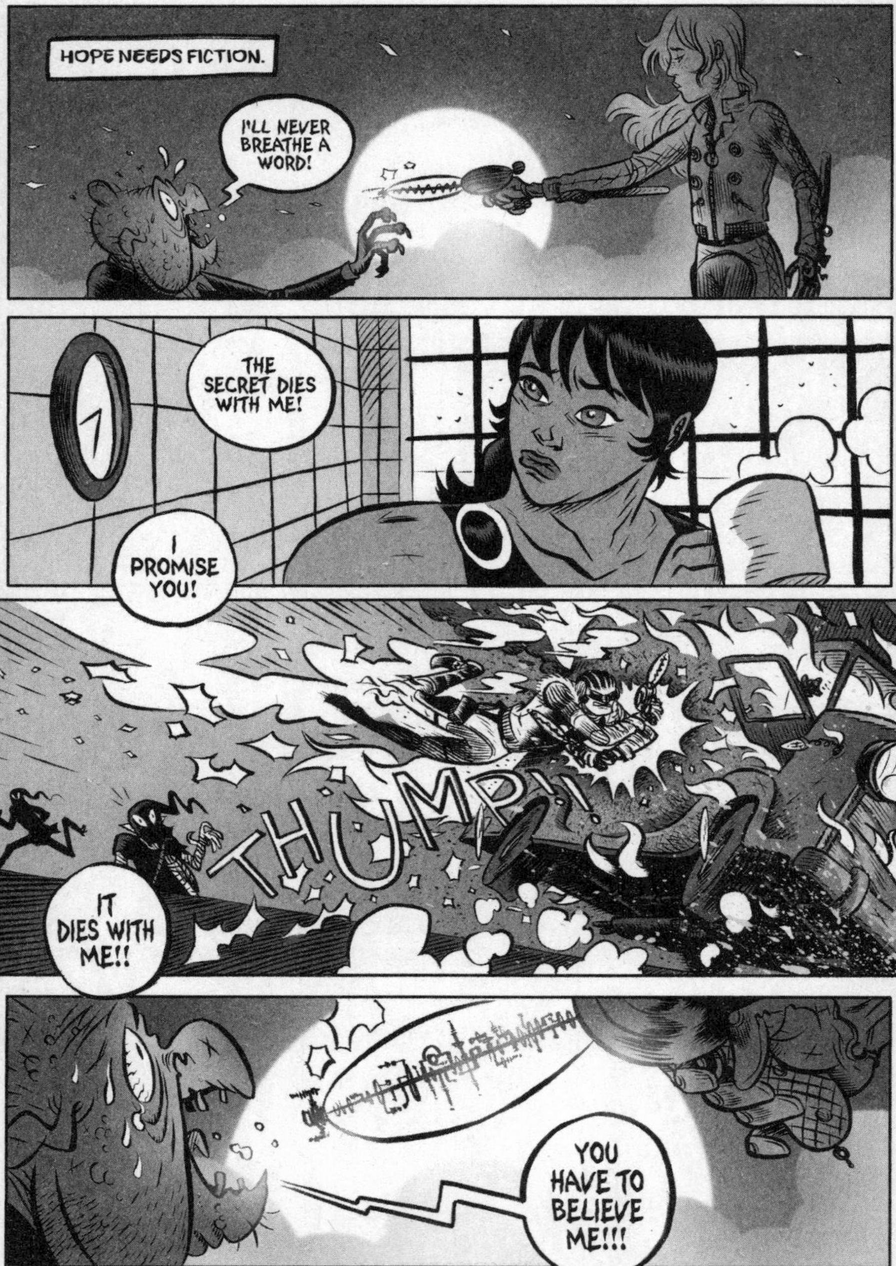
HOPE NEEDS FICTION.
I'LL NEVER BREATHE A WORD!
THE SECRET DIES WITH ME!
I PROMISE YOU!
THUMP!!
IT DIES WITH ME!!
YOU HAVE TO BELIEVE ME!!!

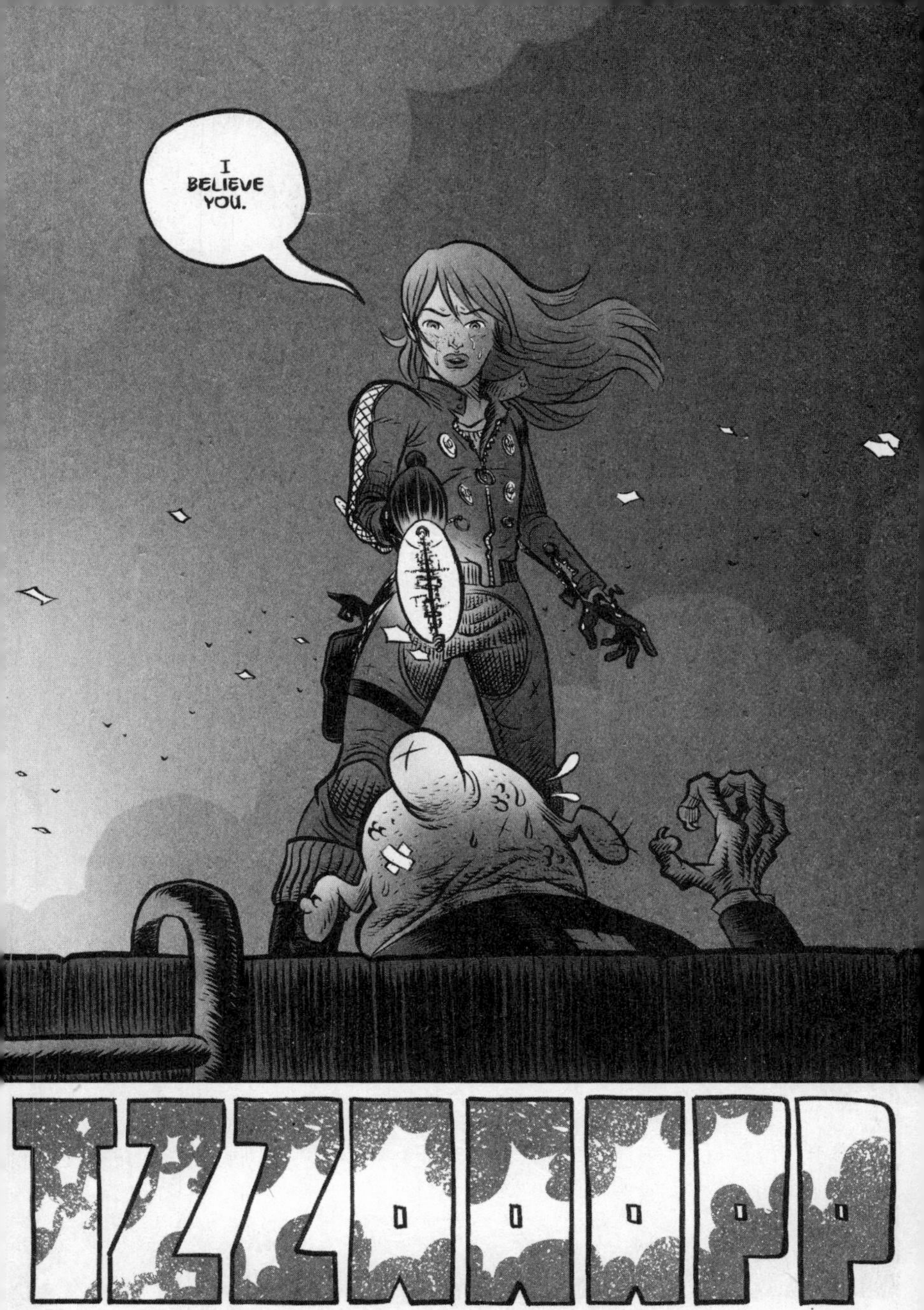
I BELIEVE YOU.
TZZOOOPP

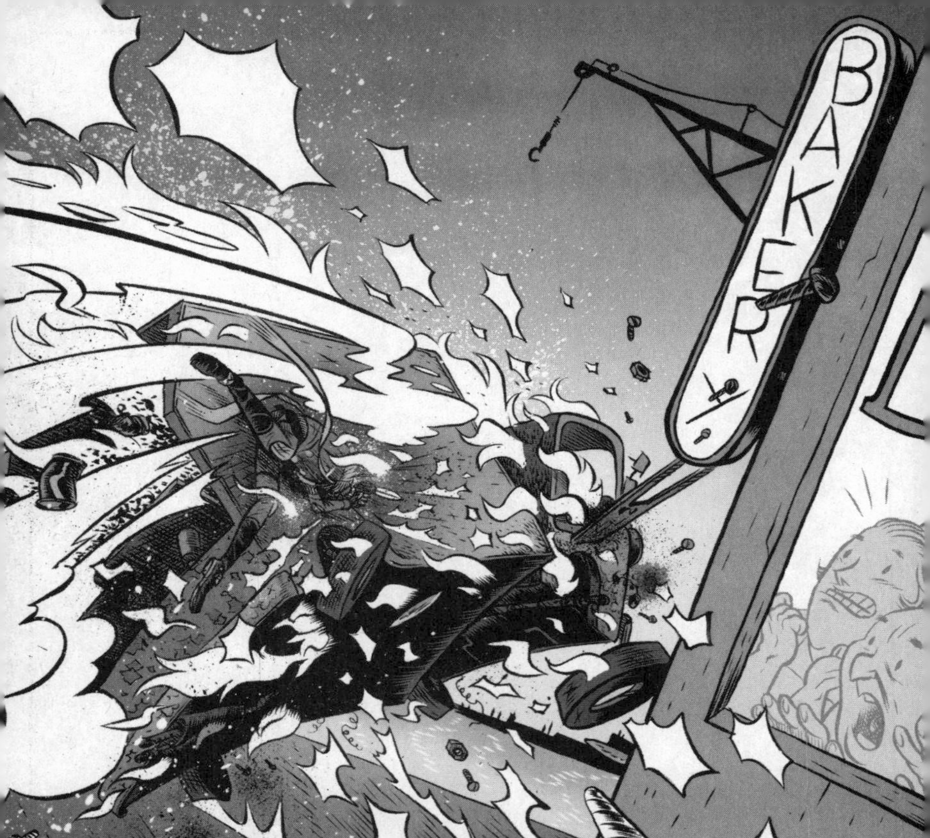
BAKER
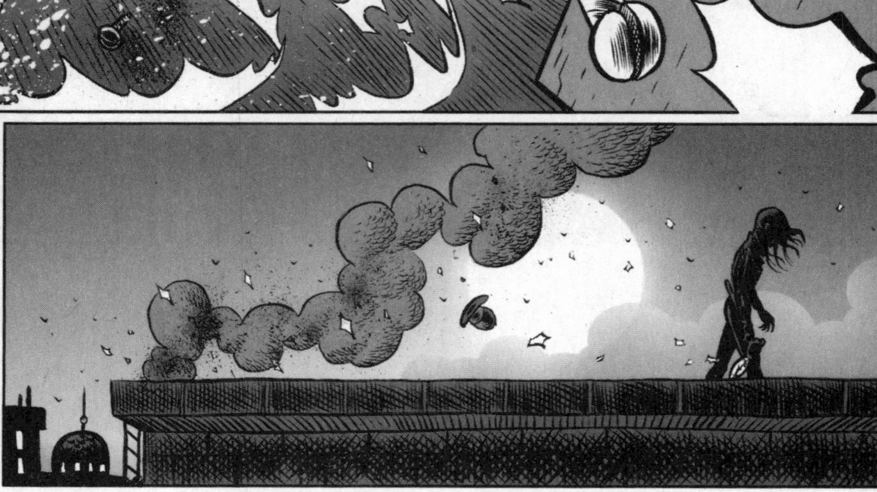

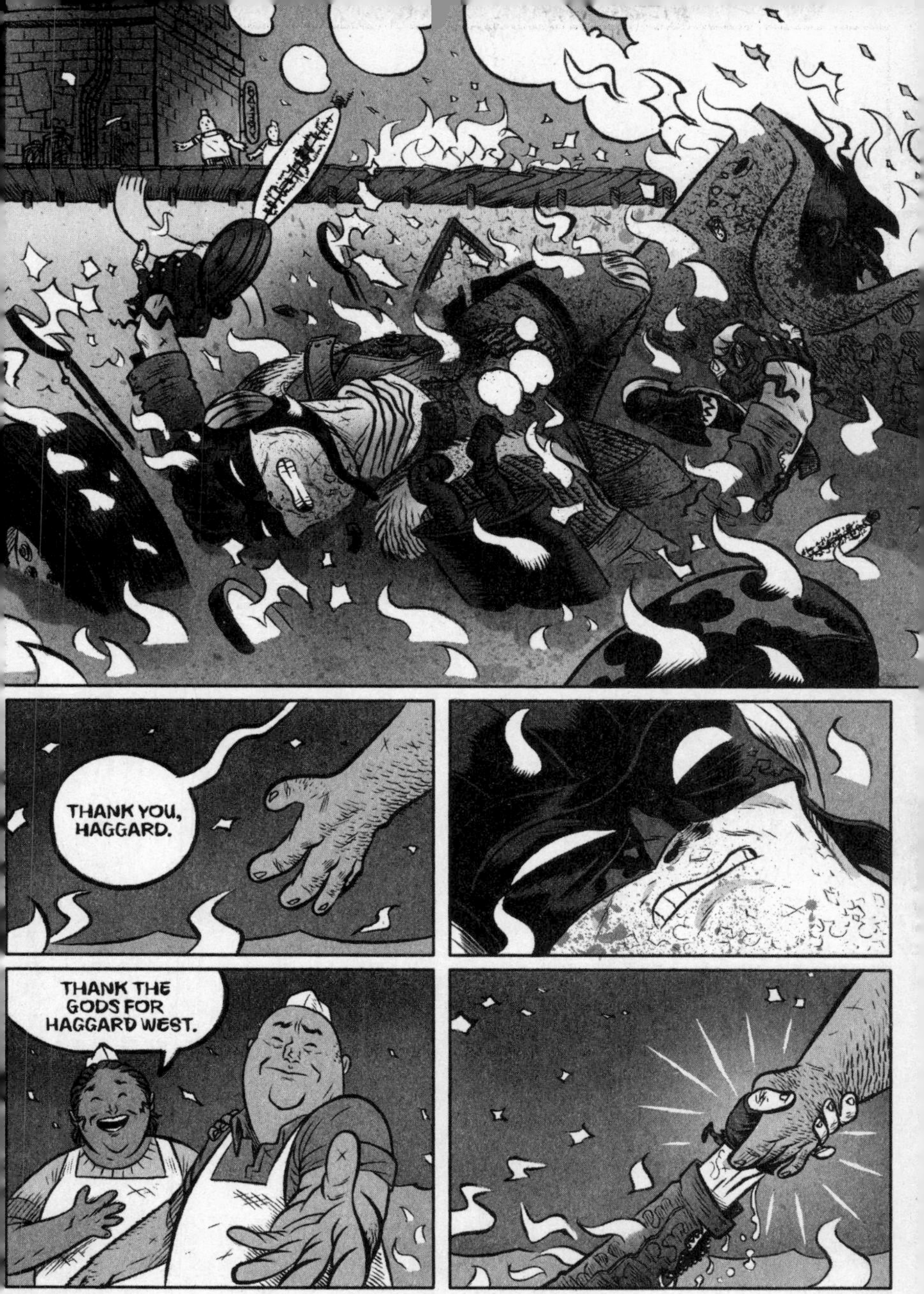
THANK YOU, HAGGARD.
THANK THE GODS FOR HAGGARD WEST.

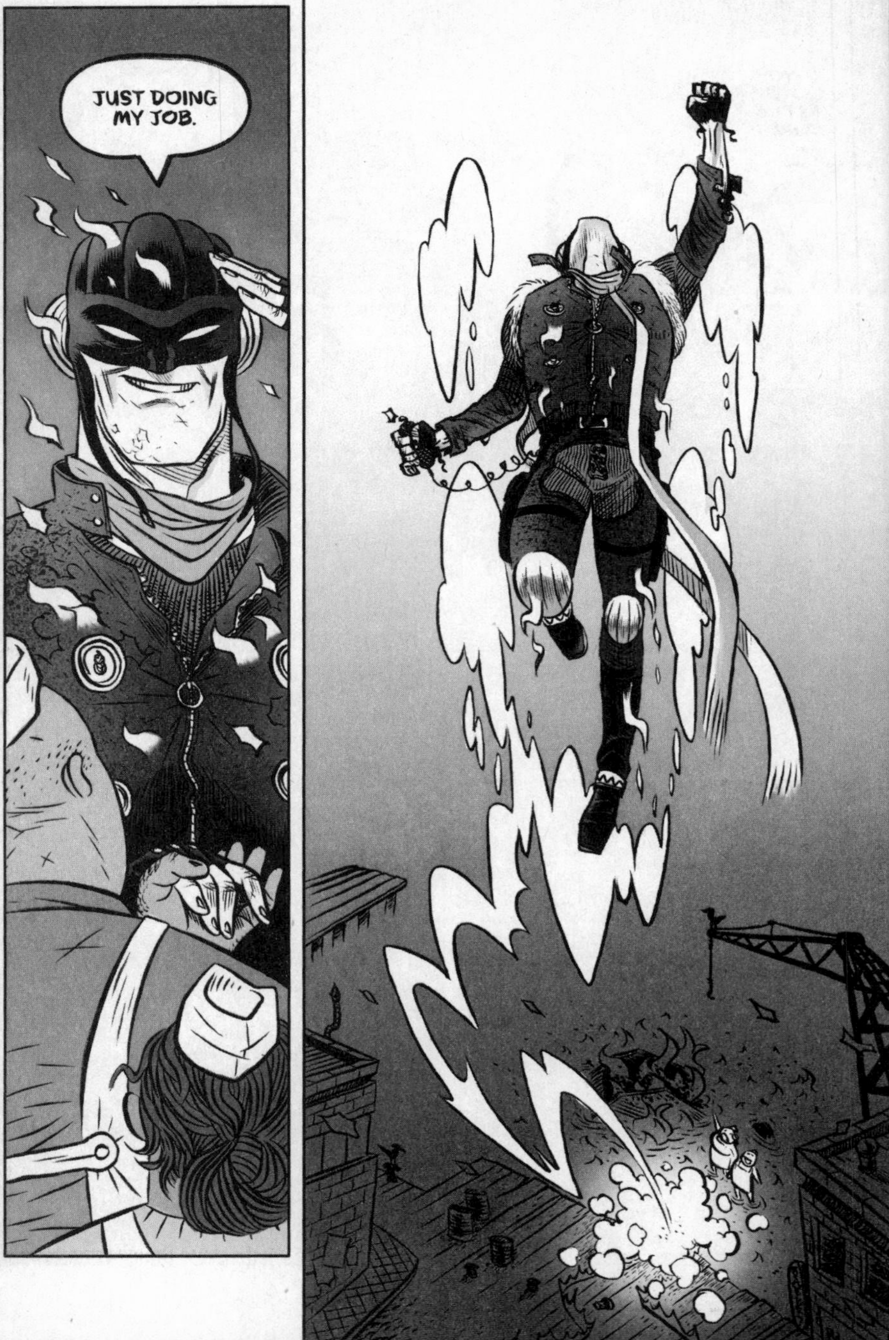
JUST DOING MY JOB.

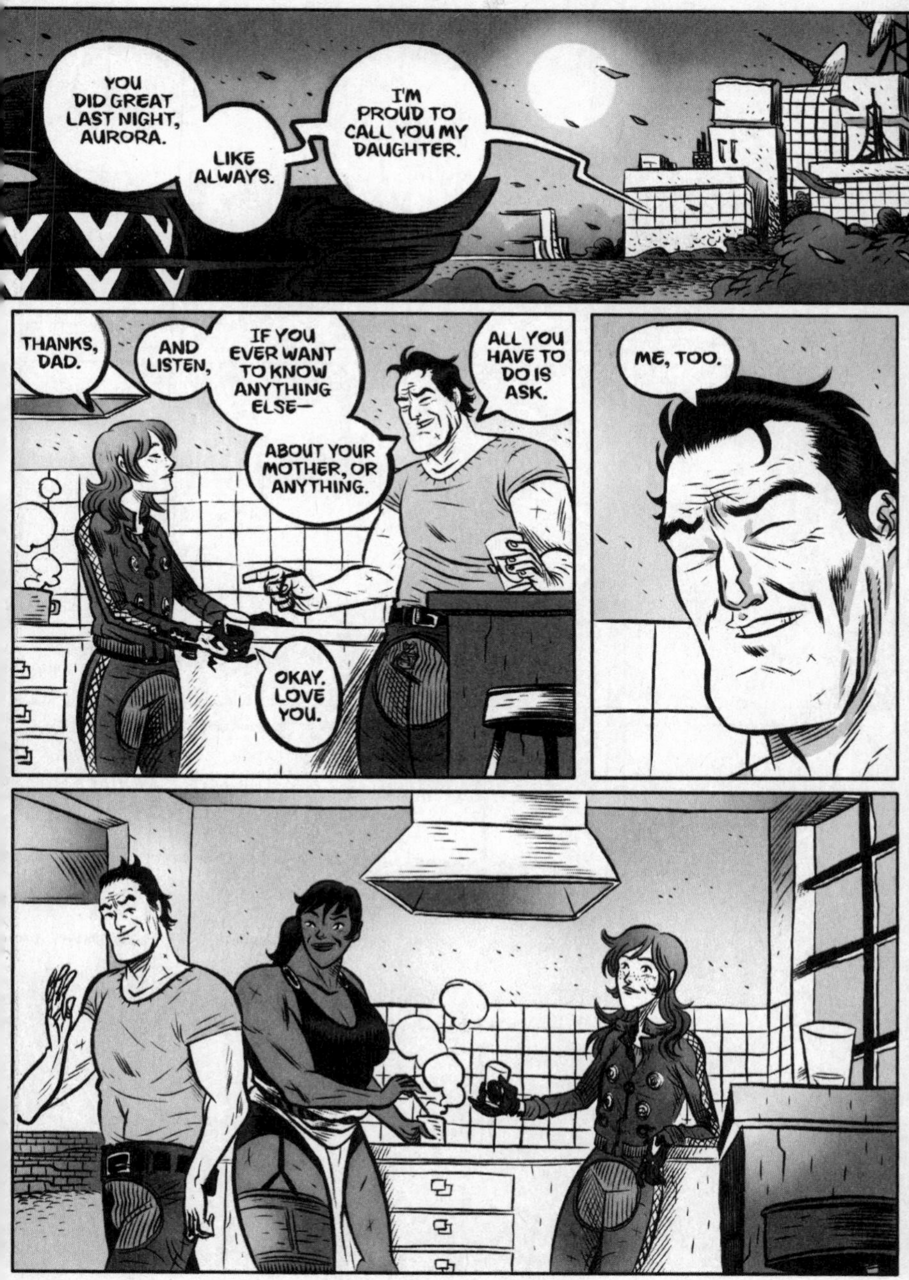
YOU DID GREAT LAST NIGHT, AURORA.
LIKE ALWAYS.
I'M PROUD TO CALL YOU MY DAUGHTER.
THANKS, DAD.
AND LISTEN,
IF YOU EVER WANT TO KNOW ANYTHING ELSE—
ABOUT YOUR MOTHER, OR ANYTHING.
ALL YOU HAVE TO DO IS ASK.
OKAY. LOVE YOU.
ME, TOO.

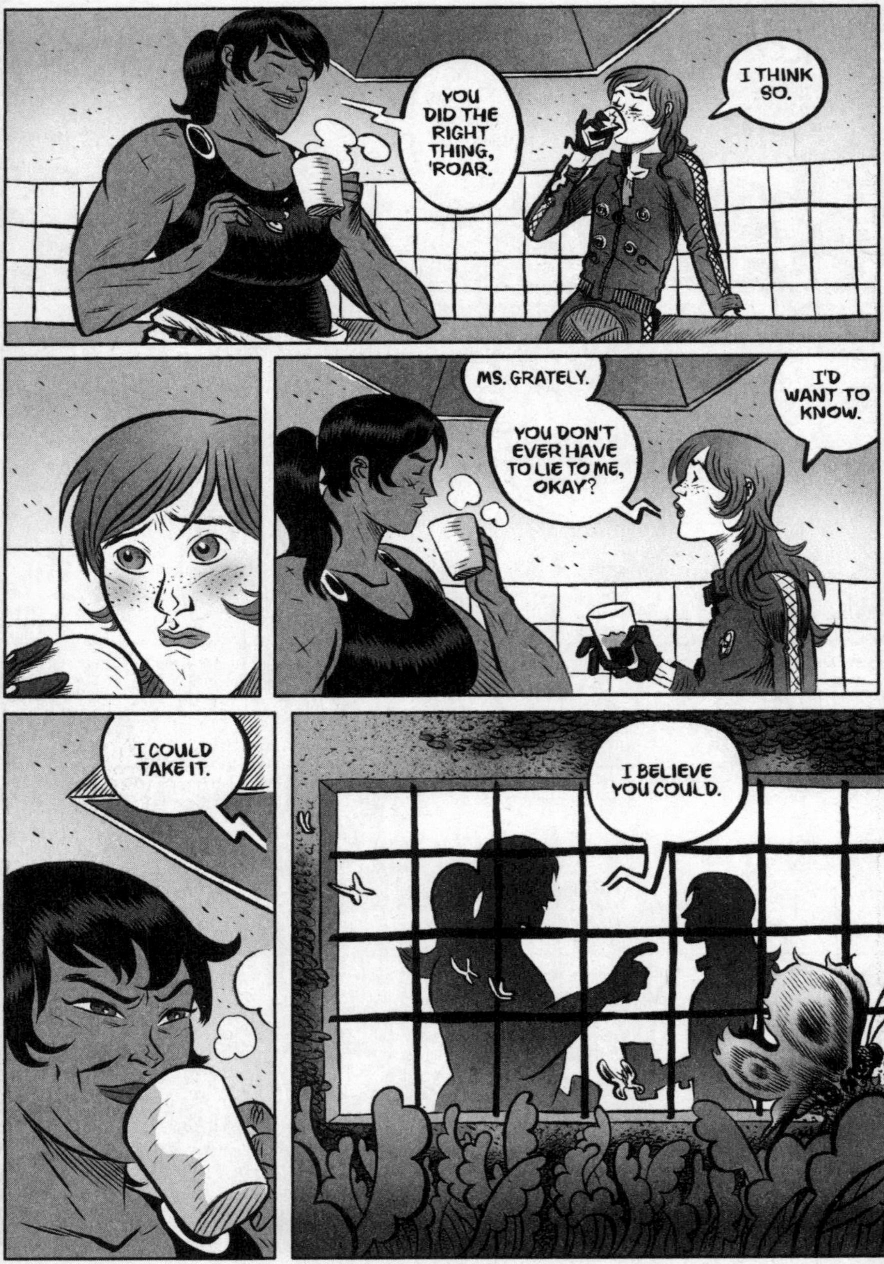
YOU DID THE RIGHT THING, 'ROAR.
I THINK SO.
MS. GRATELY.
YOU DON'T EVER HAVE TO LIE TO ME, OKAY?
I'D WANT TO KNOW.
I COULD TAKE IT.
I BELIEVE YOU COULD.

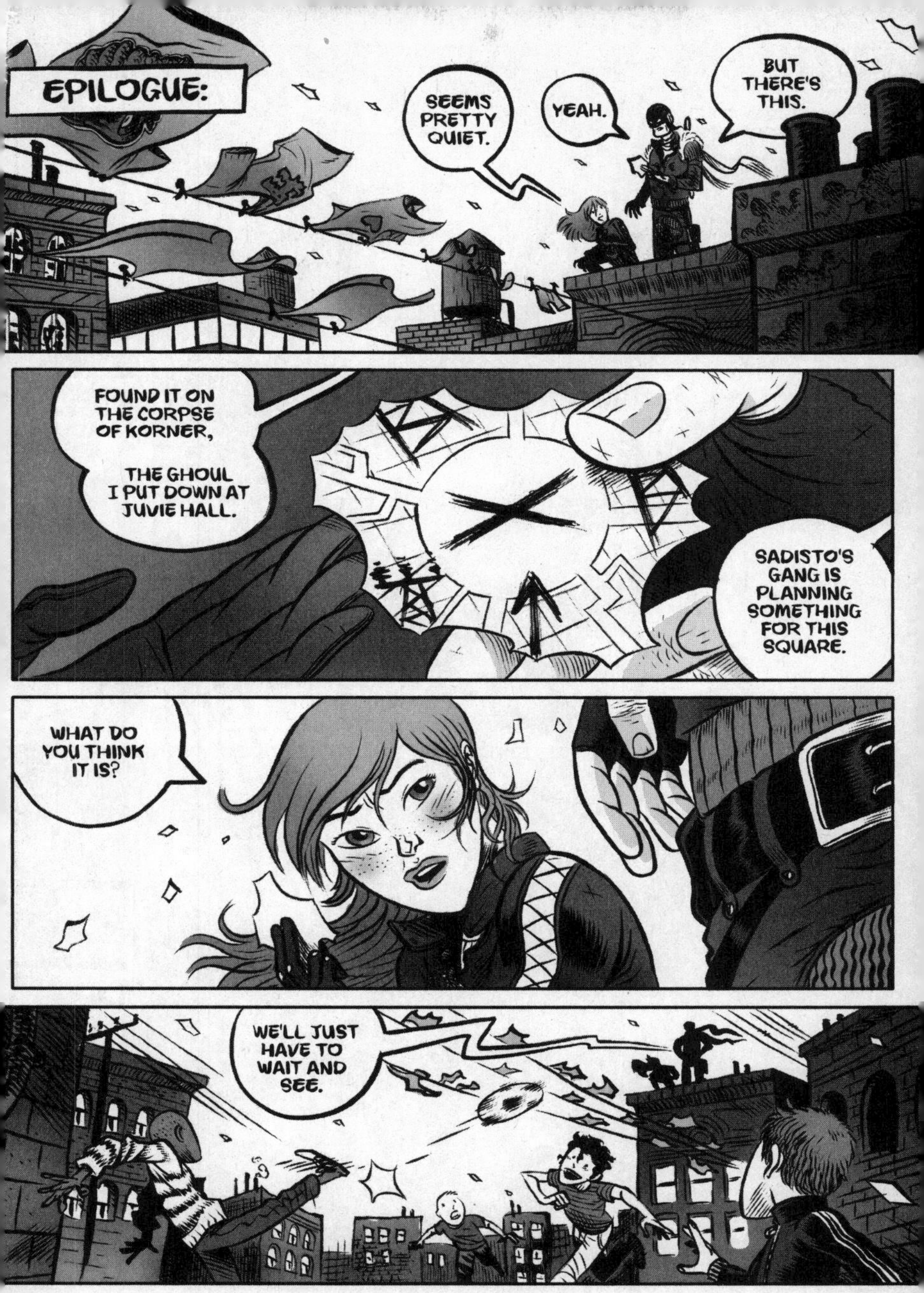
EPILOGUE:
SEEMS PRETTY QUIET.
YEAH.
BUT THERE'S THIS.
FOUND IT ON THE CORPSE OF KORNER,
THE GHOUL I PUT DOWN AT JUVIE HALL.
SADISTO'S GANG IS PLANNING SOMETHING FOR THIS SQUARE.
WHAT DO YOU THINK IT IS?
WE'LL JUST HAVE TO WAIT AND SEE.

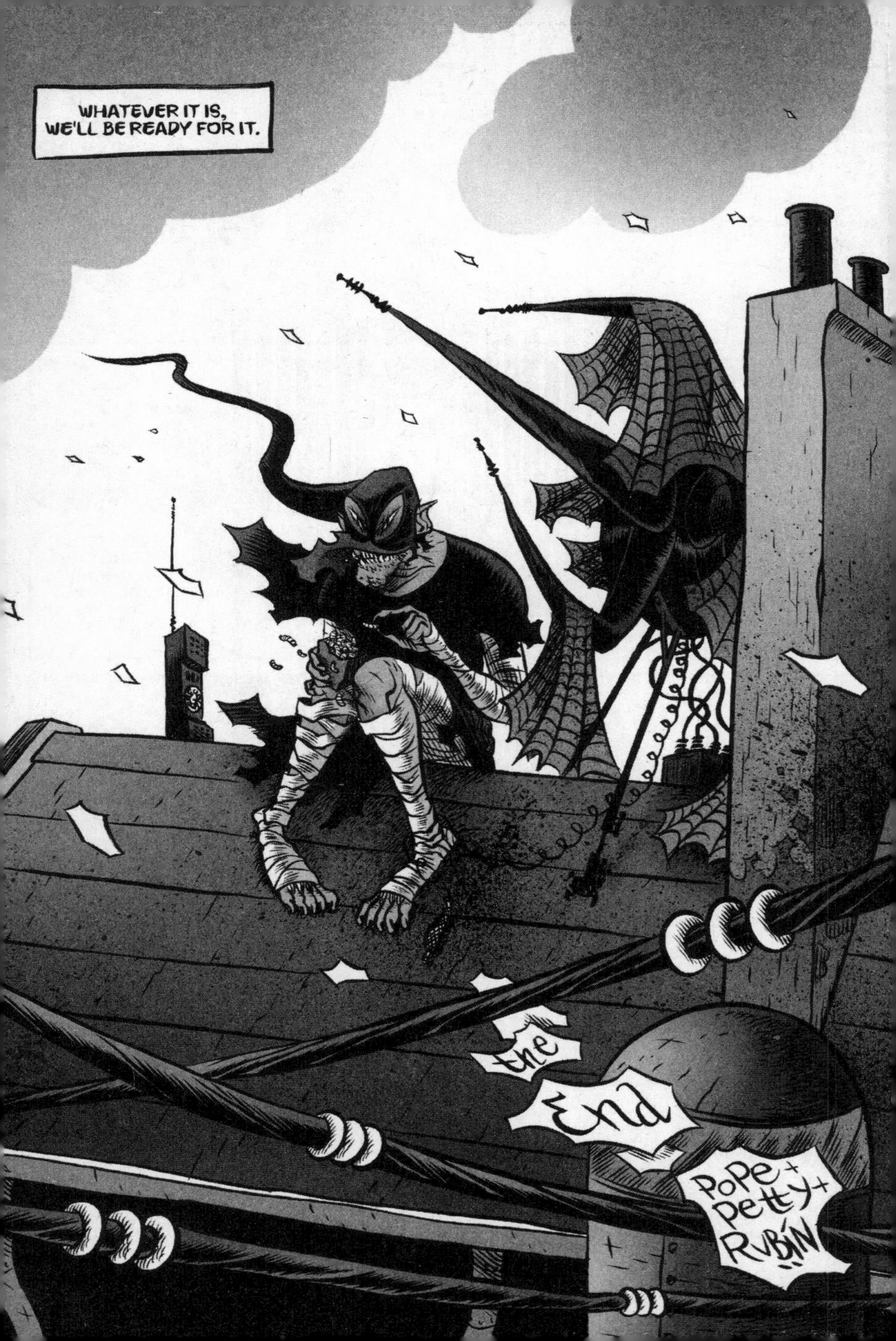
WHATEVER IT IS, WE'LL BE READY FOR IT.
the
End
Pope + Petty + RUBIN